MAGPIE LANE

Also by Lucy Atkins

The Missing One
The Other Child
The Night Visitor

MAGPIE LANE

lucy atkins

Quercus

First published in Great Britain in 2020 by Quercus
This paperback edition published in 2021 by

Quercus Editions Ltd
Carmelite House
50 Victoria Embankment
London EC4Y 0DZ

An Hachette UK company

A CIP catalogue record for this book is available
from the British Library

PB ISBN 978 1 78429 383 3
EB ISBN 978 1 78429 384 0

This book is a work of fiction. Although some of the settings are real,
the people depicted, businesses, organizations, places and events
described are fictitious and any resemblance to actual
persons, living or dead, events or locales
is entirely coincidental.

10 9 8 7 6 5 4 3 2

Typeset by CC Book Production
Printed and bound in Great Britain by Clays Ltd, Elcograf S.p.A.

MIX
Paper from
responsible sources
FSC® C104740

Papers used by Quercus Editions Ltd are from well-managed forests and other responsible sources.

For my sister, Jenny.

Goosey goosey gander,
Where shall I wander?
Upstairs, downstairs
In my lady's chamber.
There I met an old man
Who wouldn't say his prayers,
So I took him by the left leg
And threw him down the stairs

— Nursery Rhyme, Anon

Chapter 1

They are waiting for an answer. What do they want me to say? Perhaps they think I am a stalker, targeting the president of an Oxford College on his early morning jog. I have an urge to laugh which is inappropriate. There is nothing funny about this, nothing whatsoever. Felicity is missing. The whole country is looking for her.

I stare at the Oxford United mug that Faraday has put in front of me. My mouth is dry but I can't pick it up because my hand will shake. The surface of the tea is growing crinkled and rubbery but I leave it where it is.

It feels absurd to be sitting here with mugs of tea. Surely they should be out there looking for her.

But they are looking for her, of course. This is them looking for her.

–So, what *were* you doing all the way down there, last July, so early in the morning? Faraday repeats the question, studiously unthreatening.

I force myself to look into his jowly face. –I was thinking, I say.

–Thinking?

–Yes. I meet his eye. –Thinking.

Faraday glances at my cooling tea. He is around my own age,

with the thighs and shoulders of an ex-rugby player, and he is keen to put me at my ease. He has done all sorts of solicitous things already – asked if I was comfortable, explained that they will be videoing our interview, reminded me that I am free to leave at any time. I waved away his statement about legal representation – I am no more of a suspect than anybody else, perhaps less so than some, and despite multiple theories put forwards by the British press and public, nobody has the faintest idea what has happened here. They do not even know if there has been a crime.

The other detective, Khan, sits silent and motionless next to Faraday with a biro poised over a yellow lined pad. She is younger, perhaps in her thirties, slim and athletic, with cropped hair still damp from the shower, scrubbed skin and the top button of her shirt done up in a gender-neutral way. So far she has not said a word, except for a quiet hello. Perhaps she has been instructed just to sit still and write everything down.

Faraday raises a meaty fist, pops a belch into it and shuffles his papers. –So, what were you thinking about, he asks, –down there on your own so early in the morning?

And so back we circle, back again to the mathematical bridge at dawn.

I was thinking, in fact, that my life had been a failure. This may sound like self-pity but it was simply a conclusion based on solid evidence.

I had risen before sunrise that day after a particularly restless night and as I set off down Observatory Street, I had no desti-nation in mind; I just needed to walk. This is not unusual for me – I often walk through Oxford as the city sleeps; it is some-thing of a compulsion. At that early hour the city pavements are otter grey and hopeless, dotted with burger wrappers and stains of student vomit, but above them the ancient buildings have already begun to glow, to broaden their shoulders and pronounce their status to the world. Even before the sun has made it to their honeyed stones, they have begun to emit a subtle, confident light.

As I walk, I inevitably think about maths, my enduring passion in life. I have been working on the same mathematical proof for a few years now, and I tend to make the biggest leaps in my thinking while I walk. But on that particular day I wasn't thinking about my proof at all. I was thinking about Oxford, my life and what to do next. I was about to turn into St Giles' churchyard when a fox trotted out in front of me. For a second she paused, and I met her amber eyes. I felt a peculiar energy pass between us, as if she was telling me not to turn into the gate. She rippled off across St Giles', then slid behind the ecclesiastical College bins in search of a priestly chicken bone, while I carried on towards the city centre, and, as it turned out, my destiny.

The rough sleepers in the doorways of Cornmarket were oblivious to me, and as I came down St Aldate's beneath the studded barricades of Christ Church, a workman in a luminous jacket didn't even turn his head; I felt that I was invisible, a roaming ghost, searching for something I'd never find.

I paused on Folly Bridge and looked at the surface of the Thames, which was stroked by mist. The sky behind the boathouses was the colour of a field mouse, striated with pinks. It had been a very hot July and the grass in the meadow had turned to dust – geese ranged like a herd on the savannah, and above them in the chestnut trees a wood pigeon repeated its husky three-note call.

Moving on, I passed Salter's Steamers and turned onto the Thames path, falling into a brisk stride. The dawn chorus was muted, and I could hear the distant hum of early commuters on the ring road. At Iffley Lock I turned off the towpath onto the mathematical bridge, where I stopped. The air was clammy; I felt the presence of rain.

Set over a rolling channel, the mathematical bridge is a complicated wooden structure made up of tangential timbers and shaded by low-hanging branches so that at certain angles it seems to be part of the trees. The more famous bridge at Iffley is a pretty, photogenic eighteenth-century stone structure, marked with a brass bull's head. People take photos on and of it, but they rarely pay attention to the mathematical bridge, which is slightly odd – subtly out of place and somehow temporary, though it must have been there for a hundred years.

As I looked into the tangled weeds I found myself wondering, not for the first time, what on earth I was doing in Oxford. It was not clear how a small decision taken more than two decades ago had come to shape my entire adult life. My thoughts were dark, but I was probably at a bit of a low ebb – the Philosophy don, her neurotic wife and their fragile son had been taxing even by Oxford's standards – and it is always particularly hard to say goodbye to a baby, not least a sweet one like him. I'd just turned down a couple on sabbatical from the University of Utrecht and since the Philosophy don's house had been allocated to a new College family, I was technically both unemployed and homeless. I was far from destitute, though: I had my savings and my car, and I was free to go wherever I chose. The main challenge was locating the energy to care.

This wasn't anything as mundane as disappointment – my hopes and dreams had been cauterized twenty-six years ago – I simply felt I'd reached the point in life where the downward trajectory really begins. I could find more work in Oxford – finding clients has never been a problem. The University is essentially a vast community of transients, many of whom are burdened by inconvenient offspring. But although I had spent plenty of time within its ancient walls and cloisters, I had no connection to it. Nor did I feel, after all these years, that the city was my home. I was the perpetual outsider, neither 'town' nor 'gown', at best an adjunct. Perhaps if I'd taken a different turn at St Giles' that day, ignored the fox and circled back to Observatory Street, I'd have packed my bags and left for ever – but then I would not have known Felicity – and that, of course, would be unthinkable.

But it is really not a good idea for me to think about Felicity at this point, with Faraday and Khan staring at me, waiting for their explanation.

I try to remember what else I was thinking that day. Home. I was definitely thinking about home – increasingly I'd felt Scotland tugging at my hem and I remember thinking that perhaps it was time to go back. If I belonged anywhere, it was there, in the landscape of my childhood. My father's friends and colleagues were mostly dead or senile, the village shrunken, the Kirk where my ancestors lie was up for sale, the big house derelict, my own generation mostly dispersed. Even if I did meet someone I once knew, they probably wouldn't recognize me: I am not the pretty young thing I was when I left. My hair is not bright auburn any more, it is a dull brown, iron-streaked, coarse and straight as a mare's tail, all my curls having fallen out overnight over two decades ago. I have crow's feet now, and a line between my brows that probably makes me look a bit forbidding in certain lights; I am, of course, no longer slim.

But this is not about me or Scotland, or what happened there all those years ago. This is about Felicity – an anxious, silent eight-year-old who vanished from the Master's Lodging in the centre of a city of 154,000 inhabitants, none of whom, apparently, have a clue as to where she is – though, judging from the media reports, quite a few are prepared to offer an opinion.

Not least, her father.

I certainly do remember when I first spotted Nick – a tall shadow cutting through the bright green foliage at quite a pace. He came off the path towards me and hesitated when he saw me but it was too late, he was committed to crossing my bridge.

The wood made a hollow tap-tap as he ran onto it and the planks sighed and wobbled dramatically beneath us. Nick is a striking presence: over six foot tall, broad-shouldered, long-limbed and lean, with dark hair swept back off his forehead. He barely glanced at me, just gave a brief nod, but I recognized him immediately. I'd seen his picture in the University *Gazette* and the College magazine – College members seemed to talk of little else but Nick Law.

Of course what Faraday and Khan really want to know is: was my presence on the bridge that morning a coincidence? Perhaps Nick is suggesting that it wasn't. But of course he is probably saying all sorts of wild and panicky things about me now. How could it have been anything but a coincidence? I couldn't have known that he would run to Iffley Lock at five-thirty in the morning. It was his first day as College Master – there had been no time to form habits – we wouldn't have exchanged a word had his foot not slipped just as he passed behind me.

He pitched sideways – I turned, he twisted – I shot out both hands to catch him and for a second we stood face to face, strangers dancing on a mathematical bridge at dawn. I saw the sweat on his forehead, the delicate broken capillaries on his cheeks, and felt the heat coming off his body as he stepped backwards, shocked. 'So sorry! I don't know what happened there—'

'Algae, it needs a good power wash.' I glanced at his trainers: Nikes, no real grip, unlike my sturdy boots.

'Well, yes, God, it's lethal.' He wiped his forehead with his running shirt, breathing at me through dragon nostrils. His voice was accusatory. 'Are you the lock-keeper?' I laughed and his face clouded.

This sort of thing actually happens to me a lot – usually in College grounds, sometimes in Oxford parks. It might be my functional approach to fashion, but people seem to assume that I'm in charge. 'I was just admiring the bridge.' I patted the railing, which was soft with lichen.

He arranged his features more benignly then. 'Ah, right, yes, of course, this bizarre bridge.' He wiped his brow on his T-shirt and glanced sideways at me. 'It's actually modelled on one that was held up by mathematical calculations alone – did you know that? The one Isaac Newton designed in Cambridge. The only thing that stopped it falling into the water was geometry. Then some students took it apart to see how he'd done it and they couldn't calculate how to put it back together again, so they had to add the nuts and bolts.' He smiled and dropped the end of his T-shirt, putting his hands on his hips. 'This one came later, of course – 1920s, I think.'

I saw that he was the kind of man – normal for Oxford – who pulls out facts in order to establish dominance. He would not, I suspected, take kindly to being told that his story was nonsense, a tall tale made up two hundred years ago by Cambridge students. Newton had nothing to do with the original mathematical bridge; he'd died over twenty years before it was even built.

Nick straightened, perhaps sensing that I wasn't his ideal audience. 'Right then,' he said. 'I must press on.' He turned away.

'You're Dr Law, aren't you?'

He looked back sharply as if I'd accused him of something. Perhaps I had. I named the College where the Philosophy don had worked and asked if he was its new Master.

'Ha! Well, yes, I am indeed. Guilty as charged.' He came back and thrust out a hand. 'Nick Law.'

I didn't offer my name but he seemed not to expect or need it. I told him I knew the College well and named the Philosophy don. I said I'd spent the best part of a year working for her and before that, at the same College, for a visiting theologian from Zagreb. 'I've heard a lot about you,' I said.

'All good, I trust.'

It was not, in fact.

Nick's appointment had not been a unanimous decision for the Governing Body. The younger Fellows believed that a dynamic and well-connected media man like him could transform the College's ailing fortunes, lure big donors, win over disgruntled staff and woo the student body, but many of the older Fellows were outraged at the idea of a fifty-three-year-old BBC director taking charge of their precious six-hundred-year-old institution. They were unimpressed by Nick's celebrity contacts – the very notion of celebrity was an abomination to them. They said he'd alienated people at the BBC and was known for bullish, bullying behaviour. Others, meanwhile, simply felt that a 'media type' could not possibly appreciate the delicate, esoteric needs of this particular Oxford College. The fact that he came with a glamorous young Scandinavian wife and small daughter made him an even more inappropriate candidate in their eyes, but of course they couldn't use that against him, not openly, so they merely growled that he lacked 'gravitas' and that his appointment would be 'divisive'.

After much bitter wrangling, the Governing Body was unable to reach a consensus, and so a bizarre Oxford custom was invoked: an independent expert known as 'the Visitor' was brought in to make the decision for them. To the visceral fury of his opponents, 'the Visitor' chose Nick.

He certainly seemed nothing like the outgoing Master. Nick was at least two decades younger than Lord Eaves, for a start, and distinctly more dazzling. Lord Eaves represented the end of a dying tradition of eminent white men who take a Head of House appointment to kick off a prestigious semi-retirement. The venomous fissures in the Governing Body and the depth of the College's financial woes had proved too onerous for Eaves, and he was ousted in a vote of no confidence after trying to liquidate College assets. Since the Master before him had only lasted a year, the College was now on very shaky ground indeed. I wondered if Nick had any idea what he was getting himself into.

He gave a confident smile. 'You're thinking I don't look terribly Masterly, aren't you?'

'I'm not sure I ever saw Lord Eaves in Nikes.'

'Ah well, I own several very nice pairs of brogues too. I even wear a suit sometimes.'

I waited for him to move on, but he didn't and I realized that he was expecting me to say something admiring.

'Well, it's quite something to run an Oxford College,' I offered.

'Oh yes, yes, an honour.' He gazed at the water. 'Such a privilege to be here. My wife and I feel terribly lucky.'

The surface of the water frilled as a grey goose paddled under the bridge to the bank and began to jab at the weeds. 'I hear you have a little girl too?' I said.

'Ah, yes, yes, you've done your homework, haven't you – I do, that's right.' He blinked rapidly. 'Felicity. She's . . . well . . . ah . . . she's . . . um . . . eight.' He puffed out his cheeks. 'She's . . .

she's . . . very . . . um . . .' He gazed at the goose, seemingly unable to express exactly what his daughter was.

This is when I felt the first prick of curiosity – I wondered what it was about this little girl that could interrupt the smooth flow of his words. He straightened. 'Anyway, it's awfully good to be back. I was a graduate student here, many moons ago. Would you believe I proposed to my first wife on this actual bridge? She's the one who told me that nuts and bolts story.' He patted the railing and looked away sharply, as if he'd surprised himself by revealing this to me, a stranger. It explained his early morning pilgrimage, anyway. He glanced at me sideways and arched an eyebrow. 'I do know that's not true, by the way – though I have to say I believed her for many years.' He glanced at the sky. 'Right then, it's about to rain. I should crack on. I'm sure I'll see you in College – um – so sorry, I don't think I caught your name?'

I told him.

'Ah, Dee, yes – and I don't think I actually got your connection to College?'

'Well, I don't have one.'

His brows lowered. 'Oh, but I thought you said—?'

'I was working for a College member, a philosopher, but she's gone to Harvard now.'

'Oh, right, okay, yes, so you're a philosopher—'

'I'm a nanny.'

I caught a flash of irritation on his face, presumably as he realized he'd just wasted valuable minutes attempting to charm an insignificant childcare worker. I waited for him to move on but he didn't. Three more Greylag geese appeared from under the bridge, necks tall, eyes sharp, treading water beneath us. He gazed at them a moment, and then, suddenly, I felt the full beam of his attention. 'And who did you say you nannied for, in College?'

I named both the Philosophy don and the Zagreb professor.

'I suppose you have another job lined up, do you? Another family to go to now?'

I shook my head. 'I'm taking a wee break.'

'Ah, yes, well, you have a family of your own to look after, I suppose—'

My fingers tightened around the railing. I am used to this, of course, but that doesn't make it any easier. 'I don't have family commitments, no,' I said.

'Well!' His voice boomed, making me jump. The geese slid back under the bridge. 'Do you know, I think this might be synchronicity – or fate – or perhaps predestination. The thing is, um, Dee, my wife and I are actually in a bit of a bind at the moment. We've just lost an au pair and it's the school summer holidays. The move from London's been very – well – my wife runs her own business in London, and my daughter's . . . well . . . she's . . . it's . . . Anyway, we're urgently looking for help right now, even temporary.'

I was about to tell him that I was leaving Oxford for ever but he interrupted me. 'Of course, I understand this is out of the blue – me pouncing at you on a bridge – but maybe you'd consider popping into the Master's Lodging for a chat? Absolutely no commitment. Maybe later this morning, even, if you're free? My wife's there right now, in fact. She's doing some rather major renovations – she'd love to show you round, if nothing else.'

I sensed a desperation in him that went beyond the practicalities of childcare, and I wondered what on earth a man like Nick Law could possibly have to feel desperate about. I had no intention of working for him – he was obviously high-handed and domineering, way too much trouble – but I'd never been invited inside a Master's Lodging before and it was hard to resist. I told him I might be able to pop in later that morning, just to say hello.

'That's excellent, that's really excellent, Dee. What time's best? Eleven?' He turned the question into instruction. 'Come at eleven.'

And so our lives converged on the mathematical bridge that day in July, seven months ago now – though it feels like a lot longer. Some might say a mysterious force pulled us together – there was a need, the need was met – but I of all people do not believe in a benevolent deity or a universe that provides. In my experience, quite the opposite is true.

But of course none of these thoughts are remotely relevant to the investigation of Felicity's disappearance. Faraday and Khan are waiting for my answer, so I ask if they'd be able to remember exactly what they were thinking at any given moment, seven months ago. Faraday opens his mouth to reply, but I haven't finished talking. –I believe it was raining that day, I say. –I was probably just wishing I'd brought a coat.

Chapter 2

Faraday nods, and says, –Fine, fine. Maybe we could try to get a picture of your role in the family then? He touches an indentation on his ring finger as he speaks, a ghostly noose in the plump flesh. –What were your first impressions, Dee? Did this seem like a normal home to you?

I think about this for a moment.

–There's nothing remotely normal, I say, –about the Master's Lodging.

I had often passed the house – a white Tudor building set just outside the Porter's Lodge. Though it is in the very centre of Oxford, the College is one of the more discreet. Its gates are away from any main streets, set down a cobbled dead end – easy to miss unless you know it's there. I was about to lift the brass knocker when the Chapel bells began to clamour behind me. The sound filled my skull, crushing my thoughts. After a pause, eleven slow, pompous strikes sounded. I waited until the last one was over and was gathering myself to knock when two builders burst out. They stomped off across the cobbles, leaving the door open for me – they probably assumed that I was staff. I peered inside. The oak-panelled hall was strewn with builders' paraphernalia – sharp tools, bags, bits of timber. The air was veiled with dust, there was a smell of scorched metal and I heard crashing sounds, the whirring of drills, a demonic sawing. Even if I had used the heavy brass knocker, nobody would have heard me.

I was wondering if I should just go away again when a woman in a tight white shirt and baggy trousers appeared at the end of the hall. She spotted me and bounded down the corridor – a neat, packed cell of energy, limbs flexing, brown eyes wide, wavy blonde hair rippling in a high ponytail, showing off an absurdly beautiful face. My first instinct was weariness.

'Dee! You must be Dee? Hello! Hey! Come in. My God, is it still raining? You have no coat! You're soaking!' Her lilting Scandinavian accent made every other word sound like a joyful cry of surprise. 'I'm Mariah – the Head of House's spouse.' She laughed at her own quip and thrust out a hand, leaning in as we shook, her elbow jutting at a vigorous, sporty angle. 'Have you been standing in the rain for long? I'm so sorry! This crazy noise! It's insane here – but, hey, come in, please, come in.'

She made off down the hall calling over her shoulder, 'Nick's just gone to his College office, but come in, come with me, I'll show you round and we can try to find Felicity; I think she's upstairs somewhere.' She led me up a wide oak staircase where two workmen were unhooking oil portraits of elderly men looking solemn and foolish in ermine-fringed robes. There were faded rectangles further up the wall where other portraits had been removed. 'Yes, yes,' she followed my eyes, 'they have to go – I can't stand to have all these disapproving old guys staring down at me like that.' She shook herself and skipped off, ponytail swinging. 'Where *is* that girl?'

I followed her up, squeezing the water from the ends of my hair when she wasn't looking.

She was waiting for me on the landing. 'She's probably hiding – she does that a lot – she can't handle this noise but it looks way worse than it is, I promise.' I could see into a master bedroom behind her where workmen were ripping up a maroon carpet, throwing up clouds of dust. The atmosphere felt manic, like a TV home makeover show where teams of builders tear down walls and battle with plywood, against the ticking of a make-believe clock.

Mariah steered me towards a second flight of stairs, much more narrow and steep. 'This house was a total museum, Dee, you wouldn't believe it – I just have to get rid of basically everything.' We were on the attic floor now, walking along a long, low-ceilinged corridor, with two doors on the left, and a dark dead end ahead. 'It was worst up here though.' She bounced words at me over her shoulder like ping-pong balls: 'Dark, dark, dark and dusty and incredibly cluttered, my God! It was like one long tomb up here, covered in oil paintings and thick, heavy curtains blocking the light out. Just terrible!' She pronounced 'just' as 'yust'. 'And I said to Nick, I'm Danish! I can't live like this! Could you, Dee? I'm like a plant, I need light and space or I just shrivel up and die.'

The floor up here, I noticed, sloped to the left, as if the top of the house was about to slide off into the lane below. Mariah tried to push open the first door but a builder was drilling on the other side so she beckoned me towards the second door. 'The thing is, the Lodging isn't a private house at all – oh, watch your feet –' she stepped neatly over a hacksaw, 'it's a workplace too – a lot of people are going to be coming in and out. We'll be entertaining here from October when term starts, so it's got to reflect who we are, you know, it's got to feel modern and, like, actually *alive*. At least, that's my excuse –' she waved a hand –

'for all this. But you know what, I'd be doing a total renovation anyway. Honestly, you just couldn't live here how it was.'

She led me to a modest eaves room, with a bell tower directly opposite its window. 'So, this is going to be the nanny's room.' The carpet must have just been removed, because the parquet floor was unfinished, ancient and blackened, strewn with rusty tacks and dust. The scorched metal smell was even more powerful and I saw that the builders were working on an en suite.

There was no sign of a child, but she seemed to have forgotten that we were looking for Felicity. 'So that's the bathroom there, between the two bedrooms. You can get into it from both sides – a little bit strange, I know, but hopefully that works out okay. If I was going to live here for ever I'd do something better with it, but it'll be fine for a year or two – ' she glanced at me, 'or, you know, however long we're here.'

College Masters, I happened to know, were expected to commit to at least four years – unless ousted, which was rare – though, given the troubles with this College, perhaps a genuine hazard.

I followed her back down to the first floor landing. Dust gritted my eyeballs and teeth and my head was beginning to throb. She thrust out an arm to stop me as the workmen heaved the chest of drawers out of the master bedroom, and then we followed as they manoeuvred it down the stairs, painfully slowly. At the bottom step she guided me into a modern glass extension.

The windows were steamed and streaked with rain so I couldn't see the back garden clearly, but the light was soft, tinted peach, and as Mariah closed the door the noise receded. 'We're staying in College this week, thank God. Did Nick warn you about all this work? I hope he did. Anyway, Dee – is that short for something? Diane? Deirdre? – here, sit, sit. Oh, look at you, you're still so wet from the rain! But it's warm in here with the glass, isn't it? At least this room doesn't need any work. It's beautiful, isn't it? The Master before Lord Eaves had it built. She was the only woman – can you even call her a "Master"? – in 600 years, can you believe that? She came from New Zealand, so I guess she needed the light too.'

I had come to look after the Zagreb professor's little girl just as the Governing Body decided that the New Zealander was 'not a good fit'. I remembered that I'd once passed her in the Porter's Lodge. Her face had been set in a rictus of despair, like one of the unhinged gargoyles on the College battlements.

Mariah perched on the arm of a chair and gestured at a white couch, surrounded by vases of frothing roses. I sank into it, gratefully.

'So, Felicity must have gone with Nick. He has lovely offices – do you know them? In the main quad. It's kind of a shame the Lodging's out here, isn't it, not inside. But I guess it's a question of space.' She dug in her trouser pocket, pulling out her phone. 'So I'm going to text him and tell him you're here. I wish I could give you coffee but they're just tiling the kitchen right now so—' She shrugged, phone in hand. 'But, hey, look, I should probably tell you a bit about Felicity before they get here. I mean, she won't say hello to you, so don't take that personally. She just doesn't speak.' Her lilting voice made everything sound playful, as if she was sharing an amusing anecdote. 'She really doesn't speak at all.' She flashed a smile and lifted her phone again, clicking at it. 'I'm not exaggerating.'

I assumed, of course, that she was.

She touched her lower belly with one hand as she put away her phone. There was something protective in the gesture that made me wonder if she could be pregnant. She wore brogues with no socks and her ankles were fine and lightly tanned and she jiggled her supporting foot as she asked about the Philosophy don and my previous work. I told her I'd lost count of how many families I'd been with over the years in Oxford. I explained that I tended to work for visiting professors, anything from a term to a year's sabbatical, but rarely longer. I preferred it that way.

'Hey, I love your accent. It's Irish, yes? No – wait – Scottish? Yes, Scottish. Nick's mother was Scottish. Oh my God, Dee, you're completely perfect, truly! Felicity needs someone experienced, really, and . . .' Her eyes widened and she patted her belly. 'Nick already told you, I guess?'

My instinct was right, then. 'Actually, he didn't.' I reached for my bag.

'Well, yes, of course it isn't public yet. He doesn't want me to say anything because I'm just eight weeks so, you know—' She cleared her throat. 'I'm thirty-eight so maybe it's a bit more risky for me, I guess.'

She looked a lot younger. I got to my feet, tucking the end of my shirt into my jeans. 'I don't think I'm the person you're looking for,' I said. 'I really can't commit to anything long-term.'

'Oh no, hey!' She leaped up. 'Wait! God. No, no, please. Sit down. Sit. Please. We just need someone to help with the tran- sition – we just really need someone to focus on Felicity right now. We're both so busy, and anyway, I'm just going to take the baby to work with me at first – I'm my own boss, I can do that.'

I tried not to smile. Had she ever, I wondered, actually met a newborn?

'No, no, Felicity's the one who badly needs your help,' she continued.

'Badly?'

'Okay, look, I probably need to explain her a bit more. There's nothing wrong with her mentally – she's just super, super shy and anxious and, well, she doesn't really speak. She's always been silent, ever since she was a toddler – it's not trauma or anything – I mean, she didn't talk even before her mother died.'

'Her mother's dead?' This information came as a shock. The way Nick had spoken about his first wife on the bridge had made her feel very alive – almost as if she'd been standing behind him smiling at her little bridge hoax.

'Ah, yes, yes, Ana died four years ago.' Mariah's voice had dropped and she began to fiddle with the end of her thin belt, flipping it this way and that against her leg, making sharp little slaps. 'After a long illness.' I noted the formulaic phrase: cancer, then. 'But that's not why Felicity doesn't speak,' she was saying. 'She's had a therapist in London for that – it's called "selective mutism". Like, extreme shyness. She'll grow out of it eventually, it's really not a big problem, I just wanted to give you the heads-up, you know, so you don't think she doesn't like you or something. I mean, she never said a word to any of the au pairs either. That's probably why none of them stayed too long.' She laughed, but stopped almost immediately and her pretty face became grave. 'I guess it can be a bit hard not to take her silence personally, but you know,' the jiggling foot intensified, 'it's just the way she is right now. We just have to be patient.'

I was no expert on selective mutism but I had the feeling that most selectively mute children were able to speak to close family members. 'Sorry, can I just be clear – she doesn't speak to you, yourself?'

'No. I mean, *literally* she doesn't speak to anyone except Nick – though right now she's not speaking so much to him either; this move from London's been hard for her. She's not good with change.'

'What about school? Can she talk to the teacher – the other children?'

She shook her head. 'But we're thinking a fresh start will be a positive thing, you know. Once she's settled, things are going to get a lot better. But hey, look, I don't want to put you off. My God! Really. She's a great girl. She's clever and talented, super creative, you know, and really cute. She's not completely weird or anything, please don't worry about that.'

'I wouldn't think of any child as weird.'

'Well, yes, exactly. There, see? You'd be perfect for her.' She tucked a loose strand behind her ear; three diamond studs sparkled in a row along her neat lobe. I wondered how convenient it had been for her to take on a bereaved and silent stepchild. Her relationship with Nick must have developed quite rapidly. But of course, at her age, she probably felt she couldn't hang around too long if she wanted a baby.

'Anyway, Nick's put his foot down – no more Danish au pairs.' She laughed. 'We need a grown-up now.'

'Yes, well, it does sound as if Felicity might benefit from someone with a bit of experience.'

'Exactly. We all would, to be honest with you, Dee. I have no idea how I'm going to make this work. My business is in London – did Nick tell you that? I restore historic wallpaper – I have a studio there, and I work with organizations like the National Trust, you know, museums and stately homes, so there's travel. That's why we need someone here for Felicity. There's also going to be a lot of entertaining here in the evenings – and I mean a *lot*. I don't know how much you know about the Master's job, but it's seriously social. Nick's going to be hosting dinners, cocktails – things like that – three, four times a week here. I'm going to have to be in two places at once, basically, but Oxford's term is only eight weeks long – or ten if you count, what do they call it, ninth week and zero week?'

'Noughth week.' I managed not to say that although I had never worked for a Head of House before, I'd been in Oxford for over two decades, so was fairly familiar with the University schedule.

'Noughth.' She moved her lips around the word as if chewing toffee, and laughed at herself. 'God, I'm trying to get my head round all the vocabulary – it's basically a new language. I mean, "Michaelmas term" and "Hilary term" and "subfusc" and "manciples". Even College Masters aren't just Masters, are they? They're Presidents and Principals and Wardens.'

'And Provosts and Deans.'

'Yes, my God!' She belly laughed, as if I'd told a fantastic joke. 'Anyway, Nick will have meetings here too during the day sometimes – you know, the, um, Government Body that runs the College and things.'

'Governing Body,' I offered.

'Yes, that, exactly – so basically it's going to be busy here, but we'll keep the public stuff downstairs, in the dining room, that grand one on the right as you came in the front door? And the living room at the front. These back rooms – the kitchen, this room – will be private spaces. In summer we'll open up the garden, but nobody's going to be going upstairs, for sure. We're making that a definite rule. Except the College cleaners – what do they call them—?'

'Scouts.'

'Right, yes, weird – I thought "scout" was for kids. Anyway, they'll come to clean, and there's the head of catering, too, Angela – you'll meet her – she'll be over here a lot arranging the entertaining. She's also going to take care of our meals – mine and Nick's – but, you know, it's nobody's job to look after a little girl. The College staff never had to deal with a child in the Lodging before. So, that's why we need you. You'd take her to school, pick her up, make her meals, entertain her in the holidays, supervise her homework, put her to bed and sometimes stay here alone with her when we're both away overnight. It'd be really well paid, of course. Are you happy cooking for her? Just simple things, nothing special?' She'd already slotted me into the role. 'And you could live in, yes? Nick said you don't have a family of your own? Were you a live-in nanny before?'

I told her about the Philosophy don and the lease of the Observatory Street house coming to an end and she beamed as if we'd made a deal. 'This is amazing, Dee.' She pronounced the 'z' as an 's', straightening her arms and spine and unhooking her leg. 'Honestly, Nick's right, it feels like kind of a miracle he met you. You're like Mary Poppins, dropping onto our roof!'

'Well, I'm not sure—'

'You're exactly the person we need right now, seriously. So, hey, what do you think? Are you interested? I mean, we're going to have to check out your references, obviously, but it'd be so good to have an adult like you after the au pairs. I had to be like the mother to those girls.'

I gazed at her. The speed with which she'd decided that I was the right person to look after her silent and bereaved step-daughter, unsupervised, for long hours, when I hadn't even set eyes on the child – when they knew nothing at all about me – was astonishing, even for a desperate parent. But perhaps when you are as privileged and beautiful as Mariah, things do drop into your lap in this way: solutions, staff, help – miracles.

Until that moment I'd had no intention of working for them, but as Mariah beamed manically at me, it occurred to me that it was not the adults who desperately needed my help, but the poor child. This anxious, silent, displaced little girl, I suspected, needed me more than her parents could possibly imagine. I decided that I would wait and meet her – I felt I owed her that much, at least.

Chapter 3

The main problem with my line of work is that children come with parents, and parents come with opinions, thoughts, urges and impulses – most of them entirely misguided.

This is why I have stuck to short-term positions for visiting professors – jobs with a built-in end point, and, ideally, a solid language barrier. I have no desire to become a part of anybody's family – that would feel delusional, and a bit humiliating. In fact, I turned down the University of Utrecht couple purely because they couldn't stop talking about how their last nanny had been a 'beloved family member'. The children, of course, are a different matter. For however long I'm in their lives, I do my very best to make things better for them.

As Mariah and I sat in the garden room that first day, the door flew open and the screech of drills filled the air, making us both jump. Nick stepped in. It took me a second to notice that there was a child behind him. Her thin arms were wrapped around herself, and her eyes were fixed on the floor, so all I could see was a dark nebula of curls. I took a sharp breath. The curls seemed familiar, somehow precious, and for a moment I couldn't take my eyes off them.

Nick wore a white shirt, black jeans and tortoiseshell glasses.

His damp hair was combed back and his forehead bulged as if his capacious brain was exerting a dangerous pressure on his skull. 'Ah, Dee,' he said. 'You made it.' Both Nick and the child were wearing white tops and dark bottoms. However, while his jeans were immaculate and pressed, her leggings were baggy at the knee and tatty. Her feet, in pink flip-flops – clearly unsuited to a building site – were bony and pale and I saw lines of dirt under the toenails, which needed trimming.

'Ah, there you are! Shut the door!' Mariah leaped up.

Felicity's body gave a shudder as the door slammed. She shifted her head and a giant green eye blinked at me, momentarily, from a heart-shaped face. Then she ducked her head again and began to scratch behind one ear, viciously. A wave of emotion that I could neither identify nor explain moved silently through me. I wanted, very badly, to reach out and still her scratching fingers, to touch her crazy puff of hair.

I knew, then, that I should leave. This family was all wrong – too troublesome, too tense, too complicated – but I could not bring myself to go. I needed to see Felicity's face again; I needed to know that this child was all right.

'So, Bun, this is Dee.' Nick scooped one arm around her shoulders, easing her forwards. 'My daughter can be rather quiet . . . um . . . she's a bit shy, but she's—'

'It's okay.' Mariah cut him off. 'I've done all that.'

They exchanged a glance.

'Ach, well,' I said. 'I can be a bit quiet myself.'

Felicity's ear flooded with colour. I felt that she didn't want me to look at her and certainly didn't want me to speak to her – she didn't want to be spoken about at all, in fact – so I asked Mariah and Nick when the Lodging's renovations were expected to be finished.

'Well, they'll be done with the downstairs, more or less, by the end of next week and the attic rooms are nearly there,' Mariah said. 'Being Master, Nick can get a huge workforce – it's amazing, actually. So – ' she grinned intensely – 'we'll basically have you as soon as you can move in.'

Nick's eyes flickered from Mariah to me and then back to Mariah again. 'What – we're all settled? Already? Really?'

'I think so, darling. Dee's got tons of experience; she's been a nanny for years in Oxford, to all sorts of children.'

Nick turned to me and said, in a patrician tone, 'My wife's a force of nature, Dee, please don't let her bulldoze you.'

'I'm not easily bulldozed,' I said. 'But I do wonder what Felicity thinks of all this.'

'We haven't discussed terms and conditions yet,' Mariah said, loudly, to Nick.

'Right, but—'

'You can get Sally to sort all that out, though, can't you, darling?'

Nick's face softened as he nodded at his wife, then leaned over Felicity. 'So, Bun, Dee might help us out, how about that? She's very nice – she's looked after lots of children before.' She didn't react, and he straightened again. 'Of course, we'll need references from your former employers – before we settle anything.'

'Oh, Nick, don't be so bossy. She's happy to give references, aren't you, Dee?' Mariah reached out and ran a hand through his hair, disrupting the combed lines. She turned to me again and Nick put his free arm around her and they leaned against each other, a little family tableau – mother, father, daughter. If they'd stayed that way, I think I would have left, but Felicity wriggled out and vanished behind Nick. She peeked at me around his hip, shoving her hair back with both hands. There were shadows under her wide-apart eyes, which were the deep green of a ficus or a fern exposed to a sudden shaft of sunlight. Her face was bone white. She vanished again behind her father.

I knew I should have made my excuses and left, but it was as if tiny hooks had sprouted from my heart and attached themselves to this small, vulnerable being. I wanted to know her – I wanted it more than I'd wanted anything in a very long time.

'I don't think we met the College couple you worked for last?' said Mariah. 'Did they leave already?'

It really was an extraordinary way to introduce an anxious child to her new carer. Felicity had barely managed to look at me, let alone adjust to the idea that I was to be her new nanny – and she certainly had not agreed to that, or to anything else – but Nick and Mariah were nodding and smiling, and I saw that beneath all this confidence and rapid decision-making, they were as anxious and unsettled as their child. They were desperate to be rescued, I felt – though from what, I had no idea. I decided that I must, for Felicity's sake, stay and find out.

Chapter 4

Faraday would now like to know how much I told Mariah and Nick about my 'background' when they hired me. I feel myself stiffen. Of course I knew they'd look me up on their database, I was fully prepared for that, but even so the question feels threatening.

Perhaps this discomfort is visible on my face, because he leans forward and becomes weirdly unctuous. –Listen, Dee, we've all made mistakes in life, and at this stage we're looking into the backgrounds of absolutely everyone who's had regular contact with Felicity. There's no blame here, no blame at all. We just want to find this child, okay?

Khan says nothing. As she jots something down, the only section of her body that moves is her hand.

I have never consciously covered up my past. If people ask I tell them the truth: that I grew up in an old mill in rural Scotland, an only child with just my father, who was a gamekeeper for most of my childhood. I never knew my mother, and I left Scotland at the age of twenty, after my father died. I have never seen any point in going into any of the other long-ago, private and frankly irrelevant events in my past. If I told employers any more than that, then they might feel sympathetic to the young girl I once was, but doubts would inevitably creep in. They would find themselves lying awake at night, wondering if I'd told them the whole story, wondering if I could, perhaps, be guilty of something really wicked.

This sort of thing would make my job impossible and since I have no need for sympathy – and every need to earn a living – it would be entirely self-defeating to mention it. In fact, I didn't discuss my past with a single person until that night with Linklater in the Turf Tavern, when it all slithered out so unexpectedly.

But I must not think about that. Now is definitely not the time to think about Linklater.

I look Faraday in the eye and tell him that Nick and Mariah never asked about my background but that I gave them my references, which were glowing.

I assume Sally contacted the Philosophy don and the Zagreb professor, because that evening as I was sitting alone in Observatory Street, my suitcase packed by the door, trying not to scatter crumbs from the biscuits and cheese I was eating, Nick rang to finalize the arrangements.

'Well,' he said, 'you come highly recommended.' The monthly salary he mentioned was more than double what the Philosophy don had paid, and he offered generous holiday pay too, and overtime for weekends and evenings. I assured him that this wouldn't be necessary. I lived really quietly, I said, I preferred to be at home. The salary was more than enough to cover overtime – I could be there for Felicity whenever she needed me.

'Absolutely not,' he huffed. 'No, no, I wouldn't dream of it. This is an unusual position, a demanding one – the overtime stands.' I heard papers shuffle. No doubt he felt that the more he paid me, the more he could demand of me – and presumably College was covering the cost.

'Look, I just want to be clear, I hope you understand,' he said, suddenly gruff and efficient, 'that Felicity isn't your average eight-year-old. You might find her a little, um, challenging at times. As you know, she lost her mother four years ago, after a long illness, so she's had rather a tough time of it. She's been seeing a child psychologist in London and over the years we've worked on various approaches to try to get her speaking – CBT, behavioural, that sort of thing – none of which have made much difference. We've recently made the decision – with the blessing of her London therapist – to take a break from therapy for now, so at least you won't have to be taking her up and down to London every week. We'll probably find a psychiatrist here in Oxford for her if the situation doesn't resolve itself. There's a school of thought that medication can be helpful.'

I said nothing. I suspected that what his daughter needed was what all children need: love, attention, safety, acceptance – and patience.

'Her new school has been briefed, they're very supportive, but you don't need to be concerned with any of this. Your role's simple. All Felicity needs from you is consistency: good routines, meals at the same time, that sort of thing.'

'Right.' I wondered if he was about to mansplain my job to me. He would not be the first.

'You mustn't expect or pressurize her to speak.'

'No,' I said. 'That's clear.'

'Good, right then.' He sounded almost embarrassed suddenly, as if he'd been forced to confess intimate physical symptoms to a new doctor. 'I'll have Sally, my PA, send you over a basic contract. Three-month trial period okay with you?'

We agreed that I'd start at the Lodging when I got back from my holiday.

'Excellent, well, my wife's delighted.'

'And Felicity?'

'Oh yes, yes, she's thrilled.'

This, I felt, was extremely unlikely.

He didn't mention how he felt about hiring me and I didn't ask, because I assumed that he felt very little. I was a human resource to be settled and with my box ticked he could move onto his next major staffing issue, which I happened to know involved sacking the Senior Financial Bursar who'd made some appalling decisions, heavily influenced by an under-the-radar alcohol problem.

I finished my oatcakes, swept up the crumbs and carried my suitcase out to the car. I felt neutral as I locked Observatory Street for the last time, posted the key back through the letterbox and got into my Fiesta. If nothing else, I am an expert at shutting down my emotions when it comes to departures.

Faraday does not ask about my holiday and I see no need to tell him about it. Instead, I mention that their decision to hire me had seemed rapid, almost irresponsibly so, but they were desperate, and desperate parents make impulsive decisions.

A shifty look crosses Faraday's face, and I can tell that he has young children of his own. If he is divorced, then perhaps he doesn't see them as much as he'd like to. Perhaps he too has made hurried and impulsive decisions about their care – left them with people he barely knows, or those he knows to be flawed. Perhaps, like Nick and Mariah, he is guilty of distraction and absence. These factors, I realize, are likely to make him touchy, despite the approachable persona he is trying to convey. I will have to tread carefully. Nobody, after all, wants to be reminded of how precarious parenthood really is – how parents fail their children all the time in small ways and big, and how, in the blink of an eye, those failures can prove catastrophic.

Chapter 5

As if he can hear my thoughts, Faraday shifts uncomfortably on his seat, which seems too small to support his hefty body. His fingers sandpaper his stubble. –Okay. Right then, Dee – so, I'm wondering, did you notice any tensions in the family, when you started? Anything strike you as a bit off?

'Tensions' would be putting it mildly, and from the moment I started most things about this family seemed a bit 'off'. Mariah greeted me on my first day. She flung open the door almost the moment I knocked, as if she'd been waiting in the hall since I left. She was wearing crisp white linen – both top and bottom – but her face was more pallid, puffier beneath the eyes. Ten days without childcare had taken its toll.

'Dee! Hey! Welcome, welcome! How are you? Come in, come in. How was your vacation? I forgot where you went, was it Cornwall? Wales? I sent Felicity over to breakfast in College with Nick, so you can unpack and get settled in, okay?'

I probably looked surprised.

'Oh hey, don't worry, she can't wait to see you; I just thought, you know, it would be easier to get you settled in here first, unpack and whatever. As soon as you're sorted, Nick'll bring her over from College. You want me to send one of the guys to

get the rest of your things from your car? Did you park round
the back? I emailed to say come to the back gates – save you
walking round the front in this heat – but maybe you didn't
register that? Sorry, Dee. Too much information!'

I told her that I did register the instruction but that the back
gates were locked.

'Oh, shit. Sorry. I told the gardener to unlock it but I guess
he's a bit touchy with us. Nick had to move him over here from
the main College gardens – he'd been there over thirty years
and was becoming kind of impossible to manage. It was too
expensive to fire him and he's retiring next year anyway, but
he's not happy.'

I wondered if this level of indiscretion was a Danish thing.
I'd heard the Danes were direct. I wanted to warn her that an
Oxford College is no place for transparency. 'So anyway –' she
was saying, '– your car's open still? One of the guys can go get
your things.'

'This is all I have.' I nodded at my big old suitcase, which
seemed ample to me.

She frowned at it. 'But – you – that's it? That's all? Oh.' Her
eyelids fluttered. 'Oh, right. Okay! Yes, well, you move around
a lot, don't you? You need to keep things simple. God, I wish I
could do that.'

She ushered me into the hall, talking about clutter, then
asking again how my holiday had been, then instructing me
to keep my shoes on. 'We don't want nails sticking in your
feet.' She bounded upstairs, past decorators who were attacking
the Elizabethan oak panelling with electric sanders. The panelling stopped at the top of the stairs and the first floor landing
was covered in bald patches. When I looked closer, I saw that
layers of paint had been scraped off to reveal sections of old

wallpaper. The whole wall looked as if it was suffering from a nasty pigment disease. Mariah saw me looking. 'Yes!' she cried. 'It's really exciting, there's an original William Morris there – Bird & Pomegranate – you know the one? We're going to take it down to the London studio to restore it, then we'll rehang here. It's a bit of a mess right now – there'll be lots of bleaching and crazing and tears to fix, but it's going to be completely gorgeous. It's a lot of work, though, and we've got so much on right now, so it's going to look a bit unfinished up here for while I think, sorry.'

As businesses go, restoring wallpaper seemed particularly pointless to me.

'In Nick's Chiswick house I found this tiny bit of eighteenth-century chinoiserie behind the fireplace – just the size of a penny.' She continued talking as she led me up the attic stairs. 'I took it to my studio and analyzed the dye and the pattern and the paper composition, and I managed to work out the maker and date. I had the blocks made up and I recreated it – we did the whole room. It was stunning! There was a huge feature on it in *Homes & Antiques*.' She paused on the top step, perhaps to allow the momentousness of this achievement to sink in.

'Really?' I said, mildly.

But she was determined to win me over. 'Wallpaper can tell you everything you want to know about the people who lived in a house – their social status, their finances, their aspirations – I mean, the thing about wallpaper – ' her pretty brown eyes shone down at me – 'is unlike history books or letters or diaries, it doesn't lie.'

It took enormous restraint not to point out the obvious: that wallpaper is famous for papering over the cracks. Instead, I nodded, trying to look only mildly interested – I certainly didn't want her going on about wallpaper night and day thinking she had a captive audience. It is important, I find, to establish these unspoken but vital rules very early on.

The attic floor reeked of gloss paint and my eyeballs prickled as we walked into the room that was to be mine. It was a muggy day, and the top of the house felt airless and still. The decor was certainly minimalist. The only non-white thing other than the stripped floorboards was a grey rug. 'I thought you'd have more things of your own.' She glanced at my case. 'But just let me know if you'd like any particular cushions or artwork or anything, you know, I'd be really happy to—'

'Oh no,' I said, 'I don't need anything.' A shaft of sunlight hit the floorboards in the corridor behind her and I thought I saw something flit across the doorway, but I was tired, having driven overnight without any sleep – and my break had not exactly been restful. I also hadn't eaten since a sausage roll at 5 a.m. in a service station on the M6 and I never do well without food.

'Right, well, I'm going to let you settle in – no rush – then we'll get Felicity back here and we can have lunch together, okay? There's a kitchen now, thank God. And I'll talk you through our routine, how everything works, okay? Yes?'

She vanished and I began to unpack, folding my jeans, jumpers, fleeces and shirts into the chest of drawers. Parents always want to tell me how things are going to work. But it generally doesn't take too long to establish that that's for me to decide, not them.

The rest of my suitcase contained my books, papers and journals, some of which I stacked on the bedside table. I had done very little work on my proof while away, and I was keen to get back to it. People assume that you have to be a genius to succeed as a mathematician but a proof is more about tenacity and imagination than anything else. You have to believe, against all the odds, that you can create something new and amazing that transcends what anyone believes to be possible or correct. No matter how insane or unattainable that goal might seem, you have to pursue it, relentlessly, for as long as it takes.

I lined up my walking sandals and felted wool slippers – a gift from the Philosophy don's wife – under the bed. I tossed my sponge bag onto the bed, slid my photo album into the drawer, stowed my suitcase on top of the wardrobe and looked around. I took my boots off then and climbed up to unhook the ugly Oxford spires etching – I certainly didn't need a reminder of the pompous city that lay on the other side of these four-hundred-year-old walls.

The starkness of the room didn't bother me. It was way more restful than some of the cluttered or bizarre spaces I've been allocated over the years. The worst was the Albanian astrophysicist, a chaotic and neglectful single father, overweight and scrofulous, who hired me to care for his four-year-old son, Luca, a sweet, shy, undernourished child with complicated allergies for whom I felt a monstrous and debilitating pity. The astrophysicist had been allocated a one-bedroom College flat and wanted me to sleep on the sofa in the living room while he and Luca shared the bedroom. I drew the line at that, so he gave me his bed and squeezed himself onto the sofa bed. It was all very awkward. I cared for the little boy meticulously, but those six months felt interminable. There was never a mention of a mother, and sometimes at night the poor wee mite would creep in beside me, weeping softly, and I would have to carry him back to his own bed, kindly but firmly, and stroke his hair until he fell asleep, knowing that if I allowed my heart to open so much as a crack for him, I'd be completely undone.

Generally, I think fondly about the children I've cared for – I wonder where they are now, what they look like, what their lives have turned into. But I try not to let myself think about Luca, because whenever I do I feel a terrible guilt, as if somehow I could have rescued him, and did not.

The chemical paint smell in the hot bedroom was heady, and as I threw open a window, the Chapel bells began to clamour and clang. The sound was shockingly close – centuries of accumulated joy and sadness trembling through my skull and tangling there, before buzzing away into the ancient stone. The sound made me think of the line from a poem – 'bell-swarmed' Oxford. I looked at my watch, a quarter past ten. They must ring every fifteen minutes. I should be used to this in a city where the sound of bells fills the sky numerous times a day, but I'd never lived this close to a Chapel before – I was eye to eye with several panicking gargoyles.

I felt a little dizzy so I went into the bathroom, bent over the sink and scooped water into my mouth. My chest was constricted, perhaps because I'd allowed myself to think about Luca, and I had to lean on the sink for a moment or two until the discomfort passed. A floorboard by the doorway of Felicity's room gave a creak and I turned, thinking she'd come up – expecting to see her peeking round the door. It was open a crack. 'Felicity?' I went over and pushed it, gently, in case she was standing behind it, but the room was empty.

It was freakishly tidy – as if no child had ever set foot inside it. I wondered if this was some brutal Danish design ethos. The surfaces were all clear except for a collection of objects on the bedside table – mostly pebbles and feathers, arranged, I saw, in a perfect logarithmic spiral that ended in a lovely vole's skull, smooth and curved like a little white spaceship. I picked it up and held it for a moment. The bone around the eye-sockets was frilled and delicate, completely intact.

The shelf above the bed was filled with classic children's literature and on the end sat a framed photo of a woman and baby. It had to be Felicity and her mother – they had the same eerie wide-apart eyes. The woman's long dark hair was centre-parted and she was seated behind a bookshop counter with Felicity perched in front of her, about eighteen months old, a pretty, chubby thing with wild black curls sticking up madly all over the place. The hair was so exactly like my own daughter's that I almost found it hard to look.

I focused on Felicity's little face instead – so bright and full of life. She looked as if she might burst from the glass right into my arms. I wondered how this cherubic mite had turned into the ghostly and shaken being I'd encountered in the sunroom. I remembered, then, how the social worker used to call my baby 'our pretty wee troll' because of her hair. It felt insulting, but I couldn't object, because even though I was young, naive and inexperienced, I was not stupid: I knew it wasn't just my actions but my reactions that were under scrutiny. I could not seem to be touchy, prickly or even slightly aggressive.

I sat down heavily on the end of Felicity's bed and as I waited for the sickening sensation to recede, I focused on calculating as many digits of the square root of two as I could. The past will come up at me from time to time like this, demanding my full attention, but it generally goes away again fairly fast, and mental arithmetic sometimes helps – I tend to give myself little tasks, like multiplying two very big numbers in my head, or seeing if I can instinctively come up with a large prime number, then checking by trying to factorize it. But at this particular moment, square roots did not work, so I focused instead on

Felicity's mother's face. It was striking, almost mannish, without Mariah's crowd-pleasing prettiness, but with a presence that felt more profound. Her chin was tilted down and her eyes were enormous and haunted, looking up into the camera lens. She made me think of a pre-Raphaelite muse, but of course that was probably because of Mariah's incessant talk about William Morris wallpaper.

I put the photo back on the shelf and gazed around the immaculate room. An old nursing chair tucked beneath the eaves was almost exactly like one in the kitchen at Mill House. I went over to it and noticed, behind it, a small black eye in the painted wood panel: a keyhole. The little door had no handle or latch. I pushed the chair aside and tried to stick a finger in the rim but it wouldn't budge.

I heard something swish in the doorway, then, and I turned, guiltily, expecting to see Mariah, but the space was empty. It was either a breeze coming down the corridor from an open window somewhere, or it was Felicity who'd come up to find me, but had lost her nerve. I crossed the room and looked out: the corridor was empty. Somewhere on the floor below I could hear hammering. A builder bellowed, an urgent warning cry.

I composed my face, smoothed my hair and pushed my shoulders back. It was time to go downstairs and find out what could be done about this frightened little girl who spied at doorways, made no mess and saw the world in spirals.

Chapter 6

Mariah was standing at the top of the main staircase, talking on the phone and running her fingers over a patch of wallpaper as if stroking a lover's skin. Felicity stood a few feet closer to me on the landing, gnawing at the side of her thumb. She spotted me immediately and froze. She was wearing cut-off denim shorts and her legs, two long bendy stems, seemed intensely vulnerable. There was a painful sensation – a kind of swelling in my chest – as I gazed at her little shocked face.

'Oh Dee! You *are* here!' Mariah spotted me and said to her caller, 'I've got to go now, sorry. I'll call you back.'

She hung up and started talking about lunch, and how she'd take me through the practicalities. Mid-sentence, she glanced at Felicity's feet and said, 'I told you so many times to put shoes on, honey, there's nails and splinters everywhere.' Felicity stared at her bare feet. I realized that I needed to get her away from Mariah, and from the workmen and paint fumes and the hammering and crashing. Maybe we could go out into the garden. She might be more relaxed among trees and flowers.

'So, Angela's put out lunch for us,' Mariah was saying. 'Just cheese and salads, a bit basic, I hope that's okay?' Her phone jangled. 'Oh, God, just a moment, sorry, there's a panic going on at my studio.' She answered it, became brusque, said something about paper archives, then turned and went downstairs, giving her caller rapid, energetic instructions.

Felicity was still next to me, still staring at her bare feet.

'Do you maybe want to show me the garden?' I said. 'I've heard it's very pretty.'

She didn't even twitch. I could see that she wouldn't want to go anywhere with me right now, I was far too scary.

I tucked my shirt into my waistband and put a hand into my pocket, drawing out the little box I'd wrapped in tissues and brought back to Oxford. I hadn't intended to use it so soon, but it was clear that a distraction was needed. I held out my hand and began to unwrap the layers, revealing the old ring box, its black leather cover worn and tattered round the edges. 'I brought you this wee treasure to look at – it's been in my family in Scotland for years and years, and I thought you might like to see it. What do you think's inside?'

She glanced up at the box, but quickly fixed her eyes back on her feet.

I unpeeled the last bit of tissue and held my hand out. She looked up again.

'Do you want to open it,' I said, 'or shall I? Whoever opens it gets good luck.'

Tentatively, she reached out and touched the black box. 'That's it,' I said. 'Just lift that tiny gold catch there.'

She took a step closer and lifted the catch, levering open the lid and peering inside.

Her skin was the palest pink, with delicate, wheaten freckles across the bridge of her nose. I kept my hand steady, as if feeding a wild animal. 'What do you think it is then?' I said, quietly.

She touched it with the tip of her finger. I saw that she'd

chewed away painful raggedy strips of skin around her nail. 'It's a tooth, of course,' I said. 'A wee, witchy tooth.'

She pulled her finger back and looked up at me with vast, peculiar eyes, then gave her ear a rapid, fierce scratch.

'It belonged to my great-great-great-great-great-grandmother. They thought she was a witch because she used to have strange fits where she pulled things out of her mouth – balls of hair and straw, or lumps of coal and chicken feathers – and, presumably, this tooth.' I smiled.

Felicity's face was no longer so pallid. 'You can take her out of the box,' I said. 'It's really good luck to hold her. If she was a witch, she must have been a good witch because this tooth protects you from all the bad things.'

Very carefully, she picked the tooth up. It was a canine, ridged and stained the colour of tea, quite long – who knew if it was even human? She peered at it in the palm of her hand.

Some people are terrified of heights, not because they are afraid of falling, but because they are afraid that they might jump – they are lured by *l'appel du vide*, the call of the void. The same goes for anxious children, or some of them, at least. A pilot light flares behind their eyes when something unexpected happens and you know it's not the world that frightens them, but their own imaginations – their self-destructive impulses. Felicity, I felt, was one of these children. She looked more alive already as she stared at the tooth, which squatted in her palm. The tips of her black curls seemed electric now.

She put it back in its box very carefully, then spun round and ran downstairs after Mariah. Her footsteps were silent – her body seemed to make no impact at all on the ancient timbers of the house. She hovered at the kitchen doorway, looking up at me, thrilled by her moment with the tooth.

Mariah was standing in the hall still giving instructions on the phone, tapping her fingers on a sanded wood panel. I slid the tooth box back in my pocket and came downstairs, whistling and running my hand down the bannister, which was gritty with dust.

A workman came out of the dining room and hovered in front of Mariah with a drill hanging in his fist. Two more manoeuvred a steel ladder down the stairs, past me and along the hall so that Mariah, still talking, had to walk in front of them to get out of their way. For a moment it looked as if they were going to chase her into the lane, but at the last minute she disappeared into the front room and they took the ladder out the front door, leaving it open so any passer-by could just walk in. The Chapel bell gave a single, sonorous clang. The vibration passed down the hall and right through us. The effect on Felicity was dramatic: she hunched and covered her ears as if someone had punched her in the head. When the sound had faded, she straightened, but her cheeks were drained of colour again.

A passing builder paused and gave her a paternal smile, nodding at the table behind her, where Angela had laid out food. 'Ooh, that for me, then, love?'

It was like watching a child in a fairy tale turn to stone. All expression, all signs of life, slid from her features and any remaining light emptied from her eyes. 'That for me, then?' he repeated, no doubt thinking she hadn't heard, but she didn't even blink. The only movement in her body was the tiniest flicker of one eyelid. 'Right, that's a no, then.' The builder went away down the hall in a huff, his steel-capped boots echoing on the floorboards.

I could see why he might think the Master's daughter was haughty, but I have met some snobbish children in my time and this was something else entirely – this was closer to terror. I wondered what could have happened to the poor child that she'd react so violently to a stranger's friendly words. She slid into the kitchen, sat at the table, scratched her ear twice, then folded her hands on her lap and stared at them as if willing them to stay where they were.

Mariah appeared. 'Sorry, sorry, sorry! Right, did you wash your hands, Felicity?'

Felicity stared at her hands.

'Did she?' Mariah turned to me, exasperated.

I glanced at Felicity then nodded. 'She did, indeed.'

My fingers tightened around the tooth box in my pocket. I didn't feel bad. A little fib, after all, is sometimes necessary to win the trust of a nervous child.

Chapter 7

I had expected the police to focus on the day Felicity actually vanished, but Faraday's questioning seems resolutely general. He has not even asked me what I think has happened to her. I suppose they want to build a more detailed picture of the family and my place in it, but if I were on the other side of this table, I would definitely want to talk about the day Felicity disappeared.

The three days since she vanished have felt both surreal and quite traumatic. When a child goes missing, things move very rapidly indeed – particularly when it is the daughter of an Oxford College Master. The biggest shock has been the intensity of the media interest. But even the presence of police in the house that first day felt horrifying.

Two officers came to the Lodging as soon as Mariah phoned to report Felicity missing. When I got back from London and dropped my overnight bag in the hall, I heard deep voices in the kitchen and the unfamiliar static of a police radio. Somewhere upstairs the baby was crying. As I reached the kitchen doorway, I glimpsed bulky black jackets, reflective vests. One was sitting at the table opposite Mariah, with his back to me, filling out what looked like a form. Mariah's face was contorted with fear.

Reality crashed in on me, then, and I had to step back out into the corridor.

Mariah had phoned me in a panic when I was on the Oxford Tube. She couldn't find Felicity, she'd cried, did I have her? It was hard to take in at the time, but now I was back at the Lodging and the police were in the kitchen, it hit home as it hadn't before: Felicity really was not here. Nobody knew where she was. She had become a missing child – a high-risk missing child.

The baby's desperate cries were intensifying and I could hear them in stereo – coming from upstairs and piped through the baby monitor into the kitchen – but nobody was paying any attention to him. I put out a hand to steady myself on the panelling. I was going to have to find the right expression, the correct voice and manner to deal with this.

Mariah must have spotted me because she got up and rushed into the corridor and came at me, desperately hanging onto my arms. 'Dee! Oh my God, oh my God, where is she? She's just vanished!' She looked deranged; her skin was blotchy, her hair electrocuted, her eyes pink-rimmed and incredulous. Clearly one of us was going to have to stay in control. I felt myself seal off the panic that had been threatening to take hold of me. I straightened my spine and guided her back into the kitchen where the investigating officers were waiting.

As they introduced themselves, Mariah continued to weep. The baby monitor piped tinny, rhythmic mewling and I felt them taking in my fleece, jeans and boots as they asked what I'd been doing in London, and when I'd last spoken to or heard from Felicity. I probably didn't look like someone who'd been to see the Royal Shakespeare Company, or stayed the night in a Bloomsbury hotel.

While they were asking when I'd last had contact with Felicity, whether she'd been talking to anyone online, what friends she might see, whether she had any social media accounts – Snapchat, Instagram, Facebook, a phone of her own, a laptop? – Mariah yelped something about the baby and lurched out of the room. I told the officers that Felicity was eight years old, of course she wasn't on social media – and that she had no friends – no, really, none. I heard Mariah stumble up the stairs and moments later her high voice erupted on the monitor, mingling with the baby's cries. There was no way she was going to be able to calm him or feed him in that state. I said I should probably go and help her for a moment but would come straight back down and answer their questions.

In truth, as much as Mariah needed my help, I needed to get out of the kitchen. Everything suddenly felt dire and very frightening. I knew I had to stop myself from thinking about where Felicity was – I couldn't allow my thoughts to go there, because if I did that, then everything would spiral out of control. I forced myself to partition off the panic. I counted the stairs as I went up them – sixteen treads – two to the power four.

The police would probably initially assume she'd run away, but when they heard more about her personality and realized she'd never do that, they would start looking at the family for answers – at Nick first, I thought, as I hurried along the landing into Mariah's room – they always looked at the father first – but they'd also turn to Mariah, and then at some point, to me, too. They'd have to consider everybody Felicity was close to.

But I was rushing ahead of myself. It was vital not to do that. I needed to keep a clear head. For Felicity's sake, I must not allow this fear to take hold and rip through me. I took a breath and stepped into Mariah's room.

Chapter 8

Faraday would now like my opinion on the nature of Felicity and Mariah's relationship.

Presumably they are well aware of the state Mariah is currently in. They will need to establish quite how bad she really is – and therefore, how far things could have gone between her and Felicity.

–Could you tell us a bit about the two of them together? Faraday offers an approachable if weary smile. –How do they get on?

–Well, Felicity can't speak to Mariah, so . . .'

Khan looks up sharply, but as usual, it is Faraday who asks the next question. –It must have been a bit strange for you, coming into a family where the child doesn't speak to her mum?

–Stepmother, I correct him. –And Felicity doesn't speak to anyone except her father – and me, now.

–Right, yes, she's supposedly mute, isn't she?

–Selectively mute.

–So she's decided to talk to you but not Mrs Law?

–Selective mutism isn't a *decision* not to talk. She physically can't speak to people. It's about anxiety and fear – like a phobia.

–But she can speak to her father and to you, you say, so doesn't that mean there's an element of choice?

–No, I just told you, it's an emotional and physical response to fear and tension. It's a kind of prison for her. She couldn't speak to me at first either, but now she feels safe enough with me that her voice sort of frees itself.

They must surely understand the basics of selective mutism by now, they really can't be this clueless. I wonder why they want me to explain it to them like this. Perhaps they're testing to see whether I fully understand the condition – whether I could have been frustrated enough, taken it personally enough, to crack and do her some kind of harm.

–Right, well, this selective mutism must be very hard for Mrs Law to deal with, says Faraday.

–Yes, I say. –Very.

–So, why do you think Felicity's still so anxious around her then, after, what, four and a half years?

–Well, I suppose things between them are complicated.

In fact, the lunch we had together on the first day told me pretty much everything I needed to know about their relationship.

The catering manager, Angela, had laid out food for us on the kitchen table – salad, a separate little jug for dressing, couscous, smoked salmon, Brie, condiments in little ceramic pots, sliced French bread and a bowl of hulled strawberries. Mariah sat down and helped herself to some salmon, talking earnestly about Felicity's likes, dislikes and suspected allergies. First came a list of foods Felicity would not touch: anything slimy or lumpy, almost anything vegetable, no fish, little meat except chipolatas, nothing with seeds or spices. Felicity gnawed the tattered skin around her thumb, which could, I felt, be her only source of nutrition if Mariah was to be believed.

I nodded, as if taking mental notes, and wondered if there was something actually wrong with Mariah. She was rolling up slices of smoked salmon as she spoke, sprinkling them with dill, but not eating them. I made myself a Brie sandwich with a nice dollop of fig chutney. The couscous had the downtrodden air of having loitered on a buffet, but I spooned it onto my plate anyway. It had been a very long time since the service station sausage roll and I was starving even if they weren't.

After the food rules came instructions about how much time Felicity could spend on her iPad daily, how long she must spend outside and what were considered to be appropriate activities. There was even a rule about how many pages I was meant to read to her at bedtime (a minimum of ten). I pretended to listen as I ate, nodding occasionally. Felicity had begun to rub and scratch behind her ear again. To distract her, I put a bit of baguette on her plate and pushed the butter towards her. In London, Mariah was saying, there had been an unfortunate incident with a dyspraxic au pair on the Serpentine, 'So probably no water sports, Dee.'

I heard myself snort at this, and Felicity stopped scratching. She glanced at me, shyly, sideways. I widened my eyes at her and as she stared back down at her plate I saw a smile flit across her mouth. I knew then that I could connect with her, words or no words: she was nowhere near as locked in as Mariah believed.

Mariah didn't notice any of this. She was talking about Felicity's sensitivity to loud noises, as if the child was not sitting at the table in front of her. 'This house isn't ideal – the Chapel bells are obviously hard, though thank God, they don't ring at night between eleven and eight. It's like she has the whole world turned up to the maximum volume all the time, you know? It's exhausting.' She meant for her, not for Felicity.

Felicity stopped scratching and reached for the lemon. She squeezed it onto her bread. Mariah's instructions were now becoming tiresome so I asked about the little door in the panelling in the bedroom. 'Oh, that?' Her eyes lit up. 'Yes, that's actually a little tiny room – she's not allowed in there, though.'

Until that moment, the skin between Felicity's eyebrows had been crumpled into an anxious Pi sign, but at the mention of the little room, her face suddenly flattened to neutral. I dusted crumbs off my fingers. 'Why? What's in there?'

'Oh, nothing, nothing,' Mariah waved a hand, 'just some old newspapers from the 1930s and a load of dead bees. The builders found piles of them in there, but no sign of a hive. I've got a pest guy coming next week to check it out. But the thing is, we think the space in there was originally a priest's hole.'

'A priest's hole?' I put a big juicy strawberry on Felicity's plate. She looked at it warily.

'Yes, like a secret little place to hide illegal Catholic priests in Jacobean times. It's very exciting if it is one, and it really might be – the original part of this house was built in 1603. The builders found it behind a panel up there last week. There are actually quite a few priest's holes in these old Oxford houses. Catholics were banned in Elizabethan and Jacobean times so they were literally hunting down priests and executing them. I want my friend who's an architectural historian to come and have a look at it, but he's in Florence for a couple of months so . . .'

'It must have been used since the seventeenth century,' I pointed out, 'if there are newspapers in there.'

Felicity picked up her strawberry and put it into the middle of the lemon-juiced bread. She shook salt over it and glanced up at me as she put the saltcellar down. I wondered if she was testing me to see if I'd intervene. It was a good sign – she might be afraid and mute, but she had gumption.

'Yes, of course.' Mariah finally popped a tiny piece of salmon into her mouth. 'There's some Victorian wallpaper in there under the paint, too. So someone made it nice to be in – maybe for children. It was probably a nursery room at one time.'

'A hidey hole?'

'Yes, maybe, I think so.'

I glanced at Felicity, who bit into her lemon juice and salted strawberry sandwich then winced as the acid hit her ragged cuticles. She stuck a finger in her water glass. Mariah didn't notice. 'That wallpaper's actually the other big reason she can't go in there,' she said, casually. 'It's nothing to worry about, but it – well, it might be a little bit toxic.'

'A *little bit* toxic?'

'Well, yes, the pigment looks like it's Scheele's green – that bright green colour. It was popular in Victorian days but it has arsenic in it. It's not always lethal – William Morris himself had it in his house, actually. It's kind of exciting, if it is a Scheele's green, but please, don't worry; I mean, it's going to be fine if it's just left alone. I've damp-tested the walls and it's dry up there, so nothing's going to come into the air. I wasn't going to say anything to you, I didn't want you to worry about it. I can't deal with it right now, with everything else I've got going on, so until I've had the chance to sort it out, the priest's hole's going to stay locked, okay?'

Strawberry juice trickled down Felicity's chin.

'Oh, Felicity, you're eating. Great.' Mariah finally noticed her. 'You have . . . Here, honey—' She held out a napkin. 'You have something there.'

Felicity ignored the outstretched hand. Her jaw tightened, her brows lowered.

'See!' Mariah turned to me with an exasperated laugh. 'For her, I don't exist.'

Felicity's expression remained doggedly neutral, but I sensed that Mariah was genuinely hurt, and that her laughter covered something more painful and complicated than the day-to-day difficulties of food, mess and silence.

Seeing them at lunch that day, I realized that it wasn't just the noise of drills or hammering or the bells or the moving of furniture, the dust and toxic wallpaper that made the house feel so fraught. It was these two. Something between them was seriously misfiring. They seemed to be tangled in a pattern of suspicion, neediness and frustration – maybe something darker, too, something more alarming. I leaned over, picked up a napkin and pressed it into Felicity's palm. Her stained and tattered fingers curled around it and for a moment we were holding hands.

Chapter 9

After I have tried to explain to Faraday and Khan that Felicity's difficult relationship with Mariah was probably tied up with the loss of her mother, her complex feelings about her father and a general anxiety about the world, their focus turns, inevitably, to her behaviour at night.

Specifically, and not surprisingly, Faraday wants to discuss her sleepwalking.

–Did they warn you about her sleep problems?

I say that yes, Nick briefed me, though he did play the situation down somewhat. Either that, or he had no idea what his daughter was going through in the night.

He called me into the sunroom on my first day to talk me through the 'bedtime routine' – I assume he and Mariah had decided that this particular briefing would be better coming from him. He was sitting on the white sofa, long legs crossed, crystal glass in hand, a stack of papers on the coffee table. I refused his offer of a whisky and sat down on the armchair opposite him.

'Oh? I thought perhaps you might appreciate this, with your Scottish background – it's Talisker, thirty-year-old.'

'I'm not much of a drinker,' I said, though I knew exactly

how special it was – my father would have murdered for a thirty-year-old Talisker. Perhaps Nick was trying to establish dominance by showing me that he casually drank from £400 bottles of whisky. It seemed like overkill, if so. He made dutiful small talk, asking – with one eye on his open laptop – how my first day had gone, whether I was comfortable in the attic rooms, and had everything I needed.

'Good, good.' He straightened. 'So, Felicity's bedtime routine: I'll try to be here to put her to bed when I can, but realistically I have a lot of evening commitments, so in all likelihood it'll be you most nights.'

I reassured him that this was what I'd been expecting.

The 'routine' involved sending Felicity up alone to get her pyjamas on and brush her teeth. 'She can drag her feet,' he said. 'I give her half an hour, then get more military.' He gave a brief, tense smile and I realized that, in fact, he was uneasy, possibly even nervous. 'I read to her, then it's lights off by nine.' He paused and looked at his whisky tumbler. 'Now, look, I'm sure this won't bother you, but I should also give you the heads-up that she's not a terribly good sleeper.'

'Ah well, that's okay, nor am I.'

He blinked. 'Right. Okay. Yes, well, you might hear her talking in her sleep and possibly moving around from time to time. She's been known to, um, wander about a bit, but it's nothing to be too concerned about. She's never been good at night. Her mother used to let her come in bed with us, which is probably the root of the problem. My first wife believed in "attachment parenting". Are you familiar with that theory?'

'Yes, of course.'

'Right, yes, well, Ana "wore" Felicity for the first eighteen months, almost never put her down, breastfed her until she was three and a half, never took her near a playgroup, refused to leave her crying at night. She was very intense about motherhood.'

All parents, I felt, ought to be intense if it meant not leaving their babies to cry alone at night. On the other hand, I had to admit that the clients of mine who believed in baby-wearing and breastfeeding their pre-schoolers did tend to be the least sane on the whole.

'The sleepwalking used to be more serious. We had to put a bolt on the front door in London as she did get out of the house once. She was found walking along Chiswick High Road at three in the morning, which was – ' he gave an almost imperceptible shudder 'alarming. But of course she'd just lost her mother so she was . . . ah . . . somewhat discombobulated at the time.'

His choice of 'discombobulated' with its connotations of perplexity or befuddlement was bizarre – surely 'distraught' or 'grieving' would be a more accurate way to describe the mental state of a recently bereaved four-year-old. But Nick was obviously keen to distance himself from his daughter's anguish. A discombobulated child could, in theory, be 're-combobulated' with the imposition of order, logic or reasoning. A child whose mother has died, on the other hand, would for ever be altered by loss.

'There's a bolt at the top of the front door here,' he was saying. 'So, that's one thing to remember, please, um, Dee, if you're ever alone with her overnight: do make sure it's bolted. She hasn't done it for a while but I suppose she always might. It's probably genetic – her mother had the same, ah, insomniac tendencies. But you don't need to know all this. Mariah wanted me to mention it to you because some of the au pairs did, um, find Felicity's night-time antics a little unsettling. I'm sure you've seen it all before, though, you'll just be able to ignore her.'

I nodded, though nothing would possess me to ignore a little girl who was wandering around the house alone in the middle of the night. I would have to stand on tiptoe to slide back the bolt, but an eight-year-old, even a sleeping one, was perfectly capable of climbing on a chair to do the same.

When I mention this to Faraday and Khan, they both nod, vaguely, as if they can't help but agree.

'Yes, you'll take it all in your stride, I'm sure.' Nick rested his eyes on my face and I felt as if I'd been given a warning. The signet ring on his little finger clinked against the cut glass as he picked it up. 'No, it won't rattle you.' He took a sip and put the glass back down, soundlessly, next to his papers. 'That's why I hired you.'

I had the sudden perplexing sense that we were on the brink of an argument, though I had no idea why, or what about.

'Losing her mother has had a lasting impact, obviously, but she'll be fine when she settles here,' he said, as if closing the discussion.

'Could I just ask –' I said, 'it was cancer your wife died of, was it?'

His body didn't move, his expression barely changed, but his skin flushed a livid, mottled scarlet and behind his heavy rimmed spectacles his eyes turned to granite. He glanced at his watch, and uncrossed his legs. 'I'm not sure my first wife's illness is relevant. Now, it's getting late—'

'Well, it affects Felicity so it's releva—' I began.

He cut me off. 'You've been very clear that you aren't here for the long term. Now, I should go up and put my daughter to bed.' His colour subsided as rapidly as it had risen, but as he loomed over me I felt a quiet violence emanating from him. My question had exposed vulnerability, perhaps an unhealed wound, and he could not bear me to have seen that. He paused and turned with one hand on the doorframe, fixing stern eyes on me. 'Oh yes, ah, Dee, one more thing: can you read to her every night even if she says no, please. Ten pages, minimum.'

'Yes, Mariah said.'

'Right, well, she won't read on her own – ah – um – Dee, but there's a shelf of classics above the bed so please just work your way through them.'

As I followed him out into the hall, it struck me that leaving me on an instruction, inserting my name with the fillers 'ah – um' as if he couldn't quite summon it to mind, were control techniques. I was almost flattered that he felt the urge to control me. Perhaps he felt that I had the potential to become a rogue employee. Or perhaps he simply sensed that, on some level, he'd met his match.

Chapter 10

Khan is staring at me so intensely now that I wonder if she's about to speak. But she doesn't.

–Is this going to take much longer? I glance at my watch. –Surely we'd all be better off looking for her than just sitting here talking? I really don't know what I can tell you that can possibly help.

–I understand why you'd think that, Dee. Faraday's voice is mild but firm, calling my attention back to him. –But I can reassure you we've got a huge deployment of officers and resources out there searching Oxford. Other than the ongoing enquiries round the city, we've got foot officers with dogs in all the parks, and down the river banks and the canal, and the helicopter's out again. The Fire Brigade's got a boat on the river. She's top of the news, print and TV, and Dr Law's doing another press conference this afternoon. We've got a huge team on this – and public sightings are coming in all the time – #FindFelicity's all over social media. We're going to find her, okay? But if you can just answer our questions, and help us build a clearer picture of this little girl and her family – what might have gone on here – then you're going to be a big help. Okay?

I think of all the curious strangers who are right now camped on the cobbles outside the Lodging, blocking the entrance to the Porter's Lodge, and I feel panic rising again in my chest. They began to appear on Saturday after Nick gave the first press conference. At first there were just a few of them, but more came quickly and by the evening, the lane was full of camera crews, reporters, photographers and bystanders with lenses fixed on the windows and doors. Right now, Mariah and Nick are trapped behind the blinds for a third day, under intense scrutiny. Angela sends over meals while Nick bellows into his phone, marshalling every high-level media contact he can think of to get his child back: 'We need to get this on top of the news' – 'Tell him to get this to News 24'. Mariah, meanwhile, paces the corridors separately with their howling infant, shadowed by the family liaison officer, who offers tea and toast, gives updates, writes things down. The attic is horribly empty. None of the reporters ever lift their heads or lenses that far, and I can peek round the blind and watch them, unobserved.

As I stepped out of the Lodging today to get into the police car, I hit a wall of flashing light, jostling bodies – cameras and microphones shoved into my face. 'It's the nanny!' 'Dee!' 'Dee!' 'Where is she, Dee?' 'What's happened to Felicity?' The uniformed officer who came to drive me had to shield me for my own good as I got in, but the arrangement of our bodies – me effectively bundled into a police car – put me in a position of guilt. These photographs will have to go somewhere. I am probably emblazoned across the Internet already.

Children go missing all the time, roughly 140,000 of them a year in Britain alone – I have looked up the statistics – but there is something about Felicity's disappearance that has sparked a national frenzy. Perhaps it is because she is the daughter of the Master, the Head of House, and his beautiful Scandinavian wife, a new mother herself: the perfect family in a photogenic Oxford setting that is shorthand for a certain kind of British privilege and status. And perhaps because of that, there is something darker going on here, too. Vile comments are appearing beneath the #FindFelicity postings on social media – accusations, suspicions. The mob is turning.

The walls of the interview room seem to sway – I start to feel clammy and queasy. I must not think about what's going on outside this police station, even outside this room. I close my eyes. The situation has escalated into something bigger, noisier and more overwhelming than anything it could have been possible to imagine.

–Are you okay, Dee? Faraday says. –You look a bit peaky.

I open my eyes again.

–I know this is really stressful, he says. –You're bound to be worried. Do you need a break? How about another cup of tea? That one's a bit cold. Are you hungry at all? Fancy a ham sandwich? There's a vending machine – not great, to be honest, but—

–Can we just get on with it?

Khan raises an eyebrow.

–No problem. Faraday shuffles his notes. –Right. So. Felicity not talking – it must be a bit tricky, looking after a child who won't – sorry, can't – speak. I expect you got a bit frustrated at times, too, did you?

I force myself to focus on the question, and not its implication.

Felicity's dedication to not speaking was certainly mighty in the beginning. For the first few weeks she made no verbal sounds whatsoever in my company, but I'd done my research and I knew this silence had nothing to do with defiance or stubbornness. I could see she felt genuine terror when I spoke to her directly.

She'd freeze the way she had on the first day with the builder. It was awful to cause her such distress so I tried to ask only indirect questions and never to expect an answer. 'Perhaps a walk by the river would be better than a trip to the Covered Market?' I'd say, and watch her body language. I knew she'd not talk until she trusted me, and that in order to trust me, she mustn't feel that I was impatient for her to speak.

All this might be frustrating if you expected normality, and it could certainly be disconcerting at times, but I found it fascinating too. Felicity's silences were more than just an absence of sound. Each one vibrated at a different frequency, incubating intense emotions that I had to decode and deal with. It was like learning a new language or deciphering a puzzle. If I was impatient to hear her speak, it was only because I was curious – I wanted to know how she felt about her family, her dead mother, the move to Oxford, the Lodging. Specifically, and perhaps most urgently, I wanted to know what it was that drove her out of her bed at night.

Her night-time behaviour could be genuinely peculiar, and it was quickly obvious why none of the au pairs had lasted too long. I'd hear sudden activity in her room – a chair dragged across the floor, the thud of a hard object falling, a cry or a wild laugh, maybe urgent whispering or rapid footsteps. It was both tantalizing and eerie to hear her voice, given that it was withheld from me so stringently while she was awake. I'd get out of bed and rush through to her via the connecting bathroom and I never knew what I'd find. Sometimes she'd be lying in bed, eyes shut, feigning asleep, but other times, she'd be up and busy.

Once I found her standing with her nose pressed against the wall, sniffing the paint; another night she was crouched on the floor, absorbed in an invisible and complicated task, her fingers busy with nothing. More worryingly, not long after I arrived, I found her cross-legged on her desk at 2 a.m. with the window open, having a deep, nonsensical conversation with the gargoyles.

I have never been a good sleeper. Generally, I don't expect to get more than three or four fitful hours myself over the course of any night. I usually sit up working, reading journals or perhaps doing maths puzzles – I turn to my proof as other people do a Sudoku, a crossword, or a mobile phone. A proof is basically an exercise in proving that a certain mathematical hypothesis – something you intuitively believe to be true – actually is. This is harder than it sounds – Bertrand Russell and Alfred North Whitehead, after all, took many years and several hundred pages just to prove that $1+1 = 2$. But although my work can be aggravating at times, it has marvellous, triumphant moments and above all, it is a brilliantly diverting way to tackle insomnia.

But one night, just a few weeks after I arrived, I was sitting up, working, very late. As I worked, I listened to the night-time sounds: the bedlam cries of students rolling back to their residences, a car gunning up the High, and the conversation of the house itself – the creak and shift of ancient timbers, the gurgle of pipes, the infinitesimal contractions of newly plastered walls, stair treads popping back into place. I must have fallen into quite a deep sleep eventually because I woke, suddenly, with a cricked neck and an uneasy sense that things had been going on around me, doors opening and closing, footsteps pattering up and down the corridor and staircase, in and out of Felicity's room. I got up and hurried through the bathroom to Felicity's door, but it seemed to be jammed shut. Then I heard her cry out, 'Mummy! Mummy!'

I rattled the handle and called her name, but she didn't come.

I shoved the door with my shoulder and it gave – I burst in.

She was in bed – lying on her back like a tiny medieval knight on a tomb, with alabaster skin and her arms folded over her furry squirrel toy. The nightlight cast a soft glow on her pallid face. Everything in the room seemed to be in order, but even so, it all felt subtly wrong – as if the furniture had been caught in a criminal act and was sitting up, rigid and guilty. Her face looked odd – her skin too waxy, too flat. She made me think of an abandoned doll, her hair foaming darkly on the pillow, her face blank, locked-in. A sudden breeze flapped the curtains like the wings of a trapped bird, and I jumped.

I crossed the room and hovered by the bed – I knew I mustn't disturb her if she really was asleep, but something told me she was awake. Perhaps she'd woken herself up with her bad dream. It was hard not to just scoop her up and pull her into a hug, but I knew that would scare her so I leaned over and said, gently, 'It's only me, darling. It's just Dee, it's okay, everything's okay.' She didn't open her eyes but I felt the quality of her stillness intensify. She was definitely awake.

Behind me, I heard a floorboard out in the corridor creak and I turned, expecting to see someone standing at the door – Nick or Mariah, woken by me crashing through the door. Nobody was there. The corridor light was on and I could see the stair bannister, the newly sanded floorboards, the bare white wall. I reminded myself that in a four-hundred-year-old house things creak all the time.

Felicity's room seemed to be just as it was when I put her to bed. Her colouring books were stacked on the desk, her pens tidied into their pot, treasures lined up in their spiral on the bedside table, wardrobe doors closed, toys arranged in the cor- rect order on the foot of her bed. I'd established that her tidiness had nothing to do with Mariah. It was Felicity who kept it this way. No doubt the bedtime ritual of lining up toys, organizing pens and putting clothes away gave her a sense of agency. After all, her mother was dead: the world had proved itself to be an unpredictable place, capable of wreaking havoc. She had to control whatever she could.

I noticed then what was wrong: her desk chair was over by the bathroom door, upside down. I must have knocked it over when I shoved my way in. I tiptoed across and turned it upright, but it concertinaed in my hands. The joint where the top rail met the upright had come out. I slotted it back in but one of the spindles had cracked in two. A jagged half was still attached to the leg but the other half was gone. I'd have to buy wood glue, find the spindle and stick it all back together.

Then I noticed that the door to the priest's hole was slightly ajar. So this was why she was lying still and tense. She must have gone through Mariah's things to find the key – maybe slipped into their bedroom when I was distracted downstairs, making lunch or washing up. She knew she wasn't allowed to go in there.

I went over, toed the priest's hole door open and stuck my head and shoulders inside. The darkness was dense and complete, and an unpleasant smell hit my nostrils – something sweet and rotting. The priest's hole was no more than an arm's span wide and not tall enough to stand up straight in. There was no light or window and the darkness felt complete, solid, clammy; exerting a kind of pressure on the eyeballs. I felt as if I'd stuck my head inside a big mouth and was breathing in its halitosis.

I came out and kicked the door shut. It bounced back open. There was no sign of the key so I pressed it shut with both hands then reached out and pulled the nursing chair across to block it. In the morning I would have to find the key, lock it up and not allow her back in there.

I went back over to Felicity's bed and sat on the floor. It was hard to believe that any child would want to go into that unpleasant little hole alone in the middle of the night, even while sleepwalking. But perhaps the smell itself had driven her to steal the key and go in. Smells can bloom in the small hours just as sounds do – they worm their way into dreams, alerting primitive alarm systems.

I sat with her for a long time, until I felt her breathing ease and lengthen, and the tension around her eyes loosen.

Later, as I was climbing back into my bed, I trod on something and a sharp pain shot through my heel. I bent down, felt around on the floor and my fingers closed on a smooth wooden tube – the jagged half of the chair spindle.

I imagined Felicity armed with it, running into my room and hovering by my bed – perhaps afraid to wake me up – unable to speak in order to tell me what awful imaginary assailant was chasing her. Maybe with a different child I'd have worried for my own safety, but I felt no threat from Felicity – whatever she was running from, whatever she needed to defend herself against, it definitely wasn't me.

But I should have woken up – I should have been there to comfort and reassure her. She had come into my room in a panic, seeking shelter, but I had been dead to the world. I was no better than all the other adults in her life. She'd needed me, and I'd let her down.

Chapter 11

When Faraday asks if Nick and Mariah were 'hands-on parents', I actually hear myself laugh.

He and Khan both look at me sharply, no doubt shocked that I can find anything amusing at all under such awful circumstances. They are right, of course, there is nothing remotely funny about this; it was a laugh of despair. I think about trying to explain this, but I know it'll only make things worse, so instead I lean forwards and tell them that Nick and Mariah were hands off to the point of negligence.

After the initial controlling briefings, neither of them seemed to want to involve themselves in Felicity's daily life – they were far too caught up in their own concerns. The University term does not start until October, but right from the start, their schedules were overwhelming.

–The Master's Lodging is no place for a child, I say. –Over the summer it was mayhem; there were the builders and non-stop visitors and catering staff coming in and out all day. But in term time it got even worse. They were constantly entertaining in the evenings. That's a terrible environment for a shy child, but they didn't really seem to consider the impact it was having on Felicity. They just left her with me.

–Well, they're very busy people, Faraday says. –And they'd hired you to look after her, hadn't they?

I realize he needs evidence: specifics, numbers, facts. –In the seven months I've been there, I say, –they've only taken her for an outing twice. Once to the Ashmolean, once to Blenheim.

–Blenheim's a nice family day out, he says, wistfully.

To get her out of the house that summer, I often drove her around the Cotswolds in my Fiesta. We'd stop somewhere peaceful, lay out my tartan blanket and have a picnic. She was a dreamy companion on these trips, occupied by small things – bugs, flies, pebbles, oddities – leaving me to work on my proof, glancing up from my notebook from time to time to make sure she hadn't wandered off. When it rained, we often went to the Pitt Rivers Museum. She'd make straight for the shrivelled human heads, but when she'd exhausted those, she'd get grumpy and refuse to look at anything else.

I certainly hadn't planned to confront Mariah about her absence from Felicity's life, but the opportunity presented itself when we met in the kitchen late one night towards the end of the summer. It was gone midnight and, having reached a particularly complex and frustrating stage in my thinking, I'd taken a break to do a quick maths puzzle. The puzzle asked you to visualize holding two metal bolts parallel but with the heads at opposite ends, and then move them so that they touched, fitting their grooves together, then turning one bolt clockwise and the other anticlockwise. You had to work out whether the heads would move closer or further apart as you turned. I was stumped so I took myself downstairs, thinking I might find a toolkit containing bolts. I was poking about under the stairs when I heard the front door open and rapid footsteps coming down the hall – Mariah appeared. She looked startled to see me under the stairs, and perhaps slightly irritated too. 'What on earth are you doing in there, Dee? Why are you still up?'

I shoved the things back, mumbled something slightly incoherent and marched towards the kitchen, saying, 'I'm just making chamomile tea. I baked some flapjack today too, do you want some?'

'Oh, okay, sure – the tea, thanks, not the flapjack.' She followed me in and flopped onto the kitchen chair, kicking off her high-heeled sandals, wiggling her painted toes and pulling her hair from its clip.

'Going up and down to London like this every day doesn't leave you much time for family life.' I flipped on the kettle. 'You must be very tired.'

'God, yes! But that's the pregnancy, I think.'

'Your hours would be very long even if you weren't pregnant.'

She looked at me, quizzically, perhaps sensing the critique. 'Well, I know. But I run my own business, Dee. I have to be there. Not that I'm complaining – I love it. Nick says I'm obsessed.'

'With *wallpaper*?'

If she noticed the note of incredulity, she didn't seem to find it offensive – in fact, she seemed to take it as an invitation to tell me her life story. 'I know! I got into it by chance, really. I came to London when I was only seventeen years old – I was an au pair, believe it or not. I didn't have a good childhood, Dee; my mother isn't a stable person, she's kind of crazy, drinking, lots of men – not so nice men.' Her tone was confiding. 'I was a little bit lost, to be honest with you. I was a terrible au pair so I got a job in a bookshop – and that turned out to be Ana's shop. She sort of took me under the wing, you know, and that's how we, well, that's how . . . you know, all this happened . . .' She waved vaguely around the kitchen as if Ana had kindly donated an entire life to her.

'What was she like?'

'Ana? Oh, well, God, she was – I guess kind of amazing. I mean, I looked up to her – I felt like she was everything I wasn't at the time. She seemed . . . I don't know, just incredibly glamorous and, my God, so clever. I think she'd read every single book in that shop. I was badly educated, and I didn't look like this in those days, Dee, I was, like, ten kilos heavier,' she puffed out her cheeks, 'no sense of style, very bad hair. She helped to transform me, and I was basically in awe of her, and of course she was married to Nick, who I thought was *so* handsome – and a little bit scary, too.' She laughed, as if finding Nick intimidating was absurd. She seemed so relaxed talking about herself, confident that I'd want to know everything.

'Anyway, to make a long story short, a historic wallpaper specialist used to come in the bookshop and we'd look at the books she ordered, and eventually she offered me a job so I took it.' Her hair was loose, her face shadowed, too tired for charm now, and I suddenly sensed a seam of granite running through her – a hard-won instinct for self-preservation, perhaps.

'But you and Ana stayed in touch?' What I really wanted to ask was how she'd ended up marrying her dead saviour's husband. I wondered if they'd come together in their shared grief – or perhaps even when Ana was sick? Or perhaps, during her duckling-to-swan transformation, Mariah had seen Ana's little family and decided that she wanted it for herself.

'Yes, yes.' She lifted out her tea bag and tossed it onto a saucer. 'But you know, Ana wasn't easy; she was actually quite a complicated woman. She suffered of course, so . . . oh, I don't know . . .'

I began to ask whether it had been breast cancer but she cut me off. 'You know what, I'm way too tired to think about

Ana right now. It's really late – have to get to bed.' She got up, yawning, picked up her tea and scarf.

'Goodnight, Mariah.'

She paused and looked back at me. 'Hey, try to forgive us, okay? I know Nick and I are really busy right now, but we do love Felicity, you know. We worry about her. We only want her to be happy.'

Nick had even less of an excuse than her for being an absent parent, since he was in the Lodging much more frequently. He often held meetings around the dining room table with members of his senior management team – the Bursars, the Dean, the Senior Tutor – but he never really stopped to engage with Felicity other than ruffling her hair in passing. He seemed to be making strategic liaisons further afield, too, that summer, with other College presidents, senior university figures and influential alumni up from London. He often held luncheons at the Lodging and as we ate sandwiches at the kitchen table, we'd listen to their voices booming in the dining room next door, where College catering staff poured vintage champagne into crystal glasses and served lavish food from silver platters.

As the summer progressed, Nick grew even more gaunt and distracted – presumably as he began dealing with the tormented Governing Body. After years as a senior BBC executive, he could hardly be a stranger to overeducated employees, budgetary crises and Machiavellian egos. He must have been aware, too, that an Oxford College operates according to its own obscure principles, opaque traditions and unspoken rules. But perhaps he was only just beginning to get a sense of the rabid individuals he was going to have to control and contain.

Several of the dons would not be out of place on a psychiatric ward; at least one that I knew of was showing clear signs of dementia, and another was actually in custody having throttled a fellow mathematician to death. Some were decent and kind, of course, trying to do the right thing; but even these good ones were drawn, repeatedly, into the very quarrels they abhorred. Every don, young or old, mad or sane, poisonous or benign, was an elite nitpicker. Most also considered themselves to be geniuses. I wasn't surprised to see Nick's stress levels escalate.

But of course he would never share his thoughts on this, or anything else, with me. I might live in his house and care for his only child, but I was staff with a job to do. As long as I didn't cause any aggravation, he was content to leave his daughter's welfare in my hands. He saw no need to get to know me – he barely spoke more than a few perfunctory words to me, and almost never asked what I had been up to.

We were not completely unsupervised in the house, though. The catering manager, Angela, was a frequent presence. The Lodging kitchen was too small for anything other than domestic use, so Angela and her team came in and out all day carrying trays of food. A brisk and self-contained woman in her sixties, Angela never stood still long enough to chat, but I sensed her sharp eye on us as she came and went. She also brought Nick and Mariah's meals over on the rare occasions when they ate at home, and I'd often find her in the kitchen, ears pricked, sliding Tupperware into the fridge. She insisted on calling Nick 'Master', even when he wasn't there; she'd say things to me like, 'Can you tell the Master there's a lovely terrine in the fridge, needs eating up today'. Sometimes, as I passed the dining room, I'd glimpse her silently counting glasses, folding napkins, tweaking floral arrangements, repositioning candlesticks, or slotting doilies under fruit bowls. I began to suspect that she was Nick's eyes and ears in the Lodging, because if Felicity and I ever met

her in the hall, she'd ask, 'So, where are you two off to then?'
or 'Where have you been to now?'

But of course, Felicity and I were not always in the Lodging.
We were often out, at first just the two of us, and then, in
the autumn, as a little unit of three with Linklater, exploring
Oxford's book tunnels and secret passages, its turrets and spires
and wild, hidden graveyards. And on those days even the eagle-
eyed Angela had no idea what we were up to.

Chapter 12

'Right now, Dee. We'd like to understand a bit more about why Felicity wouldn't talk to Mrs Law.' Faraday consults his notes and takes a swig of tea. 'Four and a half years. That's a really long time not to talk to someone. Did you ever witness any rows or conflicts – anything between them that made you uncomfortable?'

Practically everything between them made me uncomfortable, but the incident that springs immediately to mind is Mariah's birthday, and the bees.

Her birthday fell in late summer and she came down that morning in an emerald silk kimono. I remember noticing that her belly, which she usually concealed in well-cut clothes, was beginning to round, and that she looked less pallid than she usually did first thing in the morning. Nick was behind her, I saw, freshly showered and dressed in his usual dark trousers and white shirt with his wet hair combed back. He could not stop touching her – a hand on the small of her back, fingers brushing her cheek or neck, a kiss on the ear.

I handed her a William Morris birthday card and noticed, laid out on the table in the dining room, a pile of croissants, a jug of orange juice and a bottle of fine champagne from the College cellars. Angela must have been in already. I was surprised that I hadn't heard her.

'Oh, thank you, Dee – hey, a birthday breakfast?' She pointed through the doorway at the dining room and turned to Nick. 'Was this you?' He kissed her on the mouth. 'I have my elves.'

They were both so jaunty. As Nick popped the champagne, he said over his shoulder, 'Felicity up yet?' Since it was seven-thirty and Felicity was always awake by six, I guessed he wanted me to go up and fetch her.

She was in the bathroom so I went over and found the birthday card on her desk. It was me who'd suggested she draw a card herself. Inside she'd just printed, 'From Felicity'. No love. No birthday wishes.

She came out of the bathroom, ghoulishly pale, with her curls scraped into lopsided bunches – she wouldn't let me brush them, though I dearly wished she would. 'What a bonnie beauty!' I smiled. 'Shall we go down?' I held out my hand and to my amazement she took it. Hers felt thin and cold, and as I led her downstairs, I felt as if I'd been given a tiny bird to hold, a wren or baby sparrow, a delicate cage of bones around a wildly beating heart.

Nick and Mariah were in the dining room. With her bare feet up on a Georgian chair, her glowing skin and hair swept up messily, I could see how irresistible she must be to him. He'd laid pastries in front of her, offerings to his Goddess, and was pouring champagne into a glass that contained just a drop of orange juice. I wondered why he felt it was a good idea to give his pregnant wife alcohol for breakfast. 'It's very weak, Dee,' he said, looking round as if he'd heard my disapproving thoughts. 'Have one yourself.'

I tend not to say I'm teetotal. People make such a boring

fuss about it. Some react with distaste, as if I've confessed that I never use shampoo or cut my toenails, others just grow wary, assuming that I'm either an alcoholic or an uptight Scottish Presbyterian, neither of which is true. It's usually easier just to accept a glass then discreetly tip it away – but not for breakfast. I do draw the line there.

Mariah smiled at Felicity. 'Oh, hi, honey.' She took her feet off the chair and sat up. 'Hey, I love your hair like that, very boho.'

'Hello, Bun.' Nick ruffled Felicity's bunches and kissed the crown of her head. She shoved his hand away. A memory of my own child's hair entered my head without warning. She loved me to brush it, even though she had tight curls like Felicity. Her brush had the softest bristles and a silver teddy bear on its handle; I never did find it. Presumably, my father got rid of it when he took her other things away. The dining room walls gave a quiver. I pulled out a chair and sat down, closing my eyes and waiting for the horrible feeling to pass. Nick was cutting a croissant, wishing out loud for raspberry jam. I said I'd get it. My legs were still a bit shaky but I was glad for the excuse to leave the room.

'What've you got there then, Bun?' As I passed the table, I saw Felicity slide the card towards Mariah, with a little package wrapped in one of the Escher print-outs I'd given her, not coloured in. I had no idea how she'd got a present, or where from. Mariah glanced at the intricate black and white tessellation Felicity had drawn on the card. 'That's an interesting pattern, darling. Look, Nick, she's a real artist, isn't she?'

'Fantastic!' Nick barely looked at it as he held up his phone and took a picture of Mariah.

'We should get you designing wallpaper, you definitely have the eye for patterns.' She picked up the package, giving it a little shake. 'Shall I open it?' She left room for an answer but of course Felicity didn't speak.

I waited, curious to see what it was.

Nick bent over and for a moment they formed a handsome family tableau, framed by the painted wood panels, honeyed light filtering through the big windows behind them. Then Nick leaned over Felicity's head and kissed Mariah on the lips – a lingering kiss. Felicity recoiled. I felt the urge to reach in, grab her and pull her to safety.

Mariah managed to rip the package open but she dropped it with a yelp and jumped to her feet, almost knocking over the Buck's Fizz. Dusty shapes scattered across the table like tiny skaters on a lacquered rink. 'Jesus Christ, Felicity!'

Nick turned to Felicity and said in a stern voice, 'What on earth are these?'

Felicity had frozen – we all knew the look: a transparent shell had closed around her.

Usually when this happened, Nick would distract her, take her out of the room, smooth things over – but not this time. Mariah's cleavage spilled from her kimono as she leaned over Felicity, who stared at the floor. 'Where did you get these bees?' she snapped. 'Tell me! Where did you get them?'

Felicity did not move.

'You know where she got them, don't you, Nick?' Mariah straightened. 'The priest's hole.'

'But it's locked, isn't it?'

The bees had been an anomaly – the pest man was unable to fathom where they'd come from; there was no sign of a hive or entry hole. But Felicity must have nipped in and grabbed a few handfuls before he took them away. I wondered where she hid them.

Mariah had turned back to Felicity. 'Did you take the key from my bedroom? Did you go through all my things to find it? Answer me, Felicity! Oh my God, just for once, answer the damned question!' She was near to tears, her face at Felicity's level. Felicity squeezed her eyes shut.

Nick put a restraining hand on Mariah's shoulder. 'It's just a few bees, my darling.'

Mariah's voice shook. 'But she knows she can't go in that priest's hole.' She turned and swept off into the kitchen, the ends of her gown fluttering like patterned green wings.

The bees and their dusty residue lay scattered across the table. As I gazed at it, the velvet mahogany surface seemed to ripple, but it was just the light from the chandelier, moving impercep-tibly as Mariah's displaced air fingered the crystals.

'Clear those bees up, Felicity.' Nick's voice was flat. 'Then put that key back where you found it. You aren't allowed in the priest's hole. It's not safe in there and you know it.' He turned to me. 'This is your responsibility, Dee. We gave you very clear instructions: she isn't to go in there.'

Felicity couldn't defend herself because she couldn't speak in front of me, but I could feel her distress that Nick had sided, so instinctively, with Mariah. It was possible that she'd actually wanted to share the bees because they interested her – she found them beautiful – but neither of them had considered that. Nick was still glaring at me as if I'd masterminded the whole trans-gression. I lifted my chin and met his gaze. He looked away first, spun on his brogue and followed Mariah into the kitchen.

I bent to Felicity. 'Ach, it's okay, pet, don't worry.' Her lips were still pressed together. 'You didn't mean to upset her, I know that. You just wanted to share the amazing bees, didn't you? But don't worry, darling, it'll all blow over soon enough.'

Her bottom lip wobbled.

I held out my arms and she took a tentative step towards me. I moved to her, folded myself around her; I felt her hesitate and then she pressed her face into my stomach. It was wonderful to hold onto her at last – I suddenly became calm, as if a loose piece somewhere inside me had slotted back into place. She kept her arms rigid by her sides but I felt her lean against me, and I wondered if she felt the same. Her shoulder blades stuck out like fragile angel wings and suddenly I wanted to pick her up and carry her away from this house – away from them both. After a moment more she wriggled out of my arms and swiped her fists over her damp cheeks. I reached out and tucked an escaped curl behind her ear and our eyes met. I smiled at her, and her tense features softened. We were allies now.

I sent her off upstairs to wash her face while I swept up the bees. As I walked into the kitchen to throw them away, I found Nick and Mariah kissing, showily: Nick was hunched over Mariah with his back to me, one hand digging through her hair, the other clawing her exposed breast; her head was tipped right back. I ducked out into the hall to the sunroom and flung open the doors, tipping the bees into the flowerbed.

I'd overheard couples at night, of course, dull bumping, the creaking of bed springs, sighs and groans, but Nick and Mariah were in a different league. Their passion seemed desperate and feral, but also slightly stagey, as if they had something to prove – not to the outside world, perhaps, but definitely to each other.

When I came back in, Felicity was still upstairs, Nick had gone over to College and Mariah was standing by the shuddering kettle looking forlorn. I suddenly felt a bit sorry for her. It can't be easy to have a silent and troubled stepdaughter – it was little wonder if she felt despair from time to time. Four and a half years of not being spoken to must feel gruelling. Then again, that four and a half years also seemed like proof, if not of negligence, then of a certain hopelessness on Mariah's part.

She saw me and grimaced. 'Dead bees, Dee? She really does hate me, doesn't she?'

'What? No, I expect she just wanted to share them with you because she's interested in them,' I said.

'Oh God, seriously?'

I nodded. 'She feels bad about it now, though.'

'Well, maybe she should – she stole that key. I keep it in my jewellery box. She must have come into my room and gone through all my stuff to find it.'

'But I think most children would find a secret den irresistible. Wouldn't you, when you were her age?'

She turned away and gazed out the window. 'I didn't have that kind of childhood, Dee.' She dropped a tea bag into a mug and stared at the billowing kettle steam. 'You know, she's punishing me, I think.'

'For what?'

I expected her to say, 'for taking her daddy away' but she muttered, 'She knows that wallpaper isn't safe.'

'It's probably hard for a child to believe something made of paper can be dangerous,' I said.

She gave a weak smile. 'Yeah, maybe. I guess even William Morris had trouble believing in poisonous dye. When the doctors started warning people about it, he said they had "witch fever".'

'What does that mean?'

'Oh, you know, a collective madness – like in medieval witch-hunts.' She pressed the heels of her hands into her eye sockets and her voice wavered. 'Oh God, though, do you really think the bees were meant to be nice? Now I feel really guilty.'

'There's no sense in that.'

'She just presses my buttons sometimes, you know? And then I feel bad because I'm not her saintly mother.'

'Was Ana a saint?'

'Well, no. God, no. But she loved Felicity so much. She was a good mother – until the end, anyway, when she was – well, you know, um, very sick.' She lifted her mug and blew on it. 'You know I look at Felicity and sometimes I see Ana looking back at me. She's so like her it's spooky.' She straightened, as if remembering that she was talking to the nanny, and smiled brightly. 'You know Dee, Nick and I were only just talking about how good you are with her – didn't you ever want a child of your own?'

I felt the heat rise to my face. I turned away and went to the cupboard to get the porridge oats.

'Oh, Dee. Sorry!' she said to my back. 'I know, I know – I'm way too direct. It's a Danish thing. I just say what's on my mind. No filter. Nick always tells me off for it. It's none of my business why you don't have children, I didn't mean to upset you.'

We heard a sound, then, and both turned to find Felicity in the doorway. I felt a rush of relief. She really could slip up and down the stairs without a sound.

'Oh, hey, honey.' Mariah smiled at her. 'I didn't mean to get cross with you just now; I was just shocked, you know? You really can't go in there, okay? There really might be poison in the wallpaper and we don't want you breathing that in or touching it. Your daddy and me, we just want you to be safe, that's all, but I'll make it your hidey-place soon, I promise you that. Then you can put all those bones and stones and funny things you collect in there. After the baby comes. Okay?'

I could see that Felicity badly wanted to answer – she swallowed a couple of times as if she was trying to make space in her throat, and her eyes looked watery. I longed to go and hug her again but I knew it would overwhelm her.

I wondered if Mariah appreciated what a torment it was for Felicity not to be able to speak, but she seemed oblivious. She pulled out her phone. Standing by the window in a patch of sunlight, she was the picture of health and fecundity, her colours blending perfectly with the abundant summer garden – pink roses, lush foliage – while behind her Felicity stood rigid and pale, in obvious distress. 'Come here, my darling.' I held out a hand. 'I'm making my special porridge with honey and vanilla for you because I know you don't like croissants.'

I try to explain to Faraday and Khan that the real problem was that Mariah wasn't attuned to Felicity's emotional state. Whether deliberately or not, she just didn't pick up on signs, clues or tells. On that particular morning, she assumed that because she had moved on from the dead bees, Felicity had too.

–In parenting terms, she's a toddler, I say. –She only sees things from her own perspective.

–Right. Faraday nods. –So, did you see her getting angry with Felicity? Did it ever get physical, anything like that?

The only incident that springs to mind was when a garrulous American professor cornered Felicity in the hall as she was getting her coat on. It was like witnessing an assault to which everyone else was oblivious. The stranger asked where she was going and Felicity froze, one arm in her coat. She stared at the floor. Mariah stepped in and answered for her, then ushered the man out the door. When she closed it, she turned on Felicity. 'Oh my God!' she cried. 'You could at least have smiled at him, Felicity. Jesus! You can't just stare at the floor. You're not a baby any more, you're eight years old.' She grabbed the trailing sleeve and shoved Felicity's arm into it. 'It's embarrassing – people just think you're rude!' She turned and marched off, leaving Felicity cowering against the painted panels.

Mariah had lost her temper because Felicity's silence reflected badly on her, as the stepmother. As he walked away, the American professor was probably wondering what on earth Mariah had done to make the child so tense and uncommunicative, so very odd. Mariah had been made to look dubious, perhaps even harmful or incompetent. And – perhaps because she already knew she was failing – she couldn't bear that.

But if I were to try to describe this incident to Faraday and Khan, I know that I would sound hyper-critical, so I just shake my head. –There wasn't any physical violence, no, I say. –But there are other ways to damage a child.

Chapter 13

They still haven't asked about Linklater. This is starting to make me uneasy. But I remind myself that they have no reason to ask about him. They have no reason to even think about him. He only came inside the Lodging twice – and both times he didn't encounter anyone other than Felicity and me.

Mariah was in email contact with him about the house history, and she spoke to him on the phone a couple of times, but she never actually met him. And Nick didn't cross paths with him until the debacle in the street in the middle of the night – and thankfully, in all the mayhem and panic of Felicity's disappearance, he seems to have forgotten about that. No doubt Nick thinks of Linklater – if he thinks of Linklater at all – as an entirely peripheral individual. Certainly, if he's building a list of people who bear him ill will, he will have far more sinister, heavyweight or ruthless characters to consider first.

Linklater entered our lives not long after Mariah's birthday, when she announced one morning at breakfast that Nick had given her an extra birthday gift. 'It's a house detective. He's going to write up the history of the Lodging, all 400 years of it. He sort of pieces together lots of photos, plans, maps and life stories and he makes them into a lovely book. Actually, he'll

probably come and have a look this week, but you know, I can't
be here – I have to be in London every day – so can you just
let him in to look round, or whatever he needs to do, and tell
him to email me if he has questions? Hopefully he can just get
on with it. He calls himself The House Detective. His name's,
um . . .' She clicked at her phone for his contact details.

'Linklater?'

'That's it, yes. Did Nick tell you about him already?'

I told her I'd seen The House Detective advert in *Daily Info* – it
was a long-standing notice.

Felicity was sitting upright, clearly intrigued. I tried to think
what she'd most want to know. 'So, will this house detective be
able to work out if it's a real priest's hole?'

'Oh – yes, maybe; that'd be useful, wouldn't it?'

'And I suppose he'll find out about all the children who've
lived here.' I poured Felicity a glass of milk. 'Some who've been
born here too, probably.'

'Or died here.' Mariah shuddered. 'Actually, Jesus, there are
some things about a house you'd rather not know, right?'

I glanced at Felicity. Mariah seemed to have forgotten that she
was talking in front of a child who'd suffered a major bereavement, was prone to nightmares and was struggling to settle in
a strange new home. 'I'm sure he'll find out lots of *good* things
about this house,' I said, pointedly.

Mariah looked up and blinked. 'Oh yes! Yes! This is a lovely
house. Only good vibes!' She put away her phone. 'Or it will
be lovely when we finish that landing – I can't wait to get the
William Morris back up there. It's going to be fabulous. You can
watch us hang it, Felicity, if you want.'

Felicity looked unimpressed.

Linklater showed up at the house a few days later, just after Felicity and I had eaten dinner.

We were alone in the front room and for once the Lodging was quiet. Mariah was in London overnight and Nick was at a seventieth birthday celebration for the Provost of a nearby College. I had my notebook open on my lap and was puzzling over a particularly tricky deduction, and Felicity was in the corner colouring a sheet of Penrose tiles. We jumped and exchanged a look of dismay when we heard the knock on the front door.

When I opened it, a tall man stumbled backwards, his body rising like a tent pole from a flapping overcoat. As he opened his mouth, the Chapel bell let out a single, sonorous clang – half past the hour. He looked theatrically startled and blinked at the murky sky through a crooked pair of round glasses. A gust of wind whooshed at him then, sucking at the papers he held under one arm, puffing his hair this way and that. Although he was technically standing still, everything about him seemed to be twitching, like a time-lapse film of a growing plant.

'Can I help you?' I said, but he didn't answer – his bashed-up satchel was slipping off his shoulder and he lurched to catch it, shouting, 'Wah!'

I began to shut the door, thinking he must be one of the unhinged geniuses who roam the streets of Oxford in ragged clothes, anxiously muttering in Latin or weeping quietly to themselves, but he shoved the toe of his scuffed Dr Marten into the door before it could close. 'No. Wait!'

'Yes?'

'I'm Linklater—'

'Ah. The House Detective?'

He hoiked his satchel onto his shoulder and said, with exaggerated formality, 'Indeed I am.'

'Well, Mrs Law's out, I'm afraid.' Despite Mariah's instruction, I really did not want to have to deal with him.

Another gust swept down the lane, and a spatter of raindrops, and as he tried to pin the papers to his flank his satchel slipped off again – he seized it just in time, somehow without dropping the papers. I relented. 'Would you like to come inside for a moment to sort yourself out?'

He slipped through the front door and, without being invited, passed straight into the front room. Felicity had vanished, leaving her paper and pencils scattered on the rug. My note-book was open on the table. He perched on the edge of the sofa, knees together, pigeon-toed, wrestling with his papers – dropping some, peeling others off his coat and trying to stuff them into the satchel, scattering more across the coffee table and rug. Then, as if he'd successfully performed a magic trick, the papers were suddenly all inside the bag. He sat up, putting his hands on his knees. He looked keen and somehow boyish, though he was surely around my age, maybe older. His face was all crevasses and mounds, its patterns slightly uneven, but not unpleasantly so.

'Do you want to leave a message?' I said.

'A message? Why?'

'For Mrs Law – Mariah?'

'Oh.' He blinked. 'You aren't Mrs Law?'

'I'm the nanny.'

'Ah! Right. Sorry. Sorry – I thought you – but yes, of course, yes, you did say that – won't she talk to me?'

'Mariah,' I repeated, slowly, 'is out.'

'Out? Oh. Yes, ah.' He looked so downcast that I found myself offering him a cup of tea, but he didn't reply because he was craning his neck, twisting his spine at an improbable angle until he almost toppled onto the floor. 'It's true then,' he said. 'She really did Farrow & Ball the panelling and beams. And she's bleached the floorboards or something, too, hasn't she? Christ alive.' He puffed his cheeks out, squeezing his eyes shut as if his head might explode.

'Are you okay?' I said.

He opened his eyes again. They were a nice rich blue, I saw, though one eyeball seemed slightly off-kilter now. He gave a weak smile – sweet, if a little wonky – and the eye righted itself. 'I'm fine, thanks. Sorry – just a bit of a shock to see the place looking like this.'

He looked a bit wobbly, so I repeated the offer of tea.

'Oh. Tea? Lovely. Thanks. Milk, three sugars.' He closed his eyes and took a long breath. 'Thanks very much. You're very kind. Thank you.'

When I came back with two mugs of tea, the front room was empty. His papers were once more scattered across the sofa and coffee table and for a second I wondered if he could have been sucked up the chimney – the fireplace was so vast that this almost felt like a possibility. I plonked the mugs down and went back into the hall. 'Dr Linklater?' I shouted. 'Hello?'

The dining room was empty, as were the downstairs toilet, kitchen and sunroom. He could not, surely, have gone into the garden as it was now raining properly – he could only have gone up. I took the stairs two at a time and as I reached the landing I heard his voice coming from the attic floor. I ran up and burst into Felicity's room, out of breath.

She was cross-legged on the bed looking electrified. The tail of Linklater's overcoat was poking out of the priest's hole. I shot across the room and yanked it. 'What are you doing? You can't just come up here without asking! How did you even get in there?' I looked back at Felicity. 'It's supposed to be locked! Felicity – did you take the key again? We talked about this.' She looked at the ceiling. A spattering of fat raindrops hit the open window and it clattered. I went over and shut it. Now was not the time to tell Felicity off. Besides, I understood why she'd be drawn to it. What eight-year-old wouldn't be?

Linklater came out of the priest's hole backwards. The light caught his bald patch as he clambered to his feet, brushing himself down. 'Christ – I just met a spider the size of a bloody rodent.' He pushed his glasses back up his nose, then smiled, showing crooked but reasonably decent teeth. 'You know it could be – it definitely could be . . .' He carried on as if we were in mid-discussion. 'I mean this house is the right period, certainly, 1603 so – no, I think – yes, I actually do – there's a good probability that this is a genuine priest's hole. There's room in there for a priest and all his vestments, vessels, altar furniture . . .'

I glanced at Felicity who was staring at him, wide-eyed but remarkably unafraid. My outrage, which moments before had felt positively savage, began to evaporate. Linklater grinned at Felicity. 'A priest's hole in your bedroom, what a stroke of luck.'

I saw her swallow – she must have questions. I tried to guess what they'd be. 'Why did they need holes to hide in?'

'Well, there were priest hunters, you see. Ruthless bastards. Bounty hunters.' He took off his smeared glasses and rubbed them on the sleeve of his overcoat. 'Government spies. They were called "pursuivants" – from the Old French, "*pursivre* – to follow". They hunted down illegal Catholic priests, and of course Oxford was a hotbed of dissent in Elizabethan times; there were priests squeezed into orifices all over the place. The pursuivants would search every inch of a house. They'd even measure the footprint of the building inside and out, and if the measurements didn't match, they'd walk round tapping all the walls –' he tapped the panel – 'till they found the secret panel or the hidden door. And when they got him –' He drew an imaginary noose around his neck and made a choking sound, head flopping sideways.

Felicity let out the tiniest laugh. I was completely amazed. It was a sound she'd never normally allow herself to make in front of a stranger – even in front of me.

'Tortured them first, of course, poor buggers.' He looked at Felicity, obviously pleased to have a captive audience. 'Elizabethan torture was very colourful. They hung them by the arms like this,' he lifted his arms into a crucified position, 'feet off the ground, and kept them there till their hands swelled up to the size of melons, then when they passed out, they unhooked them and stuck a burning paper under their nose to wake them again. They'd vomit blood for a bit—'

I gave a yelp of protest. 'You're talking to a child!'

Linklater looked confused, then, but I realized that Felicity had come alive – she was delighted – actually smiling – her eyes wide and bright, her cheeks pink. Eight-year-olds, of course, do tend to have an unquenchable thirst for gruesome historical detail. Nick should try reading her *Horrible Histories* at bedtime instead of *Famous Five*.

Linklater nodded at the priest's hole, perhaps encouraged by Felicity's reaction. 'Some priests died in the holes, too, of course. I mean, if something happened to the person who was hiding you, nobody would know you were in here. That door might be locked from the outside with a heavy wardrobe pushed in front of it – or you'd be under a hatch in the floor, with a cupboard on top of you, or whatever. You could be screaming blue murder, but if no one could hear you—'

'Okay,' I barked. 'Your tea's getting cold.'

'But it's true. Honestly. I did a house history in Wiltshire a few years ago . . .' He glanced at me, uncertainly. 'Gorgeous Tudor manor – the owners had knocked down a wall and found a bricked-up priest's hole with an actual skeleton crouched in the corner, still clutching his wooden crucifix.'

'Dr Linklater! We really don't need to know all this.'

'Right. Ah. Yes.' He looked at Felicity again. 'No skeletons in this one, I suppose?'

Felicity shook her head, grinning.

'Ah, well.' He sighed. 'Can't have it all.'

I was astonished by her willingness to engage with him. Usually by now she'd have fled – or at the very least she'd be staring at the floor, immobile with fear. Linklater, of course, was oblivious to the effect he was having.

I was genuinely torn. It was obviously inappropriate to have him up here in her bedroom talking about skeletons and torture – I could only imagine Angela's reaction if she happened to pop into the Lodging right now – but Felicity seemed extraordinarily okay.

'Right then, Dr Linklater, why don't we continue this downstairs.' I held the bedroom door open.

'It's just Linklater,' he muttered as he passed me. 'Just the one name, like, um, Prince, or Beyoncé.'

'Beyoncé?'

'The American pop sensation.' He pushed his glasses up his nose and glanced at me; I couldn't tell if he was joking.

'I know who Beyoncé is.'

In the room behind us I heard Felicity squeak.

Linklater followed me back downstairs, darting in and out of Nick's study, the guest room, Nick and Mariah's room and en suite. At the top of the main stairs, he paused on the landing and ran his fingers over the pockmarked plaster. I briefly explained what Mariah did for a living. 'It's been like this all the time I've been here,' I said. 'I've no idea why it's taking her so long to repair the wallpaper or whatever she's doing.'

A couple of young employees had come up from Mariah's London studio at the start of August, and meticulously peeled back layers of paint to reveal a bunch of faded and cracked birds pecking at gashed pomegranates. They separated each sheet from the wall and took it all off to London where, Mariah explained, they'd wash the paper in chemical baths, mend tears, strengthen it, touch up fading and flaking pigments and then bring it back to rehang.

'I don't know why they don't just buy it new,' I said. 'John Lewis probably does that print.'

'Well, yes, that would certainly cover the wall, but would it save your soul? Would it transform society?'

'It's wallpaper.' I carried on down the stairs. 'It's not going to save anyone's soul.'

'The Aesthetic Movement would beg to differ.' He followed me down. 'William Morris, Oscar Wilde, John Ruskin? They believed that wallpaper could change the world – all Oxford men, of course, so perhaps their feet weren't *entirely* on the ground. You know, come to think of it, Oscar Wilde's dying words were about wallpaper, weren't they? "Either this wallpaper goes or I do." No, wait, actually, that's a myth, now I think about it – his real dying words were a mumbled prayer or something.'

It struck me that Linklater might go on making wallpaper associations into infinity if I didn't redirect him. 'Sit.' I pointed at the chair and shoved a mug of lukewarm tea into his hand. 'So, when will you be starting this house history?'

He seemed puzzled by my question. 'I already have. And I've

actually found something rather interesting. I've discovered that the woman who sold this house to the College back in the 1950s left her entire archive to the Bodleian Library. She was a scientist – quite an eminent one, in fact – a lung specialist, very unusual at that time, being a woman scientist. Lungs were cutting edge, with Haldane here in Oxford, locking himself in sealed chambers to breathe in gases—'

'This woman's archive?' I thought it wise to step in before he went too far into lungs.

'Ah, yes, right, exactly. The archive. It's magnificent. A lifetime of letters, diaries, academic papers, bills, receipts, notebooks, household accounts, newspaper clippings, invitations – twenty-one boxes of it. You should come and have a look.' He slopped cold tea on Mariah's pale Berber rug.

'They don't let people like me into the Bodleian.'

'What? Oh, right. Ah. Yes, well, you can do tours, though,' he said. 'I'll take you. It's well worth a visit. There are twelve million books in there – for which we have pilchards to thank, of course.'

'Pilchards?'

He tilted his head. 'Sardines over six inches—'

'I know what a pilchard is!' Either he was insane or teasing me, I had no idea which.

'Yes, well, Thomas Bodley married the widow of a sixteenth-century pilchard trader. Pilchards were big money in those days – possibly still are, come to think of it.'

I felt he was on the verge of launching into pilchards, then, so I headed him off again. 'Twenty-one boxes sounds quite time-consuming.'

'Yes. Isn't it amazing? I've already found something intriguing – first box of letters I opened. It seems she had a tenant in here during the First World War while she took a research position in Edinburgh – a young widow with twin little boys. But here's something odd: this tenant doesn't seem to exist in any public records, and nor do her twins.'

I wondered why he was telling me all this.

'They don't appear in birth or death records or on the 1911 census. They're basically phantoms.'

'Do you think she made them up for tax avoidance or something?'

'Oh no – no – I'm sure they're real people, definitely real people – there are bundles of letters from the tenant. She just signs herself "V" and they seem to be close friends. The letters I read today, she's telling Muriel about her twins – Duncan and Jonnie – how they're settling in here, and damp problems in the attic rooms, little lead animals she's bought them, things like that. Duncan sounds like a handful – in one letter she says he's got a live squirrel in his room. I haven't had a chance to go through them all, obviously, but this woman and her children definitely lived here from about 1915 to 1917. They just don't exist in any public records. Not that I can see, anyway. Very intriguing. Nice little mystery.'

Out of the corner of my eye, I caught a movement as Felicity slipped into the room. I hadn't expected her to come down and again it felt miraculous. Linklater gazed at the ceiling and it struck me that he might just be passing the time, humouring the dull nanny while he waited for the glamorous Mariah to return. I put my hands on my knees and straightened my elbows. 'Right then,' I said. 'Mrs Law won't be home till much later tonight. She's a very busy woman. She told me she'd like you to get on with it, email her any questions and then just give her the finished product if that's okay.'

Felicity and Linklater both visibly deflated. Linklater actually hung his head. I thought then that perhaps I'd been wrong – perhaps he was actually enjoying talking to me. 'On the other hand,' I continued, smoothly, 'I suppose you could always tell me and Felicity if you find something fun. This phantom tenant sounds interesting. We'd like to know more about her.'

'Would you? Really?' Linklater's face brightened. 'Excellent.'

Felicity smiled, too, then quickly covered her mouth with both hands.

'How long will your house history take, do you think?' I said.

He put down his tea. 'How long's a piece of string? It's going to take months to go through the Fitzgerald archive, and that's just forty years out of the four hundred-odd, so . . .'

I wondered if Nick was paying him by the hour. 'Well, you could let us know if you discover anything good.' I did something unusual then, something impulsive and completely out of character: I tore out a piece from my notebook and wrote down my phone number.

'Jolly good.' He peered at it and shoved it into his satchel, then gathered up all his other papers. The chances of him finding my number again seemed slim. 'Well then, I suppose I'd best get back to the Bod then, see what I can dig up.'

As I showed him to the door, he paused and turned to Felicity, who was standing behind me. 'Hey, you know that nursery rhyme, "Goosey, Goosey, Gander"?'

To my astonishment, she actually nodded.

'Well, it's about hiding priests: "Upstairs, downstairs, in my lady's Chamber" – old men saying the wrong prayers. It's about priest's holes and pursuivants. Bit alarming when you think about it – but then again, most nursery rhymes are.'

Felicity's eyes widened. He looked at me, tapped the wood

panel and shook his head. 'This renovation's all they can talk about over the road. The expenditure's one thing, but who the hell paints over original Elizabethan oak panels and beams, and bleaches a Jacobean floor?'

He launched himself out into the street without saying goodbye and we watched him cover the cobbles with long, erratic strides, overcoat flapping, head bowed. Just before he turned the corner the Chapel bells began to ring the quarter hour, but Felicity didn't seem to notice – she glanced up at me, beamed, then spun on her heel and galloped off down the hall as if she was riding a horse.

Linklater, I felt, might turn out to be a very good thing – if he ever did come back.

Chapter 14

–So, can we go back to Felicity's sleepwalking for a minute? I'm just wondering what you did about it? Faraday sounds casual, as if we're chatting. He wants me to forget that I am in St Aldate's police station. He even stretches his legs under the Formica table and yawns a bit. But I am aware of Khan's dull gaze, her poised biro.

–Well, I did my best to comfort her, I say.

Faraday shakes his head. –Can't have been easy. Did she ever try to get out of the house?

The image of Felicity slipping downstairs in the moonlight barrels into my mind. I can see her standing on the stool, sliding back the bolt. I push this thought away – I must not go there now. It would undo me.

But Faraday has to go there. It's his job. This is probably why he looks so haggard. He has spent his career facing worst-case scenarios, both real and imaginary. Right now, he and Khan are visualizing a little girl in pink pyjamas wandering barefoot up a badly lit lane in the middle of the night; the wrong person stepping out of the shadows. Or perhaps they're imagining someone in the alley, watching the Lodging, maybe stealing a key from catering and creeping up the attic stairs as the baby's wails echo round the house. Or they are seeing a distraught little girl alone on the bank of the Isis, or Cherwell, or Thames, a pale bare foot slipping on the reeds.

–So what sort of things did she do when she went downstairs in her sleep? Faraday asks.

I force myself to focus on the question. –I found her laying out pebbles in a line down the hall, once, as if she was showing someone out the front door.

–Or in, says Khan, softly.

Faraday pretends not to hear this. –And did you talk to her about it? Did you ask her what she was up to?

–I don't think she remembers it – sleepwalkers often don't. Also she couldn't speak to me for the first few months – she's selectively mute, remember?

An impatient look crosses Faraday's ruddy face – he and Khan exchange a glance. Khan makes a note. Suddenly, her silent note taking feels infuriating. I point into the blinking red eye of the video recorder and ask what it's for if she also has to write down every word I say. She doesn't reply, she doesn't even look up, but Faraday narrows his eyes and I see what I already know to be the case: that his approachability is nothing more than a well-practised act. I know I'm not behaving correctly. I ought to be intimidated by Khan's writing, the video camera, the airless strip-lit interview room. I should be tearful and panicky. Self-mastery is a useful skill, but in a situation like this it can definitely count against you.

So I knit my brows and tell Faraday that he's right: Felicity's sleep disturbances were very worrying. I tell him she also has vivid, active dreams in which she talks to her dead mother and tries to protect herself against imaginary intruders.

But I don't admit that, although her night disturbances were not easy to deal with, they definitely brought us closer and so, in a strange way, I was almost grateful for them.

One night in particular stands out as a bit of a turning point in this respect. It was just before she started school and she was in a very bad way – jumpy, restless, eating almost nothing. I woke in the small hours with a sense of urgent misgiving and as I sat up, I felt gentle fingertips trail over my cheek.

I fumbled for the light, half expecting to see her standing by my side, but the room was empty. I flung myself out of bed, and rushed through to her.

In the dim glow of her nightlight I could see her kneeling on her bed in pale pyjamas, clutching her big toy squirrel. She lifted one hand, slowly, as I came in, and pointed at the priest's hole door. It was ajar. I began to ask how she'd opened it – whether she'd taken the key again, or perhaps never actually returned it to Mariah's jewellery box – but she put a finger to her lips, her round eyes fixed on mine.

I stood very still. I realized, then, that I could hear a faint scratching sound coming from behind the wood panelling by the little door. I marched over and kicked it shut. The scratching stopped. It had to be a rodent. I'd need to get the pest man back. I turned to Felicity.

Her face was blank. She blinked a few times, and began to rub behind one ear. Her eyes were open but suddenly I wasn't sure that she was seeing me – she seemed to be staring at something just behind me. I watched her expression change to one of terror.

I turned instinctively. Nobody was there but the priest's hole door had creaked open again, just a crack. I went back over and pushed it firmly shut, then pulled the nursing chair across to block it. If I couldn't get Felicity to give me the key then I'd have to tell Mariah and get the lock changed. But the last thing

I wanted was to tell Mariah that Felicity was still going in there. She'd be furious and Felicity would feel betrayed – it would set us right back.

I went back to Felicity's bed and knelt down next to her. 'It's okay, darling, there's nothing here. It's all fine.' She stared at me and scratched her ear again. I reached out and moved her hand away, looking into her hot palm, but she wasn't holding the key. I reached for her other hand which grasped her toy's fur, but she jerked it away, half rising from the bed. Her eyes were huge, the pupils dilated.

'It's okay, pet, it's okay.' I let go of her hand. 'Sorry. It's okay, darling. It's just me, it's just Dee. I won't hurt you. You're safe.'

I sat on the floor by her bed and sang old Scottish lullabies for a while and then, for something to say, I told her about Mill House. I described how the millrace cuts through a deep stone channel beneath the house, emerging in the hallway. 'When you come through the front door,' I whispered, 'you can look over a little wall and see the burn, and wherever you are in the house you hear it – it sounds like little children laughing.' I told her that when I was her age, and my father was out, I'd climb over the wall and down little iron rungs and walk into the tunnel along a ledge, hoping I might find a laughing child to play with. 'I suppose,' I said, 'I was a wee bit lonely.'

She had stopped scratching and was listening, apparently awake now. I tucked the duvet around her and gave her a kiss on the head, slipping my hand under her pillow just in case, but there was no key there, either. She must have a little box or pocket tucked away. I gazed at the growing collection of objects on her bedside table. I'd put the badger skull in the centre – pride of place – and I was pleased to see she'd left it there. We'd found this treasure on a walk to Godstow nunnery. I'd bagged it up and when we got home, I showed her how to scrape tufts of fur and flesh away from bone, then we'd macerated it in detergent overnight and simmered and bleached it. It came up white and otherworldly, as if no longer belonged to the earth but floated inside our heads, a shared, fantastical dream.

I hovered by her bed for a moment, but could not bring myself to leave her. She looked so small and vulnerable there in her bed, eyes shut, but probably awake and frightened. I sat back down on the floor. I must have nodded off eventually, head to knees, because when I woke, dawn was pushing through the blinds and Felicity was on her side, staring intensely into my eyes. As I struggled to sit up, I had a powerful feeling that I'd failed her.

Until that moment I'd always known what to do with virtually any child in any situation – even if all I did was establish routines and wait. I'd allowed myself to feel fond of the children in my care – every one has a place in my heart – but for obvious reasons I'd always avoided deep emotional attachments, even with sad little Luca, the Astrophysicist's boy. But somehow I wasn't managing to keep any distance from Felicity. I'd looked after a fair few lonely and miserable children over the years, but none of them had had the effect on me that she was having.

I reached out and tucked her hair behind her ear, and as my fingers sank into the curls I remembered the softness of my own baby's hair, the biscuity smell of her scalp. She'd only go to sleep if I stroked it. She didn't scream, as most one-year-olds do, when I washed it in the bath or brushed out little fine knots. I felt her weight in my arms – her slippery, hot skin, her little fat limbs clinging to me like a monkey as I lifted her out of the tub, and my lungs grew tight and heavy, as if someone had poured metal filings down my windpipe – for a moment

I couldn't breathe. I had to close my eyes and concentrate on moving my diaphragm up and down.

When I opened them, Felicity was still gazing at me. It was nearly light by then and where I'd pushed her hair back I could see an angry, flaky patch, dotted with blood, scabbing. I wondered if there were other patches too – brands of stress elsewhere across her body. She'd obviously been picking at this one with the sort of brutality with which she attacked her cuticles. It felt like self-harm. 'Oh, your poor wee ear.' I touched it. 'That must be so sore. Itchy too, I bet? But I know some cream that'll make it all better. We'll go up to the chemist today, okay, and get some and it'll all clear up.'

She gave the faintest nod and I saw her face soften and the expression in her eyes change to relief that I'd noticed – that I cared – that I knew what to do. It struck me that perhaps this wasn't as complicated as I was making it. She just needed what all children need: to be noticed, cared for, loved.

Later, when I went back into my room, I saw what had brushed against my cheek – not spooky fingers, but the arm of one of Felicity's dresses. It had been knotted to the light fitting and dangled, lopsided, over my bed. I couldn't imagine what obscure dream or impulse had made her do this, but the idea that she could be teetering above me without waking me up was alarming.

As I reached up to untie the dress, the pipes beneath the floorboards gave a violent shudder, and I heard a far off clanking somewhere further down, as if the house was talking to itself, or chuckling at us. I folded up the dress. Felicity's sleepwalking was intensifying, there was no doubt about it, and I was failing to deal with it.

Of course, I could try to explain all this to Faraday and Khan, but they would only think I was incompetent, failing to cope with a disturbed little girl. So I tell them that, while Felicity's sleepwalking was obviously a concern, it never got out of hand.

Faraday nods. –Okay, so what *do* you think's happened here then, Dee? Do you think she let herself out through that unbolted front door in her sleep?

–Well, I say, –Mariah did hear her go downstairs in the middle of the night, didn't she? She basically heard her leave.

–Yes, you said that to the investigating officers, didn't you?

–Of course, I had to.

–The thing is, Dee, Mrs Law says that didn't happen.

–What? It absolutely did. She told me about it as soon as I got back from London. She said she heard Felicity go downstairs in the early hours – she told me she saw her going past the bedroom door, but didn't go after her.

Khan leans forwards, then, and speaks, in a soft and alarming voice, –Mrs Law says she didn't say anything to you about this. She says you've made this up.

–What? Well, she's lying!

–Is she, Dee? Khan sits back again, and tilts her head. –Or are you?

Chapter 15

The night Felicity vanished, I was in London and so was Nick – though we weren't together, obviously. I made it back to Oxford only about half an hour before he did and so when I followed Mariah upstairs, leaving the two uniformed police officers to search the downstairs rooms and the garden, it was me who heard her confession, and not him.

I found her in the bedroom on her knees, staring helplessly at her baby, who was wailing in his bassinet – she'd not even picked him up. With her ashen skin, smudged eyes and tangled hair, she looked unhinged, like a mad witch, and I had the urge to give her a shake and tell her to pull herself together.

Instead, I went over and lifted the baby out of his bassinet. Through the cotton Babygro his body felt sweaty and muscular, a compact, maggoty thing, his face screwed up and puce.

'This is my fault, Dee. It's my fault.' Her hoarse and incredulous voice rose over the baby's cries. She shot out a hand and her fingernails needled my forearm. 'Oh God. Don't tell them. Please don't.'

'Tell who what?' I patted him, jiggled him on my shoulder.

She covered her face for a moment. Then she looked up again. 'I didn't bolt the front door – I don't remember bolting it.'

'Don't be silly, I'm sure we often don't—'

'I saw her—' She pressed her cheeks with her fingertips. 'I saw her go past my room in the middle of the night – just a shadow, real quick – then I heard her go downstairs.'

I felt myself grow very still. 'You what?'

'Oh Jesus, Dee,' she bawled, 'I just thought she was sleep-walking and I was so tired, I'm so, so, so tired – and I was in pain, this mastitis is coming back, I just couldn't – I couldn't get up. I was a zombie. But oh God, what if she was sleepwalking – what if she just went out the front door and someone found her there – it's so dark down Magpie Lane – what if someone just took her? Oh shit, Dee – or what if it was an intruder I saw – what if someone was in here, taking her, like Madeleine McCann? Is she murdered now? Trafficked? There are sex traf-fickers in Oxford – oh God, oh God, oh God. Jesus. She's just a little girl – it's my fault, this is all my fault.'

'You *saw* Felicity?' I leaned in, jiggling the baby harder, trying to wrap my head around what she'd just said. 'When? *When*, Mariah?'

'I don't know! The middle of the night, I don't know. He'd just gone to sleep. I was lying here, feeling so sick, so exhausted, Dee, I just – I can't—'

'You saw her and you let her go?'

'No!' she wailed. 'Yes! I don't know! I couldn't even *think*. I guess I assumed she'd just be wandering round the house a bit and I – but I can't – oh God, yes! I saw her, or someone, some-thing – oh my God. This is a nightmare, a total nightmare.' She shot out a hand and clutched at my forearm. 'This is payback – it's payback for what we did to Ana.'

I bent closer so she could hear me over the baby's wails. 'What did you do to Ana?' I felt the urge to slap her, bring her to her senses like they do in old movies, but thankfully I was holding the baby.

She seemed unable even to process my question; she just stared at me, then dropped her head into her hands and covered her ears, crying out, 'Oh God, Nick's never going to forgive me. You can't tell him – you have to promise you won't say anything about this, oh God—' She looked up. 'Please – promise me!'

As I looked into her blotchy face, I felt a mixture of pity and contempt. Felicity had vanished in the middle of the night, Mariah had no idea who had her or what they were doing to her, and all she could think about was what Nick would say.

The baby was howling in my ear – he'd be too panicky to latch on now even if she were capable of feeding him. I left her and took him out onto the landing. As I walked up and down, jiggling his bottom, my mind raced. I could picture Felicity creeping along the landing past the bedroom door – Mariah sitting up, glimpsing her as she passed, then blurrily letting her go. She could have hauled herself out of bed, called out to her, followed her downstairs and stopped this from happening. She could at least have looked out of the window. My legs grew weak at the thought of how different all this would be if she'd done that.

I flopped onto the window seat. My face was next to the wallpaper and the ripe, bursting pomegranates seemed to spread their lips to reveal their glistening crimson interiors. The gimlet-eyed birds, perpetually frustrated, spun and tangled in the criss-crossed branches. I remembered Mariah telling me that William Morris encouraged intricacy in his patterns in order to disguise the repeat. The whole wall was an elaborate lie.

I turned away from it. I couldn't lose control. I must calm down. Through the window I could see the tops of the police officers' heads down on the lawn and the gardener's white puff of hair. The baby's hungry cries were rhythmic and grating, hurting my ears. In a moment the police would come upstairs and they would want to ask more questions about where I'd been, what I knew, what I'd seen.

I saw Felicity tiptoeing down the hall and opening the front door, stepping out onto the cobbles. I saw her getting into a strange car. The baby's wails drilled into the back of my skull; perhaps he was picking up on my fear. 'Everything's going to be fine, wee man, everything's going to be just fine; we all just need to calm down. We all just need to calm down and think.'

I forced myself to get up off the window seat and carry him back through to Mariah's room. She was face down on the bed, still sobbing, and for a moment, I just stood in the doorway and watched her. Nick would blame her for this, she was right about that. He'd never forgive her. And if I told the police, they would blame her too.

But of course I would have to tell the police. What Mariah had heard and seen would give them a broad window of time during which Felicity had left the Lodging. Sleepwalking was just one possibility among many, of course, and they still wouldn't know how to find her – Mariah's confession didn't tell them where Felicity actually was. It didn't tell them if she was lost, hiding, or taken. Even so, I had to tell them. How could I not?

Chapter 16

To my surprise, Faraday doesn't want to talk any more about what Mariah did or did not hear that night. Perhaps he doesn't want to sit here and argue my word against hers. Instead, he would like my opinion on whether Felicity was 'at risk'.

–At risk in what way?

–Did you feel she needed your protection? he says, somewhat enigmatically.

–Well, yes, I say. –Absolutely.

They both sit up a bit straighter.

–What did she need protecting from, Dee?'

–Neglect, I say. –Parental neglect.

They deflate somewhat. Perhaps they want me to tell them that I witnessed physical abuse. Or maybe they want me to admit to seeing spooks and poltergeists so they can chalk me up as a dangerous fantasist.

–What sort of parental neglect did you witness? Faraday asks with a note of resignation.

I realize that it is not going to be easy to convey, in an interview, quite how disengaged Nick and Mariah actually were.

Weekends at the Lodging generally involved them leaving Felicity to 'be artistic' in her room while they worked on their laptops or entertained visitors. Nick would schedule an hour with her here and there, bringing her into his study to play chess, or walking round the garden with her. At these times he focused all his attention on her diligently, as if she was a tricky but promising tutorial student. But the rest of the time, he behaved as if his daughter was a pet to be patted in passing.

I lean my elbows on the table. –Most of the parents I've worked for are overeducated, overworked and under pressure, I say. –They're often single parents, often from abroad, so they're culturally displaced and homesick too. When I take charge of their children they're generally very grateful, but they expect to be involved – they want to know what we've done all day. Mariah and Nick just didn't. They hardly ever asked what we'd been doing or how she was. They just wanted her occupied.

–Right, Faraday nods. Khan's face remains impassive.

–It's like she hardly exists for them. Even when she's up in the night, they never seem to hear her and they never come to check on her.

I think of one night, in particular, sometime in early autumn. I'd slept fitfully and woken with a start an hour or so before dawn with the feeling – not unfamiliar by then – that I'd missed some activity. When I switched on the light, I saw that small bowls of rock salt had been placed around my bed. When I went through to her room, I saw she'd done the same around her own bed.

She must have gone down two flights of stairs and rummaged around the kitchen, then tiptoed around laying them out. I knew why she'd included my bed. She was worried that whatever – or whoever – she sensed in the priest's hole at night might come in here and menace me too. This protective gesture was unbearably sweet, but also alarming – if she could creep up and down two flights of stairs with bowls of salt without waking any of us up, what else could she do?

But if I mention this to Faraday and Khan, they will only ask why on earth she chose to lay out rock salt – and that was actually my fault. A few nights previously, as I was watching her go through her bedtime ritual – meticulously tidying pens, lining up toys, spacing out the treasures in her spiral – I'd found myself thinking about rituals for warding off bad energies. As I tucked her in, I said, 'You know, you're not the only person who feels safer if they've arranged little objects round the bed at night' and I told her about Shamanic bowls of salt.

I'd once looked after a toddler whose mother, a theologian, was working on a book about ritual and her flat was full of Shamanic texts; one positive about nannying for Oxford academics is the diverse reading matter. It might seem irresponsible to talk to a sensitive child about such things, but I felt it might make Felicity feel less alone to know that people have always been insecure at night, sensed energies, seen things and devised ways to neutralize them.

Of course, I knew that the most immediate source of her disturbed sleep was not Shamanism but school. She was barely eating, growing thinner than ever and the shadows under her eyes were now a deep violet. I decided that I must force Nick to engage with the fact that this new school was not working for his daughter. Mariah would be away for the next two nights working on the wallpaper in a Kent museum, so I decided to tackle Nick the next evening when he got back from College.

It was eleven-thirty by the time he came in from whatever function he'd been at. I was sitting in the kitchen lost in thought when I heard his key in the lock and his booming voice coming down the hall. 'No! That's just not good enough, sorry. I expect you all to treat my wife with absolute respect . . .' He switched on the kitchen light. 'Oh, for fuck's sake!' he shouted. Then he said to his caller, 'No. Not you, Fabien. Look, I have to go – I hope we're clear? Yes. Thanks. Yes. Do that.' He hung up and looked down at me with his phone hanging loosely in his hand. 'What on earth are you doing lurking in the dark?'

I explained that I'd been waiting to talk to him about Felicity. He glanced at the kitchen clock and frowned. 'What – *now*?' I told him it was difficult to catch him at any other time. 'Okay, fine, but you can always call Sally and set up a time to talk to me. But anyway, I'm here now, so what is it? Is she okay?'

'Not really, no,' I said.

As he took off his jacket, rolled up his shirtsleeves and flicked on the kettle, I told him how little his daughter had been eating, and that she was having a lot of bad nights. She was exhausted, I said, anxious and upset. School was a terrible place for her.

'But it's early days,' he said. 'Very.'

I asked whether she talked to him about school when he took her into his study, or walked round the garden.

'Well, yes, of course, a bit. She's not finding it easy, obviously,' he said, with his back to me. 'But she was never going to find it easy, was she?' He turned and looked down at me, then, clearly mustering all his patience. 'It's entirely normal for a child to be nervous when starting a new school. Any child would be. And it's clear that a child like Felicity will take longer than most to adjust. But she's eating *something*, though, I assume?'

I outlined exactly what she had eaten that evening, and said her lunch box came back full every day.

'Yes, well, it's not great but it's not nothing. She can't eat when she's anxious, she never could. Her mother was the same – easily, um, stressed.' He threw a tea bag into the mug, but didn't offer me one. 'Look, I did warn you about all this, Dee, when I hired you. And I'm also not as clueless as you might think. I've talked to Felicity – we're talking about it together – and I'm in close contact with the school. She's well looked after there, and I'm currently looking into finding her a new therapist. It's early days. As I told you from the start, what she needs are routines, consistency and patience. That's why I hired you.'

'She's a profoundly unhappy child,' I said. 'She's having a lot of problems at night, more than just sleepwalking – she's frightened. She sees things in her room.'

'Sees things? What things?'

'Well, I'm not sure, but I think she sees her mother.'

'Oh, for crying out loud, are you seriously trying to tell me she's seeing ghosts now?' He stiffened. 'Okay, that's it—' He took his phone out and began scrolling through images. 'Let me introduce you to my daughter.' He shoved the phone under my nose. 'This is the real Felicity; this is the child I see. She was like this once, and she can be like it again.'

A little freckled face appeared on the screen. It was Felicity, but much younger, chubbier, maybe three or four years old. The little girl in the video was animated – bright-eyed and pretty – with a tutu over her dungarees, bossing, chattering, making expansive arm movements. She performed a crazy dance and then gave an exaggerated curtsey. I didn't recognize the house – it must be their previous place in London. She stepped closer and the camera wobbled into her curls as she grabbed it, shouting in a high, clear voice, 'Right, Daddy, your turn!' Then she turned it around to film Nick at an odd angle, nostrils blooming.

I felt overwhelmed as I handed the phone back to him. Her voice was the biggest shock – alive with musical energy. When I pressed my ear against the connecting door at bedtime and heard her talking to him, her voice was always flat. His study was directly below my bedroom and if I pulled back the rug and pressed my ear against the floorboards, I could sometimes hear them there, too. Mostly I just heard Nick explaining chess moves. Sometimes she begged him to get her a pet.

I never had any doubt that she would speak to me too, eventually – it was just a question of time – but seeing who she once was brought home the scale of her misery. I was witnessing the culmination of a long, slow strangulation.

Nick had to see it too: the child in the video was not the child he had upstairs. But he shoved the phone back into his pocket. 'I wasn't going to show you that,' he said. 'I didn't want you to take her not speaking to you personally, but selective mutism really isn't that uncommon, and the vast majority of children grow out of it eventually.'

'She's not like that now, though, is she?' I nodded at the phone. 'With you?'

'That was filmed before her mother died,' he snapped. 'Look, I'm first to admit I've had my hands full, and the change was always going to be hard for her, but I've spoken to a lot of eminent people about her. I'm not anywhere near as negligent as you seem to think I am. Is she having a hard time right now? Yes, absolutely. But she has the capacity to be entirely normal. She's not a disturbed child – not by your attic spooks or anything else, and I very much hope you aren't doing anything to encourage that sort of nonsense.'

I opened my mouth to ask if he thought I was a half-wit, but he raised a hand to silence me. 'With help, she'll get past this, but in the meantime, she has you, hasn't she? Unless you're planning to leave us already?'

'Of course not.'

'Well, I know you said you couldn't commit to the long term.'

'I'm not leaving.'

'Right. So, was there anything else?'

It was me who had insisted that I couldn't stay, but as I looked into Nick's self-satisfied face, a seed of panic sprouted in my gut. At some point he was going to decide that I was no longer needed – and then what would become of Felicity? Nick would never understand or have time for her – he could not even appreciate that she was permanently altered by her mother's loss – and Mariah was certainly never going to love her as a mother should. And when their baby was born, she'd feel even more unwanted and alone. Who would hear her in the night if I wasn't there? Who would understand that while she could never be that carefree baby again, she could be something else, something extraordinary?

Chapter 17

–So you're saying they neglected her because they left her to you at night? Faraday frowns.

I can see I need to be more specific. –It wasn't only that, I say. –They never eat dinner together as a family, either. I eat with Felicity every night at six o'clock, even at weekends.

She was better off eating with me, though. We did maths puzzles as we ate, or watched You Tube videos on her iPad of cats doing funny things. On the few evenings when they were in the house without guests, Nick and Mariah ate much later, salads and soups, cold cuts, poached fish, casserole or game pie that Angela left out for them.

–And did anyone else ever join you and Felicity for dinner? Faraday asks. –Any friends of yours, maybe?

–No, I say. –Absolutely not.

I wonder, then, if someone could have seen us at Queen's Lane. We did go there often. And we were not always alone.

When school started, we got into a habit of stopping at the café there on the way home. A new school is tough on any child, but for a mute eight-year-old it is agony. Felicity was always dazed and traumatized when I met her at the school gates and I could tell from her full lunch box that she'd been eating nothing. It felt almost cruel to take her straight back to the hubbub of the Lodging, and so at the end of the first week, as we passed the café, I took her in, hoping to tempt her. Perhaps it was the feeling of anonymity – the white noise, the sense that everyone in the space was absorbed in something else – but I felt her relax as we waited at the cake counter. There was a little round table free by the window so I suggested sitting down. We sat at that table for over an hour that day. Felicity devoured two buns and drank a mug of hot chocolate as we silently watched people, buses and bikes go past.

We got into the habit of stopping in several times a week. We'd sit at the same table with puzzles or Pelmanism or patterns to colour; we drank hot chocolate, and ate toasted teacakes, scones and crumpets.

On the second week, a familiar figure passed by. I'd almost forgotten about Linklater – he certainly hadn't used my phone number – and when I saw him marching along clutching a sheaf of papers, his overcoat flapping, I felt a jolt of pleasure, followed swiftly by the urge to hide. He happened to glance in as he passed, and he came to an abrupt halt. He peered in at us, squinting, and then he looked pleased and waved. I waved back. He moved on, and my relief was followed by a strange sense of disappointment.

But then he turned around. He came back, swept into the café, wove through the tables and plonked himself on an empty chair at ours. He didn't say hello, or make any small talk. He just said, 'Well, what an odd coincidence!' He beamed at me, then at Felicity. 'I was going to call you – I think you're going to like what I've been discovering about your house.'

I wondered if this could possibly be true – had he really been thinking about us? He glanced at our cakes.

'Would you like one? They're very good.'

'Oh. Yes. Great. Lovely. Thanks.' He wrestled with his satchel. 'So anyway, remember that phantom tenant? The one who rented the house from the medical scientist – Muriel Fitzgerald – during the First World War? Well, I've discovered that she had an old nursemaid with her, too, a woman called Mrs Diles. I've found a whole bunch of funny letters from V about old Mrs Diles written in 1915 and 1916. Wonderful stuff. Old Mrs Diles seems to believe she's in touch with the spirit world. V actually catches her in the parlour one night holding a séance. She's also convinced herself there's a poltergeist up there, moving things around – though V's sure it's the young housemaid, or possibly the naughty twins playing tricks.'

He read us out a letter, then, about Mrs Diles' mad insistence that the poltergeist had moved her vanity case and banged on the wall in the night. He behaved as if we knew each other, as if we'd regularly talked about these former residents. It was strangely relaxing, if a little odd. I watched Felicity's face change as she listened – the colour came back to her cheeks and her eyes shone. She devoured the rest of her cake in just a couple of bites. All I could think of was that his focus on history, as well as his absolute disregard for social niceties, made her feel less threatened than she would with an adult who might dutifully ask her about school or try to win her over with humour.

V's letter was amusing and tender; she was obviously fond of old Mrs Diles, who was clearly a lunatic. She seemed exasperated but also delighted by her little boys, particularly Duncan, who sounded out of control and possibly disturbed, breaking train sets, hiding in cupboards, rejecting food. Linklater read the letters out in a deep, mellifluous voice, occasionally pushing his glasses back up his nose and glancing up at us, perhaps to check that we were as interested as he hoped. I wasn't, in fact, but I could see that Felicity was, so I pretended. When he'd finished, and got all his papers back into his battered bag, I found myself saying he should come back, and bring more letters.

He often came to meet us in Queen's Lane after that, not just after school, but at weekends too. At first I wondered what on earth he wanted from us – why he came – but gradually I began to realize that he simply enjoyed sharing his findings. His job, after all, must be a lonely one, sitting in archives all day, poring over old papers. He turned out to be entertaining if slightly erratic company, a mine of Oxford-related stories and facts. We had to stay physically alert, though, because he had a tendency to knock over cups or glasses – sometimes entire plates of food – as he gestured or pulled papers out of his satchel. Felicity and I would have to whip out our hands to catch things as they flew through the air. He'd scatter papers, too, and Felicity would crawl under tables to retrieve them for him. On one memorable occasion he caught the branch of a tall faux-fern in his satchel strap as he leaped up, realizing he was late for an Oxford Pedestrians' Association meeting at which he was due to speak on bollards. He swept out of the café dragging the plant behind him, oblivious to it crashing against tables and chairs, customers leaping up to grab tea-pots and coffee cups, hollering at him to stop. I had no way to explain Felicity's relaxed reaction to him except, perhaps, that his oddness – and the fact that he was totally oblivious to her silence – made her feel less odd herself.

But I see no need to go into any of this with Faraday and Khan. Nick and Mariah weren't interested in what I did with Felicity after school – they didn't care – and since I paid for the buns and hot chocolates myself, they had no practical need to know, either. It is clear to me that bringing up Queen's Lane will only confuse things – and things are confused enough already. So I keep it to myself.

Chapter 18

Faraday rubs a hand across his face, as if trying to rid himself of an encroaching weariness, or perhaps irritation. –It sounds like you and Felicity spent a lot of time alone together?

–Yes, we did.

–So at what point did she start talking to you then?

–That would be late October.

I remember the day she spoke to me for the first time because that was the day I found her in the priest's hole eating dead bees.

Nick and Mariah were socializing every night – hosting students, visitors, dons; dining in College or attending functions. I'd left Felicity colouring in her room while I made macaroni cheese for supper. When I called upstairs she didn't appear, so I went up to find her.

Her chair was empty; felt-tip pens lay strewn across the desk and her colouring book flipped in a freezing gust from the open window. A lurid image entered my head of her clambering onto the windowsill and pitching forwards, the cobbles rushing up to meet her. As I got to the window, a dark shape flitted along the periphery of my vision and I spun round. The priest's hole door was open. I saw movement there. I slammed the window shut and rushed over.

She was squatting inside in the semi-darkness with her back to me, her hair bubbling like tar at her delicate neck. 'Ah, well, there you are,' I said, with some relief, 'I thought I'd lost you!'

The tiny windowless chamber lined with toxic wallpaper was obviously not the ideal playroom. The horrible smell still hung in the air but fainter than it had been in the night. The bare floorboards were dusty and splintery and there was no ventilation. I noticed an oval patch on the wall where Mariah had scraped off top layers of paint to get at the poisonous green wallpaper. 'You really can't be in here, poppet,' I said. 'It's not safe in here because of the poisonous wallpaper, you know that. We talked about this!'

She didn't react. She had little objects scattered on the floorboards at her bare feet. I thought they were sweets at first, but as my eyes adjusted, I realized that they were bees.

As I peered over her shoulder, I saw that the scattering wasn't random. She'd laid them out in what looked a bit like a daisy shape, only with larger, looser petals. It was a witch hex.

A few days after I found the salt bowls in my room, I'd found her looking at images of witch hexes on her iPad – little swirling patterns scratched into the door joists of medieval churches and homes to ward off evil energies. At the time I didn't think it was particularly harmful – it is human nature, after all, to create patterns and to imbue them with significance and power – but seeing her laying out a witch hex in dead bees in the priest's hole definitely did not feel reassuring.

'Come on, darling,' I said. 'Out we get now.' I reached out and touched her shoulder but she jerked away and darted her hand to her mouth – I heard her gulp. I felt myself gag as if I'd swallowed the bee myself.

She turned her head – her expression was eerily desperate

and I had to remind myself she was just a little girl, a lonely, bereaved little girl, mute, troubled and displaced – anxious about her new school. She was intensely vulnerable and vulnerability can be uncanny in a child.

'Well, you must be famished if you're eating dead bees.' I tried to laugh. 'Come on, darling, we'll lock up this door once and for all and put the key back where you found it and we'll say no more about it.'

She didn't move. An image suddenly popped into my head of someone shoving me from behind, slamming the door and locking us in – the two of us trapped in the tiny chamber barely able to breathe, shouting and banging on the panels to be let out.

I had an urgent feeling, then, that I must get her out of there – carry her out if necessary.

And that's when she spoke. It was a little more than a whisper, but distinct and quite assertive. 'This will get rid of them, Dee. This will make them go away.'

It felt extraordinary to hear her speak. In any other circumstances I'd have been delighted by this breakthrough, but her words, though welcome, were hardly encouraging. Still, I knew that I must be matter of fact; I must act as if it was nothing unusual to hear her speak. I held out my hand, trying to keep my voice steady. 'Get rid of who, my darling?'

She turned her face away again and said firmly, in a deeper voice, to the sloping wall, 'Stay away. Leave this house.'

We stayed like that for a second or two, both frozen – my hand outstretched, Felicity crouched with her back to me staring intently at the back wall.

Then behind us the bedroom door blew shut. We both gave a start – and the spell broke. I felt immensely foolish – I'd almost allowed myself to get sucked into her childish superstitions. I was supposed to be the adult, keeping the mental chaos at bay, not adding to it.

Felicity reached out and took my hand with her small cold one. Her face had lost its terror. 'It's okay, Dee,' she whispered as she stepped back into the bedroom. 'It's worked. They've gone now.'

Chapter 19

–But how exactly did you make her talk to you? says Faraday.
–What did you do?

I am certainly not going to tell them about the dead bees and the priest's hole. –I didn't do anything. It was just a slow building of trust, I say. –I was there for her. I comforted her when she had bad dreams, I made porridge every morning, I picked her up from school and played with her and cooked food she liked and watched TV with her. I made her feel safe. I listened to her.

–How could you listen to her if she wasn't speaking?

–There are other ways to communicate with a frightened child. I hear my voice wobble, and I have to clear my throat. –Can I have some water?

–Of course you can. Faraday gets up and goes to the water cooler in the corner. He is not fat, exactly, but solid, broad-shouldered, a bit out of shape. The cheap material of his trousers and the back of his shirt are crumpled. He turns with the water. – Need a comfort break, too, Dee? –Want to stretch your legs a bit?

Perhaps I look more rattled than I should. –I'm perfectly comfortable, I say. I'm not, though. The chair is hard, my head throbs, my guts are churning – I just want to be with Felicity again, I just want all this to be over and for her to be safe in my arms.

I feel my throat tighten and glance at my watch. –Is this going to take much longer? I take a few sips of the water he's handed me. The strip lighting is making my eyeballs hurt.

–Is there somewhere else you need to be?

–Of course not, but surely there are more urgent things to do than sit around talking like this? I really haven't got anything to tell you that I didn't already say to your colleagues at the house.

Khan suddenly puts down her biro. –I can see you're anxious to leave, Dee. Her voice is level. –But you need to remember that forces in Oxford, and up and down the country, are urgently looking for this child. We want to find her as much as you do. We *will* find her. And you're going to help us do that.

I feel my face grow hot. Her tone is way more authoritative than I'd expected, more alert. –Let's get on with it then. I gulp the rest of the water and set the cup down next to the cold tea.

Faraday takes the reins back, asking if I know of any other adults Felicity came into contact with. Is there anyone else, he says, who could have let themselves in?

I peel my eyes away from Khan and look at him again. –People were letting themselves in all the time, I say. –As far as I can tell, half of Oxford has a key to the Master's Lodging.

–We've got a list of who had a key, but did you give one to anybody – any friends or acquaintances?

–Of course I didn't.

He is leaning back in his chair. The shirt button on the widest part of his belly strains. His eyes are growing more bloodshot. His question, of course, has made me think about Linklater again.

I remind myself that Faraday has no reason to know about Linklater.

Nick would almost certainly not have mentioned him to the police – or would only have mentioned him in passing – and neither Nick nor Mariah even knew he'd been back to the house after that first visit to see the priest's hole. He certainly did not have a key.

It was early November when he came back for the second time. Michaelmas term was in full swing and Nick and Mariah had gone to a College feast night. I was stirring a pot of leek and potato soup and Felicity was chopping parsley next to me. Some of our calmest times were in the kitchen like this, side by side with a pot bubbling on the hob, something delicious in it – or perhaps a beautiful bone that we were cleaning off to display in her expanding spiral of treasures. When we heard the knock at the front door our eyes met in dismay.

I assumed it was a delivery or a visitor arriving at the wrong time, or a member of the catering staff come to fetch a pot or vase or dish and forgetting the key. I wiped my hands on a tea towel and went down the hall. Felicity hung back, but when she saw Linklater on the doorstep she rushed towards us.

And for some reason, I felt pleased by the sight of him too. Since my main strategy for the past twenty-six years had been to avoid attachment, it was strange to find myself actually welcoming a visitor.

The tip of his nose was red and his breath clouded the evening air. 'The lying bastards are trying to dismantle the Victorian cupboards in the Museum of Natural History,' he announced.

I tried not to laugh. 'What lying bastards?'

'The University. There's a planning meeting in the town hall – I'm on my way there right now.'

'But aren't you part of the University?'

'Me? What? No. Not like that. Not any more. Oh crap – is that clock right? If it is, I've got to go. I can't let them—' He turned to leave again.

'Wait.' I touched his arm. 'Why did you come? Did you have something to tell us, or did you just want to share your thoughts on lying bastards?'

'Ah. Sorry! Yes, yes, right, yes, I do have something – I thought you'd like to see a letter I found in the archive today.' He began to dig in his satchel. 'Written by V in 1916. It seems she's taken herself off to London to work at Endell Street – the suffragette-run war hospital – and she's left the twins with Mrs Diles. They're five now, and she's worried Mrs D isn't coping. Mrs D's apparently had to lock Duncan in the closet in her room – I'm guessing the priest's hole? – as a punishment for throwing food.' He scanned his photocopied letter. 'V says: *"he made a terrible racket demanding to be let out and poor Mrs Diles relented after just a few minutes"*.'

I looked sharply at Felicity. Her eyes met mine, and there was something fearful in their expression that made me wonder whether Linklater's stories of the little boys might not be such a good idea after all. It could well have been an imaginary Duncan and Jonnie she'd banished from the priest's hole with her dead bees.

But Linklater was still talking. 'Reading between the lines, it sounds like Mrs D's gone off the deep end – she's panicking about a broken clock bringing death into the house, insisting there's bad energy in the attic. The twins are obviously winding her up. She tells V she's woken up in the night to find them both standing silently at the foot of her bed—'

'Well!' I cut him off. 'That's all very interesting, but we've got some leek and potato soup on the go.' I was going to have to tell him later not to talk about the twins in front of Felicity any more. 'How long's your meeting likely to take? The soup'll be ready in about twenty minutes – you could come back and have some if you want. We're making garlic croutons too. Nick and Mariah are out for the night.'

'Ah, no. Bugger. Sadly not. These meetings go on for hours and hours. And people are, um, extremely agitated about the cupboards.'

There were smears and fingerprints on the lenses of his specs and I had the urge to lift them off his nose and give them a good wipe. He reached out a hand and for a confusing moment I thought that he was going to take mine, but he touched the painted panel. 'What do you think of the campaign then?'

'What campaign?'

'To have these stripped back.'

'Someone's campaigning to have the wood panels *unpainted*?'

'A group of dons.' He nodded. 'They've gone a bit rabid over there.'

'About wood panels? How do you know?'

'I have eyes and ears in the SCR.' He tapped the side of his nose. 'The knives are out for Mariah.'

'Because of her decorating choices?'

'People feel very strongly about the Master's Lodging. But of course Ticketgate's the bigger shitstorm.'

'*Ticketgate*?'

'The Hong Kong trip?'

I must have looked blank.

'Didn't you hear about that, either?' He seemed shocked that I could be so ill-informed. 'Law's been invited to Hong Kong in the New Year by an alumnus, a young Bitcoin billionaire who might be donating a few million for a teaching Fellowship and a research fund in perpetuity – a pretty huge endowment, actually.'

I was genuinely confused. 'Isn't that a good thing?'

'Well, you'd think, but it's the plane tickets they're up in arms about over the road. Mr Bitcoin's flying him out to Hong Kong – British Airways, business class – at the start of January for a week and Law wants College to pay for his wife's ticket. He's arguing that it's appropriate to have her with him, but the Governing Body's refusing to pay because she's not strictly a College member. They say she has to buy her own ticket, which – being business class – is a small fortune.'

'But surely Mariah *is* a College member?'

'Ah, well, no. She's not enrolled as a student here and she's not a salaried staff member, either, so she doesn't exist, offi-cially. Law's outraged – apparently he lost it completely at the last meeting, yelling and banging the table. As you can imagine, that didn't go down well. I mean, maybe you can behave like that when you're running the BBC, but you definitely can't do that sort of thing in a Governing Body meeting.' He peered up at me. 'Crikey. I can't believe you haven't heard about this.'

It did strike me as unbelievable – not the conflict, that was entirely credible – but the fact that they hadn't bothered to mention to me that the two of them would be in Hong Kong for a week in January.

'Ructions then,' I said.

'Absolute carnage.' His mouth was serious but his eyes shone and I sensed that he, too, found College politics ridiculous. He glanced at Felicity, then at the clock. 'Fuck! Now I'm properly late' – and with that, he slipped away into the night, sword raised to defend his Victorian cupboards.

Chapter 20

It becomes clear from Faraday's follow-up questions – about what Felicity said about her parents when she did speak to me, and why I thought she'd begun to communicate less with her father – that Nick has been saying a lot of negative things about me. He must have been interviewed several times by now, both by the investigating officers at the house, and by Faraday and Khan here in this room. I have a strong feeling that he has been telling them I've been poisoning his child against him.

That Nick has turned against me should not come as a big surprise. As the months passed, I had watched his initial indifference towards me morph into a fairly open antipathy. All this pent antagonism erupted in my face on the day Felicity vanished – and it was really quite alarming.

When Nick got back to Oxford – just three days ago now, though it feels like an awful lot longer – I was upstairs helping Mariah with the baby, while the police were busy searching the Lodging. I was changing the baby's nappy in the nursery when I heard Nick come into the bedroom. He must have ignored – or perhaps not seen – the police officers, and rushed straight up to find Mariah.

He was hunched over the bed where she lay in a foetal position and I couldn't make out what he was saying. Spotting me out of the corner of his eye, he whipped round, got to his feet and lurched across the room towards me. He yanked his son from my arms, causing him to wail hysterically again, and then he shoved me back into the nursery and closed the door. His nostrils were so flared that I could see right up into the cavernous holes, and I could smell his aftershave, and something else too, some kind of acrid panic coming off his skin. We were far too close, crammed into the tiny nursery.

'Where's Felicity?' he shouted over his howling baby. A fleck of his spittle hit my bottom lip.

I pulled a tissue from my sleeve and wiped it off. I tried to get past him, then, but he was blocking my way. I'd seen this primitive look only once before on a man's face – I knew that the only reason he didn't have his hands around my throat was that he was holding his baby.

His features seemed to darken and swell as his face moved closer to mine. 'Where the hell is she?'

'I've only just got back myself, Nick.'

'Did you take her down to London with you?' he roared. 'Did you? Did something happen to her in London?'

'What? Okay, you're upset, we all are, but this is ridiculous,' I said. 'Listen to yourself. I haven't taken Felicity to London. If you want to know what's happened to her, you need to go back in there and ask your wife.'

He stared at me a moment longer, granite-eyeballed, then swung round and left the room. I kicked the door shut. The baby's cries receded.

My mouth tasted metallic and my ears rang. I reached out to switch off the baby monitor then smoothed my hair back and took some deep breaths.

The last time a man had wanted to kill me he had my baby in his Volvo. She was strapped in but she could see me as I ran round the car, my feet slipping on the mud, trying all the doors. She was holding up her arms for me to get her out, her chubby fingers splayed, her legs kicking, her mouth open, howling. And as I circled, trying each door, he followed, bellowing threats. The driver's door was half-open, the keys still in the ignition. I jumped in, slammed the door and pressed the automatic locks.

I leaned my forehead against the nursery doorframe. I had to get a grip – I had to get myself under control because in a moment I was going to have to go back downstairs and convince the police that the accusations they'd probably just heard on the baby monitor were delusional – that Nick's talk of me taking Felicity to London was just the ranting of a terrified father – understandable, but wholly unfounded.

I was going to have to go down and make them understand that I would never hurt Felicity, that I would do anything, in fact, to keep her from harm.

Chapter 21

Faraday flicks through his notes, apparently satisfied with my response that Felicity was speaking less and less to Nick because she was becoming more and more unhappy.

–Right, yes, you've said she's not been happy at school. In fact, I gather you kept her out of school on thirteen occasions up to Christmas. He looked up. –And only consulted her parents about it twice?

I tell him, as calmly as possible, that Nick and Mariah paid so little attention that the chances of them remembering whether I'd told them she was unwell or not are pretty much zero. –It's my job to notice Felicity's mental state and to safeguard her, I say. –And sometimes that means the odd duvet day.

He and Khan exchange a meaningful glance.

–So, Felicity's told you she's unhappy at school? Faraday says.

–Well, not directly, but it's obvious.

–Because she can't talk?

–Because she's being bullied.

–Yes, you said that to my officers when they interviewed you at the house, but we've spoken to her teachers now and they say there's no bullying. Dr Law says there's none of it, either. So who do you think's been bullying her?

–Lots of the other children.

–Lots of them? Surely the teachers would have noticed that and put a stop to it? Faraday flips through the papers on his lap and pulls out a sheet. –Felicity's teacher said in her statement that you yourself have been . . . He scans the page. –That's right, here you go: 'difficult'. You've bothered her with hostile queries, she says. Apparently you were also spotted hiding behind a wall at playtime, watching the children?

This comes completely out of the blue. I barely know how to respond. A nanny watching the child in her care is hardly a crime, but even so it's going to be difficult to make Faraday and Khan understand what I was doing behind the playground wall.

All I can say is it sounds a lot more suspicious than it was.

Felicity's teacher was young, newly qualified and not very clever. She seemed only to operate in platitudes, cooing: 'Ah, she's such a lovely girl, she's doing *so* well' when I asked for a progress report. When I demanded specifics, she'd look a bit startled and say: 'Oh, I'm sure she'll choose to talk when she's ready. She'll come out of herself, don't worry.'

I'd fully researched selective mutism by then. I knew it was a debilitating fear response, possibly bound up in complicated personality traits to do with perfectionism, imagination, anxiety, a high IQ. I understood that it was also probably genetic, though it had undoubtedly been worsened by the trauma of losing her mother. I also knew that Felicity's silence was no more about choice than any other phobia was. Her teacher, however, clearly had not done the same level of research. In fact, she appeared to know almost nothing about selective mutism.

'You wouldn't say of an arachnophobe "ah, she'll choose to love spiders when she's ready",' I said to her, perhaps a little harshly. 'Felicity's not *deciding* not to talk. She's frozen. Paralyzed. It's like having very bad stage fright.'

'But she talks to Dad, doesn't she? She obviously can talk if she wants to.'

'Selectively mute children are almost always able to talk to close family.' I stared at her in disbelief. 'Haven't you understood even the basics about this?'

She blushed and I did feel a bit bad then – she was just an overstretched, overworked young teacher, and Felicity can't have been a straightforward child in a classroom situation. It must be incredibly easy to believe there was an element of stubbornness or defiance in her silence, though of course it was nothing of the sort.

But one thing was clear: Felicity did not need to 'come out of herself'. She needed to come back to herself, to *be* herself and currently her entire environment was doing a brilliant job of preventing that.

Her mental state definitely worsened as the autumn term progressed. Every day her lunchbox came back untouched, even the juice box – she couldn't allow herself to drink as she knew she wouldn't be able to put up her hand to ask to go to the toilet. It was still a major challenge to get her to eat at home, though she'd often have a bun or a crumpet in Queen's Lane. And then, of course, there was the lack of sleep. One night in three, at least, she was up and moving about the attic in the night, fretting and panicking and seeing things.

I think of one particularly difficult night, when I heard a scraping sound on the floorboards and went through to find her trying to drag her desk up against the priest's hole door. I managed to ease her back to her bed but as I stroked her hair, she suddenly lurched up again and scrambled to sitting, moving backwards, pressing herself against the headboard and staring in terror across the room.

I turned, too, but of course the room was empty. I took a breath and put my arms around her. She felt insubstantial, a wee whisper of a thing. 'There's no one here, darling. It's just a bad dream, you're just having a bad dream.' I patted her back. 'You're safe with me. I'll keep you safe.'

She raised her head from where she'd burrowed against my chest, and stared at the space behind me, and then she gave a cry and launched herself out of bed – I had to grab her ankle to stop her going head first onto the floor.

'Mummy!' She ran to the priest's hole. Her bare feet scattered sharp bits of bone and pebbles as she shoved at the desk, then wrenched open the door. 'No!'

I rushed to where she was crouched, just inside the priest's hole. 'No, no, no.' She looked up at me, wild-eyed. 'Do something.' Her voice was desperate. She held up her hands, palms towards me, as if showing me something. I moved slowly, as you'd approach a frightened animal, crouched down and gently took both her hands in mine. 'Okay, I will,' I said, firmly. 'It's okay, darling. I've got this. I'm here now.'

These night terrors, of course, did nothing to help her cope at school. And since her teacher was never going to give me any meaningful information about what was going on there, I was forced to take matters into my own hands. I found a spot up the alley behind the playground, along the furthest wall, where there was a gap in the bricks by a low-branched sycamore, and a clear view of the playground.

Since I don't tend to feel the cold, I often didn't bother to go home when the children returned to their classrooms after lunch. I found that I could do some of my best work on my theorem on those autumn afternoons under the sycamore, wrapped in a fleece and a thick woollen scarf. I thought about multidimensional objects and filled my notebook with sketches and brain doodles, and the hours seemed to vanish. Working on a proof is a bit like wandering around a strange house in the dark – you see half-formed shapes, crash into furniture and tumble down stairs, injuring and frustrating yourself. You meet dead ends, locked doors, blunt corners – but then one day your fingers touch a light switch and suddenly you know exactly where you are, and what you must do to turn your dream into a reality – to prove that what you instinctively feel to be true actually is.

Presumably, a teacher or playground helper spotted me under the sycamore, though it can hardly have rung alarm bells or they'd have come and confronted me. After all, I sat there frequently, between the lunch hour and pick up time, lost in my work. And I'm glad I did, because what I saw confirmed to me that school was torture for Felicity.

Her teacher had paired her with a little extrovert called Nicole, who dragged her around the playground like a pet, explaining to other children how she felt or guessing what she might like to say. Felicity followed Nicole stiffly, eyes down, gnawing her fingers or scratching her ear. With her wild black curls, wide-apart eyes and pale, freckled skin, she was always going to stand out, but even if she'd been a pretty little blonde girl, she'd have been an oddity because her silence attracted more attention than her voice ever could. Children came over and confronted her all the time, saying, 'Why don't you talk?' or 'When will you talk?' or 'Can't you speak at all?' When Nicole thought Felicity wasn't looking, she sometimes made cruel faces behind her back. Other children performed jerky robot movements. Felicity was aware of it all.

Bad things happened almost every day. Some girls wrote a sign that read 'Are you deaf and dumb?' They held it up in her face. I watched a fat boy, perhaps a year six, shove her from behind so she went face down on the tarmac. I was on the point of climbing the wall, then, to scoop her up and take her home, when a playground helper noticed and went over. That day she had plasters on both knees and couldn't even eat a bun in Queen's Lane; she just sat staring at it sadly until I wrapped it up and took her home, where she climbed into bed, curled up and stared at the wall.

I made an appointment with Nick that day – I phoned his PA, Sally, as he'd instructed me to a few weeks before, when I'd waited for him that night in the kitchen and he'd shown me the video of Felicity. When I said it was urgent, Sally said he could 'give me' fifteen minutes in his College office the following day, between appointments.

The next day, I climbed the creaking oak staircase marked 'SCR Members Only'. I peeked into the Senior Common Room as I passed it, a large and light-filled space with armchairs and sofas set around an ancient stone fireplace. The oak panels were polished and there were low beams, ancient sloping floors and bookshelves stacked with priceless leather volumes. There were only three dons, all of them hunched around the espresso machine. They didn't notice me step in and I heard one say, in a strong Mancunian accent, 'I gather he's got another of his celebrities coming to Formal Hall this week. It's embarrassing, he's turning this place into a fucking circus.'

'It's not the celebrities that get me,' growled a taller, older, white-haired companion, 'it's that fucking Danish pastry.'

'Oh Christ, yes.' The third had a camp, Etonian voice. 'Ghastly cunt. We have to do something about her.' A floorboard creaked under my foot, and they turned in unison.

I went over, leaned past them and took a handful of short-bread biscuits – which I remembered from previous visits were excellent, baked daily by the College chef. 'Sorry,' the Etonian whined, 'but are you looking for someone?' I turned and left before they could gather themselves to point out that the SCR's shortbread had not been baked for civilians like me. As I walked out into the sloping oak-panelled corridor, which smelled of wax polish and burned toast, I heard one say, 'Hang on – wasn't that his fucking *nanny*?'

It was just as well I had eaten the shortbread because Nick offered me nothing. He gestured at the hard chair on the other side of his desk, shuffled his papers about, glanced at his watch, looked over his glasses and said, 'Right then, Dee, what can I do for you?' I noticed that the papers were the minutes of a Governing Body meeting. The first item was 'Alumnus invitation – Hong Kong'.

When I told him what was going on with Felicity, he nodded. 'Yes, yes, we're familiar with this pattern of behaviour.'

'Being bullied is hardly a "pattern of behaviour".'

'Sorry, Dee, but what bullying? By whom? Nobody's bullying her.'

I stared at him – had he not listened to a word I had just said?

'Listen, I'm in regular contact with the school,' he continued. 'She's being monitored by the SEN people – all the teachers are on board. We'd certainly know if anyone was bullying her. Her form teacher did mention that you're very hands-on and concerned, but you need to back off a bit now and let them do their job. But look, since I've got you, there's one thing I wanted to raise with you – the state of her bedroom. All those bones and things you two have been bringing in and putting on her floor, they're . . .'

I couldn't believe that he was telling me to tidy her room. Only someone who had never been a victim of bullying could be this blinkered. Nick just wasn't prepared to admit that bullies can go beneath the radar. He was also choosing to ignore the obvious fact that his daughter could not communicate with the staff who were supposedly protecting her. He had chosen a high-performing state primary because they wanted a more 'normal' or 'relaxed' environment after her intense, private girls' school in London, but what he failed to realize was that she didn't belong in any formal institution. He could have hired private tutors – Oxford was full of them – I could have taught her myself, come to that – but this would have been an admission of a perceived failure, and he couldn't have that. Failure was not an option for a man like Nick Law.

It made me think of an argument I'd overheard between the Philosophy don and an English Literature professor who had come to dinner just after Nick's appointment had been announced. The Literature professor said Nick was known at the BBC as someone who imposed impossibly high standards, controlled the minutiae and fired people at the drop of a hat. The Philosophy don had defended him, saying what the College needed was strong leadership, someone unafraid of change. 'You wait,' the Literature professor growled. 'You lot all think he's Mr Darcy, but this isn't *Pride and Prejudice*, darling – the man's not Darcy, he's fucking Voldemort.'

Nick had stopped talking and his expression was stern and querulous, almost identical, in fact, to the fifteenth-century College founder in the gilt-framed portrait on the wall above him.

I couldn't help but feel that Nick's obvious dislike of me had something to do with the fact that I wasn't in awe of him. A man like him – tall, striking, powerful – was no doubt used to having a rather more dramatic effect on women. The problem was he couldn't pigeonhole me: I wasn't an impressionable Danish au pair, nor was I a homely mother figure, or a subservient member of College staff – there was no way I'd be calling him 'Master'. He might also be growing jealous. In the four years since Ana's death, he had been the only person Felicity could speak to, but now I'd slipped a finger inside his father-daughter tangle and found that the threads weren't tightly woven at all. Felicity was communicating with him less and less, while her bond with me grew stronger by the day.

'So,' he said, in a clipped voice. 'Are we clear? No more skulls. No more ghosts.'

I knew that if I stayed in his office a second longer I'd say something I might regret.

I tell Faraday and Khan that, yes, Felicity was being bullied – the kind of subtle but devastating bullying that mostly goes undetected – and that I was the only person who knew the extent of it, because I was the only one who was wholly focused on her. Nick was either being naive, or deliberately obtuse because he did not want to deal with another problem.

Faraday nods as if he agrees with me. –Kids who run away from home are often being bullied at school, he says. –Do you think it's possible she's run away? He cocks his head and watches my face for a response. Khan stops writing and stares at me, too.

–All I know, I say, –is that a bullied child is a desperate child.

Chapter 22

Faraday clears his thick throat. –Fine, so maybe you tell us a bit more about the sort of things you and Felicity like to do together when she's not at school – where are her favourite places to go in Oxford?

I have already told them about the Pitt Rivers Museum and I'm not going to mention Queen's Lane, so this time I tell them about Holywell and St Sepulchre's. It is possible that we've been spotted in those places, after all.

Khan and Faraday exchange a glance, then speak at the same time: –*Graveyards?*

–They're actually really lovely places to be, I say. –Wild gardens. Full of local interest. She loves them.

Khan scribbles furiously.

I will not mention that we went to these places with Linklater. As far as I know, nobody – not even Angela – was aware that Felicity and I were spending time with him. We were seeing him fairly regularly in Queen's Lane by then, but he only came inside the Lodging for the second time one Saturday afternoon in late November. And then, once again, Felicity and I were the only ones who saw him.

Mariah and Nick happened to be at a friend's private view in

London that day and there were no parties planned, so Angela and her staff, for once, were leaving us alone. I'd just taken a batch of rock cakes out of the oven when I heard the knock on the door. I went to answer it rather grumpily, expecting to find a confused academic on the doorstep, mistaking the date, or a College lackey, perhaps, fetching or bringing something pointless and forgetting the key. My spirits lifted at the sight of Linklater waving a handful of papers. 'Well, I think I know why V's here!'

'And hello to you too.' I stood aside and gestured for him to come in.

'Ah. Yes, right, hello.' He paused, pushing his glasses up his nose and peering at me – they were still lopsided. For a moment, our eyes met. I turned and led him into the kitchen.

'I've been going through the letters again, looking for things and I found this—'

Felicity appeared at the kitchen door as he began reading the letter out loud. I'd texted him after the last time to say perhaps he'd best not talk too much about the twins, but in his excitement he seemed to have forgotten that.

I must thank you once again, my dearest, for your most generous love and support. I do not know what I would have done without you, Muriel, truly, you have saved our lives. I feel safe here in Oxford, perhaps for the first time in ten years. Even Mrs Diles seems calmer – though she is still convinced that we have a phantom. She gets up at night and paces the attic corridor with her candle, searching for it, but I don't hear a thing. I am sleeping like a baby for the first time in years. Oh, my darling Muriel, we shall be happy here in Oxford I think, until you can come – though of course I will never be truly happy until we are together.

He handed the paper to me. 'I don't think she's a widow at all. I think she's escaping a violent husband – all the talk of her life being saved and feeling safe for the first time, and the pseudonym – the twins too. I can't find twin boys called "Duncan and Jonnie" anywhere official. She's obviously run away. It explains why she's not in any public records.'

I glanced at Felicity. 'This is surely taking up far too much of your time! You should leave this and go onto some of the other former residents.'

'Oh, but it's just getting interesting, isn't it? I love a good mystery.' He glanced at the rock buns, which were cooling on the rack between a pile of thawing mince and the Le Creuset pot in which we were macerating a beautiful rat's mandible that we'd found on Port Meadow.

Felicity's voice was almost a whisper. 'What does Mrs Diles see in the attic?'

We both turned to look at her. Linklater, of course, had no idea how extraordinary it was that she'd just asked him a question. I was both thrilled to hear her voice, and anxious about where this conversation might go, and what it had already triggered in her imagination.

'A phantom? A phantom's a ghost.' Linklater glanced at the rock buns again. 'Not that there's any such thing.'

Felicity looked dubious.

'Yes,' I said. 'Mrs Diles was just a confused old lady.'

Linklater turned to me. 'It could be dementia, actually, couldn't it? People with dementia see ghosts all the time.'

'Have a rock bun.' I pushed them towards him but as he reached for one he looked at the clock above my head and yelped. 'Oh bollocking hell! I'm meant to be at Holywell Cemetery.' He threw the cake back down. 'Guided walk.'

'Well, you've missed it,' I said. 'So sit down and have a cup of tea.'

'I'm the guide—' He flew past Felicity and away down the corridor. She turned and followed him. I turned off the stove, and ran after them. Felicity was shoving her feet into boots. Before I could stop her, she'd followed him out. I ran out too, grabbing both our coats from the hooks by the door.

It was a freezing, vaporous day and Felicity sprinted ahead after Linklater, who moved surprisingly fast – he'd look quite athletic if it weren't for the chaotic flapping of his overcoat and satchel. I yelled to her to stop at the top of Magpie Lane, which fortunately she did – teetering on the brink of the High Street as buses powered by. Linklater vanished between some bicycles – I heard bells ringing, a car horn, someone swearing.

I caught up with her and got her across the road safely, but while I walked all the time, I wasn't used to running, and when she started off after him again I had to let her vanish into the mist.

In all my years in Oxford I'd never noticed Holywell Cemetery, and as I passed through the little gate, I found myself on a very narrow path, almost a burrow, through low trees that came out at a dilapidated gatehouse with a homeless encampment in its porch. I was wondering if I had the wrong place but then I saw Linklater ahead, standing next to a gravestone with Felicity and a grey-haired couple in rain ponchos and very white trainers: American tourists. As I approached I heard him say: '. . . of *Wind in the Willows* fame', and then he saw me and waved me over. The older man turned a draped, walrus face towards me and watched as I approached, but his wife kept her eyes fixed on the grave. Felicity crouched to examine something on the stone.

The churchyard looked half-forgotten, a tangled pocket of

weeds under enormous oaks and chestnuts whose remaining leaves flared against the murky sky. Many of the gravestones were entirely packaged in ivy and they loomed in the mist like crouched apes.

'Kenneth Grahame actually went to school here in Oxford,' Linklater was saying. 'He always wanted to study at the University but his guardian wouldn't let him – he made him go into banking when he was just sixteen. He wrote *Wind in the Willows* to teach his son not to show off, but that was a bit ironic, given what he did to the boy.'

'What did he do to his son?' There was trepidation in the American's voice.

'Well, his son wasn't that bright – Grahame made him do the Christ Church entrance exams six times – and when he did get in, he couldn't cope. The poor lad eventually just lay himself down on the railway line at Port Meadow and—'

The woman grasped her husband's hand, plainly shaken.

'Grahame and his wife never recovered from the loss,' Linklater said. 'Obviously.'

The Americans stared at the headstone, no doubt watching their love of *Wind in the Willows* drain into the lichen.

Linklater, either oblivious to the effect of his harrowing story, or pleased by it, slid away between the crooked crosses. His voice floated back to us. 'This graveyard's basically a snapshot of Victorian Oxford: town and gown side by side, death the great leveller and all that.'

We picked our way after him through briars and down a narrow path as he pointed at gravestones and tossed out names like Happy Families cards: 'Boffin the baker ... Salter the boatmaker ... Badcock the draper ... Gillman the bootmaker ... Venables the gunsmith and here – ' he stopped, 'lies Benjamin

Blackwell.' He made a small bow. 'Bookshop owner.' A robin fluttered away, cheeping in alarm.

The woman – plump and bedraggled – asked in a quavering voice whether there was a restroom, but Linklater ignored her and marched us to the tomb of Henry Bird, a Magdalen College choirboy who had died of typhoid in 1856. 'A very fine tomb, this one. The boy's distraught mother commissioned a very famous London architect to . . .' We gazed at the stone effigy as Linklater pointed out features of the stonework, including a small bird. The child lay on his back with his small hands clasped in prayer. The woman bent her head and began to sniff; the man draped his big arm around her. They'd both gone very pale. Perhaps Linklater did notice their distress, then, as he knitted his brows anxiously, and moved us on.

Rooks cawed and clapped in a huge, flaming horse chestnut above the next grave. 'Look, here's Theophilus Carter.' Linklater pointed at it. 'He owned a furniture shop on the High Street and used to stand on the doorstep with his top hat pushed back, greeting everyone – *madly*.' He paused, raised an eyebrow, perhaps hoping to cheer the shaken Americans up. 'The Mad Hatter. *Through the Looking Glass?*'

'Hey, is C. S. Lewis also buried here?' the man asked, while the woman blew her nose.

Linklater pointed at a tree. 'That's a golden oak,' he said. 'Extremely rare.'

'He's in Headington, on the other side of the city,' I said to the man.

'Okay, sure.' He nodded. 'Thanks.'

I decided not to mention that Lewis Carroll wrote the Alice books, not C. S. Lewis, since both authors, in my view, were equally atrocious.

Holywell was a far cry from the slick College gardens and city parks we usually walked in and I could see that Felicity was captivated, flitting through the tangled undergrowth with bright cheeks, her eyes flickering from stone to treetop and up to the goose grey sky.

We went back to Holywell with Linklater several times after this. His commentary on Oxford's thinkers and townspeople always came with snippets of information that Felicity loved – though I couldn't help but wonder if some were more accurate than others. He told us that the phrase 'stinking rich' came from the corpses of Oxford's wealthy Victorians, who'd insisted on being buried above ground so they could climb out if there'd been a mistake. He also said that cemetery space was tight in Oxford so they used to dig up medieval bones to make room for the newly dead. They'd burn the bones behind the church, he said, in a 'bone fire' – a 'bonfire.' Felicity absorbed every word and Linklater was obviously thrilled to have such an appreciative audience.

As we turned back down Magpie Lane after that first visit to Holywell, he stopped at a building and pointed at the date burned into its timbers: 1588. I'd passed this on countless occasions but had never noticed it before. 'This is Prudence Bostock's house,' he said. 'She was a young Puritan girl who got pregnant. Her Cavalier lover abandoned her and she hanged herself in this very house. People say if you come down Magpie Lane late on a foggy night you might see Prudence wandering around in a big black cape, searching for her lost love.' He glanced at Felicity, who, I was very relieved to see, looked delighted.

It was funny how she could be so spooked at night in the attic, and yet seemed to derive nothing but pleasure from Linklater's stories. It was as if she knew that his tales were safe:

daft entertainments – unlike whatever she felt in the house. Still, she was impressionable, and vulnerable. Linklater needed to be careful.

When she ran ahead of us, looking for Prudence, I said to him, 'Listen, maybe don't talk to her about ghosts. She's actually been a bit spooked in the night.'

'But she doesn't believe the ghost stuff, does she?'

'I don't know.' I looked at him. 'Do you?'

'Despite appearances, I'm not a total numpty, Dee, though don't tell that to the people who come on my ghost tour.'

I had to laugh. 'You do a ghost tour?'

'I do indeed. Dr Linklater's Spook Trail. Five p.m. every Friday from Carfax, rain or shine.' He pointed at the modern building. 'The Magpie Inn used to stand in this spot before it was torn down. Hence Magpie Lane.'

'Really? I always assumed it was named for the bird – one for sorrow, two for joy . . .'

'Three for a girl, four for a boy, five . . . um . . .' He petered out. 'I can never remember how it goes. Something about secrets.'

'Seven for a secret never to be told,' I said. 'My father used to say magpies carry a drop of the Devil's blood on their tongues.'

'Well, my mum told me if I saw one on its own I had to dot its eye with my finger, like this.' He drew a circle in the air and jabbed the centre. 'Then I had to say "Good morning, Mr Magpie" to deactivate its curse. I still do that every time I see a magpie – which is frankly a curse in itself.'

'Better to neutralize them than leave it to chance – they're evil birds.'

'Ah, no, they get a bad rap; all that stuff about stealing shiny things is basically a lie – the worst they do is swipe the odd duckling. Also they mate for life, which is always a sign of good character.'

Our eyes met for a moment – I looked away. 'Yes, well, I can't get past the Devil's blood,' I muttered.

'Yes, thanks for that. I keep picturing their hard, black little tongues now.' He shuddered. 'Anyway, this isn't really Magpie Lane at all. The Victorians renamed it because the original was such a shocker – brace yourself, Dee – it used to be Gropecunt Lane.'

Felicity was, fortunately, too far away to hear him.

'The Georgians changed it to Grove Lane, but maybe the Victorians thought even that was a bit close to the bone so they just named it after the pub. You know, until relatively recently, this was a dirty, dangerous, filthy little alley full of prostitutes and drunkards knifing each other. There was a brothel here in the eighteenth century, too, I think.' He pointed at the back wall of Oriel College, which towered along the west side of the lane. 'That's why they built thirty foot walls with spikes on top,' he said. 'To keep filthy townies like us in the gutter.'

–Dee? Faraday and Khan are both looking at me with some intensity.

Then Khan speaks, –What *does* Professor Law think of you taking his daughter round graveyards?

Chapter 23

I am able to tell Faraday and Khan that Nick had no opinion whatsoever on graveyards because he didn't know about them; and he didn't know about them because he didn't ask.

I do not, however, mention that as the first term wore on he was clearly beginning to turn against me for other reasons.

The Lodging is an ancient house; its windows and doors do not fit their frames securely, and sometimes they creak open, even when they have been closed. There are also gaps and spaces where voices can travel, swell or echo. It was essentially impossible to live there and not occasionally overhear other people's conversations. I often heard them talking about deranged or Machiavellian dons, or drunk bursars, or their social plans or Mariah's staffing issues. But some of these overheard chats made more uncomfortable listening than others.

I once heard Nick complaining about me to Mariah as I was coming along the landing late one night. Their bedroom door had popped open and they must have been on opposite sides of the room, perhaps getting undressed, because as I passed I could hear Nick's voice very clearly, 'So, how are you finding this nanny? Do you think she's okay? Angela's not sure about her.'

Mariah said something I didn't catch. I stopped and pressed my back against the wallpaper.

'I have a feeling she's going to turn out to be a bit of a pain in the neck. I didn't tell you she came into my office the other day insisting Felicity's being bullied. It's nonsense, of course. I phoned the head teacher right away and she says nothing's happening, other than the obvious.'

'Well, at least she's concerned.'

'She was also ranting about ghosts in the attic.'

Mariah laughed. 'Ghosts?'

'I know. I mean, for Christ's sake, at this rate she'll be more trouble than the bloody au pairs. Angela says she's a bit odd. I'm actually wondering if we just get rid of her now, my darling, before this goes any further?'

'Okay, wait. What?' Mariah sounded panicky. 'Wait a moment. Just wait. Okay? You can't fire her. I've got so much on – and so have you – and who the hell do we replace her with? Are you going to have Felicity in meetings with you? Because I definitely can't look after her.'

'That's not what I mean. I'm just saying she might be a pain – I mean, I feel like every time I walk into a room she's standing there staring at me like I'm the devil. Doesn't she irritate you, too?'

'No, she doesn't. I actually kind of like her, and she's so good with Felicity – I've never seen Felicity so comfortable with anyone, ever, have you?'

'Well, I suppose they do seem to be bonding.'

Mariah crossed the room. 'Did she really tell you there are ghosts up there?'

'Well, she said Felicity seems to think there's a ghost.'

'I guess this house could be a bit creepy for a child – also having a priest's hole in your bedroom. Is it the ghost of a priest?'

'No. She says it's Ana – there, see, I told you, it's bloody absurd. I've said I won't have it.'

'Okay, you know what, maybe we need to talk to her about Ana?'

'Why? No. Absolutely not! That's none of her bloody business, and the last I need is a whole lot of College gossip undermining me right now,' he snapped. 'She's not a bloody bereavement therapist, she's just a nanny – a short-term nanny at that. All she has to do is feed her, keep her safe and get her to school on time.'

'Well, she's doing all that, isn't she?' Mariah mollified. 'She's doing that really well. She's one hundred per cent reliable – the safe pair of hands. And Felicity feels safe with her. Yes? Nick? Okay? We'll look at it again when the baby's born, but for now it's all fine so let's just leave it. Okay? I just can't cope with anything else right now. Look – the door's come open again. Can you kick it shut?'

Chapter 24

Faraday asks about Mariah then. –Would it be fair to say Mrs Law has been under a lot of pressure lately?'

I nod. –Yes, that would be fair.

Presumably he needs to establish how much of a threat to Felicity Mariah actually was. Perhaps they are wondering whether Mariah didn't just let her walk out the door but actually cracked and did something to her.

–I gather she's not coping too well with the baby?

–Can anyone cope well with a colicky baby?

–I'm asking what you think her mental state is right now?

–Well, not great, I say. –She's had a very difficult time. The birth was traumatic. She and the baby almost died, they were in intensive care. He was five weeks premature so she's really anxious about him and she's had lots of problems with breast-feeding and infections and things – and of course the colic's exhausting, she's getting no sleep at all. So, she's overwhelmed. Any new mother would be.

–Overwhelmed. Right. Do you think there's a chance of post-natal depression?

–I'm not a health professional.

Khan suddenly lays her pad on the table, making a little

slapping noise. We both look at her. –You aren't a health professional, Dee, she says, in a flat and slightly sinister voice, which is particularly disconcerting after Faraday's matey chat. –But you've seen a lot of new mums, haven't you? We just want to know if, in your opinion, postnatal depression's a possibility.

I feel as if I've swallowed sand. –Could I have another glass of water?

–No problem. Faraday gets up, goes to the cooler and fills a plastic cup. As I watch him come back towards me I feel Khan's eyes on my face.

I take the water and gulp it down.

–So, Khan says, –postnatal depression?

–It's always a possibility with a new mother.

Khan looks at me for a second longer in silence. Perhaps she's asking herself how I fit into all this. As the nanny, should I not have been taking the strain of the colicky baby? She doesn't even blink. It is becoming very clear to me that she is more than just a scribe.

Faraday muscles back in. –Okay, so what about before the baby was born? Did Mrs Law seem to be settling in well to College life?

–Well, it hasn't been easy for her. She's had some issues with the Governing Body.

They must surely know all about this since they've been interviewing College members for the past three days.

–Right, Angela Phelps, the catering manager, did say there's been a bit of tension there. The decorating, isn't it? And, what, Mrs Law's dinner outfits or something? She's ruffled a few feathers, hasn't she?

–Well, yes, she's not had an easy time of it. I have the sudden urge to defend Mariah, which I resist.

She was, clearly, finding College life hard. She admitted as much to me when I found her in the kitchen very early one morning. She was staring out of the window, and when she turned I saw that her nose was red, her eyes watery. She had her hair pulled up, and very little make-up on, and there were a few little spots on her chin, which made her look younger and more vulnerable. Her pregnancy was showing by then, a neat, taut bump beneath her tight black top.

'You know what, Dee,' she said, as if we'd been talking all night, 'I used to worry a lot about Felicity, but since you've been here I haven't had to, which is a relief, because my God, this place! I had no idea—' She stopped, blinked, clamped her mouth shut and looked out the window again. No doubt Nick had told her it was inappropriate to admit to anything other than positive feelings about College in front of the staff.

'Are you okay?' I stepped tentatively into the kitchen, hoping that she wasn't going to unburden herself.

'I'm fine, no, I'm fine. I couldn't sleep.' She took a breath and cleared her throat. 'But, God, it's brutal here, isn't it?'

I wondered if that 'brutal' had something to do with a letter that had been pushed through the Lodging door the previous day. I'd heard raised voices in their room late that night – perhaps Nick hadn't been sympathetic.

The letter was addressed to *The Master* – just one sheet, folded over, without even an envelope, and with 'urgent' scrawled on it. I'd opened it up, wondering if it was so urgent that I should stop what I was doing and take it over to Nick's office.

It was written on a computer, printed on College crested paper, and signed, '*Concerned members of the Governing Body.*' They were writing to Nick, they explained, in order to raise the issue of Mariah's 'inappropriate attire' at Formal Hall. It seemed that Mariah borrowed an old academic gown of Nick's to wear over her dress. The wearing of Nick's gown, they said, was *'disrespectful'* since Mariah did not have a University of Oxford degree. Her general attire and *'manner'*, they said, was becoming *'an unfortunate distraction'*. *'Your wife,'* the anonymous complainers finished, *'runs the risk of diluting, so to speak, your impact as College figurehead, a position of dignity and authority . . .'*

Underneath Nick's PhD gown she had, I recalled, worn an eye-catching designer dress, striped like a tiger, and tall red-soled heels. Felicity and I were in the kitchen when she came downstairs and I heard Nick say, 'You can't wear my gown!' She laughed at him. 'Oh my God, Nick! Just for tonight – otherwise my belly looks too big in this dress and I can't be bothered to go back up and change now – anyway, why can't I look all serious and official at Formal Hall too?'

Formal Hall was a preposterous candlelit affair that took place weekly in term time. Since none of my employers had ever invited me to one, I'd only ever heard about it or glimpsed it through the windows of the medieval College dining hall. It is, basically, a weekly reminder that the feudal system is thriving in Oxford. The College choir sings as the Master, dons and eminent guests process down the hall in black tie and floor-length academic robes while the students, in short 'Commoners' gowns, stand to attention by long glittering tables. The Fellows install themselves at High Table – often on a platform or stage – and the Master says grace in Latin, and then sounds a gong. At least five courses follow – for those at High Table, a different wine with each – and then there's a pudding, and a 'savoury' after the pudding, and then the Fellows glide up the creaking private staircase to the Senior Common Room for their 'second pudding'.

This particularly lunatic ritual involves plates of hard fruit followed by plates of soft fruit, cheese and oatcakes; and port,

Sauternes or claret passed round to the left, often several circuits. A silver snuffbox goes round, too, and coffee, served in a towering ornate pot, with little plates of handmade chocolate truffles, and a 'digestif' or liqueur.

This second pudding ritual always makes me think of an oil painting by William Rothenstein that hung in the SCR of a college where I once spent a harrowing term looking after the maladjusted five-year-old son of a neurotic American anthropologist. 'Dessert in the Senior Common Room' depicts five solemn Victorian men sitting in a wood-panelled room, dressed in sombre suits and bow ties, with starched napkins on their laps, gilt-framed portraits of old men hanging behind them.

I had a feeling that some of the older male dons were responsible for this letter to Nick. These men, I felt, longed for a simpler, bachelor-only Oxford – days when loyal manservants served up chaffinch on toast and puddings called 'whim wham'; when each don was master of his own tiny fiefdom and there was no call for any gender-neutral pronouns, inclusivity, diversity. A time, in fact, when there were no women at all.

I had folded the letter back up and propped it on the console. But no wonder Mariah was distraught now. A formal letter of complaint sent to Nick as if he were her handler was extraordinary even by Oxford standards.

Of course, I didn't mention to her that I'd read the letter. I really didn't want to be drawn into their battles with the Governing Body. 'Dee,' Mariah turned to me again, 'I know you said you can't stay long term, but—'

'Oh, I won't leave Felicity.'

She looked slightly taken aback – perhaps I had sounded a bit vehement. Or perhaps she'd sensed the missing two words – 'with you'.

At that moment my phone jangled. I pulled it out, surprised, since nobody ever phoned me, least of all this early in the morning. I saw Linklater's name on the little screen and turned the ringer off.

'It's okay.' Mariah put her mug in the sink. 'You can answer that. I've got to go get dressed. I've got an early meeting in London.'

I wondered why she felt I needed her permission to answer my own phone.

'You know what – ' she nodded at my Nokia, 'we really need to get you a smartphone to bring you into the twenty-first century.'

'Oh, I don't want one.'

'But that old brick just isn't – I mean, you could keep in touch with all your old children on Facebook and Whatsapp and things if you had an iPhone.'

I function perfectly well without having to tell the world what I am doing. I certainly have no need to be 'liked' – and as for keeping in touch with the children I've cared for, I'm sure the ones who are old enough to use social media have forgotten me long ago, and I have no desire to be reminded of time passing and all my little ones growing up, moving on.

–So what do you think, Dee? Faraday interrupts my thoughts. –Has it been hard for Mrs Law to fit in as an outsider – as a wife without a proper College role, and all that?

–Yes, I say. –I think it's been hard. I didn't envy her.

She probably thought that if she presented herself as Nick's effervescent co-host they'd roll over and adore her. What she didn't realize was that she was dealing with a self-contained, self-serving body which was under very little pressure to move with the times. Beneath the layer of political correctness and inclusivity, its values were as medieval as its foundation stones.

The problem Mariah faced had nothing to do with home décor or clothing; it was about deep, institutional misogyny. Those old men hated her because she was a young, attractive, pregnant woman without a degree. And by wearing Nick's DPhil gown to Formal Hall, she'd inadvertently mocked the structure that made them who they were. All the little emperors suddenly had no clothes.

But even if she could see the absurdities of the institution, she still wanted to belong to it. She made me think of the hungry, bright-plumed birds on her William Morris wallpaper: her beak might gape at the ripe, bursting pomegranates, but they'd always be out of reach.

The renovation of the Master's house was her most misguided move, but perhaps she didn't realize that. I remember being in the hall when she let one of the older Fellow in. For a moment he took in the painted panels and white walls, and then he said, acidly, 'What did you do with all the previous Masters?'

'They're in storage,' Mariah said. 'Why? You want one?' I couldn't tell if she was oblivious to his censure or defiant, but I hoped it was the latter.

The Lodging was certainly a statement. With the worm-eaten Elizabethan beams and panels now a chalky white, the floor-boards stained Scandinavian blond, the fusty antiques gone and the walls relieved of glowering old men, it was unrecognizable, as if the house had risen, stretched and widened its windows to suck in the light.

But Oxford has no need for light: light is an anathema to it. Light destroys its ancient manuscripts and disturbs its concentration. Oxford is a place of dust motes, vaults and arm-span alleys, of Anglepoise lamps and dimmer switches, of creaking floorboards, and whispers in oak-panelled libraries. Its energy is stored in archives and silent corners, in book stacks and cellars. The College took one look at Mariah's airy white walls and said, 'you do not belong here'; it gathered its academic gowns and turned away.

It is interesting that Faraday should have mentioned Angela, but I suppose it shouldn't come as a surprise to find that Angela has been sticking the knife in too. Mariah's relationship with Angela encapsulated her alienation from College rather neatly.

I sensed early on that things between the two women were less than harmonious.

Towards the start of Michaelmas term I heard them in Mariah's room, arguing about a vase.

'You can't have it up here,' Angela said. 'We need it for the big displays.'

'Don't you have other vases?'

'We have plenty, but it's that one I need. You can't have it up here.'

'I can have it where I want it.' Mariah sounded astonished. 'In my own house.'

'It's not your house, actually.'

There was a pause. 'Sorry, what?'

'The Master's Lodging belongs to College and that vase belongs to College catering.' Angela emerged moments later carrying a big vase. She stopped, embarrassed to see me in the hall; I gave her a dazzling smile.

Then there were the doilies. A doily standoff might sound trivial to the outside world, but it summed up the way the non-academic staff saw Mariah – as the foreign impostor who'd never be able to understand the subtleties of College life.

I attempt to explain to Faraday and Khan that for Angela, doilies were an essential element in the Lodging's dignity – one that was firmly under her remit. She slipped them under bowls and vases on sideboards and tables. Mariah, meanwhile, saw doilies as ugly, old-fashioned and completely naff. She would go round removing them.

One day in November, Felicity and I were taking our coats off in the hall when Mariah rushed in behind us. Without stopping she called, 'Oh! Sorry! Hello! Late!' and then Nick came in clutching files and papers. He was about to say something when Angela appeared behind him with a vase of monstrous dahlias. She put them on the console, slipping a doily under them, before saying to Nick, in an unctuous voice, 'If I may, Master, I just need to speak to you about the—'

Mariah, who'd come running back down the hall to hang up her coat, saw the doily and howled. 'Jesus! Angela! I've told you so many times, no more doilies!' She whipped it out.

Angela's voice was harsh. 'But Lord Eaves always—'

'If I hear any more about Lord Eaves, I'm going to scream!' Mariah screamed, and ran off down the hall.

Felicity looked up at me, wide-eyed. I pulled a funny face, raised my eyebrows, and took her book bag to hang up. A catering assistant came out of the dining room then, with a tray of clinking glasses, almost hitting Felicity, who pressed her back against the wall. The Chapel bells began a hysterical peal and a young man burst through the front door carrying a humungous bell jar of gourds. Nick stuck out his arm, frowned and said, 'Isn't there somewhere better you two could stand?' I reached out, took Felicity's hand away from her ear and squeezed it. It struck me that I might exist purely to protect her from this ghastly family.

Chapter 25

Faraday and Khan are still looking puzzled about the doilies.

–I just don't think College staff – academic or otherwise –
approve of her, I say.

–And what about you, Faraday asks. –Do you approve of her?

–In what way?

–How about as a stepmother?

–It's not my job to approve or disapprove, I say.

I did, however, have my private opinions. You only had to
look at Mariah's social media activities to know what sort of a
stepmother she really was. I wonder whether to mention this
to Faraday.

Felicity showed me Mariah's anonymous Twitter account one
night when Nick and Mariah were having a party for the College
choir. It was around nine o'clock and Felicity should have been
falling asleep, but with the voices from downstairs echoing up
the stairwell and the organ scholar making a racket on the
harpsichord, there was no point even trying, so I'd let her watch
Coraline again on her iPad. *Coraline* was her favourite film and
she would watch it as often as I'd let her, apparently without
ever getting bored.

'Shall I read to you for a change?' My gaze travelled down

the shelf of children's literature. Despite Nick's instructions about ten pages a night, we still hadn't touched the books – she always preferred my made-up stories. As I scanned the titles, I came eye to eye with Ana. 'I bet your mum read to you a lot, didn't she?'

Felicity looked up. She suddenly seemed terribly small and sad, as if my words had sucked all the energy out of her. I understood – of course I did – what it was like to lose the person you love most in the world. I also knew that I couldn't take that pain away from her, nobody could. 'Maybe,' I went and sat next to her, putting my arm around her shoulders, 'it's hard to enjoy being read to because it reminds you a bit of your mum?'

She nodded.

'You miss her all the time, don't you?'

She nodded again.

'But your dad loves you.' I squeezed her shoulder. 'And Mariah too.'

'No, she doesn't.'

I was delighted that she'd spoken to me. 'I know it's hard with Mariah,' I said, 'but she does care about you. And you have me, now, too, don't you?'

She rested her head against my shoulder and I stroked her curls. 'You know,' I heard myself say, 'I had a little girl once and she had hair just like yours. Sometimes you really make me think of her.'

She looked up, sharply. She knew I wasn't talking about being a nanny.

I couldn't believe the words had come out of my mouth. The party below suddenly felt too loud – I could hear guests trooping around on the ground floor, high heels clipping the floorboards, booming voices and laughter and the crazed notes of Bach on the harpsichord. I had said it out loud for the first time, and the sky had not fallen.

With the intense kindness that only a little girl can show, Felicity looked up at me and whispered, 'Do you have a picture?'

I had, in fact, been looking at my old brown photo album the night before. And so I went and got it from my bedside drawer.

The pages creaked as we opened them. I pointed at one of my favourites. She is thirteen months old and sitting on my tartan blanket under a Bloody Ploughman apple tree in the orchard at Mill House. Its branches are laden with carmine-coloured fruit and she is sitting in a patch of sunlight, a tiny Buddha, holding up her hairbrush.

'Her hair is like mine.' Felicity touched the crinkly plastic.

'She loved that brush.' I stroked my baby's cheek. 'It had a silver teddy on the back but you can't see that in the photo.' I pictured my father's calloused hands tossing the brush into the back of his truck, incinerating it at the abattoir with the rest of her things.

As a child I used to believe that nothing bad could happen because my father was there – enormous, bearded, protective, as permanent as a standing stone. He would always keep me from harm. As it turned out, I was wrong about that.

But there's no sense dwelling on a parent's failings. He loved me and only wanted the best for me, and for the first fourteen years of my life I did feel safe. He used to say that it was a good thing my mother had gone because he wouldn't have wanted to share me with anyone. It must have been painful for him to send me away to school, but he was determined I should take the scholarship and better myself, even though I was lost from the moment I got there, a social misfit, soon outperforming even the brightest girls, and paying for it. But I did not blame him for that. Everything he'd known was changing; the old structures that had sustained our family for generations were disintegrating and he saw no future for me in a life of Scottish rural poverty and frustration. He was prepared to sacrifice his own well-being, and possibly mine, to get me out.

I thought, not for the first time, how disappointed he'd be if he could see me now – serving others, in a sense, just as he had. And in Oxford of all places. I'd often thought how ironic it was that I had ended up pushing a pram beneath the dreaming spires. But that was my own fault too. After I lost my child I could have picked myself up and carried on down the path he'd laid out for me – he'd wanted that, expected it – but I didn't have the stomach for it. I was in way too much pain. I remember him taking my chin once when I was quite unwell, bringing his big face close to mine, saying, 'Anger's a boomerang, Dee, it only comes back to knock you down.'

Felicity was looking at me intensely. 'It was a precious thing.' I swallowed and pointed at the brush in the photo. 'I don't know where it went.'

The familiar, suffocating darkness was folding itself over me. I put my arm around Felicity's shoulders and she pressed herself into me. Somehow she knew not to ask where my child was now. I turned more pages and when we got to the end of the album, she reached out and took my hand and for a while we sat together in silence, each of us battling to control our invisible assailants; neither of us, perhaps, entirely winning.

Then Felicity got up and went to get her iPad. She carried it back to me and I saw she'd been on Twitter. 'You aren't supposed to be on social media,' I said, putting aside my album.

She pointed at the lines of text.

It's like we're always fighting dirty little battles to grab his attention.

I saw the name of the account: *@stepmomslament*. The description read: *Struggling Stepmother. Getting it off my chest. Don't hate me.* The banner above it was William Morris' Bird & Pomegranate.

I read some of the messages – some seemed to be snippets of thoughts or experiences, others gave links to articles on step-parenting.

She's staring at me – 'get away from him, he's mine'.

'What on earth is this?' I re-read the description. The account didn't reveal the identity of its author, but with the Bird & Pomegranate design, it surely had to be Mariah's work.

Felicity kept her eyes on the screen.

She had him before he had me and she has a part of him I'll never have.

'This is awful,' I said. I'd have to ask Linklater if it was possible to find out the identity of a Twitter account.

If the house burns down, would he save her first, or me?

I leaned over and stabbed at the screen so that the Twitter window vanished. 'Whoever's writing this stuff doesn't deserve a lovely little girl,' I said.

I wondered if Nick really would save Mariah from a house fire before he'd save Felicity. I realized that I probably knew the answer to this. Felicity was blinking rapidly as if she'd just asked herself the same question. I lifted her chin and looked into her speckled green eyes. 'Stay away from social media, okay?' I said. 'This Twitter thing is toxic, and I don't want you to go on it any more. Promise?'

She nodded.

I pulled her closer and wrapped both arms around her, hugging her tight. 'Just so you know,' I kissed her curls, 'if this house burns down I'm *definitely* saving you first.'

I was very restless that night – claustrophobic. I needed to get out, to walk, to feel the cold night air on my face, to move my limbs and get far away from the attic rooms – to be on my own, and to think. But I couldn't leave Felicity up there alone.

She'd nodded off in my arms around eleven when the party died down and, when I was sure she was in a deep sleep, I eased myself off the bed and crept downstairs. The Lodging was quiet. The catering staff had cleared everything away and there was no sign of any activity – the dining room table shone in the gloom. I needed the comfort of food, so I wandered into the kitchen. I'd seen some nice-looking homemade oatcakes and a sharp, crumbly Somerset cheddar, and I knew there was a rather fine fig chutney somewhere, that Angela had brought over the previous day.

I was sitting at the table with my notebook, scribbling my workings, oatcake in hand, when I heard them coming down the hall. They must have been in the front room together, all this time, silently recovering from their party.

But as they came closer, I heard the tension in their voices. 'Seriously.' Mariah's feet pecked the wood. 'No one's treated me like that since – like I'm a stupid little girl – not for ever. I just can't stand being patronized like this, Nick, I can't stand it here.'

Nick sounded serious. 'I'm going to have words with him first thing in the morning.'

I shoved the notebook into my dressing-gown pocket and stood up just as they came into the kitchen. Mariah's jaw was tense, and Nick glowered behind her as they stopped in the doorway. 'Ah, Dee,' said Nick, with a note of sarcasm. 'You're up, are you?' He went over and flicked the kettle on.

Mariah ignored me and flopped into a kitchen chair, kicking off her heels and yanking at the clips so that her hair tumbled onto her shoulders in golden waves.

I paused, expecting them to ask how Felicity was, whether

she'd eaten much that evening, whether the party had kept her awake, but neither of them spoke. I was being dismissed – the intruder who'd strayed into their private space and wasn't welcome.

Their lack of engagement in Felicity's life was staggering. They seemed less like a family than a couple, reluctantly caretaking an inconvenient child. @Stepmomslament popped into my mind and I felt a knot of anger tighten inside my chest.

I left the kitchen without a word and as I reached the bottom stair there was an enormous thud, a bump and the shattering of glass across floorboards. Mariah and Nick rushed out of the kitchen. A photograph had come off the stair wall – their wedding portrait, in fact – it had crashed to the floor, seemingly out of the blue. Had I knocked it down? I honestly had no idea. Shards of glass littered the floorboards at the base of the staircase.

'Shit!' Mariah gazed at it. 'What happened?'

I looked at the carnage. 'The Brownie's not pleased.'

'The Brownie?' Nick's chin gave small, incredulous jerk.

'Wait, wait, I'm going to get the dustpan.' Mariah turned away. 'Don't touch this glass.'

'The Brownie?' Nick glared at me. 'Scottish folklore, Dee?'

I bent to the glass. 'House spirits,' I said. 'They don't like renovations.'

There was a moment of furious silence.

When I looked up, holding a large shard of glass, Mariah was standing behind Nick again. 'Oh my God, don't cut yourself on that.' She held out the dustpan.

'Apparently, Dee's "house spirit" is unhappy with us,' Nick said, drily.

I laid the jagged glass carefully in the dustpan then took the handle from Mariah. She glanced at Nick, then at me. 'Oh. House spirits? Yes. We have them too in Denmark.' Her tone was mollifying. Perhaps she sensed the fierce tension that had sprung up between us. 'Yes, we have the *nisse*. The Swedes have *tomte*.'

'Well, in my house,' Nick said, 'we just have humans.'

I swept up the rest of the mess and took the dustpan into the kitchen. As the shards tinkled into the bin I heard them whispering – Mariah said, 'Don't, Nick.'

When I came out again he was holding my notebook.

'It fell out of your pocket.' Mariah shoved Nick's hand towards me. I snatched it back.

'What are you working on there, Dee?' I saw a glimmer of patronizing malice in Nick's eye.

'Nothing,' I said. 'Goodnight.'

As I walked up the stairs I felt them watching me.

When I reached the landing, Nick called out, 'Oh, Dee?' I turned and looked down over the bannisters at them. 'Tomorrow, could you please, once and for all, clear those old bones and things off Felicity's bedroom floor? Thank you.'

As I passed along the landing to the attic stairs, the anger simmered inside me. I ran my fingernails along the birds and the pomegranates as I went, feeling the unruly ripples and pimples of plaster beneath the thick, priceless paper. The wallpaper seemed to represent everything that was wrong with Nick and Mariah – the extravagance of their rarified life; their substanceless parenting; their artifice and concealment. At that moment I'd have liked nothing more than to pick an edge and tear.

Chapter 26

When I've finished telling Faraday that it was clear to me that Mariah was in a dark place, both in Oxford generally, and as a new mother, he moves onto my relationship with Nick.

–I gather you and Dr Law didn't see eye to eye on quite a few things, he says. –Would that be fair?

I wonder what exactly Nick has been saying about me. He is probably trying to deflect attention from his wife who is, after all, the one who let an eight-year-old girl walk out of the house in the middle of the night. Or perhaps it's more visceral than that. From the moment Felicity vanished, Nick has been convinced that I am involved.

He began to accuse me of this as soon as he arrived back from London on Saturday, the day of her disappearance. First he cornered me in the nursery. Then, when I followed him downstairs, I heard him telling the police that I might know more than I was letting on. That was actually quite shocking.

After our nasty confrontation in the baby's room, I had tidied my hair, splashed my face with cold water and walked back into the bedroom. Mariah was on the bed, feeding the baby at last, but Nick had gone. I hurried down. I had to tell the police what Mariah had just told me.

As I came to the bottom of the main staircase, I could hear Nick's voice booming from the sunroom, 'I really don't know why you need to waste time searching the house, you can see she's not here.' They said something about standard procedure, and looking for things that might help them to locate her. The older officer asked Nick when he last saw or spoke to his daughter. Then he asked whether Felicity had a mobile phone.

'Of course not, she's only a child!'

'About half of all children under ten have a smartphone these days,' the younger officer chimed in.

'Well, my daughter isn't one of them.'

The first officer then asked whether Felicity ever used the home computer or other devices. Nick told them she had an iPad in her room. Then they asked whether she'd been talking to anyone online, whether there were any other family members or friends she might seek out. Did she have a reason to run away? Was there any trouble at school? At home? Was she jealous of the baby? Had there been any harsh words?

'Listen.' Nick sounded tense. 'I do know that when a child goes missing, the first person you look at is the father, but I've got to tell you right now, you're wasting your time if that's where you're going with this. I love my daughter and she loves me. We haven't had a row. She hasn't run away. Something's happened to her. Either she's walked out in her sleep or someone's taken her. We can go and get her iPad or whatever else you want, but you need to stop talking and get out there and find her.'

'Right, yes, your wife told us Felicity sometimes sleepwalks. Has she ever gone outside in the night?'

'Only once. Years ago. Look, we could speculate for hours, but that's not going to get her back. She has to be on CCTV some-where – someone in this city must have seen her. You need to get out there and look! An eight-year-old girl can't just vanish into thin air in a city like Oxford.'

One of the officers reassured Nick that Felicity had already been classified as High Risk. All the protocols had been activated – officers were already out searching for her in patrol cars and on foot, talking to people, checking CCTV, checking transport links. But had anything happened, anything at all, that might cause her to run away?

'Dear God, I've just told you she hasn't run away! I'm the only person she can speak to, how could she possibly negotiate the outside world?' I heard the officer say he thought Felicity spoke to me, too. 'Maybe a word or two sometimes,' Nick was dismissive, 'but my daughter's selectively mute. She can't talk to anyone at all outside the home. She's a very anxious child, a highly intelligent, highly sensitive child – she's not like other eight-year-olds, she's incredibly ... she's very vulnerable ... She's ...' His voice faltered. 'Could you give me a moment, please?'

There was a pause and the officer said something I didn't catch. 'No,' Nick snapped. 'Look, have you spoken to the nanny yet? She's got to know something. I'm sure she does. Get her back down here, ask *her* where my daughter is.'

One of the officers asked if he had reason to believe I was involved in some way.

'She's got to know something,' Nick repeated.

I did know something. I knew that Mariah saw Felicity leaving in the middle of the night – perhaps even deliberately let her go.

'Is Felicity close to the nanny?' the younger officer said. 'Could she have followed her to London?'

'What? No. Of course not. How? But the nanny could have taken her to London, couldn't she?'

'You think your nanny took your daughter to London?'

'I don't bloody know!' Nick shouted. 'Check CCTV? Ask the bus company?'

'We're checking all that right now, sir. We're taking this very seriously, I can assure you, but can I just check – are you saying your nanny might have taken your daughter down to London without your consent?'

'I have no idea – I'm just ... I just ...' There was another furious pause. 'You need to bloody well find her!'

'I know this is difficult, sir, we're doing everything we can, but I do need to clarify this. Your nanny says she was at the theatre in London, so can you just try to tell me how you think she might be involved, if she wasn't actually here in Oxford?'

'She could have come back here and got her, couldn't she?' Nick was hell-bent on blaming me, even though it made no sense to do so. 'My wife's exhausted – our baby has colic, he cries all night, doesn't sleep, she might not have heard if—'

'Your wife says she didn't see Felicity from about five p.m. last night ...' There was a pause as the officer, presumably, consulted his notes. 'She only noticed her gone this morning at about 8.45.'

'No, that's not right. Mariah would have given her dinner, put her to bed, given her breakfast much earlier than 8.45.'

'Apparently she was too busy dealing with the baby. Your wife seems a bit, um, overwhelmed, sir, would that be fair?'

'Our baby has colic.' I could hear the hesitation in Nick's voice as he absorbed the fact that there was roughly a sixteen-hour window in which Mariah had completely ignored Felicity.

'Your wife's a bit fragile right now, is she? Short fuse?'

'How on Earth is that relevant? My daughter's out there somewhere, with God knows who – someone clearly has her – something appalling is happening here, and you're asking me ...'

My wife has done nothing wrong. You have to stop wasting time with these absurd questions—'

'A lot of children this age go missing for a short time, and we do find them. If Felicity's feeling a bit jealous of the baby, this is a good way to get your attention, isn't it?'

The officer went on to say that if Felicity had wandered into central Oxford in the middle of the night, then a patrol car would almost certainly have spotted her and brought her home, so it was more likely that she was hiding somewhere – and didn't want to be found right now.

'Dear God! She has NOT run away!' Nick was livid now. 'Listen very carefully to me. There's nowhere for her to go. She doesn't speak. She has no friends. Her grandparents are all dead. My brother lives in California, Mariah's sister's in Denmark—'

'Denmark?' The officers both spoke at once.

'That's the last place she'd go, even if she could get herself out of the country, which clearly she can't because her passport is locked in my filing cabinet.' Nick's voice shook with rage.

'Would you mind just checking your filing cabinet? You'd be surprised what a clever child can do. There was that twelve-year-old Australian lad, got himself to Bali on his mum's credit card, spent four days in a luxury resort—'

'This is completely absurd!' Nick bellowed. 'She's not in bloody Denmark! Right. That's enough. I want to talk to your DCI, right now, please – and I'm also going to contact your chief constable, who I happen to have met recently.'

There was a pause during which, I assume, the officers were simultaneously making a mental note of Nick's rage, and wondering, frantically, if they had followed procedure to the letter, given that the Thames Valley chief constable would now be scrutinizing everything they did.

But it was no surprise that Nick was pulling rank. Pulling rank was his default position. The older officer assured him, again, that they were treating this as a high-risk situation. The family liaison team was on its way, he said; senior CID had been notified and were on their way too. 'When it comes to missing children, girls are most often found in or very close to home. Is there anywhere in this house, or garden, where she could be concealing herself?'

I heard Nick tell them about the shed and the priest's hole. He described it as 'a little room under the eaves'.

'Your gardener showed us the shed,' the officer said. 'We didn't see any little room, though, could you show us that?'

A radio crackled. I heard the younger officer: 'Anything from Bravo Victor yet?'

'Come with me,' Nick growled.

An intense panic gripped me and I turned and fled back upstairs. I paused on the attic landing. Felicity's door was ajar and I pushed it open, half expecting to find her sitting there with Fibby and her iPad, wondering what all the fuss was about. But of course, the room was empty. There was no sign of the cat. The duvet was rumpled, trailing off the bed as if she'd just got up. For a moment, I became light-headed – a white noise filled my ears, as if I was about to pass out. Then I heard heavy booted feet coming up the stairs. I went through to my room and sat on my own bed. The bells began to clamour and I felt disorientated, as if someone had come in and subtly moved the furniture – an inch here, an inch there; or rearranged the parquet floor into a different pattern – the boards seemed unstable, suddenly, like an Escher tessellation that shifts when you stare at it. The attic felt horribly empty. I longed, physically, for Felicity – to get her and hug her and tell her she was safe and that I'd never let anything bad happen to her ever again.

The bells had stopped but the vibrations tongued my inner ear. I heard their feet clumping along the landing.

The priest's hole was, of course, locked. I heard Nick go back down to look for the key, which I knew he wouldn't find. When he came back up, they discussed whether to force it, then I heard thuds, and the eventual splintering of wood. Then perhaps they moved to the other side of the room because I could hear their voices, deep, concerned, but I couldn't make out their words. A few minutes later, one set of feet went rapidly downstairs, and then the investigating officers came through the bathroom, and loomed in my doorway, radios crackling. The older one had Felicity's iPad tucked under his arm.

'Into animal bones and stuff, is she?' the younger officer said. 'That bedroom's quite something.'

'She collects things.' This suddenly felt too real – two uniformed police officers surveying my bedroom. I saw their eyes travel from my bedside table, across the tidy floor.

'Dr Law says she has a cat up here?'

'The bedroom door's been open,' I said. 'The cat's probably run out – she's been kept in Felicity's room so far; she's a rescue, quite new, very nervy.'

Perhaps they saw how frightened I was because the younger officer said, 'Felicity's probably just run off to scare her dad, you know. Kids do this all the time. She'll come back, don't worry. It's not your fault.'

The other officer nodded. 'Maybe you could have a look round for that cat in a minute?'

I swallowed. 'Mariah just told me she saw Felicity go downstairs in the middle of the night. Did she tell you that?'

The quality of their attention altered. 'When was this?' the older officer said.

'She isn't sure of the time, but she definitely saw Felicity pass her bedroom door. She thought she was sleepwalking. She might not want to tell you because she's worried her husband's going to be angry.'

'Oh. Why would he be angry?'

'Well, because she saw Felicity go downstairs and didn't stop her!'

'She didn't even get up?'

'No.'

The officers glanced at one another. Then the older one asked if I'd come and take the baby so they could talk to Mariah again.

Nick was in the bedroom on the phone, ashen-faced, standing by their big bay window with despairing gargoyles beyond him, saying, 'Yes, if you could ask him to call me as soon as he can. It's extremely urgent.'

Mariah lay dazed and tear-stained on the blush pink pillows with the baby on her shoulder, patting him weakly. Her breast was still half out of her T-shirt, engorged, its nipple like a big bruised eye – she hadn't noticed or didn't care. The baby was beginning to writhe and mew again. Nick hung up and turned to us. 'Not her,' he barked, pointing his phone at me. The officer replied that I was just going to hold the baby for a few minutes so they could ask Mariah a couple more questions.

'When's CID coming?' Nick snapped. 'Why aren't they here yet?'

'They're on their way, sir. Any minute now.'

Mariah, hollow-eyed, held the baby out to me and I felt Nick rein himself back in, no doubt deciding that I could do nothing to his son with two police officers actually in the house and more on the way.

The police began to ask Mariah if she'd seen Felicity go down-stairs.

'What? No!' she cried. 'I told you already – I was either feeding or totally crashed out.'

I patted the baby until he gave a burp, then slid my ring finger into his mouth. He tried to spit it out again but after a moment gave in and began to suckle.

'You saw and heard nothing at all?'

The baby began to writhe. He spat my finger out. I put him on my shoulder and stepped forwards to say something but he began to cry. The younger officer moved towards me. 'Would you mind taking him outside the room for a moment or two?'

As I walked towards the door, Nick's voice rose. 'What are you getting at? She says she didn't see or hear anything. I won't have anyone upsetting my wife. This is a monumental waste of time.'

'It's okay, Nick, it's okay—' Mariah's voice was shaking. 'I was asleep between about 11.30 and 4.30 – I was dead, com-pletely dead asleep. If she was sleepwalking and went out, then I wouldn't hear. That might have happened, I guess. But what if someone was in this house? What if someone came in and took her, like Madeleine McCann? Oh God, I can't think about that, I just can't . . .' I heard Nick hushing her but her voice rose up again, panicky. 'This isn't real, is it? It can't be. This isn't happening. Tell me this isn't happening, Nick.'

I stood just outside the door, jiggling the baby. The officer said, 'Your nanny says you saw Felicity go past your room in the middle of the night.'

For a moment there was silence.

'Of course she didn't,' Nick snapped. 'For God's sake.'

'Why would your nanny make this up?'

'Because she wants you to blame my wife!'

Mariah said nothing.

'Sorry,' the officer sounded genuinely puzzled, 'but why would she want to blame Mrs Law?'

'Just ask her,' Nick said. 'Get her back in here and ask her what else she knows.'

I took the baby into the spare room, then, over to the window, and looked out as I patted his back. I began to count the gargoyles but I couldn't focus. Now that Nick had turned on me, I'd have to watch every word that came out of my mouth because, if it came down to it, the police were always going to believe an Oxford College Master, with his degrees and awards and famous friends, above a middle-aged nobody like me, a woman without connections or accolades, without any formal qualifications unless you count Scottish Highers – and a criminal record.

Which, undoubtedly, they will.

And now, three days later, as I sit in this stuffy interview room, staring into Faraday's bloodshot eyes, I am aware that this particular dynamic is playing out, somewhere, beneath these questions. They must know about my criminal record; it would have leaped out the moment someone typed my name into the police database. They cannot possibly be unaware of it – that would be like failing to notice that the intruder in your kitchen is holding a carving knife.

And yet they have still not brought it up. Faraday's questions may seem rambling, even random, but they are not. They have planned out this interview, I realize. They are strategizing. They might not have a crime yet, but they have a criminal.

Chapter 27

–Other than the bullying, what specifically did you and Nick disagree on? Faraday presses on.

I push thoughts of my past firmly aside. It will not do to get rattled. I have known from the start that this is not an informal chat. Of course it isn't. I force my mind to stick with this question. The main thing Nick and I disagreed on was the extent of Felicity's unhappiness. Specifically, he did not take her night disturbances seriously enough. It might suit him to believe that I was inventing the notion that his daughter saw things in the attic, but he wasn't up there with us, he didn't see what I saw.

Felicity's night terrors seemed to be tangled up not just with her mother's death, but with the priest's hole itself. One night, for instance, I was sitting up in bed listening to the heave and groan of the pipes – it sounded as if the house was squeezing a monstrous slug through its bowels – when I heard a thud in Felicity's room, and a cry. I rushed through and found her kneeling just inside the priest's hole. She'd meticulously moved her treasure spiral so that it was outside the priest's hole, and she was on the other side of it from me. She didn't seem aware of my presence. Her eyes were fixed on the dark interior, something just in front of her, and I heard her say, in a high, anxious voice, 'Oh no! Wake up, wake up, wake up, wake up.'

Night terrors are such eerie states of conviction – the dreamer is lucid and looks awake, if slightly absent, and it can be hard to know what to do to get them out of it; Felicity was plainly seeing something dreadful. 'Mummy!' she cried, the second syllable rising to a pitch.

I became aware of a rapid scratching, tapping sound, then, coming from somewhere just beyond her, in the darkness. She was staring and muttering under her breath, now, as if rehearsing a complicated speech.

A feeling of urgency overcame me, and I barrelled over the spiral, scattering little bones and pebbles underfoot. I took her arms and lifted her out. She was light, and clung to me like a much younger child as I carried her out of her room and along the attic corridor.

I took her down to the kitchen – as far away as possible from the priest's hole – I'd probably have taken her outside if it hadn't been so late in November, and us just in our pyjamas. I shut the kitchen door, and put her on a chair. She looked dazed, blinking and beginning to wake up.

It was cold in the kitchen; the heating had gone off hours before. I remembered the white mohair throw on the sunroom sofa and darted through to get it. When I came back she was where I'd left her, but looking even more confused, and less absent. I wrapped her like a sausage in the throw and knelt in front of her. 'It's okay, my love, you were just having a bad dream. How about some warm milk?'

She gazed at me.

'Were you dreaming about your mummy?'

But she couldn't answer. Perhaps she didn't know.

As I put the milk pan on the hob, I thought about her scattered treasures – I'd felt at least one precious object crunch underfoot. I realized how intense my reaction had been. This house, I felt, was bad for us both. I'd never been so jumpy. It probably didn't help that I couldn't go on my walks at night any more – perhaps that was the root of my unease. But I couldn't leave her alone, even with Mariah and Nick. She might wake up and find me gone. If she had a nightmare, they probably wouldn't hear her. I didn't even trust them to comfort her, if they did hear her.

I put a mug of warm milk down in front of her. She just stared at it.

'Your dream sounded a wee bit scary.'

She pressed her lips together.

'Do you not remember what was happening?'

She shook her head.

'That's okay.' I put my hands round hers on the mug. 'You miss your mummy very much, don't you?'

Her lower lip trembled and I cupped her cheeks in my warm hands. 'It's okay to miss her,' I said. 'I know it hurts.'

The next day, after I dropped her at school, I went for a long walk in the cold drizzle along Devil's backbone towards South Hinksey. I phoned Linklater as I walked, and I told him about the sounds in the priest's hole. 'It was kind of a scratching, but also maybe tapping, too.'

'And did you tap back?'

'What?'

'Well, if it's a rat, it stops when you tap back, but if it's the ghost of a suffocating priest, the tapping will generally intensify.'

It took me a moment to realize he was teasing me.

'Could be bats, I suppose,' he said. 'The Lodging has a gabled end so they can get in. Bats can get quite scratchy, possibly a bit tappy too, who knows.'

I felt foolish then. 'Well, I'm calling the pest man back. He can figure this out.'

'Good plan. So, Queen's Lane, 3.30?'

'See you there,' I said. 'But no talk of any creepy twins and definitely no ghost stories, okay?'

As I hung up, I thought how unusual it was for me to have reached out to somebody who had, with just a few sentences, made me feel significantly better.

My well-being, sadly, was short-lived. When I came back into the Lodging, I saw Mariah's suitcase in the hall. I remembered that she'd told me she was going to Lincolnshire for a few days to work on the eighteenth-century wallpaper in the ballroom of a stately home. I was going to go and tell her there were rodents or possibly bats in the attic and that I needed to get the pest man, when I heard her in the kitchen. 'Yeah, I know, it's insane here – seriously!'

A tinny and remote woman's voice answered, 'God, Mari, they sound fucking horrendous.'

I went to the kitchen door. Mariah was filling the coffee machine and had her back to me. She was wearing boots with lots of buckles on them, and a flowing white cardigan, and her hair was roughly pinned up with tendrils coming loose. On me this hairstyle would look like a crow's nest, but on Mariah it was casually romantic. Her phone was on the counter next to her. 'Well, most of the younger dons are actually lovely,' she said. 'They're on my side. It's just a few who are so vicious.' She slotted the water reservoir back into the machine and pressed a button. It began to hum. 'I met one yesterday when I was coming back from Nick's office, crossing the main quad – he looked like he'd eaten a kilo of lemons. It's only me and him and he just walks right past me, looking the other way.'

The woman's voice echoed on the tiled worktop. 'What did you do?'

'I just shouted "Hi, hi!" and kept on walking. They're like children. They're so insular. We had this beautiful dinner here for some senior dons last week – Nick's been having issues with the Governing Body, so we made it amazing – the best food, fine wines – and we said, "bring the most interesting person you know". Guess what? Most of them brought their spouses. I'm not joking! One guy – he's a world expert in "Anachronism and Antiquity"—'

Her friend shrieked.

'No, serious – I know, you couldn't make it up. But anyway, he didn't bring anyone, and when I ask him why not, he just says, "I'm the most interesting person I know."'

They both laughed, wildly. Although the don's comment was arrogant, it surely masked something deeper and perhaps more sad. But clearly, neither Mariah nor her friend knew a thing about loneliness. Mariah took her coffee over to the sink – she still hadn't seen me – and I heard a clatter and a splash.

'Jesus Christ!'

'What is it?' her friend said. 'What happened?'

I knew what had happened. She'd knocked into the bucket of detergent in which Felicity and I were macerating a little vole.

'Oh my God. Felicity and the nanny keep bringing dead animals – stinking skulls and things – into the house and soaking them in buckets, then Felicity lays them out on her floor in weird patterns. It's horrible. Jesus, Allie, this place! How am I going to stay here two years without going crazy?' Mariah sounded despairing. 'Nick says he'll get us something lovely in California after this, but *two years*.'

I thought about Felicity, uprooted again, and taken abroad – to America, of all places. I felt unsteady, and quite sick. It was unthinkable to move her abroad. Abominable!

'Two years is nothing,' the friend was saying. 'It'll get better. I know you. You'll win them all over – who could resist you? Anyway, who did you and Nick bring to the party?'

Mariah named a handsome, well-known actor, a rakish old Etonian – I had no idea he had been in the Lodging that night, nobody had mentioned it to me. 'He adores Nick,' she said. 'I'm sure they think bringing famous actors to dinner is showy but how do they think we're going to raise fifty million pounds without celebrities? God, this place needs a kick up the ass.'

I stepped into the kitchen, then. There was a puddle of detergent on the floor.

'Okay, I have to get goi—' Mariah turned and finally saw me. '*Fy flate!* Shit, Dee! Don't creep up on me, like, oh my God!' She picked up the phone and flicked it off speaker mode, saying into it, 'It's okay, no, no, it's the nanny.'

I'm not sure why her dismissive tone irritated me so much. I have always rather enjoyed being underestimated by my employers. In all my years in Oxford I've never mentioned, even to the most patronizing professor, that I too was once offered a place to study at their venerable institution. But I suppose I didn't expect Mariah, of all people, to be contemptuous.

I shoved a dirty mug into the dishwasher and slammed the door, making the crockery and glasses clatter. Mariah looked startled. I left the room. I would deal with the macerating vole later.

I waited in the hall and sure enough, she lowered her voice

to almost a whisper. 'No, no, it's fine. She's cross about something . . . No, no. We'll do something else when the baby comes.
We've actually been thinking Felicity might be best at boarding
school – you know, the routines and things . . .' Perhaps she saw
my shadow by the doorframe because she suddenly raised her
voice and started talking about the troublesome flock wallpaper
in the Lincolnshire house and what a challenge the project had
been – how she just wished the whole thing was over.

Faraday and Khan are still waiting for me to say what Nick
and I disagreed on.

–We just have very different perceptions of his daughter's
needs, I say. –He basically doesn't understand Felicity at all –
and nor does Mariah.

Chapter 28

Faraday squeezes empty space on his ring finger. –Okay. Okay, Dee. So, if you're the only one who understands her, why would you want to leave?

–What? I say. –I didn't want to leave.

–Oh really? Dr and Mrs Law say you'd been very clear from the start that you couldn't stay.

This might have been true when I took the job, but I certainly no longer felt that way, and they both knew it. In fact, after overhearing Mariah's comment about boarding school that day, I'd tried to talk to her about staying on.

I tackled her as soon as she came back from Lincolnshire. I waited up for her. She looked pasty and drawn – her schedule would be punishing even for a woman who was not approaching her third trimester – and she seemed dispirited, I recall, rubbing her sore feet, eating the Parkin I'd baked. Perhaps I could have chosen a better time, but I'd been stewing for two days, and had to say something.

The builders had been back to turn the dressing room off the master bedroom into a tiny nursery and she asked if everything had gone okay with that. I said it had but told her that Felicity had refused even to come and look at it.

'Oh, she's jealous already.' Mariah sighed.

This had nothing to do with jealousy. Felicity had said nothing when I asked her if she wanted to look; she just went back to colouring her Penrose tiles. She was dreading the baby's arrival because she knew she'd be even more unwanted, even more marginalized when they had their own child.

Neither Nick nor Mariah seemed to have properly considered the impact the baby would have on Felicity after eight years an only child. If they'd asked me – which they hadn't – I could tell them exactly how she'd feel: ousted, insecure, raw, hurt, irrelevant, huge, awkward and excluded. The most catastrophic thing they could do right now – other than send her to boarding school – would be to get rid of the only person who gave her continuity and attention: me.

'You're going to have to stop baking,' Mariah mumbled through a mouthful of Parkin. 'I'm getting so fat. I'm never going to push this baby out if I keep eating like this. Oh God, though, I can't even think about that – giving birth.'

This surprised me. With all the exercising and herring-eating and Danish matter-of-factness, I had assumed she'd be planning some kind of drug-free water birth.

'To be honest with you, Dee, I'd love a planned C-section. Nick's probably thinking I'll push his baby out on the living room floor like Ana did, but that's a vintage Beni Ourain rug in there. Also, I want drugs. All the drugs – all of them.'

'Was Felicity really born on the living room floor?'

'Well, I think they had a birthing pool in the kitchen – I guess Ana was fierce like that, but I like my vagina the way it is.'

I probably looked a bit queasy – I have no idea why she thought I'd want an image of her vagina in my head.

She laughed. 'You don't approve.'

'It doesn't matter what I think,' I said. 'What matters is what you're going to do afterwards. We should talk about that. I wanted to let you know I'll be happy to stay on – I think Felicity needs me. I'd like to stay a bit longer, for her.'

Her face flushed and she dusted off her fingers, becoming almost incoherent. 'Yes, yes, yes, God, we need to talk about all this sometime, don't we, but I guess, the baby – and Nick and I haven't had a chance to ... you know ... work things out and such, so ...'

They could not surely be thinking of boarding school for her – not really. But I knew they could. They were more than capable of sending her away. Life would be unbearable for her, and it would only get worse. A silent child might survive primary school, to a certain extent, but a mute teenager would be a self-destructive outcast – not least at a boarding school.

'Hey, I know you're very attached to her,' Mariah continued. 'You're so caring. You'd have been such a great mum.'

The comment was so unexpected – like a punch to the head – that for a second I couldn't speak. I stepped over to the sink and turned on the hot tap. I grabbed the sticky baking sheet and began to scrub. The sink was draining too slowly, the pipes perhaps beginning to block. I made a mental note to stick some baking soda and vinegar down it. I tried very hard to breathe in and out.

Mariah was not the first person to say such things to me, but perhaps because I was already slightly overwrought, the memory of giving birth rose up and I had to steady myself with both hands on the sink. Childbirth was an extraordinary experience – not least because my mother appeared in the room. Since I'd last seen her when I was a baby, I should not have recognized her, but I did, instantly: a tall, broad and ruddy-faced presence in overalls, sleeves rolled to the elbow. I recognized her smell as she came closer – clay and salt – and when she spoke to me, her voice was familiar, too, as was the feel of her wide, cool hand pressing on my forehead. 'Wheesht, my pet.' She took me in her arms. 'Lean on me now.' I felt an enormous and overwhelming relief, the deepest peace – a feeling I'd been missing my whole life. All the fear left my body.

This was not a hallucination or visitation – if anything, I was the visitor, briefly slipping under the fence into my mother's world, because I understood then that she was dead – something I'd always known, though there had never been a body or a grave or a funeral, nothing but the strange echo in the water hall at Mill House and my father's refusal ever to look over into the stone channel at the burn. Sometimes you don't need to prove a hypothesis to know that it is true.

As the pains intensified, I felt no fear, and with a final burning heave I pushed my daughter into the world. When I looked up from her beautiful, crumpled face, my mother was gone.

I gave her my mother's name. Perhaps that was the start of it. That 'Rosie' got my father off on the wrong foot. It tore open a wound to reveal long-buried, rotten feelings that he couldn't handle. His granddaughter was nothing to him but a loud package containing all the things he'd failed to control – not through want of trying. Guilt can make people behave with irrational decisiveness.

'Oh Dee, did I upset you?' Mariah interrupted my thoughts. 'Are you okay? I'm sorry . . .'

'Ach, I'm not upset.' I smoothed my hair. 'Now then. Will Nick be with you when you give birth? Or your sister, your mother?'

'Oh Jesus, no.' She gave a weak laugh. 'My sister's too bossy; she wouldn't let me have all the drugs, and if my mother was there, it really would kill me.'

'Yes, you did say she's difficult.'

'Difficult's a nice way to put it. She lives in Marbella now with her fourth – wait, no – fifth husband.' Her face suddenly looked vulnerable, like a child trying to be defiant, and I found myself forgiving her lack of tact. 'I haven't spoken with my mother in four – no, five – years.'

I folded a tea towel. It was odd of her to get the numbers four and five mixed up when they are so different. I realized I didn't feel particularly upset any more, just a little spaced out.

'Actually, it's kind of a relief, you know?' she was saying. 'She hasn't met Nick and she doesn't even know I'm pregnant. She hates being a grandmother. She's only seen my sister's boys, like, a few times and most of them are teenagers now. Actually, that's the only thing I'm looking forward to about turning forty next year – her youngest child being forty's going to kill her.' She gave a wobbly laugh.

'I never understand why people get so het up about forty.' My own voice sounded far off. 'Or fifty, come to that. They aren't particularly interesting numbers. Forty-seven's a much more exciting number than forty.' I began to sweep up Parkin crumbs. 'Forty-seven's divisible only by itself and one. It's both a prime number and a Lucas number. Forty-eight's quite good too, actually – it's three times two to the fourth, as well as being thirty in hexadecimal.' I felt my hands grow steadier as the numbers marched across my mind shutting down other thoughts, partitioning off my guilty, angry father and my own lost baby. 'Fifty's a fairly humdrum number,' I said, 'but fifty-one, now, that's lovely: it's three times seventeen, so it's a bit odd – interesting, you know, it kind of feels like a prime but isn't—'

'You know, Dee,' Mariah heaved herself out of the chair, laughing, 'you can be *seriously* strange.' She brushed the crumbs off her belly. 'But I guess that's why you understand Felicity so well.'

Chapter 29

–So are you saying you were actually happy with this family? Faraday looks surprised. –You wanted to stay on?

I think about this for a moment. Over the past seven months I have, in fact, felt happy at times, happier than I've been in many, many years. All of these happy times have been when we were with Linklater, the three of us together.

We went back to Holywell twice more with Linklater, and Felicity never seemed more content than when we were wandering round listening to his stories about the people who lay there. She never mentioned these outings to Nick. I think she knew, instinctively, that he would put a stop to them if he found out. But I was prepared to defend myself if challenged. Felicity was learning more from Linklater about the history of Oxford – which is, of course, a history of Western thought, of literature, philosophy, politics, art and scientific discovery – than she ever could sitting inside with a book.

Linklater himself seemed more relaxed on these days out, too, less clumsy and flustered. I think he was just glad of a decent audience. His tour groups, he said, usually consisted of bored foreign teenagers taking selfies or adults asking irritating questions, trying to catch him out.

It wasn't just Holywell we loved. There were others, too. One Sunday morning in early December, as I was brushing my teeth, my mobile phone rang.

'Wolvercote Cemetery?' Linklater said, without announcing himself or saying hello. 'Eleven o'clock?'

'Today?' I said.

'Are you free?'

'We are.'

Felicity and I drove across town in the Fiesta. She was in good spirits, sitting up and looking out of the window. It was a bright, windy day, ferociously cold, with clouds dashing overhead and dead leaves swirling. She was looking almost chubby since I'd made her wear two jumpers under her coat. I had even packed a little picnic – ham sandwiches, salt and vinegar crisps, shortbread, and a big flask of tea.

Linklater was standing alone with his bike propped up against a tree. I'd pinned my hair up to keep it out of my face, and had borrowed an olive green cashmere wrap that Mariah left in the hall, so I might have looked a bit different. Linklater gazed at me as I approached and then, when we got close, he jolted back to life and seemed a bit flustered.

I had expected to tag along with a tour group but it was just the three of us. He showed us a grave containing Tolkien and his wife, Edith. 'That was a great love story.' He slipped into tour-guide patter. 'They were teenagers when they met. Both of them were orphans, but Tolkein's guardian banned him from contacting her, even in writing, till he turned twenty-one. Tolkein stuck with the ban, but he wrote Edith a love letter at midnight on the eve of his twenty-first birthday. They had four children and a happy home. And that's Edith's unacknowledged gift to the world. You couldn't write *The Hobbit* if you'd never experienced domestic bliss, could you?'

I told him I'd never read *The Hobbit*. In my fiction-reading days, I generally stuck to books for adults.

He looked affronted. 'But *The Hobbit*'s for adults!'

I did, in fact, try to read *The Hobbit* once. I'd found it possibly the most irritating novel in the whole of English literature, but I didn't tell him that. It would have felt cruel to quash his enthusiasm.

He led us off to find the grave of James Murray, the first editor of the Oxford English Dictionary. 'The Oxford post office had to install a special post-box outside Murray's house in North Oxford because his correspondence was so vast. It's still there, at 78 Banbury Road; have a look on your way home. Volunteers from all round the country used to send Murray little slips of paper noting down word usages, and he'd reply to every single one. When he died, they found three tons of paper slips in his work shed.'

'Seriously?'

'They still use index cards at Oxford University Press today. Paper ones. I know – even now! They've got a vault of failed words there. A friend of mine used to curate it. They've got all the words the OED has rejected filed away on index cards. It's a bit mad.'

'Like what?'

He thought for a moment. 'Polkadodge,' he said. 'That thing where you dodge someone in a corridor or on the pavement, you know, that little panicky dance.' He gave a little shimmy. 'Or "lexpionage"– the act of sleuthing for the meaning or origin of a word. I don't know why that failed. It's brilliant.'

When we got cold, we huddled on a bench near the Tolkien

grave where I'd left the picnic bag. Fortunately, I'd brought my blanket too, and instead of picnicking on it, we wrapped it around our shoulders with Felicity snug between us. We were quite cosy, eating sandwiches and crisps under the scratchy wool.

'Your family hunting tartan, I assume?' Linklater fingered the edge of the blanket.

'Hunting tartans are green, dress tartans are red, royal tartans are usually green but in ancient faded dyes, so no . . .' For a moment he thought I was serious but then he must have caught something in my eye and realized I was making it up, because he grinned, and so did I.

The tip of his nose was red and with his hat pulled low, he looked a bit Hobbit-like himself. He cleared his throat and glanced at the headstone. 'Poor old Edith. She never really belonged in Oxford. It must have been awful for her – all his colleagues were very snobby about her. I've always felt a great empathy for her, actually.'

'I'm sorry,' I said, 'but you clearly do belong in Oxford.'

His blue eyes squinted at me from behind his glasses. 'Is that what you think? I really don't. Do you know, something like three quarters of all the judges in England are Oxbridge graduates, and maybe like a quarter of all MPs, too – and half of our newspaper columnists. I read that somewhere reliable, I can't remember where. Probably in a newspaper column. But I mean, this place incubates overconfident narcissists, doesn't it? It's terrifying when you think about the number of sociopaths out there with Oxford matriculation photos hanging in their downstairs loos.'

'But you studied here too.'

'Well, I did, but I definitely don't have a matriculation photo in my downstairs loo. I don't even have a downstairs loo. Or a matriculation photo, for that matter. I'm not part of it, not officially, not any more. If I ever was.'

'If you feel that strongly about it, why are you here?'

'Unfortunately, there's not a *huge* demand for Oxford tour guides in other British cities. Also, I've got no money. But you could get out, though, it's not too late for you. Nannies meet a universal need, don't they? You could work anywhere.'

'Actually, I have thought about leaving. Many times.'

He looked taken aback. 'Have you?'

'I always thought I'd go back to Scotland one day.' I glanced at Felicity, who was trying to plait three bendy sticks. 'But that was before I met this one, of course.'

As I told him, briefly, about Mill House, he began to look wistful. When I'd finished he said, 'When I was eight, my mum took me on holiday to Ullapool. We went pony trekking and it was incredibly cold and wet, but I loved it. It was the last time we had a holiday together, though, because she got sick that autumn. But I've always wanted to go back.'

'Ullapool's not my part of Scotland,' I said, gently.

He cleared his throat, perhaps embarrassed to have revealed something so personal and sad. 'You know, Edith hated Oxford, too. When Tolkien retired, she got him to move to Bournemouth. He didn't want to leave, but he wanted to make her happy, and it worked because she really loved Bournemouth. When she died, he was heartbroken and he came back here – I suppose it felt familiar. He died twenty-one months later. He couldn't live without her.' His eyes met mine and I saw something tentatively hopeful in them, as if he was sliding a foot onto a rickety bridge to test a plank.

I tucked a loose strand of hair behind my ear. 'Apparently, dying of a broken heart is a physiological reality. There's actually a name for it in cardiology, but I can't remember what it is – some kind of syndrome. It happens mostly to women though.' I remembered the pain of losing my child – the physical agony of it in my body. It sometimes amazed me that I had not died – that my heart had continued, stubbornly, to beat.

'But men are capable of deep devotion too.' He flushed and cleared his throat. His eyes, I realized, were the exact colour of the cornflowers sold in bunches in the Covered Market in June. 'Have you heard of the Inklings? Tolkien, Lewis and co?' he said, and I saw that he was scrambling back to safer ground, buttoning his tour-guide coat back up. 'They used to get together in the Eagle and Child pub to talk about Middle Earth.' He turned to Felicity, who was happily munching crisps. 'C. S. Lewis wrote *The Lion, The Witch and The Wardrobe*.'

She looked blank.

'You've read *The Lion, The Witch and The Wardobe*?' He raised an eyebrow.

'She isn't keen on fiction,' I said. 'Nor am I, in fact.'

He looked aghast, as if I had just confessed that we were serial killers. 'You don't *like novels*?'

'Well, I used to quite enjoy Sherlock Holmes.'

'Oh, you're one of those, are you? Morse, too?'

'No, I can't stand Morse.'

'Thank God. Me neither. Though on the bright side, Colin Dexter did murder three College masters.'

I laughed. 'My father tried to make me read Scottish classics from a young age. He was a gamekeeper and he used to smuggle books out of the big house's library for me, things like Conan Doyle, and Walter Scott and Robert Louis Stevenson. He wanted me to better myself. Then I got a scholarship to a girls' school – no detective novels allowed there.'

'Ah. Which school?' In all my years, nobody had asked me this quintessentially Oxonian question. I named it but I had no desire to talk about my school days. I had worked very hard to forget those. 'What about you?'

'What school?' he shrugged. 'The local comprehensive in Muswell Hill – before Muswell Hill went upmarket.' He looked at Felicity. 'I suppose you're the screen generation, is that your excuse for not reading novels?'

She shook her head.

'She just doesn't like them,' I said.

He looked at her. 'What, *all* of them?'

Felicity nodded.

'Good God, child, you've read them *all*?'

She giggled and picked up her sandwich, nibbling at the crust. 'My mum owned a bookshop,' she said, quietly.

I sat very still, astonished.

'Ah-ha.' He sniffed. 'Rebellion, then. I bet she's not happy you don't read.'

I stiffened, but Felicity said in a matter-of-fact voice, 'My mummy died.'

I heard him take a sharp breath and I braced myself for awkward apologies or worse, for him to say nothing, but he cleared his throat. 'Oh, I'm sorry to hear that, Flipper, very sorry.'

'I was four.' Felicity put her sandwich back, neatly, in the Tupperware. 'So I don't remember her much.'

'My mum died when I was about your age.' He shook his head. 'Not easy. Not easy at all.' I gazed at him but he wouldn't – or couldn't – meet my eye.

Felicity pushed her hair back with both hands. 'My dad says I look like her.'

'Well, she must have been very lovely then.'

She looked pleased.

'I really am sorry about your mum,' he nodded.

Felicity nodded too and they sat for a moment side by side like little nodding dog toys. Watching them, I felt a huge, warm energy expand inside me. 'Are you going to eat that?' Linklater pointed at Felicity's sandwich. 'Because if you aren't . . .'

He had no idea of the enormity of what had just taken place. He was the first adult Felicity had conversed with – possibly ever – and she'd spoken about her mother's death. I decided not to tell him how momentous this was. It would only make him self–conscious and the last thing I wanted to do was spoil their extraordinary connection.

We met at Headington Cemetery the following Sunday, a drizzly, bitter day. We huddled by the grave of C. S. Lewis, beneath the gargantuan umbrella that Linklater used for his walking tours, eating my homemade Scotch eggs and drinking hot chocolate from the flask. 'So, Lewis was John Betjeman's tutor.' Linklater put down the tea flask. 'Betjeman the Poet Laureate? They couldn't stand each other – this was before Lewis went rabidly Christian – he'd just survived the First World War and he thought Betjeman was a sheltered dilettante. He wrote vicious letters calling him "an idle prig" and things like that. He hated Betjeman so much he refused to give him a degree.'

Later, when Felicity wandered away, Linklater said to me, 'You know, Nick Law and I were working on our DPhils at roughly the same time here, many moons ago. He was a couple of years ahead of me, so he wouldn't remember me.'

I stared at him. 'Sorry – you and Nick were graduate students *together*?'

'Not in that way, no, no. As I say, I doubt if he'd even remember me. Our paths only crossed very tangentially.' In maths, tangential paths by definition touch but don't cross but I didn't go there – though I thought, suddenly, of the mathematical bridge with its tangent and radial trussing – straight lines that together, improbably, create a beautiful curve. 'Everyone knew Nick Law though,' Linklater was saying. 'He was the Faculty wunderkind, tipped for greatness. My supervisor used to go on about his brilliance, which was somewhat dispiriting at the time, I seem to remember. He practically went into mourning when Nick joined the BBC. And now here he is, back in the mother ship, taking his rightful seat at High Table, feasting with celebrities.' There was a bitter note to his voice that I'd not heard before.

'Have you told him you remember him?'

'What? No, no, we've had no direct contact. Anyway, he wouldn't have any reason to remember me.'

'But what on earth made you take on his house history? Why do that to yourself?'

'Well, money, for a start. And also, I'm ashamed to admit, nosiness. I really wanted to know what he'd turned out like. I suppose in a way he just represents something for me, you know, some kind of unattainable existence that maybe, if I'd been a different person, I could have had myself. Almost like he's living the life I could have had if I'd got my act together, or something. I suppose if anything, taking this house history was an act of self-punishment.' He looked glum. 'The Germans have a word for this, you know: *Torschlusspanik*. It's the fear that life's passing you by and you've fucked it all up and it's too late. It literally means "gate-closing panic". In the middle ages—'

I sensed another diversion and headed him off. 'So you haven't told him you overlapped?'

'Oh. No, I haven't. And I don't intend to, either. As I say, I haven't even spoken to him. He got his PA to hire me and I've only ever seen you and Felicity at the Lodging. I haven't even met Mariah. I didn't know his first wife killed herself, by the way, Christ. Sorry about that. That really was a bit of a shocker.' He touched his wrists, and shook his head. 'I Googled her when I got back from Wolvercote last weekend – a terrible business. Poor, poor Felicity.'

I stopped walking and looked for somewhere to sit down.

'Are you okay?' he said. 'You look a bit off suddenly.'

I perched on a gravestone.

He peered at me. 'Okay, you aren't telling me you didn't know?'

'They told me it was cancer!' I thought back over the few interactions we'd had about Ana – and realized that they'd never actually told me in so many words that it had been cancer. They'd just used stock phrases like 'after a long illness'. But somehow this revelation of suicide, though shocking, did make sense. The tension that had always arisen whenever I'd asked about Ana – some sense of unspoken awfulness that neither Nick nor Mariah could deal with – fell into place. But poor Felicity. Her trauma made even more sense now too. Suicide was such a terrible abandonment. She'd have been far too young to understand the complexities of mental illness. It was incredibly irresponsible of them not to mention it to me.

Linklater seemed to read my mind. 'I can't believe they didn't tell you something like that.'

'They won't talk to me about Ana at all,' I said, weakly.

He put his head on one side. 'You know, there's this astonishing modern invention, Dee, I don't know if you've heard about it – it's called the "Interweb"? You type in whatever you need to know and the answers just pop up, like little miracles—'

Felicity reappeared from the undergrowth. 'Oh!' I got up.

'There you are!' She had burrs and brambles clinging to her trousers, and mud on her cheek, and, though thin and small, she looked healthy suddenly – full of life. Something in her energy made me think of the video Nick had shown me on his phone – that animated, happy little girl. A wood pigeon shot from the hedgerow behind her, and clattered up into the sky. She laughed and watched it soar.

Seeing her like this, you could never think that graveyards were bad for her. There was fresh air, space and wildlife too – we saw rabbits and squirrels and all kinds of birds. Once, in Holywell, we even startled a deer just as dusk was falling; it took off in great sweeping arcs over the misty graves towards Magdalen deer park, a floating phantom, improbably slow.

Anyone who saw us on these days out would have taken us for a small, rather unconventional family enjoying a chilly picnic, wholly at ease with our surroundings. We were so content in each other's company, but it was more than that; we seemed to thrive as a threesome in a way that we couldn't as individuals. We seemed to grow more substantial when we were together, to take up our rightful shape in the world. In a sense, we were family in its purest and most positive form.

Chapter 30

Faraday changes tack again: he suddenly wants to talk about Fibonacci – the cat, not the mathematician. He does this a lot, I notice, switches subjects without warning. It is disorientating, which is presumably the point – a tactic designed to throw suspects off their guard.

Am I a suspect?

Given what they know about my past, I must be.

–So, this cat, he says. –I gather Felicity's very attached to it? Did you get the cat for her, or was it her parents?

–It was Mariah. She thought a cat would help Felicity to talk to her.

–And did it?

–Not exactly.

Fibonacci was an act of desperation on Mariah's part. Michaelmas term had ended in a blaze of cocktail parties, wassailing, madrigals and feasts. Catering staff invaded the house almost every day and Felicity and I would come back to find strangers moving furniture around, laying out glasses, stringing up lights. Mariah would get back from London, run upstairs, and come down again in a glamorous dress or tuxedo, the waistband pulled low to accommodate her belly, even higher heels, red lipstick, dark eye make-up, floral perfume floating in her wake. The University term was over in early December but the primary school festivities were relentless all the way up to Christmas. All of this took its toll on Felicity's mental state. Her mood was unpredictable; she was eating and saying almost nothing, even to me, and most nights I'd find myself in her room dealing with some disturbance or other.

When I tried to talk to Nick about this, he said, 'Well, of course, she's overtired. It's the end of term. We're all overtired, Dee, but it's nearly Christmas.' When I spoke to Mariah, she said, 'Yes, we're worried about her. But what can we do? She just has to get to the holidays, then she can rest.'

They had at least finally thought to inform me that in early January they would be flying to Hong Kong for a week, leaving me with Felicity. They said nothing about 'Ticketgate' but I knew from Linklater that Nick had won this particular battle by threatening the ringleader dons individually. College was, very reluctantly, stumping up for Mariah's extortionate plane ticket.

And then, ten days before Christmas, Mariah announced, perhaps in a bizarre moment of guilt about going to Hong Kong, that she'd decided to get a 'therapy cat' for Felicity. She showed me a YouTube clip of a little boy who had been selectively mute until he got a cat. He began to talk – first to the cat, then to extended family, then to other children, then to his teacher, until finally he was communicating normally with everyone. Boy and cat appeared on *Good Morning* TV. The cat, a sweet tabby, was either drugged or exceptionally laissez-faire. 'It's a no-judgment friend that brings the child's anxiety level right down,' Mariah explained.

Cats did not strike me as particularly non-judgmental animals, but I went along with it because Felicity had always wanted a pet.

Angela, herself the owner of two rescue cats, happened to have recently taken in a tomcat that had been abandoned in College rooms by a schizoid Russian cosmologist who'd been arrested while attempting to smuggle cocaine out of Argentina. Angela's cats had taken against this interloper and so, the very next day, Fibonacci arrived at the house.

He was a hefty animal, the colour of old dishcloths, and despite Mariah's optimism, he did not at first sight seem likely to unravel four years of silence. Perhaps understandably given the animal's background, he was also not quite as amenable as the cat in the YouTube video. Hunkered at the back of his crate, he let out a low, warning yowl as Felicity opened the door.

Angela put her hands on her hips. 'Fibonacci's an old medieval mathematician or something.' She caught my eye. 'Only in Oxford.'

As Felicity reached a hand inside the crate, the cat gave an elongated moan. I stepped forwards. 'Perhaps we should give him a bit of time to get used to us?'

Angela nodded. 'Cats don't like to be hurried. They don't like change and they don't like anyone telling them what to do.'

'I can think of a few humans like that,' Mariah said, pointedly.

Angela stared fixedly at the cat crate.

Felicity crossed her legs. Her hair was sticking up and she looked a bit feral herself – I made a mental note to buy a better detangling conditioner. Mariah pressed a hand on her round belly and perched on the side of the armchair looking strained. I had a feeling that Fibonacci would have to produce a very swift miracle or his days at the Lodging could be numbered.

Felicity suddenly leaned forwards, shoved her arms inside the crate and seized the cat's struggling body. He spiralled and sank his teeth into her – she yelped and dropped him – he shot under the sofa. She grasped her arm, looking up at me with huge, shocked eyes. 'My God, Felicity!' Mariah cried. 'We *literally* just told you not to touch him!'

I gave Mariah a robust look and took Felicity into the kitchen to find the first aid kit.

'Are you okay, sweetie?' Mariah said as we passed, as if Felicity might give up four years of silence in order to put her mind at rest.

'Well, I'm going to have to love you and leave you, I'm afraid,' I heard Angela say. 'I'm sure he'll settle, eventually. I've left some instructions there on the crate. Good luck. I won't see you till after your Hong Kong trip now.'

'Yes, thanks, Angela. See you in January. Have a good Christmas.'

I noticed the hint of a smile playing on Angela's lips as she passed the kitchen door. It was possible that she had sourced an unhinged animal purely to make Mariah's life more difficult.

Mariah was slumped on an armchair staring at her phone. 'The Fibonacci sequence,' she read out loud as we came back in. 'Are you listening? Let's see if any of us can understand it. It's a sequence of numbers where you add the two previous numbers together to get the next one: 0, 1, 1, 2, 3, 5, 8, 13, 21, 34 . . . What the . . . ?'

'It's just addition,' I said.

Mariah raised an eyebrow.

'See, 0 plus 1 equals 1; 1 plus 1 equals 2; 2 plus 1 equals 3; 3 plus 2 equals 5; 5 plus 3 equals 8, and so on,' I explained.

'Okay, well, it also says here the Fibonacci sequence is "nature's numbering system".' Mariah frowned. 'Fibonacci numbers show up in leaf arrangements, flower petals, fern fronds, pine cones, shells – and even in the human body.' She let her phone drop to her lap. 'I'm sorry, what? How can numbers be in a flower and the human body? What does that even *mean*?'

'It's just simple patterns.' I tried not to sound impatient. 'And maths is the science of patterns. If you count the total number of petals on a flower, more often than not it's a Fibonacci number. Buttercups have five petals, lilies have three, delphiniums eight – all Fibonacci numbers. The same goes for the human body. One nose, one mouth, two eyes, two ears, five fingers – all of them are Fibonacci numbers.' I decided it wasn't worth getting into Fibonacci spirals. 'Maths connects apparently unrelated things in the universe; it's the closest there is to magic.'

Mariah put down her phone. 'Oh my God. Even nannies are geniuses in Oxford.' She turned to Felicity. 'Did you know Dee was so clever?'

Felicity glanced at me and – to my amazement – she nodded. But Mariah didn't even notice, she was looking at her phone again.

I spotted the gardener wandering across the lawn carrying a massive, if inexplicable, cactus. I went and opened the French windows. 'Hello?' I called. 'Are you any good with cats?' He changed direction smoothly and when he got closer, I explained that the cat had hidden under the sofa. The smell of wood smoke and tobacco on his clothing made me think of my father. He turned and walked away without a word.

'He's not going to help us, Dee,' Mariah said. 'He still hates Nick for moving him over here.' After a moment or two he came back across the lawn again, without the cactus and with something metallic in his hand. His boots left mucky prints across Mariah's pale rug – I saw her wince but she managed not to say anything. I smiled when I saw he had a tin of sardines. He cracked the ring pull and knelt by the sofa. Fibonacci shot towards the fish and the gardener pressed earthy hands around its body and shoved it back into the crate, locking the door. He stood up, muttered something that sounded like 'Cat's an eggplant', and left.

'Right. Sorry. Thank you!' Mariah called. 'Thanks.' She looked at me, eyes shining. 'What did he say? Cat's . . . what?'

Felicity had picked up the crate and was lugging it over to the doorway.

'Oh, are you taking him up to your room?' Mariah called. She then turned to me. 'He's supposed to stay indoors for at least a week, Angela said. He has to accept that he belongs here. You have to keep him shut in her room.'

I heard Felicity go upstairs one ponderous step at a time with the heavy crate. Mariah flopped back into the armchair and put her feet up on the ottoman. 'Who the hell calls a cat "Fibonacci"?'

'An Oxford mathematician,' I said.

She gave a hollow laugh. 'This place is so bizarre, don't you think, Dee?'

I shrugged. 'I'm probably used to it.'

'It's such a bubble. The College just turned down a friend of ours for a job because, they said, "he's sold his soul to London publishers and the media".' She threw up her hands. 'He's published by Faber instead of Oxford University Press! And oh my God, all the secret rules – nobody will explain anything to me. It's like if you don't already know, you don't belong here.' She gave a deranged laugh, perhaps realizing she shouldn't let me see her despair, but unable to stop herself. 'I'm getting things wrong all the time – passing the port the wrong way, wearing the wrong clothes. And they're always watching me with these beady little eyes, waiting for me to mess up. At Formal Hall I said to the guy next to me, kind of joking, "How will I know if I do the wrong thing here?" and he says, cold as ice, "We'll write to your husband". And he wasn't joking!' She looked at me, wide-eyed. I thought of the 'inappropriate' dress letter and wondered if she'd tell me about it, but she didn't.

'Nick had to do a swearing-in ceremony for a new Fellow the other day and I went to the Chapel to watch. It's all in Latin! Every word. The guy's kneeling by Nick's feet in prayer position, like this, reciting a – what do they call it – "oath of fealty" and Nick looked like the Pope – all of them are in these creepy Christian robes. I mean, what do Muslim or Hindu or Jewish or other religions think of it? It's basically a medieval Christian cult. It's weird. It's just not normal.'

'Well, it's normal for Oxford.'

'Normal for Oxford!' She laughed. 'Well, Fibonacci's going to fit right in.'

'Ach, he's just a nervy creature.'

She rolled her eyes, flopping back against the armchair cushions. 'And that's just what this house really needs right now, another nervy creature.'

Chapter 31

Faraday nods. –Right, he says. –Right. So – where's this cat now?

I could do with more water. My mouth is dry again. –I don't know, I say.

–Do you think she could have taken it with her?

Perhaps he has some sort of Dick Whittington image in his head. I try to put him right.

–Fibonacci isn't that sort of cat.

–But she's very attached to it, isn't she? If she left the house of her own volition, she'd take the cat with her, wouldn't she?

–Well, I say, –maybe not if she was asleep. This isn't an amenable animal, I add. –It's not the sort of cat you can just lug around.

The cat was certainly not the cure Mariah had hoped for, either. He remained firmly in the attic with Felicity and, since he scratched or bit anyone who came near him, he quickly became a highly effective barrier between her and the rest of the world.

On the last day of the school term, Nick flew off to an alumni event in New York, and Mariah announced that she was exhausted and would be working from home. She stayed in bed with her laptop and phone and then, late in the afternoon, came down wrapped in a long cashmere cardigan looking perky. I was

making cock-a-leekie and looking forward to an evening with
my notebook. 'I want to cook for you tonight,' she announced.
'We've been so busy. I want to do something nice for you, Dee,
a thank you for getting Felicity through this first term.'

I started to protest that I was making dinner already, but she
handed me a shopping list. 'Can you pop out for the ingredients?'

I told Felicity I was going out. 'Shall I buy some cat treats?' I
said. 'For Fibby?'

She looked up, sharply.

I'd been in the bathroom the previous evening when she and
Nick were on Skype.

'Fibonacci's a bit of a mouthful,' Nick was saying. 'Can't you
call him Fred?'

Felicity didn't reply.

'Darling? Did you hear me?'

There was silence.

'Are you sleeping any better? Dee said you've been having bad
dreams about Mummy.'

'It's not a dream,' she hissed.

'What?'

Silence.

'I didn't hear you, say it again?'

'His name's Fibby.'

'Your cat? Oh. Right. Fibby. That's nice.'

He changed the subject, telling her he'd been meeting rich
people who might give the College money when they die.
'Oxford's a big, special club and people will pay a lot to feel
like they still belong to it, even when they're dead.'

'I wouldn't join that club if you paid me a million pounds,'
she said. 'Dead or alive.'

He laughed. 'You sound just like your mum.'

Later that night, he would presumably call Mariah and report this conversation back to her. The obvious dysfunction of Nick in New York telling his wife in Oxford what the child in the room above her was saying, thinking or doing perhaps didn't escape them, but I couldn't help but wonder whether Nick might, in some small way, relish this privileged position. He must have felt excluded when Ana was alive, wearing Felicity, breastfeeding her to toddlerhood, keeping her away from nursery schools and playgroups, bringing her into the bookshop all day. Now, though, he was Felicity's number one. I'd not yet told him that she spoke to me now too – somehow, there hadn't been a good time to raise that. But I had a feeling that he wouldn't simply be glad to hear it.

When I got back from Tesco, Felicity came down and Mariah asked her if she wanted to join us for a celebration dinner. She turned and left the kitchen without reacting and I saw the frustration on Mariah's face, but it seemed obvious to me that no child would want to eat cod and chorizo. If a takeaway pizza had been on offer, who knows, but there were never any takeaway pizzas in the Lodging. Linklater and I did take Felicity to Pizza Express once, though, after we'd been down the Bodleian Library tunnels. She ate like a horse in Pizza Express.

When I came downstairs after putting Felicity to bed, Mariah was laying the dining room table. 'I thought we could eat here – make it an occasion!' Since she was constantly having occasions, this seemed utterly bizarre. I pictured us shouting at each other from either end of the banqueting table.

She served a complicated fish dish on a bed of black rice with buttered greens. It was almost nine by the time we sat down, so I was starving. She'd put herself at the head of the table, with me on her right, but even that felt mildly insane. If I ate fast,

I reasoned, it would soon be over, but when I looked up after a few mouthfuls, she hadn't even picked up her fork. Her face wore a grave expression. I braced myself for further irritation.

'I have to talk to you about something important, Dee.'

'Oh?'

'Nick had a call from the head teacher today. She's saying Felicity's missed a lot of school this term: thirteen days.'

'Oh?'

'That's a lot. You should have told us you were keeping her at home.'

'Well, you often aren't here to tell, to be fair, Mariah.'

'You could text or phone – or leave a message for Nick with Sally. Thirteen days is *a lot*.'

'Do you want me to consult you every time Felicity has a tummy ache?'

'Yes,' she said. Then she shook her head. 'Well, no. I mean, not like that. It's just you kept her off incredibly often. Keeping her off school isn't going to help her settle.'

'I couldn't send her to school,' I pointed out, 'when she was poorly.'

'She's always *looking* sick,' she said. 'Especially now she wants to be with the cat. You shouldn't have kept her at home just because she looked pale or whatever. You should have called us.'

The room was airless. The fish stank. I suddenly felt very hot.

'Well, this cat's totally backfiring, anyway.' She sounded relaxed again, as she cut into her fish with the side of her fork. There was something wrong with Mariah, I realized; something was actually wrong with the way her brain was wired. Any remotely normal human would have found this situation excruciating now – pretending to be friends when she'd just ticked me off as if I was an eighteen-year-old au pair. 'It's made her go into herself even more,' she carried on.

'They're bonding,' I said through gritted teeth. 'Wasn't that the point?'

'The point was to break down the barriers.' Mariah's fork shrieked across the plate. She found it so simple to contradict. She did it without apparent embarrassment or tension.

I found myself growing furious. 'The point,' I said, 'was to make Felicity feel more secure.'

She looked up, perhaps surprised by my tone. 'Yes, of course. I just mean the cat's not helping me to make a connection with her, you know? I think maybe it needs to go back to Angela.'

For a moment, all I could do was stare at her in utter disbelief. I shoved a clammy nodule of fish into my mouth. It slid across my tongue, oleaginous, over-seasoned.

When I looked up, she was dabbing her lips with a Christmas napkin. She shook her head. 'Yeah. Okay, I know. Bad idea. She loves that horrible cat already. I just have no idea what to do with her, Dee. I never had a mother myself, not really. I just don't know how to get through to her.'

I had no desire to hear about Mariah's emotionally deprived Copenhagen childhood. If she embarked on a journey of self-pity, I really would get up and leave.

'She's going to be even harder to handle when my own baby comes, too.'

This statement, I felt, condensed everything that was wrong with this so-called family.

She started to justify herself. 'When I moved in with Nick, she was a really cute, distressed little four-year-old and I thought I could be a mummy to her, you know? But I had no idea – I mean, she has this deep wound inside of her, I know that, but she's going to be nine in May and she's never spoken to me, or anyone except Nick. I mean, that's crazily intense, isn't it?'

'Well, she speaks to me.' I hadn't intended to tell her this way, but I'd lost all patience, all restraint.

'She what?'

I told her, briefly and rather brutally, about the bee incident, and Felicity's gradual opening up. There were tears in her eyes when I finished.

'But – my God, Dee, why didn't you tell us?'

'I'm telling you now.'

She stared at her plate, and her voice trembled. 'Can I tell you something I've never told anyone before?'

The word 'no' sprung to mind but I managed not to say it.

'Sometimes I want to give up on her. I know it's not her fault, she lost her mummy, and there's all the Freudian things about me taking her daddy away – I know the official advice is this isn't personal, but *oh my God*, it feels personal! She hates me, Dee. She hates me because—' She stopped, and looked away.

I put down my cutlery. 'Because of *what*, Mariah?'

'Ah! No—' Her hand rose and trembled in the air in front of my face. 'No, no, no. I can't talk about this, I just can't. Nick doesn't want me to. I can't talk about it, no.'

'If something happened that's relevant to Felicity,' I felt the blood rushing to my face, 'then I need to know about it.'

'There's nothing more to say. Really. But you should know, Ana didn't have cancer, okay, she killed herself.' Her face flushed a deep red.

'I know that.'

'Oh? You do? Right. Wow. Well, yes, that's public knowledge, I suppose. But Nick's—' She sipped some water. 'He's a very private man, and a College is just – you know what it's like here.

He feels we don't – we shouldn't – this is his private business, you know? He doesn't want everyone talking about it.'

'I'm not everyone!' I cried.

She jumped, and one side of a Christmas garland broke in half. The two ends dropped down and one trailed over her head like an arrow. For a moment she looked incredibly guilty, and I had a sudden intuition that she was covering something worse up, lying to me. But that was daft; we weren't in an episode of Morse.

'You aren't her therapist, Dee.' She was definitely rattled. 'You just need to make sure she's fed and entertained and goes to school.' She sounded like Nick.

'Is that really all you think I do?' I said.

Her eyelids fluttered, and she massaged her temples. 'No. Sorry. Of course not. I'm sorry. I didn't mean to – I know you do much more than that. God, Dee, I'm huge and hormonal – my back hurts and this place, I think, it's actually driving me a little bit crazy. Do you know what I mean? It's – I'm – I'm just, you know – it hurts to hear that she speaks to you and not me. That actually really hurts.'

I could think of nothing to say – nothing reasonable, at least – but that didn't matter because she said, in a shaky voice, 'The thing is, I can't even talk to Nick about any of this. He's obviously really protective of Felicity and we just end up fighting. But he's got no idea what it's like to be on the other side of her wall of silence. You're probably the only one who gets it, actually. You're the only person who can really understand what it's like to be me.' She gave a high laugh. 'Isn't that crazy?'

But I did not understand what it was like to be Mariah – beautiful, rich, privileged, adored. I didn't understand it even slightly. And I didn't particularly want to, either.

'You want to hear the worst thing?' she said.

There surely could not be anything worse, I thought.

She touched her belly. 'I think I'm going to love this baby more than I love her – I can't help it. I hate myself for this, Dee, but it's the truth.'

I glanced at the door. It would be catastrophic for Felicity to overhear this.

'I can't believe I'm saying this to you. Oh my God!' She picked up her fork, and laughed, madly. 'Shit like this is just spilling out of my mouth all the time – is this normal for pregnant women? I had this horrible nightmare last night. I opened my eyes and Ana was standing over my bed, staring down at me. I was totally terrified. I woke up screaming – Nick thought there was a burglar. It was so real. Then again, the other night I dreamed I gave birth to a wedge of cheese, and that felt real, too.' She laughed again, but her eyes weren't smiling.

I suddenly felt that I had to get away from her.

She put down her fork and leaned closer. 'Nick said you and Felicity feel Ana in the attic. The thing is, I sometimes kind of feel like she's here, too – I can't tell Nick this, but often it's on the landing at night outside my room. It's crazy, I know, but I can't help it. I just have such a bad feeling right now.' She looked excitable, slightly deranged.

I put down my napkin. 'I don't feel well, Mariah, I need to go to bed.'

'Oh!' She stood up, her belly scraping the table edge. 'I thought you're looking a bit pale. I'm so sorry. You think I'm crazy. Ignore me. Are you sick? Is it the fish? I'm a terrible cook, I know it. Can I get you some water? Bring you – oh, watch out, the plate. Hey – Dee – are you okay?'

I went for the door. I didn't want her awful intimacy and confessions. I couldn't be in the same room as her.

–So, where *is* this cat now? Khan says, in almost a whisper, jolting me out of my thoughts.

–What?

–Where's the cat, Dee?

–I should imagine it's escaped, I say. –With police all over the Lodging, all the coming and going the last three days, it probably got out of her bedroom. It could be anywhere.

–You kept the cat locked in her bedroom?

–It's a maladjusted stray. It didn't *want* to leave her bedroom.

–Well, it obviously did, says Khan. –Unless someone took it, too?

Chapter 32

−My officers didn't see a cat carrier when they searched the house, Faraday says. −Mariah said it was delivered to the Lodging in one. Do you know where that cat carrier might be?

−I have no idea. Angela brought it. Maybe she took it back.

Faraday leans over and mutters something to Khan.

I cannot allow a cat to derail this interview. −Look, I say, −Felicity's perfectly capable of leaving the house without the cat. She's only had it a few weeks.

She left the Lodging without Fibonacci the day after my dinner with Mariah, in fact. Linklater rapped on the front door just as I was drying the porridge pan. 'Fancy a secret graveyard?' He bounced on the balls of his feet.

I really needed to get out of the house. Mariah was still in bed and the thought of seeing her made me unaccountably furious. Felicity appeared in the hall out of nowhere, looking keen, if a bit fragile, blinking and wobbly; I wondered if she'd slept. Perhaps she too felt the tension in the house and needed to escape. She too grabbed her coat. I took mine, and a woolly hat for Felicity, and followed them out − they were already walking off into the foggy lane together.

'The Endell Street Military Hospital,' Linklater was saying

when I caught up with them, 'was set up by two women doctors called Flora Murray and Louisa Garrett Anderson in the First World War. In those days, hardly any women were doctors, but the whole hospital was entirely run and staffed by suffragettes.'

'She won't know what suffragettes are.' I shoved Felicity's hat on her head, pulling it low over her curls.

I stopped to tie my boot and they went ahead again, side by side, long-limbed and skinny, both in knitted hats, talking about suffrage; they could easily be father and daughter.

They waited for me at the kissing gate into Christ Church meadow – a tall iron zigzag affair, overcomplicated, like most things in Oxford. Behind them the meadow was shrouded in fog; only the very tips of the trees and their skeleton shadows were visible. Felicity went through the gate first and Linklater hung back to let me go. He was still talking. 'The army sent the most hopeless cases to Endell Street – all the butchered and traumatized boys that none of the male doctors wanted to treat – but their results were astonishing—'

'This is awfully interesting,' I said as I passed him, 'but why are you going on about it?'

'Well, that's it, you see. Last night in the Bod, I found V in an Endell Street photograph.'

There was a moment of confusion as he came into the kissing gate behind me – I stopped and his body pressed hard against mine. An electric current passed through me – he must have felt it too because he backed out instantly. When I turned, his face was scarlet. I squinted away into the fog. 'Which way then?'

'Follow me.' He shimmied through the gate. 'Up Dead Man's Walk.' He strode off, not looking back at me.

'Up what?'

'Dead Man's Walk – this path. It's called that because Oxford's medieval Jews used to carry their dead along here between the synagogue in St Aldates and the cemetery where we're actually going.'

Felicity stumbled, righted herself and followed us, hunched in her coat like a little old lady. 'How far is it?' I called to Linklater's back. 'Because Felicity's looking a bit peely-wally. She only finished school yesterday, she probably shouldn't be—'

'Just along here, not far.'

We were walking along the path that runs beneath the wall of Merton College towards Rose Lane, a familiar route since on warmer days I had walked Felicity to school this way. Now, the trees thrust witchy hands through the fog and the air was bronchial and harsh. Felicity's breath puffed around her. Her face was light grey, her eyes dark-circled like a small Victorian consumptive. 'Are you okay, my love?' I said. 'Do you want to just go back?'

Ahead of us, Linklater's foot slipped pointlessly – he wobbled as if he was on the edge of a precipice. He dressed like a student from the 1980s, I thought. Perhaps these were even the actual clothes he had worn then – the shabby overcoat, Doc Martens, that beanie. He suddenly seemed like a very neglected creature, scrambling along the foggy edges of the city.

'Do you have plans for Christmas?' I caught up with him.

'Same as always, Messiah and a vindaloo.'

'No family gatherings?'

He took a sideways leap around an invisible obstruction. 'I do my utmost to avoid my family all year, but I redouble my efforts over the festive period. My stepmother is basically Cruella De Vil; Felicity and I have that in common.' He turned to her. 'Hey, keep your eyes peeled now, Flipps, because on a foggy day like today you might see Sir Francis Windebank. He was a Royalist colonel in the English Civil War, shot by firing squad here in 1645. You'll know him because you only ever see him from the knees up. At some point they raised the ground-level out here.'

We were used to hearing these snippets from 'Dr Linklater's Spook Trail', which he billed as 'a glimpse of the other side, *only for the brave*'. I'd decided it would be unwise to take Felicity on one, though, given her tendency to see things at night.

She was looking a little spectral herself, now. We'd see this hidden graveyard quickly, I decided, then I'd get her back in the warm. We came out of the meadow into Rose Lane and arrived at the front of the botanic gardens, where we stopped. 'Et voila!' Linklater gestured over the box-hedge maze. 'The most secret graveyard in Oxford.'

So secret as to be invisible. I suddenly felt cross. Felicity should not be out in the freezing fog. This was ridiculous. Linklater was pointing to a plaque, reading out loud about how the rose garden was built on top of a medieval Jewish cemetery.

Out of the corner of my eye, I saw Felicity bow her head and cover her ears. I thought there must be a bell ringing somewhere, though I couldn't hear any. Linklater was talking about the underground passageways in St Aldates that once connected the homes of Oxford's ancient Jewish community, a network that still existed beneath the city centre. 'Linklater!' I barked. 'Stop!'

He looked at me with wide, shocked eyes. Then he noticed Felicity.

She was staring at her feet in trepidation, as if skeleton hands were about to burst through the soil and seize her ankles. 'Are there dead people under here?'

Linklater and I spoke at the same time. 'No, no, no,' I said.

'Quite a few.' He nodded.

The end of his nose was pink, his beanie set at an angle. How, I wondered, could he be so clueless? Felicity pressed her hands back over her ears and I bent to her, glad she was talking, but not glad that she was so distressed. 'Let's get you back to the Lodging now, darling.' She shook her head. She was genuinely spooked. 'There are no dead people here,' I said. 'Come on, now, let's go back.' I peeled her hand off one ear. 'Do you hear bells?'

'I can hear them whispering.'

Linklater was peering over my shoulder. 'In Yiddish?'

'She's not joking, Linklater!' I snapped.

There was a difference between the three of us eating Scotch eggs in a picturesque cemetery, talking about literature, history, philosophy and mathematics and this – a small girl shivering in the fog while the wronged medieval dead hissed Yiddish into her ears. 'Right.' I stood up. 'Time to go.' I turned to Linklater. 'She's genuinely scared, can't you see that?'

He looked appalled, and bent to her. 'Hey, don't be scared. We're all walking over dead bodies all the time. There's nothing scary about it, Flipper. They dig up medieval skeletons all the time in Oxford – and not just Oxford. I mean, the people of Leicester were parking on top of Richard III for decades. And when they dug the London Crossrail they found about 4,000 skeletons, including all the lost souls of Bedlam—'

I began to walk Felicity towards the High Street, but she yanked her hand out of mine and hurtled back down the steps towards Linklater. I caught her just in time to stop her pitching face first on to the gravel. Her hat fell off. I scooped her up.

'I'm not going back!' she howled. Her face was twisted, her nose red-tipped. 'I hate it there! I hate Mariah!'

She tore her arm from mine and stumbled to Linklater, who was walking towards us now, looking alarmed. 'I want to stay with you,' she bellowed at him. He hesitated, then wrapped his arms around her.

I wondered if she'd slipped downstairs the night before and heard what Mariah had said. She was crying properly now, with her face pressed against him. 'I – want – to – stay – with – you!'

'Well, you'd be more than welcome, Flipper. The only problem is my building doesn't allow cats, so I don't know what we'd do about that.' She looked up at him and he gave her a kind smile, wiping a tear from her cheek with his thumb. 'Also you'd probably have to sleep in a piano.'

'I want to sleep in a piano!'

I tried to peel her arms off Linklater. She felt wild and tangled. 'Poor Fibby,' I said. 'He'd be really sad without you. Come on, now. It's very cold out here and you're a wee bit poorly, I think.' I manoeuvred her away from Linklater but her legs were weak and trailing. I picked her up, then, glad to be physically strong. She gripped onto me and buried her head in my coat. 'It's okay, darling.' I patted her. 'I've got you now.'

When I got her to the steps, I looked back. Linklater was frozen by the plaque. He looked bewildered.

Back in the house she went straight up to her bedroom, crawled into bed and moulded herself around her squirrel. Fibonacci watched accusingly from his crate as I brought up hot milk and cookies and moved her colouring sheets so I could lay the plate on her bedside table. Maybe Linklater's talk of the invisible dead had sparked thoughts of her mother. If she'd overheard Mariah talking about Ana's ghost that might trigger things too. Or perhaps it was just the lack of headstones that had upset her – it was possible – probable, even – that Nick and Mariah had never even taken her to visit her mother's grave.

In the room below us Mariah lay in the big marital bed,

growing her baby, oblivious to the distress she'd caused – or perhaps not wanting to know. She did not deserve a child.

I gazed at the A4 sheet of Penrose tiles that Felicity had coloured so meticulously. The tiles cover the courtyard outside the Mathematical Institute and represent Penrose's most profound discovery. To the untrained eye, it just looks like nice ceramic paving – a pattern of big stars or flowers connected by curved steel bands – but the pattern is mathematically extraordinary. I could sit and stare at it for hours. It is made from only two different shapes of tile, each one a rhombus that achieves five-fold symmetry. These two tiles fit together in a pattern that will extend to infinity without ever repeating.

It struck me, as I looked at her coloured sheet, that the bond between a mother and child works a bit like the Penrose tiles: a pattern of different, unbreakable interactions between two distinct but related shapes that stretches to infinity. No forced separation – not even death – can destroy it, because it operates according to a logic that exists independent of geography, or time.

Chapter 33

–Right, let's move on, then. Faraday sounds brusque. –Christmas. I gather you all had Christmas day together, is that right?

–What's Christmas got to do with anything? I say. –This all feels like a waste of time.

–Bear with us, Dee. We're just trying to get a sense of life for Felicity in the past few months. This is going to help us find her, okay? He smiles, but only with his mouth.

So I say that yes, we did all spend Christmas together: Nick and Mariah had intended to take Felicity to Mariah's sister in Odense, but at the last moment they cancelled, so we all ended up together.

There was a picture on the mantelpiece of Mariah's sister, husband and their four Viking sons grinning on a sandy beach, all bellowing good health. While I was disappointed that I wouldn't be able to cook lunch at the Lodging for Linklater, I could only imagine how stressful Christmas in Denmark would have been for Felicity with these huge alien strangers. Mariah was exhausted and needed a rest – not least because they were leaving for Hong Kong the week Felicity started back at school. They didn't seem to have factored Felicity's needs into any of their travel plans, but that was no surprise.

Nick seemed relieved to be let off this particular trip. He looked haggard and it was clear that things at College had not improved. As I passed their bedroom door one morning, I overhead him complaining to Mariah about a College committee: 'They'll pass an unwise multi-million-pound budgetary decision in five seconds, but try to move a fucking bike shed and they'll quibble for months. Christ, darling, maybe we really should think about California sooner. I mean, I knew this was a mess, but . . .'

'Seriously?' She sounded hopeful.

'Well, why not? We'll have to see the rest of the academic year out, but I could put out some feelers.'

It was all I could do to stop myself bursting into their room and shouting, 'What about Felicity?'

Later that morning, I was baking mince pies when he came into the kitchen. 'Just getting a coffee,' he said. He tended to announce his intentions when he entered any room with me in it, as if to warn me that he wouldn't have time to interact. Perhaps he was under the impression that I might like to chat. He shoved a pod into the coffee machine. 'I assume you're heading off to Scotland for Christmas?' He pressed the button, drowning any chance of a response.

I reached for the rolling pin. Nobody had, until that point, thought to ask me about my Christmas plans. It was as if I only existed when they needed me. Even so, I assumed they'd realize I was staying, since I'd said nothing about going anywhere else. It was hardly my fault if they'd cancelled their trip at the last moment.

When the buzzing stopped, I said, 'I was planning to be in Oxford.'

'Oh.' Nick picked up his coffee cup, very carefully. 'You aren't going away? But we wouldn't want to keep you from a family knees-up, that would be very sad for you.'

'I don't have family in Scotland,' I said.

'Don't you? No parents?'

'Both dead.'

'Ah. No extended family?'

'I'm the only child of an only child. I have an uncle on the Isle of Lewis but I believe he's a maniac. We aren't in touch.' I had only met my father's brother once, when I was very small. It had not been a positive experience.

'Gosh.' Nick took a sip of coffee. 'Well, I suppose flights are expensive at this time of year, but if you did want a holiday somewhere and money's an issue, um, Dee, I'm sure we can help you out. You'd need to be back here by New Year, of course, because we fly to Hong Kong, but Mariah's been through all that with you, hasn't she?'

I looked him in the eye. 'Money's not an issue.'

He leaned back against the counter. 'Well, you must make whatever plans suit you, but it'd be awfully dull for you here, I'm afraid. We're planning a very quiet one this year because Mariah really needs the rest. Of course, you must do whatever you want. I expect you have plenty of friends you could go to in Oxford.' He pushed himself off the counter. 'Right. My car's waiting. Let us know what you decide.'

On Christmas Eve, Nick accosted me on the landing. 'I should put the stocking on her bed tonight, I always do that.' I nodded and went up again to get it from its hiding place. I'd told Mariah that I'd do the stocking and had been collecting little presents for weeks: hair-ties, sweets, pens, cat toys, a vintage microscope, a jar of buttons with needles and thread, a maths puzzle book, and some curiosities I knew she'd love: a hag stone I discovered many years ago on a beach in Galloway, a glass eye and a weasel's skull that I'd found in a junk shop in Banbury, and the witch's tooth in its leather ring box.

Nick, who was waiting on the landing by his room, took the wrapped stocking from me without asking about its contents.

I didn't fall asleep until dawn, but there were no disturbances that night other than Nick's swift footsteps. When I woke up and went into her room, Felicity had already ripped open the stocking and was waving the feathery cat toy at Fibonnaci, who shot under the bed. I went over and gave her a gentle hug, wishing her Happy Christmas. She showed me the witch's tooth. 'It's just like yours,' she whispered in awe.

'Well, it was mine,' I said. 'Santa asked if he could give it to you, and I said yes, so now it's yours.'

She gazed up at me.

'Now she'll keep you safe, too,' I said.

She slipped the box into her pocket.

Nick and Mariah were not downstairs until eleven, by which time Felicity and I had eaten porridge and she'd opened my present – a yellow hooded raincoat, just like Coraline's.

They bustled about, turning on King's College carols, making scrambled eggs, pouring champagne, touching each other constantly. I took Felicity into the living room and laid a fire. After a bit, Mariah came in with a champagne glass. 'Well, I should give you your present before you go off to see your friends.'

'What?'

Nick came in. 'Dee, you're still here.'

I stared at him. 'Where would you like me to be?'

'I thought you said you were spending today with friends.'

'No,' I said. 'I didn't say that.'

'Oh,' he said. 'Really?'

'You're welcome to stay and have turkey with us, Dee.' Mariah shot Nick a look. 'Oh, and thanks for doing the stocking, by the way.'

I saw Felicity's chin jerk up.

'Yes, thank you for that.' Nick stood behind Mariah and rested a hand on the back of her chair.

'But I had nothing to do with it!' I cried. 'It's Santa you need to thank.'

They glanced at each other and both of them had the decency to flush. 'Ah, yes, good old Santa, didn't he do well?' said Nick. Mariah gabbled something about Saint Nicholas and how she always opened her presents on Christmas Eve. Would her baby, I wondered, get presents on Christmas Eve, but not Felicity? And would they, when that child was eight, forget that he or she still believed in Santa?

'Now we need to give you your presents!' Mariah cried. She rushed to the tree. 'This one's from Felicity.' She handed me an envelope.

Felicity looked down at the buttons, which she'd laid out in a complex repeating pattern. She'd not even bothered to try on the bracelet they gave her, which had a tiny real diamond on it. She was eight – she liked voles' skulls, witch teeth, buttons and cats. She had no interest in jewellery.

The envelope contained tickets to *Richard III* at the Barbican in February, and a receipt for a Bloomsbury hotel room. It clearly had nothing whatsoever to do with Felicity. I thought of Linklater's comment about the King's body found beneath the Leicester car park, and then I wondered what Linklater was doing, right at that moment, alone in his flat, just a mile or so away. Perhaps he was thinking about us. 'It's just before the baby's born.' Mariah glanced at Nick. 'We thought you'd need a break – a thank-you for all your hard work. It's an all-female production; it's supposed to be amazing.'

Was this, I wondered, their way of dismissing me? It was far too much, I said. Nick shrugged. 'Our friend's on the board of the RSC, she's been very kind.'

Mariah handed me a small wrapped box. 'And this one's from all of us. A big thank you,' she cleared her throat, 'for rescuing us all these last few months.'

Presumably they'd decided to wait until they got back from Hong Kong to formally dismiss me. No doubt they didn't want me disgruntled and alone in the house with Felicity while they were on the other side of the world.

I pulled off the wrapping to find a white box with an Apple logo on it. 'Welcome to the twenty-first century.' Mariah laughed. 'Don't look so scared! It's reconditioned, don't worry, not brand new or anything.' She came closer and I smelled her delicate perfume, her freshly shampooed hair. I protested that I couldn't possibly accept a gift like this.

'You'll need it for wherever you go next,' Nick said.

Mariah shot him a look. 'Have you got your old Nokia, Dee? I need the SIM card so I can set this up for you.'

I went upstairs. My old brick phone was on the chest of drawers. I saw a text on it from Linklater wishing me a Happy Christmas, adding:

If you change your mind, a vindaloo awaits. Also, I stuck something in your car late last night. You shouldn't leave it unlocked!

I deleted his message and took the old phone down to Mariah. She switched the SIM card, talking about the iPhone's features, clicking buttons, showing me what it could do. I wasn't paying the slightest attention. I wondered what it was about people like Nick and Mariah that made them think they could buy their way

out of any awkward situation. Something was definitely wrong
with them as human beings. Nick's childhood was probably as
loveless as hers had been – it would explain why they clung
to each other with such fervour. I imagined he'd been sent to
boarding school at a catastrophically young age; had a hard-to-
please father, a cold mother. I didn't mind being excluded from
their Christmas lunch, but this passive-aggressive pre-dismissal
manoeuvring was something else.

Mariah handed me another package and I opened it, dully, to
find an olive green scarf, a cheap one from the Covered Market,
a bit like her cashmere wrap. 'Just a little extra.' She smiled.
'You have lovely eyes – if you put on a little bit of mascara and
wore this, they'd really pop, wouldn't they, Nick?'

Nick didn't look up. He'd just opened a gift that someone had
anonymously left for him in the Porter's Lodge: a biography of
Donald Trump.

I made my excuses and took the new phone upstairs. As I came
into my room, I saw something lying on my bed. The wrapping
paper, a neat, repeating zigzag pattern, had been painstakingly
coloured in felt-tip pens. I peeled it open. Inside I found a baby's
hairbrush. I turned it over. The bristles were downy and made
a hushing sound when I ran them over my fingers. There was
a silver bear on the wooden handle.

The room felt incredibly still, as if all the objects in it were
holding their breath and for a confusing moment, I felt as if
time had curled itself into a helix and Felicity had been at Mill
House – she was the one who took my baby's brush – but of
course, this brush was new, this wasn't Rosie's. I looked at the
tags: it came from a shop in the Covered Market. Felicity must
have used money from her piggy bank. I pictured her darting
down the cobbled alleys, then up Magpie Lane to the High,

dodging double-deckers and bikes and angry taxis.

How could I have been unaware that, at some point, just for a short while, I had been alone in the house while the child in my care was running through the city centre?

I barely recovered after that. When I'd pulled myself together, I crept downstairs. Felicity was just coming out of the front room and I took her in my arms, and held her tight against me for a second, trying to find my voice, trying to master the nameless and confusing emotions that were whirling about inside me. When I was able to speak, I whispered to her that her present meant the world to me, that it was wonderful. I told her I had to go out for a bit, and her parents wanted it to be just the three of them for lunch, but I'd be back soon. Maybe, I said, she could go and play with Fibby for a bit? Her head drooped, she looked miserable and she turned and went slowly up the broad red stairs, trailing a hand on the bannister. I badly wanted to take her with me but of course, I couldn't. I grabbed my coat, slipping out the back door.

The frosty grass crackled under my boots and the Oxford sky was raucous with Christmas bells – the spires and chapels uniting in their festive mania, lassoing the city with sound. I stepped through the garden gate into the back alley where I saw my car, covered in frost. It seemed, suddenly, like a refuge. I opened the door and as I got in something crackled under me. I lifted myself up and found a package wrapped in paper torn from a music score.

I ripped it open. Inside was a copy of *Gödel, Escher, Bach*.

Very gently I opened the front cover – 1979, a first edition. I turned the precious thing over in my hands. It was smooth, only slightly tattered; extraordinary. I lifted it to my nose and breathed the musky scent of old paper, hints of smoke and chocolate. I'd been trying to explain this book to Linklater just a few weeks previously – how it explores the deepest ideas in maths using parallels in music and art. I'd made a solid attempt to explain Gödel's Incompleteness Theorem as the notion that there are no set of mathematical truths or axioms that will prove or disprove all mathematical statements. After all, I told him, even in simple school arithmetic it is impossible to prove or disprove every hypothesis. There will always be things that are obviously true, I said, but that you just can't prove.

Linkater engaged valiantly, and I think he may have understood what I was talking about.

He must have searched out this first edition in a rare bookshop, and probably paid a large sum of money for it. I opened it again; the spine creaked and a scrap of paper fluttered out – a note. He'd written, in surprisingly attractive handwriting, *Happy Christmas, Dee. Go to page thirty-five.*

I turned to page thirty-five. A different hand – faded ink, definitely not Linklater's – had scribbled in the margins, *What the fuck does this even mean?!*

I wrapped the book up and put it in the glove box, locking the door. I couldn't drive. I needed to walk. Linklater's gift had left me reeling. It was overwhelming. It was perfect.

When I got to the High Street there was hardly a soul. I passed the Radcliffe Camera towards the Bodleian, walking fast, feeling as if I was lurching through a dreamscape, profoundly alone. Somehow I found myself at St Sepulchre's. Linklater had brought us there a few weeks previously, and though I'd lived in Jericho more than once, I'd not known the graveyard existed. Like Holywell and Wolvercote, it had been created in Victorian times after a cholera epidemic filled the city's graveyards. Linklater said it was his favourite. He'd shown us Icelandic scholars, College presidents and politicians, lying beside saddlers and ropemakers, coal-heavers and confectioners, and all their poor dead babies between.

When we had come with Linklater the place had felt magical, with sparkling frost, and robin redbreasts chirping gaily. Now, I wandered through it alone in the darkness and it was desolate. In the flats above, someone flung open a window and I heard salsa music and laughter, and further off beyond the wall, drunk carollers sang 'Ding Dong Merrily'. Somehow, I found myself at the Hale children's grave, a modest slab whose inscription had been almost erased by time. I crouched down, running my fingers over the grooves in the cold stone, feeling the dents of each name and date. In the space of just a few years, these Victorian parents had buried five baby girls and a boy – the eldest just two years old. Their mother had loved them no less than I loved my child. If she could survive such devastation, who was I to feel anything?

My baby, after all, was alive and well – a healthy and hopefully happy young woman in her twenties with a pretty face, dimples, thick curly hair and almond-shaped eyes like mine. Right now she was probably waking up to a West Coast Christmas with no idea that a stranger was hunched in a graveyard on the other side of the Atlantic, longing for her still, shattered and broken by all the lost years.

I had intended to walk to Banbury Road to thank Linklater for the book, maybe eat his vindaloo, but I realized as I stood up that I couldn't do it. I couldn't face him. He would know that something was wrong. I didn't have the strength to experience whatever emotions were coiled inside me. As I turned and made my way back across the knotted graves, I counted my own footsteps – I needed to make everything inside me silent again, because the alternative was unbearable.

I walked the periphery of Oxford for hours, circling the dark canal paths and back alleys, going under bridges, along towpaths, through allotments. When I got back to the house it was late – Nick and Mariah were on the sofa watching TV. There was no sign of Felicity, though a witch hex in buttons had been laid on the rug. On the screen I recognized a scene from *Rear Window*: James Stewart was taking flash photographs of a man with bottle-top glasses.

Mariah lay on her side, asleep with her head in Nick's lap, her belly slack beside her. Nick had a whisky glass in one hand, his crystal decanter on the coffee table. It was the first time I'd seen them together like this, so ordinary. Nick's free fingers were tangled in hers. He stared at the TV, his brows lowered like a raptor. He must have recently thrown more logs on the fire because the grate was blazing and the wood spat and crackled. A fat ember shot out and fizzled on the rug and I smelled scorched wool, but I didn't move to extinguish it. I saw the fibres begin to smoulder, then catch – flames fingering towards the sofa and roaring to life to engulf them where they lay. I blinked. The ember was gone. All that remained on the rug was a small charcoal fleck.

Nick didn't turn his head, though I knew he must have heard me come in – he must sense me standing by the door. He kept his eyes fixed on the screen as the Hitchcockian carmine washed intermittently over his face and Mariah's, darkening their cheeks and their pale entangled hands.

Chapter 34

Faraday is staring at me with raised eyebrows and I sense that he has just asked me a question. I have to ask him to repeat himself and he says, with exaggerated patience, that he would like me to 'talk him through' the week Nick and Mariah were in Hong Kong. –Can you tell us what you did together, he says. –Where you went, who you saw?

–We did very little, I say. –Felicity was sick that week.

He clears his throat and consults his notes. –Right, I gather you kept her off school again. Dr Law says you refused to take their calls, and Angela Masters says you were behaving 'strangely'. So, what was going on, Dee?

–Nothing was 'going on'. I told you – Felicity wasn't well.

Khan suddenly leans forward. I am so unused to her speaking that her voice unnerves me – her tone is hard and assertive. –But you still made her get up and do maths in the middle of the night?

It takes me a moment to realize what on earth she's talking about. And then I wonder who told her. Mariah? Nick? If so, then they are deliberately presenting me to the police as an unstable person, which seems rich, given Mariah's recent state of mind.

Nick and Mariah flew to Hong Kong on the Sunday, and Monday

was the first day of Felicity's school term. I found her in the bathroom at five-thirty that morning, bent over with stomach pains. Naturally I phoned the school to say she had stomach flu. Since I was proxy parent, I assumed this was my decision to make.

With Mariah and Nick away and no pressure to go to school, I was expecting Felicity to recover, but in fact she was sad and listless. She barely ate and wouldn't speak. She rearranged all the treasures into a different pattern on the rug. She lay on her belly and stared at the cat. I suppose I wasn't myself either. The knowledge that when they got back from Hong Kong they'd probably be getting rid of me – and that I might never see Felicity again – weighed on my mind. I lurched from one possibility to the next, helpless and trapped. The day passed in a disjointed haze.

She was still under the weather on the Tuesday so I kept her at home again. I phoned the GP who said that I should bring her in the following day if she didn't improve. She wouldn't play cards with me that day, or watch *Midsomer Murders*, and didn't even look interested when I took up the tibia I'd been cleaning off – a beautiful smooth bone that I'd found on Port Meadow, absolutely perfect. I told her it might have belonged to a cat but she just stared at it, dully, until I put it away.

The cat crouched in the corner of the room, watching me come and go, his fur ruffled, his face indignant. I felt that at any moment he could leap across and sink his fangs into my jugular.

She seemed better on the Wednesday; she had more colour in her cheeks and she ate her porridge, but since she had eaten so little the previous two days I felt it would be wiser to keep her at home just to be sure. I was convinced that the root of the malaise was her dread of school; I couldn't blame her. This was confirmed when, that night, I woke to find her standing at the foot of my bed, staring at me. The bathroom light was on so I couldn't see her face, just her silhouette in a pale nightdress, with her wild hair standing up in a black, electrified halo. I scrambled to sit up. 'What's the matter, my darling? What is it?'

My legs felt shaky as I got out of bed and went round to her. She was shivering, I saw: I wondered how long she'd been standing there, watching me. I touched her arm; her skin was icy. 'God, you're freezing,' I said. 'Poor wee mite.'

'They're in my room.' Her voice sounded flat and eerily detached. 'Get them out.'

'Who, darling?'

She couldn't tell me but it seemed likely that she'd been dreaming about Duncan and Jonnie again. Linklater had definitely not mentioned the twins since I'd warned him about this, but such things will lodge in a child's mind, stubborn as tics.

I knew I should lead her back through the bathroom and into her room to show her that the twins were imaginary, but at that moment all I could think was that we both needed to get out of the attic.

I wrapped her in my tartan blanket and as I led her along the corridor, I had the eerie feeling that someone was standing behind us, in the darkest part, down at the end, watching us leave. I knew, rationally, that this was nonsense, but I didn't turn to look; I hurried her downstairs and into the kitchen, shutting the door.

She had a vacant look, as if she was stuck somewhere between wakefulness and sleep. Her schoolbooks were in a pile on the table next to her. Maths has saved me from many a nightmare, waking or asleep. Sometimes I find that my unconscious brain has hit on a solution in my sleep that has stumped me for weeks – I've even woken up to find that I've scribbled an important and accurate step in my notebook and I only know it was me because it's my own handwriting.

Nick and Mariah have always lazily assumed that because Felicity likes colouring books she is artistic, but she never draws anything freehand. What interests her are shapes – lines, form, structure, repeating patterns. Felicity, I suspect, is a mathematician.

It really isn't possible to 'make' a child to do fractions at 4 a.m. Felicity took the pencil from me willingly, almost with relief, and as soon as she started, her odd energy seemed to quieten. Perhaps the concentration required to convert simple fractions to decimal allowed her to bypass the fear. As I made toast and heated up the milk, I kept an eye on her sweet face – the little line etched between her brows and her sprinkle of wheaten freckles – and I thought how similar we were, she and I.

There is a concept known to mathematicians as isomorphism, where two complex but apparently different structures can be mapped onto one another exactly so that each part of one structure finds a corresponding part in the other: a teacup, for instance, is equivalent to a doughnut because one shape can be morphed exactly into the other. If it were possible to map our essential selves, I felt that Felicity and I – ostensibly teacup and doughnut – would turn out to be isomorphic. Every part of me, I felt, had its equivalent part in her. Neither of us really fitted into the world, but somehow we fitted each other.

She looked up at me, tired but calmer, and obviously awake now. I eased the exercise book out of her hands. She had done all six fractions correctly. I slid buttered toast and a mug of warm milk in front of her.

When they fired me, and they would, how would I bear to leave her? She would be so alone without me, so misunderstood.

Who else would think to comfort her with fractions? 'Shall I tell you a wee real story?' I offered. 'While you eat your toast?'

She gave a feeble nod. I wondered if she even remembered whatever dream or visitation had pushed her to my bedside.

I had recently discovered that she liked me to embellish little news stories that appear in the margins of the newspaper – little ordinary tragedies or oddities. I thought for a moment, then a story occurred to me.

'One day a sixty-four-year-old man was driving towards the crossroads in a small town a long, long way from here.' I sat down opposite her. 'The lights were red but he didn't stop and a lorry smashed into his van. Lots of people saw it and ran to the wreckage, trying to pull him out of the crumpled van. The lorry driver got out without a scratch but the man died at the scene.' I clicked my fingers. 'Just like that.' I reached for a piece of toast, bit into it. 'Which is where the real story begins.' I chewed. 'Because sometimes stories have to be told backwards, don't they? The man was distracted because his daughter was in trouble and he blamed himself, as parents do. He felt he'd failed her. She'd reversed a car into someone and the police were saying it was deliberate.' I finished the toast, licked my fingers. There was a bit more colour in her cheeks and she'd nibbled a corner of the toast. 'She'd reversed into this man because he was trying to take her baby away from her. He was the baby's father and he'd been telling everyone she was a really bad mother.'

Felicity lifted her mug and our eyes met over its rim. I felt sure that she knew who the girl was. 'She did it because she was frightened and angry, and, truth to tell, she'd had a bit to drink. Nobody believed she could be a good mother, even after a year of showing them she could. That's why her dad was distracted in his van. He saw the flash of the lorry's headlamps and heard the horn, but it was too late – or perhaps he didn't want to stop. He had demons of his own. His childhood had been brutal, his brother was mad and he, himself, had once done a really terrible thing – something that he could never forget or forgive himself for. When he pressed the accelerator, he'd had enough. And look, there you go – we're back at the beginning again. The beginning which is also the end.'

I looked down at my hands, which lay limp, reddened and work-worn, on the table between us. An enormous darkness rose up in me, then, blotting everything out. I had to close my eyes. After a moment or two I felt her soft fingers patting my hands. I opened my eyes. She was offering me her toast. I took a bite. 'Thank you, pet,' I mumbled. The toast was hard to swallow.

I give Khan a condensed version of this, leaving out my story. She says nothing, but writes it all down.

–What else happened that week they were away, Dee? Faraday says. –Why weren't you answering any phones?

–That, I say, –was just a misunderstanding.

Felicity was in no fit state for school the next day after being up half the night. My priority was to keep her eating. I baked scones and Parkin and honey cake, her favourite treats, and took them up with glasses of milk or juice. I did some cleaning – I'd told the College scouts not to come, the last thing we needed was any more intruders. As I cleaned Nick's study, I looked through his papers – minutes of Bursarial or Fellowship or ad hoc committee meetings – dreading the moment when I'd find boarding school brochures, but there were none. What I thought might be one turned out to be an audit of the College wine cellars, which included a bottle of brandy worth £2,000, and six bottles of Krug worth £6,000.

Angela let herself in that evening as I was dicing chicken for soup. She marched up the hall and stood at the kitchen doorway with righteous, folded arms. 'So you are alive, then.'

'Apparently so.'

'The Master sent me over. He says you aren't picking up the phones. He's asked me to come and check what's going on.'

The iPhone was upstairs in my bedside table, turned off. I had no use for it. I had taken the Lodging phone off the hook, I remembered, on the Monday, so it wouldn't disturb Felicity as she slept. I had even switched off my Nokia; I still could not communicate with Linklater, not even by text.

'Well, as you can see, everything's fine,' I said to Angela, and sliced into the glistening breast. 'I'm making chicken soup.'

'Well, you'd better phone him – he doesn't sound happy and I've got better things to do than come over here checking up on you.' Angela glanced at the knife, and retreated.

When I went upstairs with the soup, I saw that Fibonacci had graduated to the foot of the bed. He lifted his head and stared at me with cold defiance, guarding his small queen. I put the tray down on the desk. As I drew the blinds, Great Tom's mournful chimes began to sound. Linklater had pointed them out to us one evening as we walked back to the Lodging after climbing St Mary's spire at night – a friend of his had let us up there. Oxford's time zone is officially five minutes and two seconds behind Greenwich Mean Time, so Great Tom rings every evening at 9.05 p.m. It rings 101 times, he told us, once for every student who was enrolled at Christ Church in 1663. This nightly farrago seemed to me to embody the entire narcissistic psychopathy of Oxford: a city mired in the past, saturated with self-importance.

As I stood at Felicity's window, I felt as if I'd forgotten something vital – as if I'd left a gas ring burning, or the front door open. And then I had an odd realization: what was missing was Linklater.

We hadn't seen him since the rose garden. I had ignored his Christmas day message. And even worse than that, I hadn't yet been able to thank him for *Gödel, Escher, Bach*.

I had no words for how I felt about the book. No man, other than my father, had ever given me a gift before and every time I imagined contacting him to say thank you, I froze. I didn't reply when he texted on Boxing Day to ask if I'd looked in my car. I didn't reply when he texted at midnight on New Year's Eve, asking if he should appear on my doorstep with a lump of coal, or when he texted on New Year's Day, asking if everything was all right, or when he said he was sorry if he'd upset me by taking us to the hidden cemetery. I switched off my phone. I did nothing.

Now, staring down at the slick cobbles, I wanted to see him very badly.

But he didn't come to the Lodging that night, or the next day, which was a good thing, really, given what happened to the cat.

Chapter 35

When I went into Felicity's room early the next morning she wasn't there. The priest's hole door was wide open.

I found her crouched with her back to me. She'd propped up a torch and its glow made odd, flickering shadows on the sloping walls. A sickly, ferrous smell hit me as I peered inside – not the usual rotten stench, something more active. I expected to see a new witch hex or another superstitious arrangement of bones or insects, but what I saw was the cat, lying in a nest of jumpers and T-shirts, panting and glassy-eyed. My first thought was that Felicity had done something horrific in her sleep.

Then I noticed slime, muck and wetness around the animal's tail, and some dark liverish lumps by the armpit. I reached past her and touched one – it was damp and sticky. I grabbed the torch. I saw tiny, clawed legs – there was something poking out of the cat's rear end. I gently lifted the tail and saw a bulbous amniotic sac. 'Oh dear God, he's having kittens.' I caught my own pronoun. 'She. Fibby's a she.'

I'd seen cats give birth before and it was definitely not meant to be like this. The cat wasn't trying to lick the kitten that was poking out of her. She didn't seem interested in the two little bodies either. There was no straining or contracting, just a lot of panting. She was exhausted, possibly even giving up.

'Has this been going on for a long time?'

Felicity nodded, frantically.

'How long?'

The anxiety was stopping her voice. She'd once said to me that when she tried to speak, her bones felt like glass. At that moment, she looked as if she might crackle and shatter.

'An hour, darling?' I said. 'Two? Three? All night? Felicity?'

She nodded again.

'Why didn't you wake me? Right, budge over, let me in.'

She scooted over against the wall – I reached past her and lifted the cat's tail. This kitten plainly needed to come out. I gave the torch to Felicity and told her to point it at the bulging amniotic sac. A tiny black nose and claws were visible through the veiny membrane. It was slimy and hard to get a hold of, but I wedged my fingers round it and pulled – gently at first, then more firmly. I felt the cat's birth canal suck back. I tugged again and after a moment's resistance the kitten slid out. I rubbed the amniotic sac off its head and fluid gushed onto the T-shirt. I recoiled. It was a poor, malformed thing, its face grotesquely swollen, its closed eyes bulging like an alien's, presumably from having been stuck halfway out of its mother for hours. I laid it by the cat's muzzle, just in case, but Fibby looked at it, sniffed it, then just lay back down. She knew.

I rubbed the two other little bodies, wiped their little noses and slit eyes. Their whiskers were only damp stumps of cartilage. They were both dead too. I turned to Felicity. Tears were rolling down her cheeks and her mouth was twisted. 'Oh, pet.' I stroked her cheek. 'Sometimes this just happens. It's just nature – none of us can do anything about it.'

Of course, there was a possibility of more dead kittens still inside the cat – we were going to have to get to the vet. I scooped the kittens into a T-shirt and backed out of the doorway. I could feel the three little nodules in my hand through the thin cotton shirt. I felt slightly sick.

Felicity stayed in the priest's hole. I could see the knobbles of her spine poking through her jumper. She looked incredibly fragile. The cat made a feeble attempt to get up then flopped back down. Felicity stroked her head.

'It's okay,' I said. 'It's going to be okay.'

The smell of death filled the priest's hole.

Felicity's head whipped round and her eyes were wild. 'They did this.'

'What?' I realized she was talking about Duncan and Jonnie. 'Oh, sweetheart—'

'I saw them go in here. It was dark and I was too scared to stop them. They killed the babies.'

Engaging in this would only validate her imaginings. 'Nobody was here, darling,' I said, very firmly. 'Nobody. You just had a very bad dream.' I made my voice solid and reassuring, but a part of me felt that on some level she was right – no new life could survive in this attic.

I went and stood over the toilet, clutching the stained T-shirt. Then one by one I dropped the dead kittens into the pan. I stared at them for a moment. I thought that perhaps I should have flushed after each one but it was too late for that. I pulled the chain. My hands, I realized, were trembling.

I drank water from the tap. I needed to calm down. Six-year-old Edwardian twins were not haunting the attic. Back at the priest's hole, I steadied myself with both hands on the low doorframe. 'We need to take Fibby to the vet now.'

Somehow I got us both dressed, got the cat into the crate, and all of us out of the priest's hole and into the garden. The gardener was wrestling with a dead clematis – the ragged strands lashed in the wind. He must have seen something in our faces because he dropped it and came straight over. I explained what was happening and he unlocked the back gate for us, took the cat crate from me and carried it to the car. I felt a flood of gratitude for this simple, wordless gesture of solidarity – my throat tightened and I felt as if I might cry. I had not cried in front of anyone for many years and the idea made me panicky – I felt as if a fissure had appeared in the stone that encased my heart, and at any moment it might crack and then everything would pour out – all the mess and shame. As I slammed the car door, it struck me that the gardener had tried to warn us about this the first day the cat arrived. I had misheard 'pregnant' as 'eggplant'.

The visit to the vet was a bit of a blur. An X-ray found no more kittens. There was medication and instructions to keep the cat inside, in a 'low-stress environment' with food and water – no bright lights, no loud noises; reassurance that sometimes these things happen – abnormalities, still birth.

Back at the Lodging, as I sat on Felicity's bed waiting for her to come out of the bathroom, I phoned a locksmith. I wouldn't need to tell Mariah. I would just pay for the priest's hole lock to be changed myself. I should have done it months ago.

When I have finished telling Faraday and Khan about the cat's miscarriage, Khan licks her lips – actually licks them – and says, in her emotionless way, –I think those kittens were born alive.

–But I just told you—

–Did you flush live kittens down the toilet, Dee?

I feel as if she's punched me in the chest. –What?

A horrible thought flashes into my head that Felicity had told

Nick that I did this – that somehow in the shock I hadn't shown her clearly enough that they were dead. It had been obvious to me – I grew up in the countryside; my father was a gamekeeper most of my childhood and then worked at an abattoir; I know a dead animal when I see one. But I could not remember what I said to her as I carried them away, if I said anything at all. I must have been very stressed indeed.

Khan is waiting for my answer.

–Why on earth would I do a thing like that? I try to sound calm.

–Well, here's one theory, she says. –Felicity's very attached to that cat, isn't she? You might be able to take Felicity to London with one animal in a pet carrier, but you weren't going to be able to take her with a cat plus newborn kittens. You'd never get her to leave the house quietly without them, so you drowned them.

I realize, then, that this is coming from Nick and Mariah. It has to be. They are throwing around wild accusations in order to make me look mad and dangerous. I suddenly feel cold, though moments before the interview room felt hot and stuffy. I straighten my shoulders. –I did not take anyone to London. You can trace all my movements on CCTV, can't you? And I certainly did not kill the kittens. This is ridiculous.

Then I realize that of course Khan is just trying to derail me. She's the bad cop. She wants to get me angry and push me to say things I will regret. What kind of twisted lunatic would flush live newborn kittens down a toilet?

–Do you really think I'd do something that insane? I say.

–I don't know, Dee. Khan tilts her cropped head; her dark eyes remain steady on my face. –Would you?

Chapter 36

My hands have begun to shake again so I fold them on my lap. –Listen, if I was a child abductor, I say, –I'd have done it that week, wouldn't I? With Nick and Mariah on the other side of the world, I could have taken her anywhere I fancied. It would have been several days before they'd even know we'd gone.

Khan stares at me with narrowed eyes, and says nothing.

Faraday taps his pen on his knee and clears his throat. –If I'm being cynical here, Dee, I suppose I might say you wouldn't do that, not on this particular week, because if you took her that week, then we'd all know it was you, wouldn't we?

I look at him with his big slumped shoulders and his pudgy eye bags, and I wonder what it must do to him to look at strangers like me all day, day after day, and try to imagine the very worst thing that they are capable of.

I feel Khan's eyes on my face too but I don't look at her.

–Let's get back to the day the kittens died, Faraday suggests. –You had a bit of a confrontation with Angela that night, too, is that right?

He explains that Angela has told them that when she came to the Lodging for the second time, I 'went mad' and 'used awful language'; I seemed 'agitated' and 'very frustrated'.

If I did seem a bit off that evening, it was because of the upset with the kittens, and the fact that Angela just marched into the house without knocking. The sight of her standing on the landing as I came out of Nick's study almost gave me a heart attack. It had been a very stressful day.

'Right. The Master's wondering what's going on here,' she said officiously, folding her arms over her quilted navy bosom, not even bothering to explain what she was doing in our house. 'Apparently you're still not answering the blinking phones?'

I found myself plunged into a sudden, violent fury. 'Get out!' I bellowed. 'Get out of this house!'

Angela's jaw dropped – she stepped backwards and teetered on the top of the stairs, grabbing the bannister just in time to stop herself plummeting backwards. 'Where's Felicity?' She sounded shaken.

I quivered with rage. 'Where do you think she is?'

Perhaps it was something in my face, but Angela shoved past me and galloped up the attic stairs, her buttocks wobbling inside her slacks. I had never seen her move so fast and for some reason – again, perhaps stress – I found the sight of her bottom funny; I began to laugh.

Ten minutes later I found myself standing in the sunroom. I had no memory of getting downstairs, but I now felt perfectly calm.

A moment later, I heard the front door slam.

I did plug the home phones back in then. I dialled Mariah's mobile and began to pace around. She answered after just a couple of rings.

'Dee? Is that you?' She sounded throaty. 'Oh my God! We've been trying to call you! What the hell's happening? Jesus, Dee.'

'Nothing's happening. Angela's just been here. Felicity's asleep.'

'But why haven't you called us back? Seriously, you can't just not pick up!'

'Yes,' I said. 'The home phone was unfortunately unplugged, and I haven't had my mobile switched on.'

'But that's just—'

I really did not want a tedious debate at this point. I'd walked upstairs and I was standing on the landing outside Nick's study again. 'There's nothing to worry about,' I gazed at the William Morris wallpaper. The birds looked desperate, ravenous.

'Okay, listen, it's seven in the morning here – Nick's just gone to a breakfast meeting – but he's going to Skype Felicity when he gets back, and you've got to make sure she has her iPad switched on and is waiting for him. Okay?'

'Actually, she's been a bit under the weather.'

'What?' I heard the shift in her voice. 'But you just said she was fine. What's wrong with her?'

'Just a tummy bug.'

'Was she sick at school?'

I walked into Nick's study to get away from the wallpaper and stood at his desk, a vast, sturdy antique walnut piece with an inlaid leather top, which was scored and scarred by the nibs of pens in the hands of very important men. I gazed at his papers, each stamped with the College crest: the minutes of a Security subcommittee meeting; a draft contract for a new bursar; a document laying out the case for moving the College bike sheds. I picked up a paperweight with a baby scorpion petrified inside it.

Mariah was still bleating. 'What are her actual symptoms? What's actually wrong with her?'

'She's really fine.' I put the paperweight down.

'Can I talk to Felicity? Let me talk to her.'

I tried not to laugh – not just at the idea that I should go up to the attic and wake her, but at the notion that, after four years, she'd suddenly start talking to Mariah. 'It's eleven o'clock at night, Mariah; I told you, she's fast asleep.' I picked up a paperknife with an ivory handle, and touched the sharp end against my fingertip. Mariah launched into a diatribe about keeping them informed. I moved the phone away from my ear and looked at the ceiling with its pale, painted beams. I followed their lines out onto the landing. After a moment or two I put the phone back against my ear.

'Are you still there? Can you hear me?'

'It's not a good line.'

'You're sounding a little bit weird right now,' Mariah said. 'Are you okay? You have to—'

My patience ran out then. I held the phone away, looked at it for a second, then hung up.

I suppose I was very stressed. I was still carrying the paperknife and somehow as I turned, I must have stumbled, and the tip of the blade stabbed into Mariah's wallpaper, gouging the splayed lips of a pomegranate. The tear was circular, little more than the size of a child's thumb, but it went deep, through the lining papers to the plaster.

I pressed the torn area back down. The ghost of the lining showed round the edges but you'd have to be looking closely to notice it. If I told Mariah about it, she'd have to remove a whole section, take it back to London and have it repaired or remade – and goodness only knew what sort of a job that would be. If I said nothing, then in all likelihood the tear would sit in the pattern for another hundred years. Damage is only damage, after all, when it is observed.

Chapter 37

The morning they were due back from Hong Kong, I was sitting in the kitchen when a text from Linklater pinged into my phone. My spirits lifted.

In Bodleian – found something SENSATIONAL. Have to go to planning meeting tonight, but can we meet tomorrow? It's about the twins, so best without F?

I was about to reply when I heard a key in the front door – Nick and Mariah. I put the phone away and came into the hall. When I saw Mariah's gravel-coloured skin and puffy face, I was shocked. 'I just need to—' She gave a faint smile and staggered to the living room, where she flopped on her back on the sofa, still in her coat, shielding her face with one arm.

I carried her bag down the hall and Nick followed with two bigger suitcases.

'Felicity's in her room,' I said as we reached the bottom of the stairs.

Without a word to me, he dumped the cases and ran upstairs, two at a time.

He burst back into the kitchen ten minutes later as I was making tea for Mariah. 'She won't talk to me – she won't tell me anything. What the hell's been going on?'

I attempted to explain that she'd been a bit under the weather early in the week but was fine, just upset. I described, briefly, what had happened to the cat, but Nick did not seem interested in that.

'Was she sick at school then?'

'She hasn't been to school.'

'What? You gave her another day off?'

'Actually, she had to be off all week.'

Mariah appeared at the door behind him, both hands on her belly. She came past him and flumped into the chair as if her coat was lined with lead.

'You've kept her off school *all week*?' Nick lowered his brows and stared at me.

I wondered how he'd feel if I followed him over to his elegant College rooms, stood beneath the oil portraits of old white men and told him how to do his job. 'As proxy parent, I felt it reasonable to make that call.'

'You're not proxy anything, you're the bloody nanny. We've told you very clearly that you must consult us if you feel she can't go to school. It's absolutely unacceptable to ignore our calls. You were completely AWOL and we were extremely concerned. This is just – it's ridiculous, frankly. Look, I'm afraid this just isn't going to—'

'No! Nick – ' Mariah sounded panicky ' – we talked about this – I have such a bad headache. Please. Stop now!'

I stood still, my hand on the kettle. Presumably, as they sat in Business Class, they had made a plan of how and when they would get rid of me. Perhaps they had drawn up a list of boarding schools, or drafted an advert for a new nanny. My only hope was that Mariah could be won over – I was, after all, her best buffer against Felicity. Nick wouldn't see it that way, though. To him, I was just staff – replaceable. The precariousness of my situation was impossible to ignore.

Nick went over to Mariah, bent and touched her cheek. 'Sorry, my darling, it's okay. Are you all right? You look done in. You should go to bed.'

She nodded, weakly. 'What's that horrible smell?' She covered her face and bent forward. I wondered if she might be sick on the floor I had just mopped.

Nick took her hands, gently. 'Come on, let's get you to bed.' He glanced back at me. 'Don't go anywhere. I'll talk to you in a minute.'

I turned back to the sink.

As he eased Mariah up, Nick must have spotted the bucket behind the door in which I was soaking the flesh off a couple of our treasures. 'Christ alive! Get rid of that bloody thing right now!' His phone began to buzz, an angry wasp circling the space between us. As he went into the hall with his arm around Mariah, I heard him answer it with a curt, 'Sally? Yes, yes. I know. I'll be over there in ten, fifteen minutes. Give them coffee – tell them our flight was delayed.'

I heard them going up the stairs, step by step, like fragile octogenarians. I got out my phone and sent a text to Linklater.

Can we meet now?

His text pinged straight back.

Yes! QL, 15 mins?

Nick came back down not long afterwards and I heard him stride down the hall. I was relieved that he didn't come back to the kitchen to harangue me. He slammed the front door so hard that their mended wedding picture in the hall trembled and shuddered. He had seen his daughter for a total of ten minutes.

Chapter 38

When I went up, Felicity was sitting in the semi-darkness staring at *Coraline* with the cat on the bed next to her. 'How are you feeling, my darling girl, any better?' She gave a nod and I stroked her face and told her I was just nipping out for a bit and that she must drink the milk and eat the cookie I'd brought her before I got back.

She mustn't worry, I said, I'd only be half an hour. If she wanted me she should phone me, as I'd only be five minutes away. Mariah was downstairs, and her dad would be back soon too. In her small hands, the glass of milk looked huge. I felt very bad not taking her with me but I had to see Linklater alone this time.

He was waiting for me at our table in Queen's Lane and when he saw me, he gave a beaming, lopsided smile, raised his hand and half-stood up, his thighs knocking against the tabletop. He looked hopeful and pleased, if a bit nervous. I'd felt he might be cross with me – hurt by my silence and my rudeness – but there was no trace of anger or resentment in his kind face. I felt my spirits lift.

We ordered tea and crumpets and I told him briefly what had been happening since Christmas.

He shook his head. 'Jesus, Dee, no wonder you didn't call me back.'

Something in me let go a bit and I found myself telling him how I felt about Nick and Mariah and the decisions they made for Felicity. I didn't hold back. 'They're breathtakingly awful parents,' I finished.

My words seemed to have quite an effect on him. 'Ah, God, the poor child.'

'I know.'

'Do you know what people at the BBC say about Law?' He pushed up his glasses. 'He had a reputation as a manipulative bully. Apparently he was aiming for the top job but when he realized he'd never get it, he took the College position in a massive huff. No one thinks he'll last here – he's way too ambitious. He wants to be Master for the cachet, but he'll soon be off.'

'I've heard them talking about America,' I admitted. 'How they can even consider moving Felicity to another country's beyond me.'

He shook his head. 'She's such a sweet kid, this is awful.'

'They really don't deserve her.'

'Well, at least she's got you.'

'She won't have when they fire me,' I said. 'And they will.' I told him how Nick had turned on me in the kitchen – teetering on the brink of dismissing me before Mariah intervened.

Our eyes met and I knew he understood the situation – he saw how inadequate they were, the damage they were inflicting on Felicity, and how precarious everything had become. It felt drastically unfamiliar to unburden myself to another human being like this but suddenly I understood why people did it. The circumstances hadn't changed, but I did feel slightly less tangled and panicky.

'Anyway,' I said. 'Tell me what you found in the Bodleian? You said in your text it's sensational?'

'I've had an astonishingly fertile week.' His face broke into a grin.

'Go on then.' I smiled too.

He'd made a breakthrough, he said. 'I know who V is. It's quite exciting. She met Muriel through the suffrage movement in Edinburgh – I'm pretty sure of it. I found a report in *The Scotsman* from 1915 about a young, upper-middle-class mother who'd vanished from her home in Edinburgh with her four-year-old twins. Her name was Vida Wallace – I've found her on the same WSPU register as Muriel. V's "The Runaway Wife". I found another little cache of letters, tucked into some financial folders, and it looks like Muriel planned to join them in Oxford. These letters are quite different in tone, lots of endearments and odd phrases which I'm pretty sure are coded references to their sex life.'

'Really?'

He nodded. 'I think Vida and Muriel were a couple. I think they were planning to set up home together – maybe intending to escape to America where Muriel could get a research position. But then the war started, and obviously they couldn't go anywhere, so our V fled here with the twins to wait it out.'

'Well. That *is* interesting. And did you find anything on old Mrs Diles?'

'Yes, I've got her too. Leonora Diles – she didn't use a pseudonym. She wasn't old at all, though. I found her in Scottish records. She'd only have been about sixty-five when they came here to look after the boys.'

'Don't tell Felicity any of this, okay? She's still having nightmares about those twins. Maybe you could move onto another era now or something?'

'I could, but it's such a good story, isn't it? They're just an unconventional little family, trying to be together.'

For some reason, I felt the blood rush to my face. 'It is a good story, yes.'

His expression turned more serious. 'Listen, Dee,' he said. 'Were you cross about the hidden cemetery? Or did I offend you in some way, giving you that book?'

I looked away.

'It's just, you haven't answered my messages, and I thought maybe the book was all wrong or something. I'm really sorry if it was.'

'The book –' I stared at my hands, 'the book is perfect. It's better than perfect.'

'Well, it's slightly foxed, as they say.'

'Slightly foxed?'

'It's what booksellers call the scuffed-up, spotty pages, you know? A bit worn and battered.'

I felt a pressure inside my chest and I couldn't say any more.

Without any warning, he reached for my hand. Startled by his unexpected touch, I pulled away. His cheeks pinked and he looked down and fiddled with his spoon, crossing and re-crossing his legs. I felt my own face burning. I hadn't meant to yank my hand away – it had been an automatic reaction; I was so unused to being touched by anyone other than children or babies.

We'd never sat facing each other like this before, either. We'd always been walking or sitting on gravestones or with Felicity and a pack of cards or a bunch of letters to distract us. The situation suddenly felt incredibly intense.

Thankfully, our tea and crumpets appeared and we were able to fuss around with them – moving plates, finding space on the tiny round table. The moment of excruciating awkwardness had passed, though I still felt the warmth of his hand on mine. I unfolded the little butter pat, not looking up. I would have to eat fast, as I needed to get back to Felicity.

'You know, before I stop on V and the twins, there's one puzzle I do want to try and solve.' He tapped the spoon against the table. 'The last thing I've got in the archive is a telegram from V to Muriel saying, "Come to Oxford. *Very urgent.*" And that's it. End of correspondence. I want to see if I can find out what happened here in June 1917.'

I'd buttered my crumpets but he hadn't touched his. I pushed his plate towards him. 'They're getting cold.'

'Oh, crumpets!' He looked pleasantly surprised, as if he hadn't been there when we ordered them – as if he hadn't even noticed them arriving. I wondered how he managed to look after himself at all.

'You'll be doing this history for all eternity,' I said, 'if you get into every resident in this much detail. I mean, the Lodging's over 400 years old.' He wasn't listening – he'd become flustered by practicalities, pushing his plate around, trying to organize the teapot, milk jug, cup, saucer, dropping his teaspoon, bumping the table edge with his head as he rose from the floor. It seemed best not to intervene. I smoothed my hair back. I probably looked an absolute mess, but Linklater was not the kind of man who'd notice that, or care. 'Aren't you getting a bit sidetracked?' I said. 'By this one bunch of tenants?'

He looked up from buttering his crumpet. 'The sidetracking's the only thing that makes this work bearable, Dee, at the end of the day.'

'What? I thought you loved all this?'

'God, no. I mean, this is a good one so far, but really the house histories just keep me from my real work.' He slopped tea over the saucer as he lifted the cup.

'Your Oxford tours?'

'What? No. My DPhil.'

'But I thought you already had one?'

'Technically, I'm still working on it.'

'Really? But you've never told me that! You said you weren't part of the University.'

'Well, I'm not really – it's sort of, well, I mean, the research is sort of my own thing now.' He gazed at his plate.

I understood that we had touched on something painful. 'What's it about?'

'Um, well, it's about the comments people have scribbled in the margins of a Milton pamphlet.' His cheeks flushed again. 'It's called "*Critic on the Edge: Marginalia in Milton's* Areopagitica".'

'Marginalia? As in Fermat's last theorem?'

'Yes, yes, exactly! The famous scribble in Diophantus's *Arithmetica*.' He recited Fermat's actual words: '*I have discovered a truly marvellous proof –* '

We finished the quote together: ' *– which this margin is too narrow to contain.*'

For a moment we grinned at each other across the crumpets. Then I felt my face heat up again. I looked away.

'You're not solving Fermat's Last Theorem, are you?' He took a big bite of his crumpet.

'Andrew Wiles did that in 1994,' I mumbled. 'That's why we have the Andrew Wiles Building here; you probably cycle past it every day.'

'Oh yes. Right. That. Of course. So what *are* you working on in that notebook of yours?'

'You'd have to be a mathematician to understand it.'

'Well, Dodgson was a mathematician and I understand his books.'

'Who?'

'Dodgson. Lewis Carroll? He was a Maths don at Christ Church.'

'Right, well, it's not *Alice in Wonderland*, I can tell you that. I'm working on a proof, but don't make me try to explain it.' I stuffed the last of my crumpet into my mouth and swallowed it almost whole. 'Tell me about your thesis instead.' I reached for my tea. I knew I was going to have to get back to the Lodging, I couldn't leave Felicity much longer, but just for a moment more, I wanted to feel like a normal person, sitting in a coffee shop.

'Well, it's about the act of reading, really.' He began to explain and as I watched his face, his bright blue eyes, it was as if someone had turned up the volume and colour in the café, sharpened all the edges, intensified the smells – it felt vertiginous, extraordinary.

'Reading isn't a one-way process,' he was saying. 'It isn't just the author's thoughts pouring into your brain. It's a dialogue between you and the author, and you and all the other readers of the same work, past, present and future. And these reactions *in the moment* are captured in all the scribbles and doodles and outbursts you find in the margins of a book. I found a brilliant one yesterday in a collection of postmodern essays – scrawled down the side of the page: "*You're all cocks. Sort out your lives!*"'

His thesis sounded a bit pointless, but that was pretty much the standard criterion for an Oxford Arts PhD. Perhaps he realized that he needed to talk in order to keep a sense of normality between us. If he did, it worked, because I was already calmer.

I managed to speak again. 'When do you think you'll finish it, then?'

'Well, I suppose that depends on how long it takes to do

the Lodging. The last house history took almost six years.' He grinned. 'It was a work of genius, but . . .'

I gulped the last of my tea. 'Is Nick paying you by the day?'

'Ha, if only. Flat fee. Same as always: £350.'

'You got £350 for six years' work?' I had to laugh, then.

'Ah – yes – *yes* – laugh away, but I do other things too, obviously. There are the tours, the odd gallery assistant shift at the Ashmolean, some godawful American summer schools. My funding ran out years ago, that's the real problem.' He bumped the cup down on its saucer. 'If it wasn't for the small matter of paying the College rent, I'd have finished years ago,' he said.

'Wait – you live in College?' I realized I'd always pictured him in a tiny Victorian flat somewhere up the Cowley Road.

'Well, no – I mean, yes – well, sort of. I've been there since I was a full-time graduate student. I just keep paying the rent and I suppose I've never been flagged up in anyone's system. It's massively cheaper than anything else I'd find in Oxford, that's for sure. I mean, a flat up Banbury Road these days would cost about a million quid. Plus, I've been there twenty-seven years; it's my home.'

'Wait, sorry – are you saying you've been doing the same thesis for *twenty-seven years*?'

'Well, um, kind of. On and off.' He looked a bit glum, then, as his failures crowded in on him.

But I was relieved. He wasn't a failure. Or if he was, then so was I. He was just like me – wandering in that hazy territory between town and gown; a lungful of Oxford diesel, a borrowed gasp of hallowed air.

'Anyway,' he said. 'I should probably crack on. I've got a private ghost tour to do. Hey – why don't you bring Felicity? I'm taking them to the Castle dungeons, there's a 900-year-old crypt down there. I get people believing a little child is brushing past their legs. They get very excited. She'd love it.'

'But it's a private tour?'

'Oh, that's okay, I'll just introduce you as my, um, err, family . . .'

I felt agitated again. I reached for my scarf. 'The last thing Felicity needs right now is more ghosts, Linklater.'

'But she loves ghost stories. I've seen her. Don't all children?'

'She's not like other children. You must have noticed that! She has awful night terrors involving her mother, and also these twins now. She's an incredibly sensitive, incredibly anxious and impressionable child who's suffered a huge loss.' I thought about confessing that I too sometimes felt uneasy in the attic rooms these days, but I knew he wouldn't take me seriously, and nor should he. 'She's just deeply unhappy in that house.'

'Yes.' He nodded. 'And so are you, I think.'

Our eyes met. His expression was so concerned and sympathetic that I found myself feeling exposed all over again – barricades I'd taken decades to construct were crashing down all over the place. Friendship really was exhausting. Fraught. Terrible. No wonder I'd avoided it. I dragged my coat off the back of the chair.

'I think I understand how Felicity feels,' he said.

'I doubt it. Her situation's pretty unique. She's selectively mute, bereaved and bullied, and living in an Oxford College with two narcissists.'

'She's selectively mute?' He frowned. 'What do you mean?'

I was about to express disbelief, when I realized that I'd never actually spelled this out to him. I'd probably just assumed that, as a professional reader between the lines, he'd have worked it out by now. But why on earth would he? She'd started speaking to him so early on.

I tried to explain, then, that Felicity wasn't just shy – that she actually spoke to nobody at all, other than him, me and Nick – though she hardly spoke to Nick these days.

'Seriously? Christ.' He looked genuinely shocked. 'I mean, I knew she was quiet and had trouble making friends, but selectively mute sounds serious. I mean, my God, the poor thing. Was it the shock of losing her mother?'

'People always think children go mute because of a trauma, but actually, that hardly ever happens,' I said. 'Her mother's suicide didn't help, but she's also probably just made this way.'

Linklater looked out onto the High Street at the buses powering by, the students weaving through the traffic on rickety bikes. He suddenly looked a bit forlorn. He'd kept his overcoat on but it was unbuttoned to reveal a shabby jumper that needed mending round the neck, and beneath that the frayed collar of a checked shirt. 'Have you ever been married?' My question surprised me as much as it did him. I hugged my coat and looked for the waitress.

'Oh, good God, no.' He laughed, then stopped. 'Well, almost, once, a long time ago, but she called it off a fortnight before the wedding. She wanted more of an earner, I think. I've steered clear since then, more or less – nobody too serious, anyway. It was all too – you know – just too – well, I suppose I'm not really cut out to withstand that level of pain at the end of the day. I've kind of, you know, stuck my head in the sand on that front, so to speak.' He cleared his throat.

The waitress came with the bill. I took it, but he grabbed it out of my hand. 'No. No, no, no. Jesus, Dee. This is mine.' He got out his wallet, peered at the bill, looked comically shocked, then threw down way too much cash.

I got up and put on my coat. 'Thanks for listening to me.'

His eyes were intense. 'Really, Dee,' he said. 'It is the very greatest pleasure. The *very* greatest.'

I felt joy bloom in my chest.

The sky was darkening as I left the café, but as I crossed the High, past the Examination Schools and down Logic Lane, I was only dimly aware of the rain starting to fall. At my car I stopped. Bits of me were flapping about and I needed to gather the edges back together, sew up all the seams before I could go back into the Master's Lodging to face Nick and Mariah. I climbed in, locked all the doors and sat listening to rain drumming on the roof. All around me, in the gloom, possibilities opened like bright, sudden flowers.

Chapter 39

Khan has not taken her eyes off my face. –Did you damage their priceless wallpaper? she says.

I frown at her. –Did I do what?

–Mrs Law says that you ripped off a large section of her original William Morris wallpaper.

–Are you serious? I cannot keep the incredulity out of my voice. –It was Mariah who damaged that wallpaper!

When I walked through the front door after seeing Linklater in Queen's Lane, I heard Mariah calling my name. Her voice was high and panicky, as if something dire had happened. My first thought was that she'd done something to Felicity. I should never have left them.

I shot up the stairs.

Her room was half-dark, hot and slightly stale – I saw the mass of her belly shrouded in the pale duvet. 'A little boy died here!' Mariah's voice trembled from the bed, close to tears. 'A little boy was murdered in this house!'

I walked over. 'What?'

'That house detective person just phoned – I'd forgotten all about him. He was asking for you, for some reason, he says he's trying your mobile but you won't pick up. Why's he phoning *you*? I was sleeping – he just woke me up and he told me to tell you a little boy was murdered here. A little boy was poisoned in this house! In the First World War! Oh my God, a . . . little . . . *boy*.' Her words dissolved into sobs.

I tried to soothe her. 'Ach, I'm sure lots of people have died here,' I said. 'It's a 400-year-old house.'

The room was boiling and the air smelled sweet and sickly. 'But a child was *murdered here*!' Mariah wailed. 'This is so horrible. So horrible. It makes sense now, the atmosphere in this place. Don't you feel it? You have to!'

I hushed her again. What was Linklater thinking, telling Mariah this disturbing news over the phone – calling the house at all, in fact?

'I just feel – I don't – this is just – I can't—'

I leaned over her bed. 'Shhh, now, Mariah, it's just a daft story – just one among thousands that anyone could pluck out of the Library stacks. Who really knows what happened in this house? Who does? Nobody. Now, don't get yourself in a state, think of your wee baby.' As I looked into her eyes, I had a sense that something else was wrong with her – this was not just the shock of hearing about some little poisoned boy. Her skin looked dank and almost slimy, like paper on a humid bathroom wall. She struggled to sit up. 'I was dreaming,' she babbled. 'When that house detective called, I was having this horrible dream – Ana was outside my room, on the landing out there, tearing up my wallpaper. I could hear her tearing it off the walls. Oh God, I can't bring a baby to this place, I can't, I just can't!'

Late pregnancy can be an unsettling time, with heightened senses, strange sensitivities. 'Now, now,' I said, 'pregnancy dreams are very vivid, it's normal.'

'This doesn't feel normal,' she said in a low voice. Her enormous belly heaved as she got out of bed.

There was something about the way she moved that made me wonder if she could be going into labour. 'Are you having pains?' I asked. She stood in front of me. Her yoga pants were pulled low and her T-shirt had ridden up to reveal an oval of taut white flesh, two eyelids blinking over a sightless albumen. It was still five weeks until this baby was due. She began to lumber towards the door.

'Mariah?' I said. 'Come back and lie down now.'

'I have to check something.'

I followed her onto the landing where she stood running her hands up and down the wallpaper, pressing at the birds and open pomegranates, the tangled green foliage. She began to move her fingers towards the doorframe, instinct taking her to the very spot I'd damaged with Nick's paperknife. Then she started to pick at the spot with her fingernail, ripping at it.

I stepped in front of her and seized her hands. 'Mariah! Stop.' Her breath smelled off, slightly acidic. Her hair was wild – she looked like a patient in a psychiatric ward. I tried to smile, reassuringly, as I took her hands. 'Come and lie back down now, you're not thinking straight. Come on. Let's get you back to bed.'

Her eyes bulged – she tried to wrestle her hands out of mine. 'No. No. No. Let go. Let go of me,' she cried. 'Get off – you're scaring me, Dee, let go!'

Chapter 40

–So, let's just get the timing straight, says Faraday. –This was all happening on the day her baby was born? He glances at Khan. –Childbirth can do funny things to a woman, can't it?

–No, I say. –No. I took her to hospital the next day.

As we drove up Headington Hill, Mariah's face was going grey, and by the time we got to the hospital, her lips were a strange, ethereal blue. She massaged her belly and dialled Nick's number repeatedly, but he had left for Paris early in the morning – just one day after they got back from Hong Kong. He was not due back until the following day, and he wasn't picking up.

When I looked in the rearview mirror, Felicity's fearful eyes stared back at me. I'd had no choice other than to bring her – I'd phoned Nick's office, hoping Sally would be there, but she was in Paris with Nick. I'd phoned the Porter's Lodge, asking them to find Angela – I couldn't, obviously, get Linklater, and I didn't want to wait; Mariah wasn't bleeding but she was uncomfortable, and something told me it wasn't right. So I put Felicity in the back seat of the Fiesta.

She would have been aware of Mariah's growing panic and she certainly must have seen the dark stain on the back of Mariah's long pale cardigan as she got out of the car, and I called for help and a nurse came running. Then the hospital staff were getting Mariah onto a gurney, a young doctor shouting, 'Where are her blue notes?' – everyone moving very fast.

I thought of Nick's expression when he arrived at the hospital an hour and a half after us. His usual self-control had gone and I was faced with a gaunt and panicked being, extravagantly afraid.

He barely acknowledged Felicity, who sat by me, clinging to my hand. 'Where are they? Is she okay? Are they okay?'

I told him, as I had several times already on the phone, that they were in intensive care: Mariah had lost a lot of blood but was stable, and his son, though tiny, was strong and healthy. A nurse led him away. I squeezed Felicity's hand. Her bottom lip wobbled. This was no place for her to wait – I decided to take her back to the house.

But I forgot about the front seat and as she got in, she put her hand on the blood and recoiled, holding it up to me, aghast, like a tiny Lady Macbeth. Her hands began to shake, wavering in the air by her face, but instead of wiping them, instinctively, on something, she stood still, holding them up and staring at me, as if she wanted me to separate her hands from her body.

Back at the empty house, I put Felicity to bed; she was a slow-moving shadow, not speaking, hardly there. I sat with her for a long time, stroking her curls. The usual creaks and groans of the Lodging seemed brief and muted. The whole of the attic floor felt too still, too taut, as if the house was holding its breath, and we were suspended inside its skull. Her freckles seemed so delicate to me, as if fairies had tiptoed across her nose. Her mouth was too large right now, her eyes a little too big, too wide apart, her chin too pointed, but one day she would grow into these features and she would become a striking woman, like Ana.

I thought, then, of my own child's adult face. I could see

in photographs that she was like me around the eyes, though her cheeks were softer, rounder, and her hair straightened and glossy. People always put happy pictures on social media, but Rosie did look happy – and she still had two dimples by her mouth when she smiled. Although her hair was once black and wild like Felicity's, their characters were different in so many ways. Even as the tiniest thing, Rosie was a robust and solid buccaneer, pink-cheeked, toddling by her first birthday, swash-buckling the furniture, galloping on my knee. I made mistakes, I know that – what new mother hasn't? But neither of us deserved what we got.

I heard a floorboard creak in the doorway behind me, and turned my head. Nobody was there of course, but even so, I felt observed, and disapproved of.

Outside Felicity's window, I heard heels clacking on the cob-bles, and the vulpine yelps of students returning to their halls of residence. Everything in Felicity's world had changed yet again, and not for the better. In the attic corridor – or perhaps on the stairs – I heard the tap-tap-tap of a contracting pipe, and it sounded like rapid little footsteps running up and past the room. Somewhere further down in the house, I thought I heard a door softly close.

Chapter 41

–Did Felicity give you any indication she was unhappy when this new baby arrived? Faraday asks. –Was she distressed? Withdrawn? That sort of thing?

–Well, yes, I say. –Of course. It definitely hasn't been easy for her.

Felicity did not take well to her brother. His screaming was a torment for her – the pitch and volume of it, the tension in his small, tight body as he passed from room to room, up and down the stairs, round the garden. It didn't help that Mariah guarded him jealously whenever Felicity was around, clutching him to her as if she was a predator come to snatch him. The situation was disastrous – as I had always known it would be.

They brought him home after just ten days in the hospital. He was remarkably healthy, if teeny, with raw, peeling skin, though it no longer had the same translucence as when he'd first been born. He was in fine fettle, unlike his mother. She was still physically weak from the birth, of course, but there was a new fragility about her, too. I would find her sometimes, struggling to feed him bottles of expressed milk – she had the liminal, haunted look women get when they have come face to face with their own mortality.

He screamed, a lot. All night, every night, his mechanical cries – 'alas, alas' – rang through the floorboards and I'd lie in the attic room wondering if she wanted me to go down and rescue her – change his nappy, feed him her expressed milk, do something – anything – to make him stop. Sometimes I did go, and with tears streaming down her face she would hold the poor mite out to me; a writhing, sweaty package, cheeks puce, eyes screwed up, fontanelle bulging. But then she'd come and take him back, just minutes later, as if she couldn't trust me to keep him alive.

Nick became spectacularly absent, both day and night. Hilary term was underway and he often slept in College, leaving Mariah to deal with the baby alone. I couldn't go down every night – I had to draw a line somewhere. I was determined to put Felicity first, even if it now suited everyone to forget that particular detail of our agreement.

After a few weeks of this Mariah was obviously beginning to unravel. It had been a struggle for her even to sit up at first, then the caesarean stitches became infected and she was in a lot of pain, oozing pus and on antibiotics. She developed mastitis and I had to make her poultices, feed her ibuprofen, help her with the breast-pump. A colicky infant can turn even the most glamorous Scandinavian into a ragged lunatic, and she wandered the corridors with her unwashed hair hanging lank around her puffy-eyed face; her spongy stomach draped over sick-stained yoga pants. She burst into tears frequently. Angela brought meals as usual, but she only ate the sweet things – cakes, cookies, chocolate puddings. Sometimes I'd walk into a room to find her staring vacantly at her screaming baby as he writhed, hungry, on a blanket. But she was always reluctant for me to take him away, as if he was a hideous, unruly part of her, manifest, but still attached.

I found it relatively easy to detach myself from the screaming, which took up hours of every day, but the sound was torture for Mariah. Every corner of the house was filling up with her despair – and I understood this. A mother tunes into her baby's cries on a frequency that others cannot possibly comprehend.

Nick was out most evenings, powering through Hilary term. He moved the entertaining over to College since it was not possible to have alumni cocktail parties, entertain the rowing squad, or hold committee meetings in a house haunted by rhythmic howling, and, after the knocker had woken the baby too many times, he got Sally to pin a laminated note to the front door, redirecting unknowing visitors to the Porter's Lodge. Consequently, in those early weeks the Master's Lodging was a cauterized wound. Nobody came.

Given that I was going out of my way to help Mariah, I'd assumed they'd shelved their plans to get rid of me. It therefore came as quite a shock to find out that they had not.

One morning a few weeks after the birth, as I was making Felicity's porridge, they came into the kitchen midway through a discussion about the Shakespeare tickets – that date was looming, just a fortnight away. Nick was saying he'd have to be in London that night too: the Bitcoin billionaire was arriving from Hong Kong to finalize the endowment. The timing was awful, he knew that; he'd tried to move it, but the donor was only in London for one night and wanted both a dinner in Knightsbridge and a meeting in the City the next day with lawyers at 6.30 a.m. before he flew to St Andrews for a spot of golfing.

'I really don't mind not going to *Richard III*,' I said. 'That's not a problem.'

They both looked at me, briefly, then carried on talking to each other. In a flat voice, Mariah said he should go to his meeting. 'You can't lose £5 million because of me. It's hardly the first night I've been on my own here, my God, Nick.'

'I know that, darling, but I haven't left you with Felicity as well, without Dee. I don't like that. Felicity's not doing very well right now, either, is she?'

'She's never doing well!' Mariah cried.

'Look, Dee just said she'll stay. I'll get Sally to rebook the hotel and get the theatre seats for another night.'

'No, Nick!' Mariah said. 'Didn't you hear me? No, no, no. I'm not a baby! I don't need anyone to stay here with me.'

'But—' Nick started to argue, gingerly, that it wasn't necessary for her to be alone with Felicity too.

I thought I heard Felicity's footsteps on the stairs so I stepped out into the hall. I did not want her walking into this.

Behind me, I heard Mariah hiss. 'I can't stand being stuck in here with her watching me all the time – like I'm doing it all wrong, like I'm a terrible mother because I can't stop him crying and I can't feed him properly. I can't do anything right.'

'Isn't she helping you with him?'

'It's not that!' Her voice was shrill. 'I can't explain it, Nick, I just don't – I have a bad feeling all the time – when she holds him, I feel so tense, you know, so worried, even though I'm desperate for someone to take him.'

'I think new mothers always feel that way about their babies, my darling. Ana would hardly let anyone so much as look at Felicity – even me—'

'Ana was mentally ill!' Mariah was close to tears. 'That's not what I'm saying, why can't you listen to me?'

'You're not used to being at home all the time, darling; it's probably hard to adjust to that.'

'Stop calling me darling. Stop talking to me like I'm a child. Listen to me.'

'I am listening to you. You're exhausted, and I've not been here for you enough. I'm so sorry, my poor darling.'

'I'm not your fucking poor darling!' she screamed. The baby woke up, and gave a high, thin wail.

There was a pause.

Nick's voice grew muffled, presumably as he took his son. 'I'm worried about you, Mari. I really think you need to talk to the doctor: hormones, and no sleep can be—'

'I'm not mad!' she bellowed over the howling. 'Don't say these things to me!'

I hurried upstairs to head Felicity off.

Later that day, Angela was in the kitchen. Since their Hong Kong trip she had been even more stiff with me, but this time when I came in, she turned with a smile. 'Leaving us, then, are you?' She was holding a plate of lemon tarts, each one decorated with a curl of rind.

'I've just got in.' I put my shopping down. I could hear the baby's cries floating down the stairwell.

'I don't mean that. I mean *leaving* leaving. I hear the Master's looking for a new nanny.' She slid the tarts into the fridge.

'Well, you hear wrong,' I said. 'I'm not going anywhere.'

As I put away the ingredients for the honey cake I had planned to make for Felicity, I felt shaken, as if someone had whispered in my ear the date of my own execution.

His absenteeism – given his supposed concerns for Mariah's mental health – really was remarkable. And it was not just Mariah he'd failed to support. He had spent almost no time alone with Felicity since his son was born – he'd not once put her to bed or played chess or gone for a walk round the garden with her. Whenever he was in the Lodging, he was dealing with his screaming infant and rapidly unspooling wife. Mariah, meanwhile, had no patience with Felicity any more. She was liable to lash out for the tiniest infraction – shoes in the hall, a book bag on the kitchen floor, not eating her peas, or eating her peas too slowly, coming downstairs too fast, or not fast enough.

I'd seen other parents go through this – they were not the first and wouldn't be the last – but it was clear that Mariah was neither a safe nor reliable pair of hands.

My strategy, as ever, was to keep Felicity out of the house as much as I could. I took her to Queen's Lane almost every day after school, and Linklater often joined us.

The first time we met as a threesome after the baby's birth, he waited until Felicity went to the loo then said he hoped his account of the poisoned child had not put Mariah into labour. He looked genuinely worried. 'Your stories are excellent, Linklater,' I said. 'But even you can't cause a placenta to detach.'

He looked relieved. 'I was phoning for you. I might have been a bit over-excited.'

'Okay, well – tell me quickly – which child was poisoned?'

'Duncan.'

'Oh no.'

'Yup, he was six. There was a huge scandal – it's quite extraordinary – wait for it: Mrs Diles did it.'

He stopped. Felicity was coming back towards the table.

'Shall we play Old Maid?' I said.

After that we ate crumpets, drank hot chocolate and played a lot of card games – Snap, Happy Families, Gin Rummy, Racing Demon.

Of course, the baby's colic would stop eventually, Mariah would start to sleep again and the trauma of the birth would fade with its scars; she'd return to her personal trainer, her designer dresses and heels. Nick would reopen the Lodging doors and they would emerge intact with their beautiful son – the flawless family. But Felicity would always be left to one side, the unwanted extra – troubled, like her mother, liable to spoil their image.

But it would be impossible to explain any of this to Faraday and Khan. To them, this would just sound like the normal adjustment process of a blended family welcoming a colicky newborn.

–Felicity definitely felt marginalized, I say. –Nick wasn't around and Mariah has been hard on her. Mariah's been very edgy, not at all stable. It's been a really difficult time for Felicity.

Khan scribbles this down and Faraday nods. –And what about you? Were you able to be there for her? This sounds like way more than a full-time job.

I tell them that I don't have much of a social life.

This is true. I almost never went out in the evening. I only went to Linklater's rooms for the first time quite recently, in fact.

His rooms were on the top floor of a mammoth Gothic revival house set back from the Banbury road in a gravel forecourt. At first sight it looked ludicrously posh, but up close the burgundy front door and the rack of bicycles clearly signalled College ownership. There was no *Linklater* on any of the buzzers – the top bell was marked *H.L. Birdy*, which made me smile. I'd looked him up, of course. He might have teased me, but I did in fact know how to operate Google. I could see why he might feel that people would take him more seriously if he went by his middle name.

I rang *Birdy*, keeping my finger pressed down as a February wind swept up the drive and cut through my fleece. My ungloved hands were stiff and the bottle of Merlot I'd picked up in Tesco threatened to slip onto the cracked porch tiles. I could hear faint, hysterical violin music floating from a high window. Eventually, I gave up and pressed the bell below *Birdy*; its resident, *Kuznetsov*, buzzed me in without query.

I found myself in a spacious entryway that smelled of Dettol, with a fire escape plan on the wall above a set of well-stuffed pigeonholes. As I climbed up the echoing stairwell, the violin grew louder, and by the time I reached the top floor it was blaring. I bashed on the door but of course he couldn't hear me. Eventually, in a pause, I was able to bark, 'Linklater!' There was a scrabbling sound, a thud, a yelp of pain, and the door was flung open.

He seemed to have blow-dried his hair; it stood up in a disconcerting halo. I smelled shampoo and shaving foam as I stepped past him and a whiff of not-unpleasant soap or aftershave. I was about to say hello but the violin music started again.

I probably should have been prepared for his rooms, but the disarray was positively majestic. The entire floor, and every surface, was cluttered with books and papers and files. The low ceilings sloped on both sides of a dormer window beneath which sat a sofa stacked with books. A bunting of mismatched socks hung along an old column radiator and I realized that what at first sight I'd taken for a large table was actually a battered baby grand, taking up about a third of the room. That, too, was covered in books, files and papers. Behind the piano, just, I could make out a low double bed piled with clothes and more books, but you'd have to climb under or over the piano to get to it. The bookshelves were crammed – books two deep, upside down, sideways, back to front.

Linklater scrambled back across the room to turn the record player down, then faced me beaming. I smelled burning. There was a smoky haze coming from a kitchenette to my left. He sniffed the air. 'Oh shite.' He scrambled back over the debris.

I followed him into the kitchenette where he was peering into a pan. The smoke alarm hung slack-jawed on the ceiling above him, its battery removed. In a surprisingly agile, muscular move, he hopped onto the draining board and cracked open the top window. A pineapple sat in the sink, balanced on a stack of dishes.

When he was down again, I handed him the wine. I'd brought it out of politeness, but was beginning to think that I might need a glass.

'Tesco's Finest. Marvellous.' He opened and closed drawers.

'It's a screw top.'

'So it is, so it is.' He located a wine glass on the toaster and another in the sink, waved them both somewhere near the cold tap, filled them to the rim and handed me one. Our eyes met and I was struck, not for the first time, by what a pleasant blue they were – not Covered Market cornflowers after all, but the colour of the Galloway sky in full summer. He raised his glass and his right eye opened a little wider than the left. 'You look, um . . . really . . . um . . . Did you, um, do something to your – you look—' He waved a hand towards my head, flushed and took a slug of wine. 'Delicious.' I wasn't sure if he meant the wine or me.

No man had noticed my hair for years – not that I was aware of, anyway. It used to attract plenty of attention when I was young and it was a cascade of auburn curls. So did the rest of me, in fact. Men would shout lewd things at me as I walked down Edinburgh streets behind the other girls, who took this as evidence that I was giving out all the wrong signals. Linklater's gaze, thankfully, was much more gentle.

I had, in fact, popped into the hairdresser after I'd dropped

Felicity at school that morning. It was the first time I'd set foot in one for years, and I was pleasantly surprised at how it came out. The price tag, on the other hand, was monstrous, so I wouldn't be troubling them again. I bumped into Mariah on the landing as I was heading out. 'Oh my God!' For a moment she sounded almost like her old vivacious self. 'You look amazing! Do you have a date?'

'I'm just meeting a friend.' As I zipped up my fleece, I quelled the urge to go back upstairs and stick my head under the tap.

'So . . . um, how's the baby and things?' Linklater cleared his throat. 'Any better?'

'Still loud. Still tiring.'

He shook his head, as if babies were a cause of grave concern, which, of course, this one was – but I didn't want to talk about the baby – not yet. 'So, tell me about this poisoning,' I said.

His face lit up. 'Christ, Dee, I've got so much to show you – fascinating stuff, honestly. I've found newspaper clippings from 1917 about little Duncan's murder. It was a proper Oxford scandal. Dreadful business.' He seized a can from the countertop, ripped the ring pull and tumbled olives into a pea-green bowl, the kind found in College refectories. He held it out, I waved it away, he took one himself, then another, then three more, chewing fast. 'They aren't actually very good.' He peered into the bowl. 'Bit plasticky – I didn't have time to go to a deli – shall I stick some Tabasco on them?'

'Why don't you show me the newspaper clippings?' I suggested.

He managed to locate a laptop and a couple of files from the carnage and gestured for me to take the space he cleared by straightening his arm and sweeping everything from that patch of sofa onto the floor. He hummed, rather tunefully, as he opened up his computer. I noticed a collection of vinyl next to a record player and a dying fern. He favoured classical violin music, jazz, and a few bands I vaguely associated with the 1980s. I'd never embraced music myself. As a teenager all I'd really cared about was maths, but Thelonius Monk once said that all musicians are subconsciously mathematicians, so perhaps Linklater and I were more alike than we seemed.

I picked up the sleeve of the record that Linklater had been playing. He nodded at it. 'Schumann killed himself after he wrote that – the violinist he wrote it for thought it was cursed and gave it to the Prussian State Library with instructions that nobody could play it for a hundred years. But Schumann's grand-nieces had a séance where Schumann, rather handily, appeared to them and told them they must perform it in public –'

His capacity for sidetracking when nervous was appealing, but potentially limitless. He could never have been a mathematician. His mind was interesting, but it had no discipline. I took a sip of wine. It was excellent. I took another long sip. I had quite forgotten that I like wine, even a £6.99 Tesco Merlot. I interrupted him eventually. 'So, come on then: Mrs Diles?'

'Ah, right! Yes, well, brace yourself.' He thrust a photocopy at me. 'That's the *Oxford Chronicle* from 1917.'

POISONED CHILD, SUSPECT IN CUSTODY!

I scanned the article.

'She poisoned Duncan's shortbread?' I pushed it aside. 'Seriously? That's a wee bit far-fetched, isn't it?'

'Well, actually, there was a case not long before this where a man and his housekeeper died from eating arsenic shortbread sent by an enemy – though if you're foolish enough to eat anything your enemy sends you – but anyway, there's actually a very solid theory that people used to poison each other a lot in those days. Arsenic was fairly easy to get hold of and it looks a lot like sugar – you can just bake it into a biscuit or stick it in a cup of tea and it sort of shimmies round the body like an infectious disease and then—'

I cut in. 'But why would Mrs Diles kill Duncan? Even if he was a maladjusted pain in the neck, it's a bit extreme, isn't it?'

'Quite. Here—' He handed me more murder trial cuttings.

In all of them, Mrs Diles was portrayed as ugly, bestial, bolshy, superstitious and cunning. She appeared to have entered a well-established club made up of women throughout history, young and old, who have unconventional opinions and no desire to please anyone other than themselves. Mrs Diles was a witch – and the witch must burn.

Linklater shook his head. 'They hanged her for it.'

'Of course they did.'

'Maybe she did poison little Duncan – he was the naughtiest twin, wasn't he? Remember there was that letter where V says Mrs Diles put him in the priest's hole as punishment?'

'I do.'

'But we also know there was damp in the attic at that time, don't we, so if she did that a lot, or if he used to sneak in there himself—' He took his glasses off and rubbed his eyes. He looked naked without the protection of the smeared lenses; younger too. 'I mean, sadly I don't, um, have children of my own, but Mrs Diles was V's childhood nanny; V would have known her incredibly well. If Mrs Diles was dangerous, then surely V would know it – and no mother would leave her little boys with someone she'd even the slightest doubt about, would she?'

I thought of all the loving parents over the years who had left their little ones with me on the strength of a brief interview and a few words of recommendation from people they'd never met. I could have done anything, taken their children anywhere, been anyone at all. None of them were even aware that I had a criminal record. That level of trust, when you think about it, really is delusional. 'You'd be surprised,' I said to Linklater, 'what parents do when they urgently need childcare.'

As I refilled our glasses, I found myself telling him that Felicity sometimes let herself into the priest's hole at night. I found myself telling him about everything then – the bad smells and broken chairs, her forays into my room, her attempts to protect us both with witch hexes and salt bowls; her night terrors; that I'd had to change the priest's hole lock to stop her going in there.

'Poor child.' He shook his head. 'And poor you, too.'

I went on, then, telling him more about Nick and Mariah, and as I talked I drank, and by the end of it I was quite animated. Linklater, it turned out, was an excellent listener, and – whether loosened by the drink or the quality of his attention, I could not seem to stop talking.

He asked how I came to be a nanny in the first place, and I told him – briefly – about the lorry hitting my father's van, and how I came down to London soon after.

In fact, that is a dark period of my life that I usually try to forget. I rented a miserable room in Hounslow and worked at a call-centre, taking some night shifts as a carer, too – since I hardly slept any more, it would have been silly to waste time lying in bed. I met my first client in an Ealing playground where I used to eat my lunch. She was desperate – a single working mother who needed someone to pick up her four-year-old son from nursery. When I said I'd help her out, she offered me a rent-free room. I stayed with her for almost a year before she moved abroad. She knew an American who was coming for two terms to Oxford University with a four-month-old baby; the American, a Middle English professor, had been allocated a two-bedroom College flat and could also offer me rent-free accommodation.

At first I found it uncomfortable to push a pram past Oxford students who were only a few years younger than me. As I passed libraries, Porters' Lodges and halls of residence, I'd look away, afraid to glimpse the ghost of the person I almost became: erudite, high-flying, fulfilled.

Eventually, though, I mapped a different Oxford – one of parks and swings, duck feeding, community centres, church halls, messy play. And since the flat was full of books, I began to read again. The American's sabbatical ended, but she'd heard about a visiting lecturer from Rome whose toddler had special needs. The Italian had no space for a nanny so I rented a room in the North Oxford home of a retired mathematician, a hoarder with five cats and rooms stuffed with mathematical journals and texts, which I began to work my way through: despite everything that had happened, it took very little to reignite my passion for maths. Oxford clients came and went and I was never out of work. I'd grown up self-sufficient, cooking and cleaning from a very young age, and I was surprised by how chaotic these families could be, how delighted they were when someone imposed a modicum of order. Perhaps high-achieving academics make hapless parents – or perhaps my clients were particularly disorientated and displaced.

I was only ever asked for a police check once, and when that happened, I found an alternative employer.

I had no desire for a life of my own – I'd tried that and it had almost destroyed me. Using my landlady's library login, I began to download journals and books and to study in earnest, focusing only on areas that interested me. I did not want to enter formal education – even if I could have brought myself to reapply to the University, it seemed far too late. I was no longer the naive young girl from rural Scotland who'd once been offered a place to study at the finest university in the world.

It did not feel like a relief to tell Linklater about this, even in the sketchiest of terms. As I talked, I felt the frustration and sadness building inside me again. These what-ifs only ever brought chaos. Open any door in my head and you'd find a room crowded with guilt and regret – and in each room a grate in which embers of self-destruction smoulder, ready to flare and burn.

I suggested to Linklater that we open a third bottle of wine. 'Let's go mad,' he said. 'A friend of mine's Keeper of the Wine in College – they've got half a million pounds worth of fine wines down there, but who cares: we've got Tesco.'

The later part of the evening does get a bit hazy. We talked about Scotland. I remember us looking at Google Maps together. I also have a fleeting memory of showing him @stepmomslament – he said the lack of apostrophe made it hard to take seriously. Then he reached out to tuck a strand of hair behind my ear. And I panicked. I pulled away and staggered to my feet, asking where the loo was.

'I have to go,' I said. 'I can't stay here all night talking nonsense with you.'

I have an image of his face falling – the confusion in his eyes.

I counted sixty-seven copies of the *TLS* and twenty-three rolls of toilet paper in his tiny bathroom. Each roll had been started, but not finished.

Chapter 42

I woke in my own bed at dawn the next day, roused by the sound of a delivery van reversing down the lane towards the Porter's Lodge. I experienced a rush of elation, followed by a sickening headache and a clutch of shame. Many years ago I had made the decision not to drink alcohol again. I had let myself down. My head throbbed, my mouth was dry, the baby's wails rattled through the floorboards; the evening came back to me in fragments.

I remembered leaving Linklater's rooms in the early hours and almost falling down the stairwell; insisting, repeatedly, that I wasn't a child, I wouldn't be walked anywhere – then I was weaving down St Giles' past the Lamb & Flag where Hardy wrote *Jude* and Morse drank real ale. I have a fleeting memory of dithering at Martyrs' Memorial and then I was halfway down Broad Street, teetering along a wide, deserted, sepia wasteland. I recall staring at a lamppost outside Balliol on which a tattered poster heralded a student production of *Dracula* and thinking – perhaps not entirely logically – that this was a bizarre coincidence, since Oscar Wilde, when at Balliol – or Magdalen? – had been engaged to the woman who would later marry Bram Stoker. And I turned to tell Linklater that the whole of English literature was one big Oxford cocktail party, but of course he wasn't there; I had refused to let him walk me.

As I wove through the heart of the city, my head swarmed with connections, quotations, footnotes and circularities – every last one of them placed there by Linklater. I remembered him saying once that virtually every stone in Oxford has had a poem written about it.

As I passed the Sheldonian, the bearded stone heads seemed to swivel their eyes to follow my progress, and then I was standing outside the Bodleian, scanning the slatted windows for the ghost of Charles I, who paced the stacks at night, pulling out books. I remember marvelling at the thought of all the book tunnels that stretched beneath the city – a honeycomb of ancient, subterranean stacks, vaults and chambers – and thinking that these effectively formed another plane: that Oxford was two worlds, one superimposed on the other. Then I remembered when Linklater took us into the Bodleian book tunnels and told us we were standing on the site of a gruesome murder – and that the weapon had been a heavy iron Gladstone bookshelf. When he noticed our stricken faces, he grinned. 'In a crime novel.'

I remember being in the alley by St Mary's, under the Narnia streetlamp, staring at the bronze lion's head door knocker which Linklater insisted was the inspiration for Aslan, then wandering down Magpie Lane, looking for, but not finding, Prudence.

It struck me that I had only known Linklater for a fraction of the time I'd lived in Oxford, but he had altered my perception of the city for ever; it was a richer, more interesting and layered place now. But I still did not belong in it.

When I put my key in the Lodging door, it wouldn't open. The lock turned, but the door remained shut. I tried and tried again – rattled the knob – flummoxed, thinking I was going to have to walk all the way back to Linklater's rooms again – but then I heard the heavy bolt glide and Nick was looming in a burgundy dressing gown with a tasselled belt. I started to speak but he raised a finger and nodded at his shoulder, where the baby was draped like a dead rabbit. I stumbled up the front step, righted myself and tiptoed past them. I felt Nick's eyes on me as I took off my boots, steadying myself on the wood panel. I recall noticing the grandfather clock: it was almost half past three.

Linklater sent me a text as I was falling into bed.

Did you make it? I wish you'd let me walk you.

YES, I wrote, and switched off my Nokia.

Nick was in the kitchen early the next morning. He must have been pacing the house all night because his eyes were hollow, his skin the colour of cheese rind. He had a minimalist sense of humour at the best of times, but was obviously not amused by my late-night return. The baby was still on his shoulder, asleep and sweaty-looking, bud-mouth open, as if he'd only recently howled himself into oblivion.

'I didn't expect you up so early,' Nick said, acidly.

'A delivery van woke me.'

'Yes, twenty-five cases of wine for the College cellar. Possibly not what you want to think about at this moment.'

I went to the sink and filled a water glass.

'By the way,' said Nick. 'Mariah just told me that before she went into labour she heard from that house detective chap, something about a dead child. She says it upset her.'

'Oh?'

'Yes, apparently he phoned her up to tell her. She says he sounded excitable. Has he been bothering you at all? I'm afraid I don't know much about him, but if he's one of those nutty, would-be academics who is going to start pestering us, then—'

Perhaps because I was not thinking too clearly, I instinctively leaped to Linklater's defence. 'I believe he's very well-respected in Oxford. In fact, I believe you two were graduate students here at the same time.'

I suppose I wanted to show Nick that Linklater was of his intellectual calibre, and not to be dismissed as a 'would-be' anything. It was childish and stupid, and I regretted the words the instant they came out of my mouth.

Nick looked surprised. 'What? Dr Linklater? No, I don't think so.'

I said nothing. My head was thumping. I felt sick.

'What's his first name?'

'I have no idea,' I muttered.

Nick frowned. 'Linklater . . .' I could almost hear the names spooling through his memory banks. There was a pause, then he barked, 'Not Birdy?' The baby's head snapped up; he pushed it back down. 'You have to be kidding me. It's not Linklater Birdy, is it? What was his first name – something daft and literary. Dickens . . . No, Hardy! Hardy L. Birdy? It's not Nerdy Birdy, is it? It can't be.' He gave the laugh of a man who had never failed at anything in his life. 'You're not telling me I've hired *Nerdy Birdy* to do the history of the Master's Lodging?'

'Well, I don't know if it's—' I began to backtrack, but he wasn't listening.

'But no, it can't be Birdy. The house detective I hired lives in College accommodation on Banbury Road, I remember noticing the address. Birdy can't possibly still live in College accommodation – I heard he never even finished his thesis.'

'I really don't think—'

But Nick wasn't listening to me. His massive brain was still flicking through its deep storage. 'If he *is* still in College rooms, then Richard Nailor needs a good kick up the arse.'

'Who's Richard Nailor?' My head spun.

'My bloody Domestic Bursar.'

I drank some water, then, and wondered if I might throw up.

Chapter 43

–You must have been under a lot of pressure, Dee, says Faraday. –What with Mariah behaving erratically, and the new baby, and Felicity in a bad way?

–Well, it's my job, I can handle it.

–Can you though, Dee? Khan's voice is quiet and low; her sharp features are alert and she is terribly still, like a fox encountered in a dead-end alley. –Can we talk about that William Morris wallpaper you vandalized. Why did you do that?

This is totally not what I am expecting.

–Okay, I put both hands flat on the tabletop. –I don't know what Mariah's been saying to you, but she's the one who attacked that wallpaper, not me. I admit that I once stumbled when I was carrying a knife and I took a tiny piece away, just the tiniest piece, but I fixed it. I certainly did not tear those strips off it. She did that.

Faraday comes in then with weird and unconvincing empathy. –The size of the damage doesn't really matter, Dee. Perhaps your frustrations with this family just boiled over? I wouldn't blame you if they did.

Mariah must have told them that I tore her wallpaper, in order to cover up her own dangerous instability.

I saw how bad she was the evening I went to meet Linklater in the Turf Tavern. He had phoned the day after our night in his rooms, hesitant and awkward, making a stammering suggestion that we meet at the Turf. I said I couldn't leave Felicity for the second night in a row. He suggested the following evening. 'I think we should, um, finish that conversation,' he said, cryptically. 'I really think we need to. Don't we?'

I agreed, though I had no idea what conversation he meant. The entire night felt unfinished to me.

The evening I was due to meet him, I came down from the attic and found Mariah on the landing with her back to me. She was scrabbling at the wall with her fingernails. There was no sign of the baby. I stopped at the bottom of the attic stairs. 'Mariah? What are you doing?'

She turned and held out her hands. A strip of wallpaper draped through her fingertips like a piece of flayed skin. Paper flakes were scattered around her bare toes.

'What have you done?' I said.

Her shrill voice made me jump. 'She's ripped this whole section – it's ruined!' She muttered something that was probably Danish and stared at me with bloodshot eyes. 'It's not a nightmare – my God – it's real. *She's here.*'

I walked towards her, holding out my hands, but she backed away, pressing her spine against the ruined wall.

The spot she'd attacked was exactly where I'd had the accident with the paperknife – only it was bigger now. A whole pomegranate had been shredded in half.

'Who's here?' I said, as calmly as possible.

'Ana!'

'Mariah.' I stepped closer. 'Ana's not here. Ana's dead.'

'I know! She's dead because of us!'

'But it's not your fault. She was very ill.'

'Oh no, Dee. That's wrong. It was our fault. We could have stopped her.' Her eyes filled up with tears and she stared down at the wallpaper fragments in her hands.

'What do you mean? How could you have stopped her?' I stepped forwards. I had always felt that Mariah and Nick were demonstrating that they were obsessively in love in order to prove – or justify – something, though since the baby came that seemed to be coming apart. Mariah turned back to the wall, picking and pressing the paper, muttering to herself in Danish.

I try to explain all this to Khan but she just says, in the same sinister and emotionless voice, –Dr and Mrs Law say it was you who tore up that wallpaper.

–Why on earth would I do that?

–Because you were angry with them, bitter, resentful. They were about to fire you.

–Oh, for God's sake! Mariah's the one having a psychotic post-partum breakdown, not me.

–Are you sure about that, Dee?

An image of myself on the landing with the paperknife flashes through my head. I won't tell Khan, for obvious reasons, that perhaps my little torn section is what triggered Mariah's para-noia about Ana.

I got Mariah back into her room, then I phoned Nick, who was in his College offices, and told him he had to come back to the house immediately. I said Mariah seemed to be hallucinating and she needed him, and I couldn't be there because I was going out. I hung up before he could ask any questions. I ran up and checked on Felicity again – thank goodness she was fast asleep. I would try not to be long. I waited by the front door with my coat on until I heard Nick's key in the lock, and I stepped out as he barged in. 'She's upstairs,' I said. 'The baby's been fed. She's in bed. She's been seeing Ana's ghost and tearing up her own wallpaper.'

I was almost an hour late by the time I got to the Turf, but Linklater was waiting for me, his long legs crammed under a corner table by the crowded bar. After what had just happened, the sight of him nursing a pint in the warm, dimly lit pub filled me with relief. I realized that things between us weren't confused at all. They were beautifully simple.

He leaped up, beaming, and began pushing through the bodies to get to me, ducking so he didn't hit his head on the low beams. I wondered if he was about to kiss me on the lips but he hesitated, no doubt remembering my sharp exit from his rooms, and pulled me into a strong hug. I smelled his musty overcoat, his shaving soap and his laundered shirt. 'Wine? Beer? Spirits? Food?' He moved back. I told him to sit down and save the table while I got the drinks in.

I ordered myself a large glass of Merlot – at this point it would have felt unreasonable not to drink alcohol – and another pint of Abbot for him.

'You look . . .' He glanced at me as I put the drinks down on the sticky tabletop. 'Ah . . . You look . . .' He waved a hand in my general direction. I'd clipped up my hair earlier, and had also grabbed Mariah's green cashmere wrap as I left the Lodging. It struck me that he might be on the verge of offering a compliment. 'You look . . . um . . .' He lost his nerve. 'Dee, are you okay?' I wriggled out of the cashmere.

The pub was noisy and hot and we had to lean in to hear one another. I told him what had just happened.

'Did you ever Google Ana's death?' He got out a battered device and tapped at it, then passed me the screen. On it was an article from the BBC website reporting on the inquest. The reporter ignored her career as a bookshop owner and poet, and referred to her as the 'wife of senior BBC executive Nick Law' who, aged forty-three, had taken her own life after suffering from bipolar disorder for many years. She died 'from a number of cuts to both wrists'.

'I assume they were having an affair and Ana found out,' he said.

'Well, Mariah obviously feels very guilty. She genuinely believes she's come back to destroy the wallpaper.'

'People see ghosts because they need to see them.' He sighed. 'I've learned that from my Spook Trail. After virtually every tour someone hangs back and tells me exactly where, when and how they've seen their dead husband, or beloved mother, or tragically lost child. It's heartbreaking in a way, but maybe it's comforting, for them.'

'Well, I don't think Mariah's comforted. I think knowing a little boy was poisoned in the Lodging has sort of pushed her over the edge.'

'I should stop this house history,' he said. 'I'll just tell them I'm not doing it any more.'

I waved a hand. 'The house history's neither here nor there.'

He looked uncertain.

'Mariah's just exhausted, Linklater,' I said, 'she's totally over-whelmed by the baby and College and all the pressure she's been under trying to make this life work. She needs help but she's not our problem.'

'Oh?'

'No, I don't care about Mariah. It's the effect she has on Felicity that I care about.'

'I know.' He nodded vigorously. 'You told me everything the other night, remember?'

I glanced over my shoulder. Oxford is, in essence, a village and it definitely would not do to be overheard. I knew that I was going to have to tell him about my conversation with Nick, but I couldn't quite bring myself to start. I felt I'd betrayed him, in some way, even though I'd been trying to defend him. All I could hope was that Nick would be too busy to follow up on it.

'So, you're off to London the day after tomorrow?' He wobbled his glass, turning it in circles.

A bunch of rugby players was laughing and drinking and bellowing next to my ear – some of their heads actually touched the low-beamed ceiling. I drained my wine. The ceiling seemed to lower an inch.

Linklater shimmied to the bar to get me another, and as I sat alone with the hubbub, I felt depleted, like a climber huddled in a bivouac while an ice storm raged. I'd been working my way towards a summit through thin oxygen for months in challenging weather conditions and now I somehow had to gather my last reserves for the final push.

There was a bleach stain on the breast of my shirt, I noticed, like a teardrop of milk, as well as some tiny, priceless flakes of William Morris wallpaper. I brushed them off.

Linklater was back, putting another large Merlot in front of me along with two packets of sweet chilli crisps and some pork scratchings. He wove behind me – his cheeks were rosy, his eyes bright in the gloom. 'Thing is,' he sat down, 'I know what it feels like to be Felicity in this scenario – I know what it's like to be the unwanted stepchild.'

'Do you?'

'My stepmother disliked me intensely.'

'Yes, you said she was difficult.'

'Not just difficult, an awful human being, truly – though sadly not clever enough to be interesting with it. When my mum died, she got her teeth into my dad within a month, and he didn't know what hit him. She was his secretary.'

'What was your mum like?'

He looked startled, as if nobody had ever asked him this before. 'Oh, she was lovely. Quite cultured, and very funny. She had no formal education at all – she left school at fifteen – but she used to take me to plays and art galleries and stuff. She was very, um, affectionate. My dad was different. He's not a bad man, but he was – well, is – quite weak, ground down by life, I suppose. Doesn't really approve of the arts – or me, come to that.' He looked at the ceiling and gulped his beer. 'But anyway, what I'm saying is, I get what it might feel like to be Felicity in this scenario.' He gave a small burp with his mouth shut. 'My stepmother had a baby when I was twelve. It was pretty isolating, I remember.'

'Oh, you've got a sibling?' I don't know why this surprised me. I'd somehow always imagined that Linklater, like me, was an only child.

'She's an accountant in Kent. Divorced, two kids. I never see her – we have literally nothing to say to each other. I don't see my dad very much either; he's frail now, he's almost ninety, and I definitely don't have any desire to see my stepmother. When I was thirteen, she told me she prayed every night I'd get cancer and die like my mum.'

I looked at his hand curled around the pint glass, and imagined what it would be like to reach out and hold it.

'So, I kind of know what it feels like to be replaced. And I know what it's like to be excluded from your own family unit.'

I nodded.

'That's probably why I always wanted to have a child of my own.' He gazed at me, steadily. 'I suppose I thought if I was someone's dad, I'd never let them feel like that – if that makes any sense? Too late now, though.'

'It's never too late for men.'

He opened his mouth to say something, hesitated, then picked up his pint and took a sip. He seemed to gather himself, and his eyes met mine. 'Dee, can I just ask . . . um . . . Did you ever want children? Is that a regret for you too?' He looked up at the ceiling as if spooked by the intimacy of his own question.

I was surprised that he'd taken so long to raise the subject. 'Do you really want me to answer that?'

He lifted his pint again, nodding keenly.

Perhaps it was the rapid consumption of wine – or maybe it was because he'd shown his vulnerability too – but for the first time in my life it seemed feasible to share my awful secret.

The confession slithered out of me. 'I lost my daughter when she was seventeen months old.'

We both stared at the table in shock, as if my sentence was a living thing, twitching there between us. Neither of us knew what to do with it.

Then he came to life. 'Ah, Dee! No. Oh God, I'm so sorry. How did she die?'

I raised my eyes to meet his. 'She isn't dead. She's grown up. She lives in America.'

'But . . . what? How?'

'Her father is Texan, a Maths lecturer, transplanted to Edinburgh when I met him. The school sent me to him for tutoring for my Oxbridge application when I was sixteen, and when I was seventeen I had my daughter. He was in his forties and married. He and his wife took her back to Texas with them when she was seventeen months old.'

'You gave her up?'

'They took her.'

His face contorted. 'But that's kidnapping.'

'Parental abduction. There's a loophole in Scots law where one parent could take a child out of the country without the other's consent. It basically makes abduction perfectly legal, even though in England and Wales it's a criminal offence. It's even got a nickname: the "kidnapper's charter". Actually, there was a campaign to review it, so I don't know if it exists any more – I can't bear to think about it.'

'Jesus Christ, Dee. But what about the Texan's wife? Surely she wouldn't . . . I mean . . . she took in his *love child*?'

'There was no love, believe me.'

Linklater caught something in my voice. 'Did he – oh, Dee, he didn't—'

'It wasn't technically rape, as such, but I was sixteen, and he was forty-three so . . . Anyway, they didn't have children. I can only assume his wife wanted a baby so much she was prepared to take mine.'

'Did you go after them? Did you take them to court? Did you try to get her back?' I saw a flicker of doubt cross his face as he wondered if I was the sort of person who'd give up on my child.

I took an enormous mouthful of wine, swallowing and putting the glass down very gently because otherwise I knew I could crush it in my fist. 'I was a teenager, Linklater. I lived with my father, I had no job, no money, and I had a criminal record.'

'Fuck, Dee. You have a criminal record?'

'A fairly minor one. I'd had a bit to drink and we had a situation. He tried to take my daughter in his car, and I got in and reversed over him – just his foot; I deliberately ran his foot over. I broke it quite badly. He had me arrested for drunk driving. But the point is, by the time he took her to Texas, I was an eighteen-year-old single mum with a criminal record. He'd also been telling social services for months that I was an unfit mother, which was a lie, but no lawyer would have touched me, even if I'd known how to get one.'

'But what about your father – didn't he do something?'

'He thought she'd have a better life in America. The thing is, I'd been offered a place here, at Oxford, just before she was born, and my father was desperate for me to take it. He didn't believe I could look after her and come here. Maybe he was right about that. He was so adamant that I couldn't do it, and I suppose, when they took her from me, he convinced me it was selfish to try to get her back. He said she deserved two loving parents with money and jobs and a nice house. They could give her everything she needed and, I mean, what life would she have being raised in a remote Scottish mill by a penniless teenager? So . . .' I tailed off and stared into my glass. The room span.

'Fuck, Dee, this is the worst thing I've ever heard.' He looked shattered. I wanted to reassure him that it was okay. But of course it wasn't.

Since I'd never told anyone the truth before, I had never seen it written on someone else's face. The effect on me was overwhelming. I felt myself float up and dissociate from my body – I hovered above the table looking down at us, a woman in a man's white shirt, facing a man in glasses, kind-eyed, aghast, radiating sympathy. My own hideous failings tangled around me. I should have got her back; I should have fought for her – I should never have listened to my father. What sort of a mother allows her baby to be taken? Even animals will die to stop that happening.

A rugby player bumped into my chair. I rejoined my body.

'Do you have any contact with her, now?' Linklater said. 'She must be, what . . .'

I cleared my throat. 'She's an adult with a life of her own and she doesn't want contact. I know where she is – I wrote to her, more than once. She replied, asking me quite politely to leave her alone. She said she's had a good life, and she doesn't want to be in touch. I suppose they've said things to her about me, I don't know—'

'Jesus Christ, Dee. I'm so sorry.'

I nodded as another wave of pain hit me.

'So, wait – did you do a degree here then? In the end?'

I kept my eyes on my empty glass. 'I did not, no. It took me a good few years to put myself back together and by that time, it was too late to take up a place here, even if I'd wanted to, which I didn't.'

'But that's terrible.'

'No, it's not, I'd have hated it.'

'So what in God's name are you doing in Oxford then?'

'One of life's little ironies, I suppose. I've been meaning to leave ever since I came, but somehow I've never quite managed it.'

'Well, you're not alone there,' he said. 'I think seeing Law, in all his power and glory, has kind of finished me off too. I don't belong here either. Never have.'

I looked at him as he drained his pint. 'Maybe people like us don't really belong anywhere.'

'Or, maybe . . .' He took a breath, put his glass down, then looked into my eyes. 'Maybe we belong together?'

The noise and sticky pub heat subsided – even the rugby players no longer seemed so loud or intrusive.

But I was suddenly overcome by a profound exhaustion. I got to my feet, unsteadily. 'I have to go – I have to get back to Felicity – I can't leave her there on her own.' I picked up the cashmere wrap, moving out from the table, as if through an incoming tide.

'But Nick and Mariah are in, aren't they?'

'Exactly.'

As I came down Hell's Passage – barely a shoulder-span wide – I felt disorientated and shrunken. The pressure around my heart, which had been there for so many years, had eased, but there was suddenly too much space around it. It was a peculiar feeling – close to relief and yet very frightening, as if all the rules and restrictions had dissolved – as if anything could happen now.

As I stumbled out of the passage into New College Lane, towards the Bridge of Sighs, a gust of wind hit me from the side and I staggered. Some passing students laughed, thinking that I was drunk and falling over. I wasn't drunk, and I wasn't falling. I might have been exposed and vulnerable, but somehow I was still standing.

Chapter 44

–Are you okay, Dee? Dee? Do you need a break?

I lift my head from my hands. It takes me a moment to remember where I am – in a horrible little hot interview room at Oxford police station, facing two hostile detectives. I push back my chair and get up. I have no idea where I'm going, I just know I can't sit here for another second, answering their sly questions, feeling their scrutiny and suspicion.

Faraday stands up too. –Shall I get you another cup of tea? He is suddenly solicitous, his hard-eyed persona rapidly covered over.

–I have to go now.

–Go? Oh? Right. Well, you're free to go at any time, you know that, but you can help us find this child. If you go now, that's going to tell us something – well – I don't think you want to go, really, do you? How about you stretch your legs? Have a bit of a break? Toilets are just down the corridor on the left. I know these questions can be stressful – this is a really difficult time for everyone, we get that.

As I walk down the corridor, I pass an open door into an empty office. A police officer has been looking at the *Daily Mail* on a desktop and Felicity's picture catches my eye. It is the same school photo they are using in all the campaigns – one taken when she started in Oxford. She looks like a terrified wax work. And then I see my own face, next to hers, staring back at me. I come to a halt, and reverse. I am on the front cover of the *Daily Mail*.

It is not a flattering picture. A photographer must have snapped me as I escaped the Lodging the night before – the background is dim and hazy. I look haggard and hunted and my eyes, startled by the flash, are positively ferocious. Under different circumstances, the headline – NANNY MCFLEE? – might even be amusing, but the subtitle – *Questions asked about Nanny's trip to London* – definitely is not.

I stagger to the toilets, find a cubicle and lock the door, leaning my forehead against its slimy surface.

Nick must have been talking to the press about me – or Angela has – or someone else in College. I know how this works: society turns on the one who doesn't quite fit. I don't look like a nanny. Nannies are supposed to be young and sweet and pretty – Princess Diana in a see-through skirt, or a magical Mary Poppins, or, at a pinch, a plump and jolly Mrs Doubtfire. I am none of these. I don't quite fit anywhere, in fact. I never have. Linklater is the same. So is Felicity. We only really fit together. But now, of course, we are not together. I am alone. The media will hunt me down. Everything I've done will be analyzed, twisted and misread. I think of the innocent Bristol schoolteacher a few years ago, accused by the tabloids of murdering a young woman, photographed on his doorstep with wild eyes and mad white hair, looking just like a killer. And then there was the man in Portugal, the one with the strange wonky eye in the Madeleine McCann case, branded a paedophile, investigated, exonerated – his life ruined. #FindFelicity has become a witch-hunt, and I am the witch.

I realize that I am going to have to go back into the inter-view room and persuade Faraday and Khan that I am not the person they think I am. But perhaps they've already made up their mind about me – I have felt darker things moving in the shadows beneath Faraday's questions from the start.

It is possible that they've been storing up Linklater – and that when I go back in there, they'll start to ask me about him. They'll want to know why I haven't mentioned him before. I have lied by omission. Perhaps Nick has said something to them about the incident outside the Master's Lodging – what happened after Linklater and I had been in the Turf Tavern. That would be hard to explain away.

When I got back to the house after the Turf that night, everything was eerily quiet. Even the baby wasn't crying. I crept upstairs and as I got halfway up the attic staircase, I felt a freezing draught on my skin. I began to run, knowing that something wasn't right. Felicity's bedroom door was wide open and I rushed in. The first thing I saw was her empty bed, duvet tossed onto the floor. Then I saw the cat, huddled by the priest's hole. Then I saw the open window above her desk, and Felicity on the windowsill with her back to me.

She was facing the gargoyles and she was half out of the window – not holding onto anything, her legs dangling, nothing between her and the cobbles two floors down. I froze. If I moved or called out, I might startle her and she might fall, or jump. For a second I stood in horror, unsure what to do. Then adrenaline took over. I hurtled across the room, onto her desk and seized her with both arms, pulling her backwards, to safety.

I dragged her onto the floor, and wrapped myself around her, encasing her almost entirely. 'What were you doing?' I cried. 'You could have fallen out; you could have been killed – oh Felicity!

What were you thinking?' After a moment or two she wriggled out of my arms. She looked shocked, and wide awake.

'Darling, listen to me, you can't do that ever again.'

All the tense lines of her face warped and melted, and huge tears began to fall.

'Oh love, it's okay, I'm not angry, you just really scared me.' I pulled her back into my arms again. 'It's okay. I'm here.' I rocked her for a while, then wiped her face and my own. 'What happened? Why were you sitting out the window like that?'

'I saw my mummy.' She hiccupped.

'Out the window?'

'On the other roof, with the stone man.'

I led her to her bed, and then I went back, closed the window very firmly and drew the curtains to shut out the gargoyles. I went back to her and got onto the bed with her, and put my arm around her again. 'You miss your mummy so, so much,' I said. 'I know you do. She'll always be with you, in your heart, but she isn't here, not in this room or out there, or anywhere you can see. You're dreaming about her, and you're hearing her voice – and maybe also other voices too – because you miss her so very, very much and you feel scared inside. I know what that's like. I know how awful it is to want someone who isn't with you any more.' I kissed her curls. 'But you have me now. I'm here, and I can't have you falling out of windows, okay?'

I felt her nod. Then she said, 'I don't just see my mummy though.'

'Who else do you see?'

'Duncan and Jonnie. They go in the priest's hole.'

'Well, that's the same thing, sweetheart. There are no little boys here – they aren't real – but the feelings inside you that make you see them are.'

'But it's definitely them. I know it is.'

'You know, if you think about that logically, it can't be true. The thing is, one of those poor boys, Duncan, died when he was little. We know that for sure. But Jonnie lived to be an old, old man. Linklater told me this. We didn't tell you because we thought you might be upset. But if you were really seeing their ghosts, then you'd see Duncan as a little boy and Jonnie as an old man, wouldn't you?'

She knitted her brows and thought about this for a while. Then the tension in her face dissolved.

'See? There aren't any ghosts. What you're seeing up here comes out of your imagination, and your dreams. I promise you that, okay? You're seeing these things because of what happened to you when you were little. When your mummy died, a part of you started to feel scared all the time. And when we feel scared and alone, we often have bad dreams, and we see things. Do you understand what I mean?'

She nodded and I was glad, not for the first time, that she was such a clever child.

'But I'm not going to let anything bad happen to you,' I said. 'You know that, don't you? I'm here for you. You're safe with me. I love you, okay?'

'I love you too, Dee,' she said, quietly.

We lay there for a long time and eventually I felt her knots loosen as she fell asleep in my arms. I wished I could sleep, too, holding onto her like this, but, although I was exhausted, I was still wide awake. As I gazed down at her face, I saw her eyelids flicker and a little smile appeared in the corners of her mouth. I wondered who she was with in her dream right now. Was it me? Or Linklater? Or Fibby? Or all of us together?

Linklater's words came back to me then: we see ghosts because we need to see them. But perhaps sometimes these ghosts are the last things we need to see. Certainly, there have been many times when, had my own mother reappeared, taken my hand and walked me to a window, I'd have gone out of it without hesitation.

The act of telling Linklater my secret after decades of silence had left me feeling unwell. When I was certain that Felicity was asleep, I slipped out via the bathroom to my own bed. I didn't bother getting undressed. I knew I wouldn't sleep despite the exhaustion in my bones. As I pulled my notebook out of the bedside table, my hands fumbled and the new priest's hole key jangled out of the deep pocket on its back flap. I was tempted to take the key over to the window and toss it out into the street. Ghosts or no ghosts, that little chamber was a bad place. About a hundred years ago, it had poisoned a small boy. It would be better if nobody went in there, ever again.

Chapter 45

A few hours later I became aware of scattering, pinging noises against my windowpane.

When I went over and pulled back the blind, I heard a muffled yelp below.

Linklater was on the cobbles, frantically waving up at me.

I grabbed my fleece and crept downstairs, along the landing past Mariah and Nick's room, where I could hear the baby mewling, and down the broad red staircase.

I slid back the bolt and opened the door; Linklater was wavering in the lane, his nose red, his glasses crooked. 'Jesus, Dee, I didn't think you'd ever wake up!' I stepped out, half closing the door behind me.

'I've been texting and calling you – fucking hell, Dee – I've been—'

'Linklater!' I hissed. 'Stop shouting – it's the middle of the night. What are you doing here?' He was, I saw, a bit drunk.

'This. This! Look. I've got a fucking eviction note!' He shoved a crumpled letter at me. 'When I got back from the pub, it was in my pigeonhole. The fuckers have changed the locks on me. They're throwing me out of my own home, Dee. I've lived there basically all my adult life. It's all I've got and they've locked me out.'

I glanced at the paper.

Dear Mr Birdy,

It has come to our attention that you are …

I was aware of Mariah and Nick in the room just above us. 'Let's talk about this tomorrow.'

'What? No – wait – what? Where do I go? I just told you – he's locked me out of my fucking rooms!'

'They can't have changed the locks already, surely?'

'Yes! They've done it!' He waved the paper under my nose and I had to grab his hand to hold it still so I could read it. It was signed by Richard Nailor, the Domestic Bursar. 'What I don't understand is how they found out I was still in College rooms – I thought they didn't even know I existed. It can only be his orders – Law's – he must have looked me up in the College records by my real name, the fucker!'

I pushed the letter back at him. Now was not the time to mention the conversation I'd had with Nick in the kitchen, though at some point I'd have to confess that this was entirely my fault. 'Didn't you think about this when you took the job? Didn't you think he might recognize you? Or work out who you were from the address or something?'

'The house detective stuff is all under H. Linklater, and no – I didn't think about that—' He clutched his cheeks. 'Not for a second. He must have an encyclopaedic memory if he connected the name Linklater to my real surname. But he probably does, the cunt.' He shouted this last word, looking up at the house.

'Do you really want him to come down? Because I can hear the baby crying, they're awake up there, and if he hears you, he's definitely going to come down. Do you really want that?'

'Yes, why not? Why the fuck not?' He stuffed the letter into his pocket. 'I can tell him to his face what a wanker he is. All my stuff's up there – all my papers, my books, records – my bloody piano. He can't just change the fucking locks after twenty-seven years.'

'And you'd like him to come down to discuss this at 3.15 in the morning, when he's been up all night with a colicky baby?'

He gazed at me from behind his crooked glasses. 'Probably not.' He ran a hand through his hair. 'But, Jesus fucking Christ, the man's a total—'

I saw his eyes widen and then I heard Nick's voice behind me. 'What the hell's going on?'

I turned. There was a light behind him so I couldn't see his expression, only the outline of his broad shoulders. 'What do you think you're doing, shouting obscenities outside my house at three in the morning?'

Linklater took a step back, then drew himself up again. 'Where do you want me to go? You changed my fucking locks, Law, you wanker.'

Nick peered at him. 'Birdy?'

'Linklater. You can call me Linklater.'

Nick laughed. 'Oh, do go away.'

Linklater took a step forwards. He was a couple of inches shorter than Nick anyway, and standing on the top step, Nick now appeared preternaturally tall. But Linklater was not cowed. 'This is a public street; you don't own it. I can stand here if I want to.'

'If you don't go away right now, I'm going to call the police.'

Linklater laughed, madly. 'You know what, Law, you're basically just a cunt. You always have been and you always will be. I'm sure it makes you feel like Lord of the Manor to kick the serfs, but you're a tenant too – you're just a fucking tenant at the end of the day – and the way things are going, they'll be changing your locks, too, before the year's out, you *twat*.' He screwed the letter up and threw it at Nick, then swept off round the corner.

Nick stood very still. Then he turned his head and looked down at me. 'Why are you out here?' I was about to point out that I'd only been trying to help, when Mariah appeared at the end of the hall, clutching her mewling baby. She switched on the outside light – Nick and I blinked at one another, suddenly slightly embarrassed.

Mariah's hair hung around her face in limp tangles, and she looked confused. The baby's cries grew longer, taller – and Nick hurried to them, holding out his hands. 'It's okay, darling, don't worry. It's nothing, just an idiotic former student. Here, let me take him.'

I didn't follow them in. I darted forwards, seized my keys from the hall table then went after Linklater.

I found him squatting in Magpie Lane with his back against the towering wall, his head in his hands, glasses dangling from his fingertips. He looked up when he heard my footsteps, and gazed at me for a second. '*Fuck*.'

'Yes, well, I don't think you'll be getting your rooms back any time soon,' I said.

We looked at each other, and then we both began to laugh. I knelt in front of him and he clutched my arms and our laughter rose and bounced off the ancient stones and then he grabbed my face and he kissed me – a passionate, deep, alcoholic kiss that made every atom in my body explode.

When we finally pulled apart, he gazed at me, blinking. 'Sorry. Sorry – I – Jesus, Dee.' He put his glasses back on. 'The thing is, I definitely love you.' He put his glasses back on.

'Now might not be the best time for this,' I said. Everything in the lane was alive and twitching – each glistening cobble, each ancient brick and the impossibly bright, star-punctured sky stretching out above us, topping the spires.

'No ... right ... yes ... probably not,' he said. 'Oh God, what the fuck do I do now?'

'Well, clearly you won't be sleeping in my room. Haven't you got a friend who can put you up?'

He thought about this for a moment. 'Other than you, the only person I can wake up at this time of night is my mate who lives near Banbury, and he's on sabbatical in Madrid for the next two months, so I think I'm officially buggered.' He pulled his overcoat around him and a haunted look crossed his face. 'This is how it happens, isn't it? You hear about people like me, who start out full of promise and end up living on the streets.'

'Don't be so dramatic.' I laughed, shivering and tightening my fleece. 'You've got me.'

I was suddenly struck by how much we had in common: we had both been in Oxford for decades and yet didn't fit anywhere; neither of us had a home of our own, or anybody to fall back on. Except each other. We had each other.

Gently, I reached out and lifted his glasses off his nose again. He looked surprised, then shy – I think he thought I was going to kiss him for a second time. That crossed my mind too, but everything already felt chaotic enough, so I ducked my head, pulled out a corner of my shirt and busied myself cleaning his specs, breathing onto them and wiping off the fingerprints and smears. I handed them back to him. 'There's only two or three hours left of tonight,' I said. 'You can sleep in my car. It's parked by the back gates. I'll get you some blankets. You can sleep for an hour or two and then go and have a fry-up at Queen's Lane. When I've got Felicity off to school, we'll make a proper plan, okay? You won't be homeless.'

I gave him my keys and he wandered off while I went back to the Lodging. I crept in as silently as I could. It was freezing outside, but the house wasn't warm either. There was no sign of Nick or Mariah and I could hear the baby's rasping cries on the floor above. I took two picnic blankets from under the stairs, a couple of Mariah's shot silk Ikat cushions from the sofa, and, as an afterthought, Nick's £400 whisky, three quarters full. As I went out again, I took a warming swig from the decanter – it burned my throat and spread, smokily, silkily, through my body.

Linklater called my Nokia at 5.30 a.m. I was still awake, of course, and I picked up immediately.

He'd been awake all night too – nobody could sleep in a Fiesta in February. He sounded a bit drunk. The whisky might not have been such a good plan. 'They've got blood on their hands,' he cried. 'I found Ana's sister on Facebook. She lives in Toronto, she's a teacher, a bit older than Ana, grown-up kids, likes quilting, ran a half marathon in—'

'Linklater!?'

'Ah yes, right, well, she wrote a long Facebook post after Ana died where she rips into Nick and Mariah. Ana found out about their affair and was in a really bad way. She was bipolar so everyone knew this was serious. The night she killed herself, Nick and Mariah were holed up in Soho House, so it was Felicity who found her in the bathroom – I mean, Jesus, Dee, no wonder they've been shifty about giving you the details. They left a four-year-old alone with her plainly suicidal mother.'

All the air seemed to leave my lungs. 'Felicity found Ana's body?'

'She did – a neighbour was going out for a jog when Felicity toddled out of the house covered in her mother's blood. You should hear what the sister says about that. She's saying Ana expected Nick back that night. She put a note on the bathroom door for him saying not to let Felicity in. He must have known she could do it, but he just left her. He actually chose to ignore his suicidal wife's phone calls.'

I held the phone away from my ear. I didn't need to hear any more details.

I thought about Felicity's reaction when she put her hand in Mariah's blood in the Fiesta seat, and I realized that in her eyes I had glimpsed not just revulsion, but terror.

Then I remembered the story Nick told me the day we met, about how Newton's mathematical bridge had been held up by calculations alone – each part exerting exactly enough force to keep it up, so that if you removed a single piece, the entire structure would collapse. When Ana told him this story, maybe she'd been warning him how precarious she felt. He'd probably dealt with a lot – maybe there were other suicide attempts, threats, ups and downs, challenges – who knew what they'd been through as a couple – but the fact remained that when he and Mariah chose to stay in that hotel room, they'd essentially made the decision to pull out a piece of wood and watch her collapse.

I told Linklater to stay in the car. I hung up, crept downstairs and made strong coffee. I shoved on a coat and boots and crossed the frosty grass to the back gate.

He looked lovely but awful – a pallid, sunken-eyed vagrant wrapped in tartan. The car windows were steamed up and the air reeked of stale farts and whisky. He'd had a good go at the Talisker, I saw. I probably should have brought him paracetamol too. I shoved the coffee flask at him and he rubbed his head and mumbled thanks.

I got into the Fiesta next to him and shut the door.

'I don't know what to do,' he said. 'I've been Googling the

accommodation thing and haven't got any tenancy rights because I don't officially exist. I've been living there under false pretences for years – they could sue me – shit, they probably *will* sue me. And I can't afford a place in Oxford – it's the most expensive city in Britain outside of London, did you know that? I'm finished, Dee. I might even go to jail.'

'Don't be daft.' I opened the flask for him, poured the coffee. 'Oxford isn't the be-all and end-all.'

We talked there for almost an hour, drinking coffee, only pausing for him to get out and piss against Nick's back wall. We were a unit now; we were in this together.

We resolved that he'd call his friend in Madrid and explain the circumstances, and ask if he could stay in the Banbury house, just for a short while.

And two days later, Felicity vanished from the Master's Lodging in the middle of the night.

So, I will go back in there to Faraday and Khan, but I will not mention Linklater, or the scene in the street that night. If Nick has, I will play it down. I will say that I simply answered the door to the angry house detective. I am a bystander, nothing more; unconnected, caught up in this family's mess.

After all, Felicity vanished while I was in the theatre in London, enduring an interminable all-female performance of *Richard III* – or half of one, anyway, since nobody in their right mind would sit through the whole thing. She vanished as I walked the streets of London fifty miles away from Oxford, tracked by CCTV. She vanished three days ago and I have not seen her since. But I desperately want to.

Chapter 46

I go back into the interview room and sit down on the hard chair. They have obviously been talking about me. Khan's eyes are cool; Faraday slides back into his benign persona. –Feeling better, Dee? Ready to tell us a bit about your trip to London, last Friday?

I wonder how much to say to them about London. Too much, and they will read things into the spaces; too little, and I will look as if I am hiding something.

I didn't sleep at all on the Thursday night. At one point I got out of bed and went to the window. I looked out at the traumatized gargoyles and the Chapel spire, inside which the tongues of the bells hung stiff and silent, and it struck me that it was little more than half a year since I'd first gazed out of this window – the blink of an eye for this 600-year-old College – and yet in that time my world had altered irreversibly, and for ever.

I was down in the kitchen before everyone else as usual. I wanted to keep things as normal as possible. I packed Felicity's lunch box, made her porridge, checked her book bag, signed a form for a school trip. She came down at the usual time but ate only a couple of bites of porridge. At one point our eyes met. We held each other's gaze – we did not need to speak any more.

We could hear the baby wailing rhythmically upstairs.

Nick came down wearing an expensive dark suit, looking haggard. It was the first time I'd seen him since the doorstep confrontation with Linklater and I was expecting him to say something snide, but he ignored me. He made coffee and ruffled Felicity's hair. 'I'm in London tonight, Bun, remember, so I'm counting on you to help Mariah, okay?' He kissed her head, briefly, then said, over his shoulder, 'When we both get back, Dee, you and I need to have a talk. I'll get Sally to set up a time.'

I spent the day cleaning Felicity's bedroom. I put away all our treasures, and tidied all her clothes. I packed my bag, and then I took a long walk across Port Meadow. Linklater called me from his friend's house in Banbury. I walked for a long time and as I walked, we talked.

I picked Felicity up from school and settled her upstairs with the cat and some ginger cookies and her iPad. Then I kissed her goodbye.

Faraday asks question after question about what bus I took to and from London, about the theatre, the hotel, my night walk around North London. I do admit that I only sat through the first half of the play. I tell him I have no idea why anybody thought I'd enjoy all that scheming and lying and seeing ghosts – there was quite enough of that already in real life. I left the theatre during the interval, I told him, and walked all the way to the hotel, where I checked into my room, deposited my bag, and walked some more.

He wants to know exactly where I walked. I say I ate pasta in an Italian café somewhere near Holborn – an excellent carbonara. I walked for an hour or two – round Bloomsbury, Islington, maybe into Hackney; I didn't really know the area. I was worrying about Felicity, I said, wondering what was happening to her back in Oxford, alone in the house with Mariah and the screaming baby.

–But you weren't just walking, were you? Khan sits up straighter. Her voice is still quiet, but harsh. –You asked the hotel receptionist where you could buy a phone charger. She told us you seemed agitated about that.

I suppose nothing goes unobserved these days. –Yes, I say. –I did want to buy a charger. I forgot to take mine. And it's nice to have a purpose when you're a woman alone in a strange city at night.

Faraday asks how many shops I went into, and which ones. –Surely, he says, –it's not hard to find an iPhone charger in London?

–Three or four shops, I say. –I'm really not sure. And it actually is hard to find a charger when all the shops are shut.

–But you walked for two hours anyway?

I explain, not for the first time, that I like to walk when I cannot sleep. I point out that if they look – and I assume they will – then they will find me on all the relevant CCTV cameras at all the right times in Bloomsbury, Islington, Hackney.

Back at the hotel I tried, and failed, to work on my proof. I read for a bit, slept for an hour or two. Around seven-thirty the next morning, I forced down a hotel breakfast then I walked to Oxford Street. I did find a phone charger in an electronics shop there. Then I went to Marble Arch and got back on the Oxford Tube.

I was finally able to plug my phone in on the bus, and when the screen came alive, I saw that I had six missed calls from Linklater. I was about to listen to them when the iPhone rang in my bag.

'Dee!' Mariah was shouting over the baby's rasping cries. 'Is

Felicity with you? Where are you? She's not here. She's gone – I can't find her. Have you got her? Is she with you?'

I felt my stomach lurch as if the bus had gone over a precipice. 'Of course she's not – I'm in London.'

'Shit, I'm ... oh my God, Dee, I don't know where she is! I was sleeping – he slept for five hours last night – five hours! – and when I went up there, she wasn't in her room. We've been looking everywhere – she's nowhere. I don't know what to do! I just don't know what to do. Where would she go? Where are you?'

'When did you last see her?' I tried to sound calm. My heart was beating at a sickening rate.

I established that Mariah had not set eyes on Felicity since five o'clock the previous evening. She, Sally, Angela and the gardener had searched the Lodging and grounds, then they'd got a couple of catering staff and looked round College; asked porters, scouts, passing dons and students. 'I'm going to hang up now,' she cried. 'That's Nick calling back – oh God, she wouldn't run away, would she? I mean – would she? Has she run away? Or is this – does someone – wait – I have to talk to Nick.' The line went dead.

I tell Faraday and Khan that it only really began to sink in when I walked into the house and saw two uniformed police officers in the kitchen.

–That's funny, Khan says. –Because one of our officers noted at the time how calm you were.

She pauses, then, and stares at me for a second or two. –I think you know where this child is, Dee, she says. –I think you took her.

Chapter 47

It is a shock to be accused so directly.

–What? How on earth could I have done that? I was in London.

Khan's voice is matter-of-fact. –You could have come back to Oxford later on Friday night and taken her. Or you could have had someone else take her to London to join you there.

–*How?*

–Why don't you tell us that, Dee? Just tell us what's happened to Felicity.

–Are you doing this to Nick and Mariah too?

–Do you have another phone as well as the iPhone you've shown us? Do you still have an old Nokia phone?

–What?

–Dr and Mrs Law have told us that they believe you also have a burner phone.

–A *burner phone*? I probably sound incredulous. –I don't even know what a burner phone is!

–It's a prepaid mobile without a contract, Faraday says, helpfully. –It's what people use when they don't want to be linked to any device. It's not traceable to an individual.

They are making me sound like a career criminal.

–Child abduction's a very serious charge, Khan says. –If you don't cooperate, you're going to go down for a long time for this. You're obviously a clever woman – can't you understand that?

It has to be Nick telling them about burner phones. And he'll have done this because he saw my Nokia.

In the three days since Felicity was discovered missing, we have all effectively been trapped inside the Lodging. The house quickly became the epicentre of the crisis: police officers came and went all weekend, updating each other and us, gathering information. Nick was either glued to his phone, shouting, instructing, explaining, calling in all his contacts, or talking to CID officers on the phone or in his study. A family liaison officer appeared; Sally installed herself in Nick's study, making calls, working on his desktop computer; Angela brought over trays of food – all against the baby's ceaseless chorus, 'alas, alas'.

Later on Saturday afternoon, Nick went off with the police to Kidlington to do a press conference. Soon after that was done, cars and vans started bumping down the cobbles, disgorging camera crews, photographers and reporters outside the Lodging. A journalist began broadcasting live on the doorstep. I saw familiar logos – ITN, BBC, Sky News. Uniformed officers had to guard the door. It was breathtaking how fast it escalated from Mariah's first 'Where's Felicity?' on Saturday morning. When I remarked on this to the family liaison officer, she said, 'Update and escalate – that's the basic procedure when a child goes missing like this.' She elaborated, in a practical voice, about search teams, patrol cars, foot officers and dogs, house-to-house searches, helicopters, thermal imaging. Perhaps she'd been told that I was just the temporary nanny because she didn't seem to realize that her words would affect me so deeply. Seeing my face, she told me to sit down, made me a cup of tea, fed me some platitudes. As I left the kitchen, I saw her pull out a notebook.

When I wasn't answering questions about Felicity's belong-
ings, habits or movements, I stayed in my room. I followed
what was happening on the BBC website on my iPhone – finally
that device had come into its own. Nick's press conference, a
stoic but shaken plea for his daughter's safe return in which he
called her 'vulnerable and acutely shy', was replayed on each
news cycle. All I could think about was Felicity, and how badly
I wanted to see her, speak to her, hold her in my arms again.
When I looked out the window and saw that even more people
were crowding the lane, I felt I might throw up.

Nick barely slept that first night either. I heard him pacing
and talking on the phone in his study, directly below my bedroom. He ignored his screaming son, and his desperate, silent
wife – nothing mattered to him now but finding his daughter.
He and Mariah seemed to have entered completely separate
worlds. On the Sunday morning, I saw them pass on the stairs
without a word. I wondered if she'd confessed that she'd heard
Felicity go downstairs on Friday night and done nothing. She
looked broken, ghoulishly pale and dishevelled. The contrast to
the bouncing, healthy beauty who'd greeted me at the Lodging
door just seven months previously was stark.

Throughout Sunday, too, Nick liaised with the police media
team, the University, his staff. The University Press Office put
out a press release anticipating questions about security – they
needed to protect the brand. I heard Nick shout down the phone
at them, 'What's it got to do with you what I'm going to say?'

Felicity's school photo was in all of the Sunday newspapers. And
Nick, I found, had a Twitter account of his own, @Mastersvoice,
which he seemed to have previously used to broadcast College
achievements. Now it was all #FindFelicity. Most comments on
the posts were supportive, but one or two accused Nick of being

a paedophile and a murderer. And at one point he rampaged down the stairs shouting that some criminal had set up a fake Instagram account in Felicity's name, using her picture. Later, I heard the wheels on his desk chair rumble as he dragged it across the floor, and I imagined him taking off his glasses, dropping his head into his hands. It was odd, I thought, that he had not spent more time with Felicity when he had her.

Mariah's sister arrived late on Sunday. She looked like Mariah, only less beautiful – older, heavier, sportier, more weathered – a mother of teenaged boys. She slept in the guest room next to Nick's study and took charge of the baby, who still cried all night, but somehow less intensely, as if he knew he was never going to win against this new Viking woman.

I was desperate to leave, but if I packed my bags, it would look as if I was absconding. The house was unbearable, though, and in the early hours of Monday morning I had to get out – I knew that I had to walk or I'd go insane. I took my fleece off the back of the door, grabbed my boots and tiptoed downstairs.

I'd just reached the bottom of the attic stairs when Nick emerged from his study and blocked my way. 'Where the hell are you going?'

I held up my boots. 'I need to get out.'

'At one in the bloody morning?'

'Yes.' I stood very still.

He leaned towards me, and hissed. 'What do you know?'

I looked down and untied the knot on my bootlace, saying nothing. I was not going to get into a confrontation, with him in such a dangerous, deranged state.

'If you're involved in this in any way, you're finished, do you hear me? I'll eviscerate you.'

I almost pitied him. He must be in a gruesome position, if

that's what he thought. If he banished me from his house – which he must be desperate to do – I could vanish for ever. But my presence under his roof must be a torment to him. He seemed so completely certain that I was involved, though he had no evidence of that. In fact, circumstances proved quite the opposite. I was here, under his roof. I plainly did not have his daughter.

I zipped up my fleece and sat on the bottom step to put my boots on. As I yanked the laces, my old Nokia slipped from my pocket and thudded onto the landing. I lurched for it – he did too – but I got there first. I whipped it up and shoved it back into my pocket.

'What's that?' he barked. 'Is that your old phone? Are you still using your old phone?'

I ignored him.

'You've only shown the police your iPhone!'

In the room next door, the baby woke up and began to wail.

I got off the stair and pushed past him, hurried down the red staircase. He followed me. 'Give me that fucking phone!'

I marched down the hall and out the front door, into the night.

If I admit to Khan that I do still use my Nokia, then they will want to see it.

Linklater was the only person who ever contacted me on the Nokia, because he was the only person who had the number. If I give it to the police, they will see all his calls and texts and they will immediately turn on him. What the police, not to mention the media, would do to Linklater – the oddball bachelor who'd befriended Felicity and had a grudge against her father – did not bear thinking about.

There is no way I am going to give them Linklater. So there is no way I am going to give them my Nokia.

–I've no idea why Nick would tell you I have a 'burner phone', I say to Faraday. –But perhaps he'd rather you wasted time looking at me, rather than at him or Mariah?

If they decide that they have enough to charge me with right now, then they will search me and they will find my Nokia in my jeans pocket. A small, cheap piece of technology will undo me. And Linklater. It will undo us both.

But they can't arrest me. They have nothing to link me to any crime – no evidence whatsoever. In fact, they still haven't even established that a crime has been committed. Felicity could have walked out of the house – she could be lost, or hiding. In less palatable scenarios, she could have sleepwalked through the meadow, wandered past the trees to the bank of the Cherwell – slipped on the mud and reeds. Or she could have been taken from her bed like Madeleine McCann.

Anything could have happened to her – anything at all – and all they can do is ask question after question, and hope that I will give them something. There is no way they can arrest me. They have no proof.

Chapter 48

–Just tell us what you know now, Dee. Khan is menacing. –Play nice.

–'Play nice'? I almost laugh.

But she starts up again, rapid-fire, and any notion I may have had that she is Faraday's note-taker goes out the window. –Was there an accident, Dee?

–Of course not.

–Did you take her to London?

–No.

Faraday leans in, almost cooing, massaging me with his voice. –All we're interested in is getting Felicity back, Dee. That's all. From what you've said, she's a very unhappy little girl. Her mum's committed suicide, her dad's too busy for her, she's miserable at school, she doesn't get on with her stepmum – who's definitely not stable – and now they've had this baby and she's even more unwanted. I wouldn't blame you if you did want to take her away from it all, to be honest with you.

I repeat that the only crime I have committed is to fail to enjoy an all-female production of *Richard III*.

Khan's face is stony. –You can't carry on pretending you aren't involved.

–I am involved. Of course I am. I care about Felicity. She's just about the only thing I do care about. She needs me. I'm the only stable, loving adult in her life.

Khan looks at me. –Are you, though, Dee? Are you stable?

I get up again. –Right, that's it. I'm leaving.

Faraday urges me to sit back down.

I stay standing.

–It's just, from what we know about you, Khan says, still quiet and cold, –we could argue that you're the opposite of stable.

She launches, then, into a truly peculiar list of accusations – a warped version of the past seven months: I kept Felicity out of education, showed her voodoo patterns, told her there were spooks, drowned her kittens, unplugged the phones, ghosted her parents, listened at doors, smashed wedding photos, vandalized priceless wallpaper.

–You skinned dead animals and put them in her room, she finishes, widening her brown eyes.

It's obvious what she is doing. She is trying to get inside my head. She wants me to doubt everything that has happened since I stood on the mathematical bridge that day last July. She wants me to question my own sanity. This is how false confessions come about.

–You're twisting everything.

–Am I? How?

But I can see that arguing each point is only going to get me in deeper. –Okay, I say, –if I'm so insane, why did she feel safe with me?

Khan gives a sharp nod. –The thing is, Dee, she doesn't sound to me like a little girl who felt safe. Quite the opposite. When children feel unsafe they go into themselves; they clam up, they stop eating, they develop stress symptoms like insomnia

or eczema or night terrors. They don't cope socially – they with-
draw, they focus everything they've got on survival.

–But I've just spent the last God-knows-how-long telling you
it wasn't *me* who made her feel like this! It was moving to that
madhouse, being sent to that school when she couldn't speak,
facing bullies day after day, and nobody caring, nobody seeing
her, or understanding her – nobody except me.

–What's in your notebook, Dee? I see a flicker of something
nasty in her eyes.

–None of your business.

–Well, we've had a look at it and none of us can make head
or tail of it. Is it written in code?

–I never gave you permission to read my notebook.

–All those scribbles and doodles and strange signs. What do
they mean, Dee? Is it a coded diary?

–Oh, for God's sake. Give it to any mathematician. They'll tell
you what it is.

–Why don't you tell us?

–It's a mathematical proof. Or almost – I'm working on it.

–What's a mathematical proof? says Faraday.

–It's the foundation of all mathematics.

–But what actually is it? How does it work? says Khan, irritably.

I look at her. –You start with a hypothesis, something that
feels true, and you go through a complicated logical process to
establish beyond any doubt that it is.

–Is what?

–True.

–Right. So what truth does your proof – err – prove?

–You wouldn't understand. It's far too complex.

–Try me.

She looks at me with dead eyes as I give a brief and ludicrously simplified description of my proof. She has no idea what I'm talking about, of course. –Self-taught mathematical genius, are you? she says.

–Just show it to a mathematician, I growl. I must not let her derail me. She's only doing her job. This is not personal. She has thrown all these accusations at me in order to rile me, and now she is openly mocking my work. I must not allow myself to be baited. Even by my own notebook.

It strikes me, then, that we are demonstrating different aspects of *reductio ad absurdum* – a method mathematicians use for approaching a proof. I am using one form of *reductio ad absurdum*, where you try to disprove a statement ('Dee is a kidnapper') by showing that the reasoning behind this conclusion is false, impractical or ridiculous. I am trying to demonstrate that in order to believe I'm a kidnapper, you must also believe a set of completely absurd things: that I flushed live kittens down the toilet, saw ghosts, deliberately tried to scare a little girl with dead animals, and so on. Since those statements are plainly absurd, it is obvious that the theory of my guilt cannot possibly be proven. I must, therefore, be innocent.

Faraday and Khan, meanwhile, are using a second form of *reductio ad absurdum*. They are setting out to prove that the statement 'Dee is guilty of kidnap' is true by showing that if it were false, then there would be inevitable contradictions or absurdities in the reasoning. In other words, if I haven't kidnapped Felicity, then the alternative explanations – that she sleepwalked, ran away, got lost, was taken or harmed – are absurd and impractical. They have been trying to prove my guilt this way, but they are manifestly failing – because any of these other explanations remain horribly real and possible. This is why they are now flinging wild accusations around.

Khan is talking again, in a softer voice. –I think you're carrying a lot of pain, Dee, a lot of unresolved emotions. I think you've projected some of your inner turmoil onto this household.

I close my eyes. Not this. I can't do this.

She says something about my police record. 'Drink driving, driving without due care and attention . . .'

I feel the whump of the steak-fed Texan and the lurch of the car as its back wheel travels over his boot. Yes, I did drink too much that day, and reverse into the father of my child, breaking practically every bone in his foot. No, I was not sorry for it.

–And you lost custody of your little girl, didn't you? That must have been tough for you.

I grit my teeth. I want to scream at her but I must not react. I could try, calmly, to explain that I did not lose custody of my child – that she was taken from me. I could try to convey what it is like to have your seventeen-month-old daughter stolen from you – the eviscerating agony of it – but really, what will I gain, even if I do? They will only use it to prove that I must be unbalanced. That is just what they need to make the case for 'Nanny McFlee' – the delusional child abductor, the unfit mother with a criminal past.

There is no air in the room – it is very hot indeed; someone has turned up the heat. I wonder if this is another strategy to derail me – heat. I become aware, again, of the red eye of the video camera blinking at me.

Khan suddenly pretends to be reasonable. –Listen, Dee, we all understand how this sort of thing can get out of hand. Whatever the circumstances were that led up to you losing custody of your daughter, you've had a very big hole to fill. That's a lot of pain for anyone to carry around. Feelings can build up over time and one day they just get to boiling point. Sometimes we don't even know we're under that sort of pressure till it's too late. You've spent your whole life looking after other people's kids and that's got to do something to you when you're not in contact with your own daughter – that's a really big build up of pain. Maybe things just escalated with this family? You only wanted the best for Felicity, we know that. You felt these parents were negligent, didn't you? And I get that. They sound it, to be honest. So why don't you just tell us where she is, and we can all sort this out, okay?

I look down at my hands. They are the hands of a Scottish peasant, strong and broad, with red knuckles and hard skin from years of washing and wiping other people's children, other people's homes. My father's hands were leathery too, but taper-fingered, so I assume I have inherited my mother's hands. Rosie's hands are the same shape as mine – her grandmother's hands. I noticed this once in a photograph on her Facebook page. But I will never be able to give her this information. It occurs to me – and astonishingly it is the first time I have ever allowed myself this particular thought – that first my mother was stolen from me, and then my daughter.

It is possible that the pressure inside my chest will actually crack me open.

I have to go. I have to get out. I lift my fleece off the back of the chair. I cannot stay in this room a second longer. Either they arrest me, or I walk.

Faraday and Khan leap to their feet and speak at the same time:

–Where are you going? he says.

–If you try to leave now, we can arrest you, she says.

I turn and look at them both. I see their anguish, but also their doubt and powerlessness. Suddenly, I feel very calm. They know that they have nothing to keep me right now. They have no proof of my guilt. No evidence. They have no idea whether I did this, or Nick, or Mariah – or someone else entirely. Or nobody. They have nothing. Not even a crime.

–Go on then, I shrug. –Arrest me.

They both start to object – they aren't ready to do that, we just need to talk, won't I sit back down and talk?

But I have said enough. I shut my mouth and walk out of the door.

Epilogue

As I sit by the fire in Mill House, I think back to the moment our plan first took root. It was that night in Linklater's rooms, and it all started with something he said.

He was sprawled in an undergrowth of papers and books, wine glass on his belly, his head resting on an encyclopaedia, John Coltrane on the record player, and longing in his eyes – for his lost mother, certainly, but perhaps also for a future in which he could walk away from all his failures and hurts and have a second go at life.

He asked me about Mill House and so I described to him the long potholed track that leads down into the valley, and how you come round a corner and there it is, squatting over the burn. I told him how the house had been in my mother's family for four generations, and I described the water hall. 'You'd think it would make a house freezing to have an icy burn running right through it,' I said, 'but there's a big fireplace in the sitting room and an old Rayburn in the kitchen and the walls are thick Scottish granite – nothing gets through them.'

When I'd finished describing it, he put aside his wine glass, rolled over, looked up at me and said, 'Maybe we could take her there?'

I thought about this for a moment or two.

'Get her out of Oxford? A holiday or something?' He grabbed his laptop and opened it back up. 'Show me where it is.'

I hesitated, but only for a moment, and then I pointed to the spot on the map where Mill House sat, so patient and good, waiting for me to come back and make it my home again.

John Coltrane came to an end. The turnstile continued to spin and the needle to bump.

Perhaps I'd had a witchy premonition back in July that this would happen, because when I took that holiday, I drove to Scotland and worked, obsessively, on my house.

It had been months since I'd last been up, so I didn't know what to expect, but as I climbed out of the car that night, and took a deep breath of the warm night air, I felt each molecule in my body expand – I was home. As always, I was struck by the ruckus of the land – a churring nightjar in a tree by the car; the rush and gurgle of the mill burn; somewhere close a whickering badger; the 'too-wit' of a female tawny owl, an answering 'too-woo' from its mate; a distant farm dog yapping, yapping. Under the broad, silent moon I could see that the vegetable garden was a tangle of brambles. A bat swooped, a sudden phantom, gone before it was seen, and as I pushed open the front door, the smell of the water hall hit me, and I could hear the burn travelling along its channel, whispering its secret, over and over, into the cold stone.

It was in a shabby state – if left alone, a home will rapidly eat itself. This had happened to the big house, in fact. I'd walked over there on my last visit and found it nearly derelict. It had been on the market for almost fifteen years by then, empty. The kitchen door had been kicked in and as I wandered inside, I remembered my father bringing me in as a child, the hubbub

and roasting smells, the cook plucking a hot pancake off the
stove and popping it into my hands, laughing as I flipped it
from palm to palm. I went further in and stood at the bottom
of the grand staircase – forbidden territory. I didn't dare go up,
not because I was the gamekeeper's daughter, but because rot
had worked its way through the treads and my foot would go
through them like wet cardboard. The wallpaper on the landing
had peeled off like the bark of an ancient olive tree; rotting roses
rolled over themselves, curling towards the floor.

I would never allow this to happen to Mill House. Nobody had
lived in it for twenty-six years, but all that time, I'd kept it up.
It is, after all, my mother's house – the deeds have never been
changed – and every time I come through the water hall I feel
her presence, or absence – or perhaps they are the same thing.
I have always known that my father did something to her, but
a part of me – no less magical and definite – also understands
that she never left.

I spent the ten days last summer fixing and cleaning. I washed
linens and vacuumed up spiders' webs, mouse droppings and
mothballs; I put down rodent traps, scrubbed limescale and
mould, scoured the Rayburn and the fridge. I wiped all the walls
with vinegar water, mopped floors, aired rugs, polished windows.

Outside was another story. I was only able to replace a small
portion of rusted guttering and clear a few leaves from clogged
drains. I couldn't tackle the land then – an enormous task – but in
the past three weeks, since I joined Linklater and Felicity, I have
made good progress outdoors, clearing brambles and hacking
back branches, fixing the rest of the guttering, the rotting sills.
We should be more self-sufficient by the end of summer – I have
begun to revive the vegetable garden, pruning the old raspberry
canes, digging over the soil, weeding, adding manure, readying

it for when the ground warms and I can plant early potatoes and onions. I have almost finished the chicken run, too, but I still have to fix up the fencing in the field so that we can, at some point, get a few sheep.

Linklater, wearing my father's moth-eaten Shetland jumpers, generally sticks closer to the house with Felicity. Her education is mostly in his hands, though between us, we more or less have the entire curriculum covered. They have been doing Scottish history together and sometimes I see them exploring the overgrown areas near the burn looking for fossils and rocks. She and I do our maths every morning – I always knew she was sharp, but she seems to genuinely enjoy it; she really has talent.

Linklater's library skin has grown more ruddy, and hers is blooming. There's no more scratching or picking at skin any more; her cuticles have healed and the eczema patch behind her ear vanished within days of arrival. Her appetite has vastly improved too – she eats whatever we put in front of her and her body fills out a bit more each day. With her new, cropped haircut she looks boyish and robust.

Linklater tends to look after the cooking, while I do the practical tasks outside. I often catch small trout for supper and it turns out that the disastrous burnt offering in his Oxford rooms was more a result of nerves than an inability to cook. Left to his own devices with the Rayburn, Linklater does a very fine roast or fried trout, and he and Felicity are making bread most days. When it rains and Felicity is playing with her treasures, he will sit and read for hours; his concentration is extraordinary. He's working his way through all the Scottish classics my father never returned to the big house.

He looks up from his Arthur Conan Doyle, now, as if he knows

I'm thinking about him – and we exchange a smile. I can read his mind. For the first time in my life, I'm learning how to share a bed – how to touch and be touched. He is gentle, curious and passionate, and is mapping every inch of me.

I hold my notebook in one hand and lean over to toss another log into the fire. It crackles and flares. Felicity doesn't even look up. She's cross-legged on a cushion next to Linklater, absorbed by a game she's devised with some tiny bones – we've already found skeletons of field mice and moles and she unearthed a gorgeous vole's jaw from an owl pellet. Though she does occasionally ask about Nick, or want to know when we'll go back to Oxford, she hardly talks about that at all – there has never been any longing, homesickness or upset.

When she does ask about them, I tell her that Nick and Mariah are busy with the baby and College. Perhaps we will stay in Scotland for a bit longer, I say, how would that be? She always agrees with equanimity – she has never once asked to go back. Linklater and I were clear about that from the start: we made a pact that we would take her back if she ever really wanted to go, or if she seemed at all unhappy with us. If that happened, we would just have to face the consequences.

But she really is happy here. There have been no nightmares, no night disturbances, not even sleepwalking. She and Linklater, in fact, both sleep soundly.

Of course, he and I wrestle with what we have done – sometimes we talk about it late into the night, discussing notions of criminality, of right and wrong – but we always conclude that it has to be wrong to follow the rules of society if those rules are actively harming a child. I like to remind Linklater that even in something as apparently concrete as maths, things can be right and wrong at the same time; correct in one system but not in another. He can see the wonder and beauty in this notion, even if he has no real understanding of the maths.

Even the cat is happier here. For the first week she stayed under Felicity's bed, hissing and spitting, but we left the door open and gradually she began to slink out into the room, then around the house, and then yesterday she ventured into the courtyard for the first time, tail tip twitching, eyes like lasers. Linklater says she yowled all the way to Birmingham, when Felicity finally let her out of the carrier. I like to picture Felicity's little face, alight with excitement as she waited at the attic window for Linklater to arrive – the thrill she must have felt as she put Fibby in the cat carrier and tiptoed downstairs in the moonlight, flitting past Mariah's half-open door and down the red staircase, along the hall, out onto the cobbles where Linklater was waiting for her. He told me that he was beside himself with nerves as he left the car in the shadows up Magpie Lane. As he walked down to stand beneath her window he almost turned around again – but then there she was, above him, waving, beaming – and when moments later she came out of the Lodging door, put the cat carrier down and threw herself into his arms, he knew it was all going to be okay.

I occasionally head out into the world for provisions. Not locally – I drive an hour to a Lidl. I cleared out my bank account the day I left Oxford, and we only use cash now. I had to abandon the Fiesta. Linklater had to drive his friend's car all the way back to Banbury and then catch a coach up here again, but that's all behind us. I bought a sixteen-year-old Land Rover. Felicity has no desire to go to town with me, and if a hiker or anybody else happened to wander onto our land she, naturally, wouldn't say a word.

We also have the drill, which we practise daily. A whistle

from me or Linklater and she drops whatever she's doing, runs straight to the water hall, shins down the rungs and into the tunnel, holding onto the rail all the way.

Not that they have any reason to come. I have been eliminated as a suspect – they still haven't even managed to confirm that there has been a crime. 'Nanny McFlee' has died down, though I know from the occasional newspaper, or a glimpse of the TV news on my trips to Lidl, that members of the public, including quite a few 'psychics', are bombarding the police hotline with their bogus sightings. #FindFelicity is going strong, and probably the trolls are too, but there is no Internet at Mill House, so we have no way of knowing what is being said. The police continue to search and follow up leads. Among the more plausible, a medical student saw a dark-haired girl walking over Folly Bridge at three in the morning the night Felicity vanished and an Oxford waitress swears she saw a girl matching Felicity's description being pulled into a car near the station that same night. Mariah, I read in the *Mail*, has 'fled' with the baby to Denmark. Nick, I suppose, is alone in the house – though in one picture he had a hand on the small of Sally's back, which gave me pause.

If the police do want to talk to me again, they will have to find me, and if they do that, I will go back to Oxford and answer their questions. As for Linklater, it has not occurred to anyone to connect him to this. As I suspected, he was entirely marginal to Nick, who, if he were to think about Linklater at all, would remember him only vaguely as the ex-graduate student who dramatically overstayed his welcome then rightly fled in fear of litigation. Linklater barely registered for Mariah or Angela, either – or anyone else connected to the Master's Lodging. He came to the door several times, but only set foot inside twice, after all. He was the ghost that only Felicity and I could see.

I run through all this, not for the first time, as I sip my tea by the fire. And as I listen to the crackle of the logs, the cheerful gurgle of the mill burn and the distant hoot of an owl, I become aware of the one sound that I do not want to hear. My ears are finely tuned to the conversation of house and land and I quickly register the anomaly: distant car tyres popping on stones. A vehicle is making its way down the bumpy lane.

I thump my mug down and whistle. Felicity's head jerks up. So does Linklater's. He sees I'm serious, drops his book. Felicity leaps to her feet and vanishes.

Linklater and I stare at each other for a second – I see his fear. It is nine o'clock at night. Nobody would ever come down the track. We know what this is. It has happened.

We fly through the downstairs rooms without speaking – our checklist. His face is grey. I check that Felicity is in position.

We hear the car pull up, the crack of doors – driver, passenger – the crunch of feet on the stones. A loud, assertive rap – Linklater flits soundlessly up the stairs.

I take a deep breath.

It is Khan I see first when I open the door. Her hair has grown a little but is still androgynous and dense. There are dark pouches beneath her eyes. What evidence, I wonder, has she meticulously worked through to get here? –Hello, Dee, she says, quietly.

Faraday looms behind her looking crumpled. –All right, Dee. Can we come in?

I rest my hand on the doorframe.

–Why?

–Well, we've driven a really long way.

I see them both peering past me at the mill burn. –Blimey, Faraday says. –Is that an actual stream?

–What do you want?

–Cup of tea would be nice, Dee. We've been in the car eight hours. My sciatica's playing havoc.

–Listen, I say, –I've answered all your questions and I've got no more to say to you. There's nothing else I can help you with, so unless you're actually arresting me for something, you just need to go away and leave me alone.

–Can I at least use your toilet? Faraday says. –I'm absolutely busting.

I stand aside and point – fortunately it is right by the front door. Faraday goes in. Khan steps further into the water hall and looks around. –Nice place, she says. –Well hidden. Lots of land? I expect you know every inch of it.

–Well, yes, I say. –I grew up here.

She looks at me, cold-eyed. –I know you did.

I watch her gaze travel, again, to the mill burn. –Funny things those, she says. –I'm not sure I'd want a river running through my house.

–Well, lucky it's not your house, then.

She stares at the stone channel a moment longer then takes a step towards it and peers over the edge. She won't see a thing. The hall light doesn't reach down to the water, and the rungs, the channel and the tunnel beneath the house are all in darkness. She steps back again. –Can we have a quick look around the house, please, Dee?

–No.

–We're not here to harass you.

–Why are you here then? To accuse me of skinning dead things to scare a child? Or killing some more kittens?

–We do know you didn't kill those kittens, Dee. And we know those animal bones were Felicity's hobby, and you didn't deliberately freak her out with voodoo or whatever. I'm sure it was Mrs Law who tore off that wallpaper, too.

–It was.

–I believe you. I was just trying to get you to react when I said those things. You can be quite defensive, you know. Like now. I mean, it would be really good if we could just have a look around, since we've come all this way.

–No.

Her eyes harden. –We'll only come back, you know.

The toilet flushes and Faraday emerges, wiping his wet hands on his trousers. –Any chance of that cuppa, then?

–There's a pub about fifteen miles up the road. You'll have passed it on your way. I'm sure they'll give you whatever you need. I'd like you to leave now.

–Have you got anyone else here with you? Faraday says. –Only there's a man's wellies in the loo.

–My father's things are all still here.

I realize that if he'd picked my fleece off the hook in there he'd have seen Felicity's yellow Coraline raincoat underneath it. I never thought of that.

Khan looks past me, down the water hall towards the kitchen. –So you're on your own?

Fibby appears in the kitchen doorway. She has been sitting by the Rayburn. She slowly walks down the hall and into the parlour, tail raised.

–Oh, says Khan. –You've got a cat?

–I'd like you to leave now.

–Do you happen to know of an individual called Hardy Birdy, Dee?

–What?

–Maybe you'd know him by the name of 'Dr Linklater' – the house detective? I believe he had a bit of a disagreement with Dr Law over accommodation, a couple of nights before Felicity disappeared? And you followed him out? We've had a report from some students of two people matching your descriptions kissing in Magpie Lane at around the same time that night.

–Listen – I bunch my fists in my pockets. –You lot have completely ruined my life. With the press intrusion, and all those hideous photos of me in the papers and online, the information leaks at your end – nobody's ever going to employ me as a nanny again, or anything else for that matter. I can't even go to Lidl without being recognized. I can't have any sort of normal existence. I just want to be left in peace, now, to live quietly on my own land. If you think I'm guilty of something and you want to bring me in, then by all means arrest me. Otherwise go away and leave me alone.'

I step forwards and open the front door wide. There is a blast of cold air; the night sky is overcast, clouds are moving darkly towards the sea.

They glance at each other. A bubble of tension has formed around us, suspending us all.

–Goodbye, I say.

–We'll only be back, Dee, Khan says again, quietly. She does not take her eyes off my face.

–Fine.

I watch them get into their car and drive away. The red taillights travel a long way up in the darkness and then vanish at the very far bend. I close the door.

A sickening feeling washes over me and my knees buckle. I straighten and go to the mill burn. 'You can come up now, pet.'

Felicity has been hiding in the tunnel beneath the house and now she appears, walking along the ledge, holding onto the rail above the water. 'Good girl!' She climbs up and over the wall again and I hug her. 'That was brilliant!'

'Who are those people?'

'They're police officers. They want to take you back to Oxford. They don't think you should be staying here with me and Linklater.'

'Why not?' She blinks, confused.

Linklater appears at the bottom of the stairs. He looks stricken.

My legs turn papery again and I have to perch on the edge of the wall, as I don't want Felicity to see. The burn seems very loud. I turn to her with a smile.

'Did you know,' I say, 'that it's possible to drive to the very edge of Scotland and then hop on a ferry and sail across the North Sea all the way to Norway?'

'What's Norway?'

Linklater comes over. He tries to smile too. So does Felicity. We could get in the Land Rover, right now, and drive to Shetland. We could do this. It's still possible. The three of us can still be together. We have our savings and our Land Rover – we are free to go wherever we choose.

Linklater reaches out and lays his hand flat against my cheek. It feels warm and steady. There are tears in his eyes, which are a very deep blue.

'Now that—' My voice trembles and I put my arm around Felicity. 'That would be an adventure, wouldn't it? The family outing to end all family outings.'

'Dee . . .' Linklater's voice is unsteady.

'Yes,' I say. 'We can go right now. Can't we?'

He pulls me to him, Felicity wraps her arms around the both

of us and we press together, and for a moment it isn't clear
which of us is holding the others up.

Meanwhile, below us, channelled by Scottish granite, the burn
hurtles towards the sea.

ACKNOWLEDGEMENTS

My thanks, as ever, to the superb team at Quercus, particularly my editor Stef Bierwerth, whose support and kindness are unrivalled, as well as Hannah Robinson, Bethan Ferguson, Rachel Neely, David Murphy, Cassie Brown, Jon Butler, and copy editor Sharona Selby.

I am also grateful to the peerless Judith Murray, and everyone at Greene & Heaton.

Many people helped me with the research for this book and I must thank, in particular, Tom Mettyear, Mark Sparrow, Polly and Charlie Phipps, Jenny Atkins, Kenroy Vincent, Lucy Billen, Peter Kemp, Liz Woolley, Alyson McDermott, Louise Hoult and Dr Martin Crowley. Also, Sue Atkins and her friend, Bet Inglis, who gave me valuable glimpses of Dumfries and Galloway life and idiom.

The friendship of other writers gets me through many a neurotic day and I am particularly grateful to Mick Herron for all the book talk, and for putting up with my curmudgeonly ways – some people might call our hours in Blackwell's feckless skiving, but we know better. I am also deeply thankful to Amanda Jennings and Hannah Beckerman for their brilliant readings, insights, laughter and bolstering.

There are several other people to whom I owe a great debt of gratitude. I have agreed not to name them here but they generously gave up their valuable time and opened the doors to the Master's Lodgings at more than one Oxbridge College. I could not have written this story without theirs, and will always be grateful for their kindness.

Finally, as always, thanks to Izzie, Sam, Ted and most of all to John, for his endless humour, patience and love.

Lucy Atkins is an award-winning feature journalist and author, as well as a *Sunday Times* book critic. She has written for many newspapers, including the *Guardian*, *The Times*, the *Sunday Times*, and the *Telegraph*, as well as many magazines. She lives in Oxford.